TERMINATOR GENE

GENE

HUMAN RITES TRILOGY, BOOK 2

www.ian-irvine.com

TERMINATOR GENE

HUMAN RITES TRILOGY, BOOK 2

IAN IRVINE

Santhenar Press

TERMINATOR GENE

Human Rites Book Two

THIRD EDITION

Ian Irvine

Santhenar Press

Copyright © 2003, 2009, 2015, 2018 by Ian Irvine

Cover design and typesetting © Lawston Design, Lawstondesign.com

First published by Simon & Schuster Australia 2003.
Second edition Simon & Schuster Australia 2009.

Book Title/ Author Name. – 3rd ed.

PAPERBACK ISBN: 978-0-6481869-1-5
HARDBACK ISBN 978-0-6481870-6-6

National Library of Australia Cataloguing in Publication data:

Irvine, Ian, 1950-

Terminator Gene.

ISBN 978-0-6481869-1-5

ISBN 978-0-6481870-6-6 (Hardcover)

I. Title (Series: Irvine, Ian, 1950- . Human Rites trilogy 3rd ed.; v. 2).

A823.3

AUTHOR'S NOTE

The first edition of this book was published in early 2003, several years before Hurricane Katrina, following a remarkably similar path to Hurricane Jemma in the book, devastated New Orleans. If only the response of the authorities in 2005 had been as effective.

For Angus

CHAPTER ONE

Jemma was at the window again, plucking at the gold ring on a chain around her neck. She looked pale, frightened and old.

'Irith?' she said, yet again.

Irith looked up from her reader, wishing it was a real printed book as they'd had in the good old days before the sea level rose six metres, flooded half the cities of the world and wrecked the world's economy. No one had done anything about global warming until it was too late; now everyone was paying for it.

'Yes, Mum?' she said. Her mother had been on edge for months but would not say what was the matter.

Jemma went into the kitchen. Irith sighed and blanked the screen. Laying the reader on the table, she went to the window. She was small, like her mother, though more slender. Her hair was bound into an austere plait and she wore no make-up, for her mother discouraged self-absorption.

'Beauty is like a dead dog by the side of the road,' Jemma was fond of saying. 'It attracts only vultures, hyenas and maggots.'

Seven floors below, an unmarked van pulled up outside the entrance and four people got out, dressed identically. *Security*! Irith suppressed an urge to duck out of sight – she'd done nothing wrong and had nothing to hide.

'The kettle's boiling, Mum.'

'Mmm,' said Jemma, but didn't turn it off, which was unprecedented, given how obsessive she was about waste. The global sea-level emergency had flooded hundreds of coastal cities; trillions of dollars' worth of infrastructure had had to be replaced and there were five hundred million climate refugees. Taxes were sky-high and waste was a serious crime.

The officers were staring at the kitchen window. Irith shook herself and turned away. 'Mum? There's a Security van outside. I've never –'

Jemma's mug smashed on the tiles. Irith ran into the kitchen. The kettle was still boiling and she turned it off. Once the ration had been used there was no more gas until the next month.

'Mum? What's the matter?'

'He's come for me. I knew he would.'

'Mum?' Irith gripped Jemma by her small shoulders.

Jemma was like a rabbit frozen in the headlights, and now Irith heard boots thumping up the stairs. Lifts were banned in buildings less than fifteen storeys high.

'Irith,' Jemma whispered, controlling herself with an effort. 'I've done all I could to prepare you. You're fit, resourceful –'

'Mum, please!'

'Promise me you'll keep out of this.'

'No! Tell me what the matter is.'

'You can't do anything for me.' Jemma's hands caught at Irith's wrists. 'Give me your word.' Her face was cracking at the seams.

Irith went cold inside, but said, 'I'll keep out of it.'

'Promise?'

'Yes,' Irith lied. *I'll get you out of this, Mum, whatever it takes.* 'What's going on?'

They were in the corridor now, the footsteps like a slow drumbeat. Irith followed her mother into the living room. She was staring at the door.

'It's Per Lindstrom . . .'

He was the President of the Global Congress, which had been formed to try and save the world from unstoppable global warming. It was not quite a world government since Britain had led a minor withdrawal two years ago, but almost. 'What's he got to do with you, Mum?'

The front door was smashed open and two women and two men pushed inside, dressed in steel grey. The leader, a big woman with a bosom like an opera singer, was not armed, but Security did not need to be.

'Jemma Hardey?' The leader had a jaw as round as a melon and eyes like sapphires stuck in scoops of butter.

Jemma was eerily calm now. 'How may I help you?'

'Come with us.'

'I'll get my bag.'

'Stay where you are.'

The other woman marched into Jemma's bedroom. The men unpacked a scanner and the taller fellow, who had a badly repaired hare lip, walked around the room, passing an array of sensors back and forth. The other man searched the cupboards.

'What's going on, Mum?' said Irith.

'They're taking me away.' Jemma's face was expressionless, though her fingers were squirming in her pockets. 'For something that happened a long time ago.'

'Silence!' snapped the leader, poking Irith in the chest with a finger as hard as pig-iron. 'You are Irith Hardey?'

'Yes,' said Irith, swallowing.

'You have completed your course of study?'

'After I defend my honours thesis, next Wednesday.' Six days away.

'You may shelter here until that is done. Then you have one day to remove your *possessions*.' She used the word like an oath.

Jemma spun around. 'But this is my flat! I own it outright.'

The woman was inexorable. 'You own nothing. All your possessions are forfeit. Your daughter will be allocated dormitory accommodation.'

'But I need my privacy . . .' said Irith. The idea of sleeping in a cramped, airless room with dozens of women, all dissecting her mother and taking pleasure in her fall, was unendurable.

'Aren't we the privileged one!' sneered the leader.

It had not always been this way. Before global warming melted the ice and the seas rose, before the Global Congress made consumption a sin and every human pleasure a crime, her country had been a cheerful, outward-looking place. Now it seethed with envy and malice.

Irith felt sick. 'You can't do this. We know our rights.'

'The warrant is signed by the President of the Global Congress –'

Per Lindstrom again. 'Why?' Irith broke in.

'You have no right to ask.' The woman recited from a reader, 'Detention without trial and confiscation of property are legitimate measures where there is a genuine threat to national security.'

'How can my mother be a threat to national security?' Irith snapped.

The tall man knocked her down from behind and put his size-fourteen boot on her back.

'That's what we'd like to know,' said the bosomy woman. 'And if you don't desist, you will also be charged.'

Irith, though dazed from the blow, tried to get up. Jemma shook her head. *Stop. You can't do anything.*

Irith watched numbly while her home was scanned – walls, floor and ceiling. They copied everything on her laptop and boxed up all the books, files and papers in the house. The second woman came out of Jemma's bedroom carrying a bag.

'Come,' said the first officer, jerking Jemma by the arm.

She broke free, ran three steps and threw her arms around Irith. 'I'm sorry. I should have told you.' She hugged Irith tightly. Two fingers slipped inside the collar of Irith's shirt and something fell down her back, then the two men dragged Jemma out.

Irith followed them down the stairs and stood outside, watching as they took her mother away.

Eventually she realised that people were walking around her, keeping well clear, as if mere contact could taint them, too.

Rainwater trickled down her forehead. She wiped her face, then ran up the stairs. Jemma had taught her to be resourceful; Irith had trained in self-defence, excelled in the rifle club, and had been on many self-reliance courses. She had to do something.

After picking up the scattered pieces of the door lock, she propped the door closed with a chair and went into her room. Each birthday since she'd turned five, Irith and Jemma had marked the annual sea level rise on her bedroom doorway, the way normal parents would have marked a child's height. It was a link to her father, Ryn, who had died days after she was born. He had been a scientist studying the melting of the Antarctic ice sheets and, perhaps because of him, Irith loved the sea.

Jemma had taken her to the beach once, when she was little, but all the beaches were submerged now and it would take centuries for new ones to form.

Jemma and Ryn had been involved, in a minor way, in the events that had led to the formation of the Global Congress twenty-one years ago. Was that why she had been arrested? Why now, after all this time?

Irith untucked her shirt and pulled Jemma's note out. It was scrawled on a fragment of coarse paper, the kind that had once been used for newspaper, and said but three words, 'Call Levi Seth'.

Irith knew the name. He was an old friend of Jemma's, which was notable in itself, for her mother had few friends. Jemma had been to see Levi several times in the past months, and Irith had wondered if they were having an affair.

She went to the screen in the corner and sat at the keyboard, but her hands froze above the keys. Security could be monitoring everything she said, everything that passed across the net. But she had to know.

Before she could type Levi's name, the power went off. Electricity was rationed and the power would not come back on until 6 pm. She went out to the university, logged on in the library with a supposedly untraceable cashcard, searched the directory for Levi Seth, and called.

A middle-aged, bald man with heavy-rimmed glasses answered. He was Indian, she judged, from the name.

'Hello?' he said.

She pressed the image button so he could see her face. 'My name is Irith Hardey –'

'Stay there!' The screen went blank.

Was he a friend or an enemy? There was no way to tell. Opening her reader, she paged through her thesis. The oral examination could be brutal and she needed to be prepared for any question, but it was impossible to concentrate. What did they want Jemma for? Irith knew of people being taken away by Security, though she had never heard of their property being confiscated. It made her realise just how alone she was, and how helpless.

She searched for recent footage of President Lindstrom, but found only one interview, for an obscure program that was long defunct.

He was a very tall man, long in the legs and short in the body, with a gritty, compelling voice and a scorching stare. His walk was peculiar – head, shoulders and torso sloping back like the tower at Pisa, arms swinging, legs snapping.

In the interview, he was hectoring the interviewer about an ecological collapse in Central Asia, swaying as he spoke. His fingers moved constantly and his left foot jerked this way and that.

'It's just a small area,' said the interviewer, 'only a few species threatened. I don't see the problem –'

Lindstrom sprang up. 'Humanity is the problem!' he roared, pointing a long finger that shook in his sudden rage. 'Too much humanity, too greedy, too –' His larynx bobbed up and down and he seemed to be having difficulty swallowing. 'Too selfish and too stupid. You're off the air, for life.'

He stalked out, leaving the interviewer staring after him, corpse-faced.

So that's what we're dealing with, Irith thought, staring at the blank screen. *That's who's taken Mum. And he's the most powerful man on Earth.*

CHAPTER TWO

'You don't look much like your mother,' said a soft voice.

Irith whirled. The man was in his fifties, slim and dark, with saggy ears and a bald skull fringed by fluffy grey hair. His eyes looked kind, though.

'I'm Levi Seth.' He held out his hand.

'Irith.' She shook it. His grip was surprisingly firm.

'Shame about the cricket.'

England had just thrashed Australia in the Fifth Test, as they had in the previous four, the second five–nil defeat in a hundred and fifty years. The first had been in the previous series. 'I used to watch it when I was a kid,' said Irith. 'It – it was a link with Dad. Did you know him?'

'I met him a few times. Let's go for a walk.'

They went out the front door of the library, crossed the road and headed across the lawn. Levi settled on a low wall in front of the Great Hall, looking down towards the park and the main gates of the university, and checked all around.

'What happened?'

'Security took Mum.'

'When?'

'This morning, and our flat has been confiscated.'

He stiffened. 'That's bad!'

'What's going on? She said something about Lindstrom.'

He rose and she did too. His face was carefully expressionless as he paced beside her. 'What did she say?'

'Just his name. You know what it's about, don't you?'

He sighed. 'Yes.'

'Please, Levi. Mum is all I've got.'

'My former partner was just your age when she became involved in this business. It destroyed her.'

That did not help. 'I'm already involved.'

He looked over his shoulder at the clock tower. Checking for cameras, she supposed.

Levi took her arm and they strolled down towards a stand of ancient, spreading figs near the gates. He stopped between the trees, on a groundcover of ivy, out of sight of the buildings. 'Before you were born, a fanatical environmental terrorist called Ulf Bamert believed that the only way to save the planet was to eliminate humanity, and he set out to do just that.'

'What happened to him?'

'He was supposed to have burned to death twenty-two years ago.'

'Before I was born?'

'Yes. But Jemma believes that he didn't die. She thinks he had a face transplant and continued with his plan and, a few years back, became President of the Global Congress.'

'Why has he taken Mum?'

'Revenge. Jemma and I helped to thwart him a long time ago, and he's not a man to forget.'

Instinctively, Irith clutched at his arm. 'Then you're in danger too.'

'I . . . used to be an expert in systems protection, and systems breaking, but I covered my tracks pretty well. But that doesn't help if they torture the truth out of one's friends.'

'They're going to *torture* Jemma?' It came out louder than she'd intended. A man sitting on a bench across the road looked around, though he was careful not to make eye contact.

'Shh! They may be watching now.' He led her deeper into the trees.

Irith felt a flood of panic and an overwhelming urge to run away, but forced herself to walk calmly.

'What did you and Mum do back then?'

'It's *now* that matters, and now is a very dangerous time, with all the riots –'

She stopped abruptly, ankle-deep in the ivy. 'What riots?'

'About overpopulation and compulsory sterilisation. It's not on the public net, but there have been sterilisation riots in a dozen countries, brutally put down. Now the religious right in the United States has almost enough votes to force secession from the Global Congress, as Britain did a while ago, and if they do things could get rather bloody. Lindstrom isn't a man for turning.'

They walked on, crossed the road and Levi stopped on the other side. 'What are you going to do?' Irith said.

'I'll have to disappear.'

'What about me?'

'It'll be tough, but you're not in any danger.'

'Is there anything I can do for Mum?'

'It's too late. I must go, Irith. Thank you for warning me.' He shook her hand and turned down the drive towards the main gates.

'But I thought you were going to help me,' she whispered.

Irith spent the following day trying to find out what had happened to Jemma, but the response was always the same.

The official would be politely interested until she gave her mother's name, when there would be a flurry at the keyboard and the face would go blank. 'I'm sorry, there is nothing I can do for you.'

'Can you tell me who I should talk to?' she said desperately.

'I'm sorry, there is nothing I can do for you.'

She tried to call Levi again but he did not answer, and his name was no longer in any public directory. Had they taken him too?

Irith went to the library, studied until dark, then headed home.

The late news contained only one item of note.

In the Vatican today, Pope Joan announced that she planned to sell the remaining treasures from the Vatican Museum in a last-ditch attempt to stave off bankruptcy, and to refocus the Church on the needy. 'In this age of austerity and deprivation,' she said, 'the Church cannot justify the accumulation of gilded treasures.'

The news attracted little interest in an increasingly secular Europe. However, in fundamentalist America, the announcement was greeted with fury and calls to excommunicate Pope Joan.

Wednesday came, and Irith submitted to the ordeal of her oral examination. It went better than she had expected, although the external examiners were as formal as automatons. At the end they did, however, congratulate her on a fine piece of research.

Irith thanked them and walked home through the driving rain. She'd planned a celebration dinner with her friends but that seemed pointless now. Besides, she had to be out tomorrow and she had not packed.

Jemma had proudly bound Irith's personal copy of her thesis in leather – a proper, old-fashioned book – but she could no longer see the point to it. She put it in a box, along with her academic record – eight high distinctions, one distinction. She'd once fretted about that miserable distinction spoiling her perfect academic record, but only students cared about such trivial things.

The only thing that mattered was to free her mother and Irith was going to find a way. Once she started something, she never gave up. She tried to think of ways and means as she packed, but she had led a studious life and had no idea where to begin.

Hours later, she checked her watch. The power would be back on and, needing a distraction, she turned on the screen. Power was heavily rationed and inspectors could appear at any time to check if illegal appliances were being used. The punishment for a first offence was confiscation of the appliances and a month without power. For a second offence, disconnection for a year. Nobody offended a third time.

Sitting back in the armchair, she closed her eyes. She didn't want to think about tomorrow . . .

Jerked awake by a familiar voice, she looked around in confusion. 'Mum?' She was running for the door when she realised that Jemma's voice was coming from the screen.

'Welcome to the first edition of the President's Page, the personal view of Congress President Per Lindstrom. I'm Jemma Hardey.

'Today I'll be talking about the worsening population crisis and what each of us can do about it. Despite universal contraception, selfish people continue to evade their birth-control responsibilities, and overpopulation is eating the world alive. Implant removal has reached epidemic proportions.'

Jemma looked up at the camera and, fleetingly, a sick horror showed in her eyes, but it vanished and she was the stern professional again.

'Population criminals will be punished severely, though why should this be necessary? Parents, give your children the ultimate gift – sterilise them at birth. They'll never miss what they do not have –'

Irith, sickened, turned it off. Jemma loved children. How had they coerced her to say such an evil thing? They must have threatened to harm Irith.

And, presumably, they were going to.

CHAPTER THREE

Irith was woken at 6 am by pounding on the front door. Two Security officers stood in the doorway. The white-haired man with the badly repaired harelip had helped take her mother away.

'Irith Hardey?' said the other, a thin, balding fellow with a pinched face.

'You know who I am.' She clenched her fists in the pockets of her dressing-gown.

Surprisingly, he handed her a piece of paper. Official messages were normally conveyed electronically, so this had to be important. As she glanced down at it, he said, 'You must be gone by 8 am.'

Irith couldn't make out the words; her eyes did not want to focus. 'Eight am?' she said stupidly. 'But ... but the other officers said I had a day.'

'You are mistaken.'

The paper was an eviction order. 'I've ordered the removal truck for 5 pm,' said Irith. 'Where is my dormitory?'

'How would I know?'

She took a deep breath, controlled her anger. 'Could you tell me how I can find out, please?'

He scrawled a number on the bottom of the paper. 'I suggest you call right away. They're very busy, what with all the evacuations.'

'What evacuations?'

'It's on the news.' He nodded curtly and withdrew.

She turned on the screen. After last night's storms and torrential rain, seawalls had collapsed all over the coastal suburbs, and west along the Parramatta and Nepean rivers. Low-lying suburbs were flooded and thousands of people were being evacuated. It was the same story on the south coast. A village near Nowra had been washed into the sea.

Irith called the number but it didn't answer. She set the machine to redial while she packed essentials, in case they threw her out on the dot of eight. An hour and a half later, she finally got through.

'Irith Hardey,' said a bored voice. He was young, with a froth of yellow ringlets and a hint of lipstick. 'How may we help you?'

'I need to be assigned a dormitory.'

'You live in your mother's flat –'

'It's been confiscated,' she choked.

He frowned; his fingers rattled at a keyboard. 'I'm sorry. I have nothing for you.'

'Then I'll have to stay here until you find a place.'

'The flat has been reallocated. The new tenants are moving in this morning.'

'Then find me somewhere to live!' Irith snapped.

'You won't get anywhere with that attitude!' He tapped away. 'Ah, here's something.' He gave her the address. 'It's prime real estate – on the water.' He emitted a mechanical chuckle, as for a much-used joke.

Sea level was rising inches every year, which made waterfront real estate was the lowest grade of all, but she didn't appear to have any choice.

'Thank you,' she said, downloading the details into her mobile. Nobody got anywhere in this world without the 'paperwork'.

She called the removal truck to change the time. A fat man in a torn blue singlet peered at her through a dirty screen. Fat people were rare these days, because of rationing. Irith wondered how he managed it.

'I don't have any record of the job,' he said.

'I booked it five days ago. I've got the authorisation right here.' She copied it to his phone.

He squinted at his screen. 'Job's been cancelled.'

'That's nonsense. Why would I cancel it?'

'It's come from Security. What can I do?'

Irith's scalp crawled. Lindstrom had taken her mother and he was out to get her too. 'Can you suggest another removalist?'

'Sorry, lady.'

She tried the first twenty removalists in the directory. All were willing until she told them her name.

A thin woman appeared in the doorway, whining, 'The place's still full of junk.'

A big, harried man appeared behind her. 'You'll have to deal with it. I've got to be back at work in an hour.' Catching sight of Irith, he swung around at her and the blood rushed into his face. 'You're supposed to be gone hours ago. We've got to pay for the waiting time, you inconsiderate cow!'

Irith couldn't take any more. Throwing her pack over her shoulder, she picked up her suitcase in one hand and the bound copy of her thesis in the other, and walked out the door.

'Hey!' he shouted. 'What are we supposed to do with all this crap?'

Despite her genteel upbringing, Irith was tempted to tell him. She suppressed the urge, which could do her no good at all, and headed for the stairs, abandoning the possessions of a lifetime. The suitcase was incredibly heavy, the handle cutting into her palm. Outside, she looked vainly for a taxi. Because of the fuel shortage they were not allowed to cruise, and the nearest rank was ten blocks away.

She was calling one when a youth in a courier's uniform tapped her on the shoulder. 'Are you Irith Hardey, miss?'

'Yes,' she said.

'I have a letter for you, special delivery from the university.'

What could it be? She was not expecting formal notification about her honours degree for at least another week. Irith showed him her ID and signed for the letter.

The thin woman began to scream at her from the upstairs window. Giving her two fingers, Irith walked around the corner, called a taxi and opened the letter. It was from the registrar.

Dear Irith Hardey

I regret to advise that you have failed your honours project in genome engineering and consequently do not qualify for the award of a degree at the university.

Yours faithfully

Derick Umpto
Registrar

Failed! It wasn't possible. Her research had been first class – she'd already had three papers accepted for publication in prestigious international journals, and her external examiners had been fulsome in their praise. There had been strong hints about fellowships at an institute in Cologne, a university in the UK – should the sanctions allow it – and a bio-engineering centre in Hong Kong.

Irith's stomach began to throb. She sat down on the suitcase and called her supervisor, a gentle bear of a man with red wavy hair and a perpetually distracted manner. He beamed when he saw her face on the screen.

'Irith, congratulations. That was a wonderful piece of work and your defence went perfectly. It's been eight years since I've had the honour of awarding the University Medal, but I can't think of a student I'd sooner see –'

'Ben, I've been failed!' She held the letter in front of her phone so he could read it.

'That's impossible! We were unanimous in our decision. I'll call the registrar and get back to you straightaway.'

The phone pinged a couple of minutes later, and as soon as Ben's face appeared she knew it was no mistake. He looked a hundred years old.

'Irith,' he said. 'I'm so sorry. It's come from –'

'The highest office of all. And you can't do a thing about it,' Irith said caustically.

'Nothing at all.' He was in agony. 'They've withdrawn your papers from publication, too, and if I speak out –'

'Thanks for everything!' she snapped. Irith knew she was being unfair to a good man, but why should he not feel equally put-upon? She had no generosity left.

The taxi didn't come and she had to lug the suitcase to the light-rail stop. It took an hour, because she could only walk half a block without stopping. It felt as if her shoulder was being pulled out of its socket.

She waited two hours for the first train, and nearly as long each time she changed lines. It was after 4 pm by the time she reached her destination and Irith felt as if she had travelled halfway around the world. She was so ravenous that she spent ten dollars and thirty ration points on a small block of chocolate from the station kiosk. As she took it, the extravagance so shocked her that she slipped it into her pocket. Such a luxury had to be savoured.

She lurched another nine blocks to the address she had been given. It was an old Federation mansion in a street of similar houses, although the road was awash and she had to pay a boy in a rotting dinghy to carry her to the front door. In the next block, the houses were half submerged.

'What's your name?' she asked as he zigzagged up the street. Irith wondered if she were his first customer – he certainly knew nothing about rowing. She lifted her feet out of the oily bilge water.

'Mikey,' he said cheerfully. He was a perky little chap, maybe ten or eleven. Irith liked children, although she'd not had much to do with them. 'What's yours?'

'Irith.'

He pulled up in front of the house. 'Here you are. Do you want me to wait?'

She gave him a five-dollar coin. 'No, thanks. I won't be going out tonight.'

Irith heaved her suitcase onto the top step, which was awash, and rang the doorbell.

A tiny, wrinkled woman came to the door. 'Yes?'

'I'm Irith Hardey.' She showed the accommodation authorisation.

'We're full!'

'It says here that I have a place. Let me in, please.'

'It's been cancelled.' The door slammed in Irith's face.

Irith knocked again, and kept knocking. Out of the corner of her eye she could see the dinghy circling in the street. Eventually the door was opened.

'Can you tell me where I can get a bed for the night?'

The woman frowned at her. 'Look, dearie, you're out.'

'I beg your pardon?'

'You're off the list! There's no place for you anywhere. No house will dare take you in.'

'But . . . what have I done?'

'It doesn't pay to make enemies.' The door slammed again.

Irith wanted to cry. It was after five and she had to find a place to sleep. She checked her bank account, which held just under three thousand dollars. It would be gone in a few weeks if she had to pay for accommodation. And what if they took her money, too?

Her stomach rumbled; she'd not eaten anything today. She considered the chocolate. No, later. The boy rested on his oars in the street, watching. She waved and he crabbed across.

'Where can I get something to eat, Mikey?'

He reached into a fabric bag hanging from a nail at the stern and produced a yellow, leathery object that appeared to be a dried fish. 'You can have this.'

'Is that your dinner?' It looked horrible, but she was famished.

'It's okay.'

'Well, perhaps just a mouthful.' She broke off a small piece, picked the bones out and nibbled at it. It was better than she had expected. 'That's delicious, Mikey.'

'You can have it all,' he said generously.

She broke it in two and handed the larger half to him. 'Thanks, but I'm not that hungry.'

They picked every morsel off the bones, then Mikey tossed his over the side. Irith frowned; food wastes must be properly composted. But then, the world had rejected her. With an inward wrench, she heaved the bones into the murky water.

Mikey flashed her a conspiratorial grin, and it warmed her. In her world, people were increasingly careful about relationships.

'What are you going to do, Irith?'

'I'll have to find a hotel.' What if a hotel wouldn't take her either?

He was watching her carefully. 'What have you done?'

'I haven't done anything,' she said bitterly.

'You must have, or you wouldn't be in such trouble.'

Mikey took off his hat to scratch an unkempt mop of hair. His eyes were an intense violet-blue. His brown hair was sun-bleached and a salt line wavered across his brow at the level of the hatband.

'Mum did something to the Congress President a long time ago, and now he's getting his revenge.' She told him about the past week.

Irith expected him to order her out. He just sat there, watching her with those violet eyes. They were old eyes. Knowing, but not, she thought, calculating.

'Your mum must be really brave,' he said. 'Where do you want to go now?'

Any room in a one-star hotel would be two hundred dollars a night. Even the sleaziest of boarding houses would charge a hundred. The alternative, sleeping out, was not a consideration. It would not be safe.

'Do you know any boarding houses around here?'

'There aren't any.'

'What about hotels or motels?'

'That way.' He rowed up the street to the edge of the water. 'They're near the station.'

Irith got out, struggling to lift the suitcase over the side. 'Thank you.' As she hefted it, tears sprang to her eyes.

'Here, you can borrow this.' He pulled a ramshackle two-wheeled trolley out from under the bow.

She fitted the suitcase into the rusty frame. 'Thank you, Mikey.' She gave him an impulsive hug. 'How much do I . . . ?'

'Nothing. You can bring it back later.'

Such generosity, after such a bitter day. Irith felt in her pocket for the chocolate. 'Here, I've got something for you.'

'It's all right,' he said, swallowing.

She pressed it into his hand. 'Thank you. I'll see you later.'

His eyes shone, though it was only a bar of chocolate. When she looked back, at the end of the street, he was still sitting there, looking down at the wrapper as if it held a bar of gold.

Irith eventually found a hotel. The sign said 'Vacancy' but once she gave her name the woman behind the desk said, 'We're full.'

'It says outside –'

The clerk shrugged.

Irith knew she was lying but there was nothing she could do about it. As she approached the other two hotels, the signs changed to 'No Vacancy'. She would have to sleep in the park, in the rain.

She rattled back to the boat. Mikey had not moved but there were chocolate stains around his mouth. She took the suitcase out of the frame and began to cry.

A small, salt-crusted hand slipped into hers. 'It's all right. You can come home with me.'

She wiped her eyes on her sleeve. 'Where do you live?'

'Out there.' He gestured down the street towards the drowned houses.

She surveyed the mouldering scene – smashed windows, rotting doors, collapsing outhouses. 'What does your mum . . . ?'

'She's dead. They're all dead. It's only me.'

'I'm sorry!' she said, clutching his hands.

'They died a long time ago. I've never had anything since, except this boat.' Mikey spun it in a circle with one oar. His previous awkwardness must have been to arouse the customer's sympathy. 'I don't need anything else.'

She stepped over the side, right into the oily water. 'What happened to your family?'

'The house was washed away and they drowned.' He began to row down the street.

'That's terrible. When was that?'

He shrugged and rowed down the street. 'The big storm, when I was seven.' He came to an alley, turned left into it and they floated between decaying paling fences. By the time they reached the next street, the water level was up to the windows of the mud-stained houses. It was a world of ruined dreams.

'How old are you, Mikey?'

'Twelve.' He negotiated the dinghy between the branches of a fallen tree that blocked most of the alley. Ancient plastic bags were snagged over the twigs.

'But surely Welfare would have taken you in? They would have given you a new home, a new family.'

Mikey gave her a strange look. 'You don't know anything, do you?'

He looked down. The dark water had a rich odour of mud and rot. 'Welfare don't care about lost kids – don't want to pay for us. The stories I've heard –' He broke off, mouth twisted.

'How did you survive the storm?'

'Dad got me into our boat and went back for the others, but . . .' He picked at a broken toenail. 'After the water went down, I rowed out here and hid.'

'And no one came looking for you?'

'A thousand people drowned that day. No one looked very hard.'

'Where do you live?'

He swung his arm in a semicircle at the half-submerged houses: late Victorian cottages, Federation-style homes and Californian bungalows. 'There's plenty to choose from.'

'And food and clothing?' She must seem to be prying, but he inhabited a world she had not imagined. A world she must learn to survive in.

'I earn money with my boat. And I find lots of stuff in flooded houses.'

The sun was going down when Mikey paddled around a roof with half of its orange tiles missing and across to a freestanding Victorian terrace house. The water was a metre below the upper veranda. He tied the bow rope up through a gap in the iron lace, to a post. 'Tide's coming in.'

'Is this where you live?' Irith asked.

'At the moment. Mind the boards when you get out.'

Irith clambered over the bow and climbed up onto the veranda. The boards were covered in green algae and very slippery.

She dragged her suitcase across the veranda into a large room whose floor was covered in mud-stained carpet. The rusting iron bed had a water-stained mattress and a couple of mouldy blankets. On a table in the corner stood two unopened tins, a paper packet, a rotary tin-opener, a few plates and some plastic cutlery from a picnic set. There were two mismatched metal chairs with the chrome plating flaking off. Clothes were thrown over a rope that stretched across the room.

'You can have the back bedroom.' Mikey gestured through a door. 'When the tide's high, you have to walk the plank.'

Irith carried the suitcase across a landing and a plank spanning half-submerged stairs to her room. Black specks crawled on the mouldy mattress. Gloom settled over her.

They sat on the front veranda, watching the sun go down over the submerged houses. In the golden evening light the scene was transformed from a drowned suburb to a magical village rising from the sea.

'How long have you lived here, Mikey?' she wondered.

'Only a couple of weeks. I don't stay long. They know we're out here.'

She spun around. 'What? They know I'm here?'

'They soon will. You can't hide; just try not to be noticed.'

If everything she'd suffered today was some sadistic form of revenge, they wouldn't let her get away.

'I'll make dinner.' He set out two plates and a large rusty tin without a label.

'What is it?'

'No idea,' he said cheerfully.

'Where did you get it?'

'I dived down into the pantry the other day. There's lots of tins down there.'

'But the great flood was five years ago.'

'If it smells bad I don't eat it.' He opened the tin. 'Pineapple.'

Irith sniffed. The inside was somewhat corroded and the smell had metallic overtones.

Mikey fished out a chunk with grubby fingers, and ate it. 'Tastes good.' He licked his fingers and held out the tin.

Irith wrinkled her nose. She wasn't used to eating with her fingers. But then, she was in his world now.

'Thanks!' The pineapple was brown, with an acidic, iron taste and an underlying bitterness. It might upset her stomach but she didn't suppose it would do her any real harm.

She passed the tin back. He tipped half the contents onto his plate and the rest on her own. Mikey wolfed his food down. Irith nibbled at hers. She wasn't that hungry.

She leaned back in the chair and closed her eyes, trying to think of a way out. The world was in crisis. The rising sea level and wildly unpredictable weather had wrecked the global economy. Everything but the air was rationed, while human rights and freedoms, as they had existed when her mother was young, were gone. She couldn't simply move to another state, get a job and hope to make a new life. Permits were required and, even for citizens in good favour, were refused more often than they were granted.

And she could not think of a single person who could help her.

She picked up her phone to turn it off and save the charge. It rang.

CHAPTER FOUR

Irith wasn't game to answer it.

'What should I do?' she whispered.

'Chuck it in the water.'

She was tempted to, but they would have already located it. They knew she was here. She pressed the green button. Her hand was shaking.

Jemma's face appeared on the little screen. 'Irith?'

'Mum, are you all right?'

'Of course,' said Jemma in a too-cheerful voice.

'They haven't hurt you?'

'Don't be silly,' said Jemma. Again the false note. 'Are you all right?'

'I'm fine. I haven't been hurt. Mum, what's going on?'

'Oh well,' said Jemma. 'The President's Page. It's such an important position, how could I refuse?'

She was lying. Jemma had never cared about such things. She was reading from a script. Maybe it was not her at all. They could have recorded her then killed her. Image processing was so sophisticated these days that it was almost impossible to tell the difference.

'Mum, the university failed me!' Irith cried, putting all her anguish and betrayal into her words.

For an instant, Jemma's eyes went wide, but then her face dissolved back into the previous calm image. So it was her, though her answers were a cut-and-paste job and everything she had to say was pre-recorded.

'I'm really sorry,' Jemma said mechanically. 'I guess your work wasn't as good as you thought it was.'

Her mother would never have said that. She was no fool, and not insensitive either. Irith broke the connection and switched off. Jemma was alive and that was all that mattered.

They wanted her to know her mother was safe. No, they wanted Jemma to know Irith was. So why the image processing? So Jemma could say nothing that wasn't scripted. No keywords, no hidden messages. At the same time, they wanted Jemma to know how her daughter was suffering.

I've got to get away from here, Irith thought. *For Mum's sake, I've got to go someplace where they can't get at me.*

She became aware that Mikey was looking over her shoulder. 'That was Mum,' she said. 'Security took her the other day.'

'Then there's nothing you can do for her.' Mikey looked so much older now.

'I have to do something.'

He ducked away, shortly to return with a steaming cup. 'Mum and Dad used to drink tea when they were worried about things.'

It'd have to be one hell of a cup to make any difference. 'Thanks,' said Irith, setting it on the boards. 'Do you always live around here?'

The boy leaned against the iron lacework, facing her. 'I've got lots of places along the water.'

'I suppose there are thousands of drowned houses in Sydney.'

'Yeah, but not all of them are safe.'

'What do you mean?'

'I'm not the only one who's hiding.'

'What kind of people are hiding?'

'People you wouldn't want to know.' He didn't meet her eyes. Mikey looked young, but he talked old.

'Have you met them?'

'Yes.' He gave a little shudder.

'Are they all bad?'

'No. There are some nice people, like you.'

Irith smiled at that. 'How do you know I'm not as bad as the others?'

He snorted.

'What do the nice people do, Mikey?'

'They hide from Security. And from the bad people.'

Something crawled up her backbone. Had she already come to the attention of the 'bad people'? 'And what happens to them?'

'Most are caught by Security. I don't know what happens afterwards.'

Irith took a sip from her mug. The tea was so strong and bitter that she choked.

'What's the matter?' he said anxiously. 'Is it too strong?'

'It's fine,' she lied. 'Just went down the wrong way.'

Irith put her feet up on the rusting iron lace and leaned back in her chair. So there was some kind of resistance, although, by the sound of it, not well organised. Dare she take the chance of trying to find it? Even if Mikey knew, dare she put her trust in a child?

'What did you mean by caught?' she said.

'Security officers sometimes come out here in boats.'

'How often?'

He squatted in the doorway and shrugged. 'They come when they come.'

'What do you do?'

'I hide. They're not looking for kids.'

'Who are they looking for?' she said.

'People like you.'

'Do you know where I can find people like me?'

She couldn't see his eyes, but his bare feet shifted. 'They move around.'

'But you could find some of them if you wanted to?'

'I suppose so.' Of course he was reluctant. His daily life didn't bring him to the attention of the authorities, but if he became involved in resistance it would be different. And he was just a kid – don't make things worse for him. But what choice did she have?

'If you could, I'd be really grateful.'

A long pause. She felt guilty now.

'I'll have a look.'

'Thank you, Mikey. Think I'll go to bed now. I didn't sleep much last night. Thank you for everything.'

'Goodnight.' He stared over the railing and didn't move. He looked afraid.

She walked the plank and sat on the bed in her dark room.

Irith tossed the flea-ridden blanket onto the floor, though the mattress could hardly be any better. After taking off her shoes and socks she lay down, fully dressed. Her stomach throbbed, probably from the pineapple. Folding her hands behind her head, she stared at the dark ceiling. What a hideous day. And what a horrible thing to do to a child. She prayed no harm would come of it.

She woke late the next day, and ravenous. Mikey wasn't there, and neither was the boat, and she could see nothing to eat. She stood on the edge of the veranda, plucking up the courage to dive down through the murky water into the pantry.

Irith took her clothes off but, as she was about to lower herself into the water, a small boat curved around the house next to hers. It must have had an electric motor because it made no sound, apart from the hissing of its bow through the water. There were three people in it, two men and a woman.

'Don't move,' called the man at the bow, pointing a rifle at her.

CHAPTER FIVE

Irith threw herself back through the doorway. *Crack!* A bullet struck the wall above her, gouging out damp plaster. She dragged on knickers, pants and blouse. There was no time for shoes, but shoes would be no good in the water.

Now what? She was not a strong enough swimmer to get away from a boat in daylight.

'Come out!' a woman shouted.

Had Mikey betrayed her? She around the doorway with her hands in the air. 'What do you want?'

'Move to the edge of the veranda,' said the woman in a slurred voice. 'Don't try to escape.'

There was nothing in the house she could use as a weapon, and no one in sight; it was no use calling for help. Jemma had taught Irith to be self-reliant, but she could see no way out.

The men had matted hair, dirty faces and bad teeth. The woman was her mother's age, dressed in overalls, though her hair looked as though it had been hacked short with a knife. The left side of her face was twisted, as if she'd had a stroke, and the left eye stared unblinkingly. Irith shivered and looked away.

The first man pointed the rifle at her chest. 'Get a move on.'

It might be to Irith's advantage to appear hysterical. 'What are you going to do?' she shrilled.

'Get down or I'll shoot!'

Irith edged through the doorway, making sure they could see she was unarmed. The boat was only marginally bigger than Mikey's decaying craft, though in good condition. It was two metres below the veranda, the tide now being at its lowest. The man with the rifle crouched at the bow, the woman sat in the middle and the other man was at the rear, his hand on the throttle.

'Lower yourself into the boat,' he said.

Irith had a wild idea and acted on it instantly. She jumped for the far gunwale, landed with one foot on either side of the rowlock, and pushed with all the strength in her legs. The boat rolled.

The man was tossed off his seat and she belly-flopped into the water. She might have gotten away had she dived, but she didn't think quickly enough and the overturning boat slammed into her back, pushing her under. For one horrified instant Irith thought the blow had broken her back, then she went down. Against the bright surface she could see the two men thrashing, while the woman was clinging to the stern of the boat.

Irith attempted to swim away underwater, but every movement hurt and her breath ran out before she reached the side fence. She came to the surface as carefully as she could but the woman spotted her instantly.

She swam toward Irith with clumsy but powerful strokes. Irith tried to fend her off but the woman punched her in the jaw so hard that the shock went right through her skull. Irith went under again. The woman took her in a headlock and side-stroked back. The men were struggling to right the capsized craft, but from the water it was impossible. Irith watched limply, too dazed to struggle. The fellow who'd had the rifle was coughing up water.

'Tie it to the veranda post,' said the woman. 'At high tide, put another rope up to the iron lacework and pull it tight. As the tide falls it'll turn it over.'

She changed her grip to Irith's plait and swam towards the house. The tide was low enough that she could swim in through the ground floor, below the ceiling. She towed Irith up the hall to the stairs, dragged her out of the water and forced her to go up.

Irith resisted momentarily, and received a blow to the kidneys that drove her to her knees. She could not fight any more; her self-defence classes had not equipped her for such a vicious opponent.

The woman forced her across the main room and onto the front veranda. 'Get down on the boards!'

When Irith was slow to move, the woman kicked her behind the knee and she fell down. Before she could move, the woman's gnarled foot was on the back of her neck.

'Don't move or I'll kick your head in.'

'I won't move,' whispered Irith.

The men had tied the boat to the veranda. 'Swim into the house,' the woman called, 'and come up the steps.'

Presumably, they planned to stay the night. Irith half hoped they would. At least this place was familiar, and if Mikey came back it might create an opportunity to escape.

On the other hand, he might have betrayed her. She could hardly blame him if he had. He owed her no loyalty. Selling information might be his means of survival.

The men came up the stairs. The one who'd had the rifle was still coughing and gasping. He gave Irith a dark look then went across to confer with the woman. The other man thumped Irith in the ribs as he went by. It was a casual blow, not hard enough to break bones, but it made her cry out.

'That'll do,' said the coughing man. 'She's not worth half as much if she's damaged.'

Those quiet words frightened her more than the violence. Irith rolled over. 'What are you going to do with me?' she said. 'Are you going to . . . give me to Security?'

'They wouldn't pay a dollar for you,' said the coughing man.

Irith considered that. 'Then what do you want me for?'

'You're worth what any woman can do, but all too few will. People pay well for that kind of service.'

The shudder ran all the way up her back. Human intimacy was frowned upon under the New Morality. The idea of intimacy as commerce, however, was revolting.

Irith gasped for air. 'But I've never *done it*.'

Her captors snorted.

'What?' said Irith, looking from one to the other, and back again.

'You've just trebled our profit.' The woman wiped her streaming eyes. Her whole body heaved when she laughed, her shoulders went up and down, but the left side of her face remained frozen.

These people were human vermin who would happily inflict any degradation on their victims if they could profit from it.

It was their lives or hers. Irith resolved to kill if she had to.

The men began to strip down the motor and clean it. Irith was bound hand and foot, then tied to her bed. The bonds were tight; she could not get free. She could hear them talking in the front room. Her ribs throbbed, her back too. She lay in the dark, trying to come to terms with a future, and a world, she had scarcely known existed. Were they really going to *sell* her?

Jemma had taught her to always search for a way out, and Irith spent another hour wrestling with her bonds. They had been tied by experts, however, and she only removed the skin from her wrists.

The hours ground by and the night grew cool. A little too cool, since she had no covers. The moon slanted in over the little balcony. She guessed it was three in the morning.

Then something moved by the window. There was someone in the room. Had one of the men come to molest her? Or the woman?

She squinted at the shadow. It was too small for any of her captors. 'Mikey?' she whispered.

He crept to the edge of the bed. 'I didn't tell them you were here, Irith,' he said softly. 'I swear.'

'Of course you didn't.' The house was silent, save for the lapping of the tide against the back wall. 'I didn't suspect you for an instant.'

He said nothing, so after a lengthy pause she went on. 'What can we do, Mikey?'

'These are evil people. They'll kill me if they find me here.'

Something slithered over her grave. 'Who are they?'

'Looters and smugglers. And they sell people.'

It was even worse, said out aloud. 'Just cut my ropes, then go before they catch you too.'

He cut the ropes, but stayed. 'They don't want me. I'm not worth anything.'

He said it without self-pity and it broke her heart. 'Of course you are, Mikey. Where would I be without you?'

'Not here. They must've been watching me.'

'Where can I go?'

'My dinghy is tied behind the next house.'

She was still holding his arm. 'Can I come with you?'

He hesitated. 'Can you swim that far?'

'I think so.'

'All right. Slide down the veranda post into the water and head for the back of that house.'

She got off the bed with no more than a single creak, but the bed had creaked every time she moved, so that was not suspicious. They crept across the room and onto the balcony. It was bright outside. The night was still, the sky perfectly clear. She edged forward. Mikey was already over the side. He slid into the water and moved away with scarcely a ripple.

As she took another step, the boards moved, clack-clack, then a man called out from the front of the house.

Discovered! She took hold of the post but her hands slid on algae and a band of barnacles ripped through her fingers. She lost her grip and fell into the water with a great splash.

Mikey took off, swimming fast toward a patch of shadow halfway between her and the neighbouring house.

'Mikey!' she hissed. 'Wait!'

He stopped and trod water. Feet were pounding through the house. Irith tried desperately to reach him, but had only gone a dozen strokes when someone jumped, slammed into her shoulders and drove her under. A mouthful of water went down her windpipe. It hurt so much she was unable to fight back when she was pulled to the surface.

She caught one last glimpse of Mikey as he stroked into the shadows.

'Help!' she screamed.

The woman pushed Irith under and held her there until she had no resistance left.

CHAPTER SIX

Irith was towed to the front veranda, her wrists tied behind her back and her ankles bound. A filthy rag was tied around her mouth and pulled so tight that it was forced in between her teeth.

The woman sat with Irith until the electric motor was reinstalled in the boat. She was bundled in, the motor whirred to life and the boat surged forward. They wove their way through the flooded houses and out onto the silent waterway, keeping to the moon shadows. They moved cautiously, sometimes stopping to drift with the tide while they made sure it was safe to proceed. Irith was cold in her wet clothes.

They spent half an hour hiding among the flooded wharves west of the Harbour Bridge while a patrol cruised by, its floodlight playing on the decaying structures. The pier above them had once been a shopping centre. Irith recalled Jemma taking her there when she was little. In the moonlight it looked frightening.

Once it was safe to move, they cruised beneath the bridge and crossed to the north side of the harbour. Mist wreathed the water here; she could just make out the sails of the Opera House. The last time she'd been there, waves had been lapping at the front steps.

Shortly they turned north into a narrow bay with steep, wooded sides dotted with expensive homes. It was one of the most exclusive suburbs, the houses out of reach of any conceivable rise in sea level. The boat hugged the shoreline along the western side of the bay before drawing up at a private jetty just before dawn. Irith was carried inside what appeared to be a boathouse.

'What's this?' said a guard at an inner door.

'She's not for your eyes,' the coughing man retorted. 'The boss will want to see this one.'

'Who is she?' the guard snapped.

'None of your business,' said the woman they called Janna. 'Get a move on.'

The guard drew himself up to his imperial height. 'Don't tell me what to do or you'll be swimming home. Along the bottom!'

'This one's special,' said the woman they called Janna. 'Make it snappy or I'll be taking her where we're appreciated.'

The guard spat on the floor then disappeared through the door, which locked behind him. Several minutes later he came back with a pretty young woman with a pixie haircut.

'I'm Kalli. What do you want?'

Janna repeated what she had told the guard.

Kalli looked unimpressed. She surveyed them in silence, then Irith. With a curl of the lip she said, 'Follow me. Wipe your filthy feet.'

They went into a concrete passageway ten metres long, then climbed three long sets of stairs, passed along an endless hall and finally emerged on a landing outside a vast mahogany door. The young woman put her eye to an iris scanner, the mechanism clicked and she pushed the door open.

The large room was decorated with an extravagance Irith had only read about in stories of the decadent past. The walls were panelled in walnut, the polished floor strewn with ancient Turkish carpets, while stands and display cases held relics that must have been looted from the most important archaeological sites in the world.

A woman of about sixty years sat behind a rosewood table reading an old printed book – either a Gutenberg Bible or an exquisite reproduction. As they entered she placed a silk bookmark across the pages and closed the book reverently. Putting her hands together on the desk, she examined the visitors in turn before focusing on Irith.

The woman was tall, with a long nose and a big jaw that gave her a mannish look. Her broad shoulders were padded, which made her seem even bigger, though they de-emphasised a very large bosom.

'Well, Kalli?' Her voice was flat, as if everything bored her.

'Janna says she's got a special one.'

'It had better be an improvement on the last.'

Janna scowled. 'Her name is Irith Hardey and she is –'

The woman held up a hand, then said, 'Irith Hardey,' into a device on the table and tapped a key. After reading from a screen, she fixed on Irith. The bored expression was gone.

'Irith Hardey. Daughter of the teacher and lecturer Jemma Hardey, who is in such favour with our beloved Congress President that she has been chosen for the honour of reading the President's Page.'

Irith couldn't tell whether the woman was being sarcastic, ironic, or was the President's most avid supporter.

'You were a brilliant honours student in bio-engineering at the Genome Engineering Centre of the University of Sydney. Yet, inexplicably, Irith, you failed your honours year and now no one in this country will have you. Does that sum it up?'

'Pretty much,' said Irith. 'Who are you?'

'A purveyor of alternative services. You can call me Jolyen. I may be able to offer you accommodation and employment . . . so, clearly, I am your friend.'

'Professional employment?' said Irith faintly.

'The services we provide are more an art than a science.'

'What would I have to do?'

'That depends. What happened to her, Janna?'

'I had to get her out of the water a couple of times,' muttered Janna.

'Take her downstairs, Kalli,' said Jolyen, 'and make her presentable.'

'What about our fee?' said Janna.

'Later! Kalli, get them tidied up. They bring the house into disrepute.' Jolyen grimaced. 'Send Bragg down for their gear.'

Kalli led Irith to a bathroom almost as extravagant as the room she had just been in. 'Get in the shower. I'll bring you something to wear.'

Irith did not see that she had any choice, so she turned on the shower and got in. Unlike the miserly, lukewarm trickle she was used to, the water was hot, the pressure enough to sting, and it didn't cut off after two and a half minutes, or even ten. It felt like the greatest luxury in the world.

She washed her hair, got out and blew her hair dry. Her dirty garments were gone. A silk slip had been laid over a rail but no other clothes had been provided. She put it on. It was embarrassingly clingy.

The door opened and Kalli said, 'Come.'

'You said you'd bring me something to wear.'

'I have.'

Irith followed, keeping watch for ways of escape, but saw none. At the monumental door, Kalli again put her eye to the iris scanner. This place had a fetish about security.

Irith stopped inside the door but Jolyen beckoned her forward. Janna and her two companions had also bathed and changed but they still looked like brutes. Irith had never felt so self-conscious. It was a prudish world and no one but her mother had seen her underwear. Conscious that everyone could see her breasts moving through the gown, she edged forwards. The colour crept up her face.

'No need to blush,' said Jolyen. 'It's perfectly natural.'

'I might as well be naked,' said Irith.

'You might as well be.'

The woman clicked her fingers. Images moved on a huge screen mounted on the wall on her left – a woman taking a shower. Her! The screen split into four, cameras showing Irith from four different angles as she stepped out of the shower and seemed to take an eternity to towel herself dry. She wanted to die.

'Come here,' said Jolyen. 'Pull the gown up.'

'No!' said Irith.

Jolyen was beside her in three steps. She spun Irith round and pulled up the gown. Her fingers touched the bruised line across Irith's back. She flinched.

Jolyen let the gown fall. 'You didn't take good care of her,' she said coldly to Janna.

'Wasn't our fault,' Janna blustered. 'She jumped on the side of the boat. It overturned and came down on her.'

A smile touched Jolyen's lips. 'Initiative – I like that. But there are other bruises.' Jolyen touched Irith's chin, which was still swollen from the blow the previous day. 'And she's been kicked, more than once. That'll come off your fee.'

'But –' cried Janna.

'You know violence displeases me.'

'She tried to escape.'

'You should have been ready. I'll give you six thousand and not a cent more. It would have been ten if you'd taken better care of her.'

'Keep your money!' The left side of Janna's face was savagely twisted, the right as smooth as agate. 'I'll take her to Gentle George's.'

Beside her, Kalli sucked in a breath. Irith's flesh crawled, though she could not have said why.

'She's mine now,' said Jolyen in a frigid voice. 'You'll take what you're given. It's a handsome profit, considering how little you did to earn it.' She stared the trio down.

'All right,' snapped Janna. 'But next time –'

'There won't be a next time. Put them out, Kalli, carefully. Security are running around like blue-arsed flies.'

They followed Kalli out.

'What do you want me for?' said Irith, though she felt sure she already knew. The place looked like a brothel – a very exclusive one.

'You're unique, Irith. You do realise that?'

What was she talking about? 'I'm a good scientist, but there's nothing unusual about my . . . physical attributes.' Irith knew she had a nice face and a trim body, but thousands of women had better ones.

'Oh, you're one in a million. I've got a special use for you.'

For some particularly sleazy client, Irith thought, shuddering.

Jolyen pressed a recessed plate on her table and shortly a man entered. He was above average height, lean but muscular, with wavy brown hair worn so close-cropped that it appeared to be knitted to his head. Grey eyes. Big hands and feet. He handed Jolyen a bundle of goods, including Irith's phone.

'Take Irith to her room, Bragg,' said Jolyen. 'Keep a close eye on her.'

Bragg surveyed Irith like a police officer investigating the scene of a crime. 'It would be hard to do otherwise.'

Irith wanted to smack the insolent expression off his face. He put a hand on her bare upper arm. She snatched it away. 'Don't touch me!'

He chuckled. 'This one's going to take a bit of taming.' Bragg had an American accent, which was strange in itself. She hadn't met an American in years. They seldom travelled abroad since the Christian fundamentalists had come to power, closed the borders and instituted a policy of isolationism.

There was a twinkle in his eye as his fingers locked around her wrist. She tried to prise them off but they were immovable.

'Go with Bragg, Irith,' said Jolyen.

'Why should I?'

'Because I'm the only person in this country who will take you in. Without me, you'll be back on the streets, and there are people far worse than Janna out there. People like Gentle George feast on your kind.'

Irith squirmed, but she wasn't having this woman take over her life. 'I'll go to the country.'

'Country people notice everything. They'll turn you in.'

'It'd be better than being a sex slave.'

Bragg's eyes met Jolyen's and he gave the subtlest of smiles. The swine was as depraved as the rest of them.

'You're unique and you'll be well looked after,' said Jolyen. 'You should be glad of the offer.'

'I don't want it. Let me go.'

'You couldn't survive,' said Jolyen. 'Anyway, I've just paid six thousand for you.'

'I've nearly three thousand dollars in my personal account,' Irith said desperately. 'Please, take that instead.'

'Have you checked your account lately?'

'The money was there yesterday –' She gulped. 'May I have my phone?'

'Do you really want to tell Security you're here?' Jolyen pursed her lips, then said, 'You can use my terminal. It's secure.'

'How do you know?'

'This place exists, does it not, in defiance of everything our government stands for? Besides, it's been tested just this morning.' She pulled a keyboard out from under the table, got up and moved away.

Irith tapped in her account details, then the password. The account came up instantly. It contained one dollar. The rest had been withdrawn last night.

'That's it,' she said. 'I've got nothing left. I'm trapped.'

Jolyen shrugged. 'Take her to her room, Bragg, something's come up.'

CHAPTER SEVEN

Bragg led Irith on a roundabout route through the great house, as if taking her on a tour. Whipping room, jelly tanks, velvet swings, latex chamber – all the so-called pleasures of the flesh. A library contained dozens of illuminated manuscripts, not all of them done by celibate monks.

The extravagance of the place was beyond Irith's experience and she could only imagine what her mother would have thought of it. Having grown up in a world where frugality and abstinence were the greatest virtues, Irith found the place an abomination, yet a tempting one. She longed to have a little colour in her monochrome life.

Bragg, leading her past a room with laden tables, stopped abruptly. 'You're drooling.'

'I'm not!' She wiped her mouth just in case. 'I haven't eaten for a day.'

He frowned. 'Come with me.'

He turned into a room where a long table, covered in a gauzy cloth, was piled high with foods she had only seen in images on the net – lobsters, prawns, fish roe, hams crusted with herbs, all kinds of meats, cheeses of every colour and shape, a dozen varieties of fresh-baked bread, vegetables she had never seen before. Her mouth flooded.

He handed her a white plate edged with gold. 'Help yourself.'

The plate shook in her hand. This excess, when most people had so little, was grotesque.

'What will it cost me?' She swallowed mouthfuls of saliva. Irith had read all about white slavery and debt that grew higher every day.

'I don't understand.' He peeled a prawn as thick as her wrist and bit off a chunk of white flesh.

'I'm talking about being charged a hundred dollars for every meal. Of going further into debt for every day I remain here.'

'Don't be absurd! Jolyen is a kind woman.'

'So kind that she *bought* me.'

'Would you prefer to go back to Janna and her friends?' Bragg said. 'Their other customers are brutes.' Something darkened his eyes – a personal horror? He quickly turned away.

The vulnerability made him seem more human.

'No,' she whispered, and her decision was made. She had to free Jemma, and Irith would do whatever she had to, to survive. They might use her body but they would not touch her spirit.

Taking her plate, Bragg piled it high with prawns, pieces of crab, slices of glazed ham, a couple of wedges of cheese, scoops of various prepared vegetables and half a dozen slices of bread. Holding it in one hand, he took up a jug of fruit juice in the other. 'This way.' He motioned for her to go ahead.

Self-conscious in the sheer gown, Irith said, 'I'll follow you.' She would have walked across broken glass for the contents of that plate.

He shrugged and went ahead. He was moderately good looking but would not have stood out in a crowd. Broad shoulders, taut waist, big thighs and a bum Irith approved of. She couldn't admire a man with a spindly backside, no matter how fine the rest of him.

What was she thinking? He was her jailer. Irith looked away, confused.

Bragg took her to a room half the size of Jemma's flat. There were original oil paintings on the walls and her bare feet sank into carpet to the ankles.

Bragg placed the plate and jug on a desk by the window, and went to the door.

'Enjoy it. I'll be seeing you later.' He pulled the door closed behind him.

She checked it. It was locked, and the window had a silvery coating on the outside, some kind of anti-surveillance material, she supposed, plus a fine mesh of wires embedded in the glass. Protection against electronic snooping, or to stop the occupant from breaking out?

Irith took as much food as she needed, and no more, then covered the plate with a napkin and put it in the refrigerator. Waste was a crime; it was also immoral.

She explored the room. The hanging space contained two silk dressing-gowns. The drawer held scanty bed garments that made her cheeks flame. The bottom drawer was full of what she supposed to be erotic aids, some so lurid and extravagant that she could not fathom their purpose. She shoved the drawer closed and went into the bathroom.

It contained a bathtub, a spa the size of the bed, and a glass and marble shower large enough to contain a couple of armchairs. The room was mirrored all around, which Irith, not accustomed to looking at herself, found uncomfortable. The tiles were veined marble, so beautiful she could have spent hours looking at them.

She washed her face and hands, nibbled at a slice of ham, drank a glass of juice, brushed her teeth, and washed her hands again. There was nothing to do and she didn't know how to cope. All her life she had kept busy. She lay on the bed, desperately tired, closed her eyes and slept.

When she woke, a set of clothes was sitting on the chair by the door and a note said, 'Get dressed. We're going out. Bragg.'

She dressed. The clothes fitted as if they had been her own, apart from the blue jeans which were snug across the backside. The other colours didn't suit her and she wondered if Bragg had chosen them. The blouse was a strong orange, which made her creamy complexion appear starkly white. There was also a long grey jacket, blue socks and walking boots. A small grey bag held a change of clothes and spare underwear.

Fully dressed except for the jacket, she sat on the bed and kicked her legs. And waited. Bragg did not come. She went to the fridge, then looked out the window. It was late in the afternoon. There were white sails over by the Opera House. A ferry moved up the harbour, small boats bobbing in its wake.

As the ripples reached the shore, a dinghy crossing the bay lurched up and down and Irith saw a youth standing up, his feet well-spread for balance. He looked over his shoulder and she recognised the way he held his head. It was Mikey. The boy was skilled at the art of spying – he glanced at the house for just a few seconds before continuing across the bay, where she lost him in the afternoon shadows.

There was nothing he could do for her. She had to get out of here on her own, and she'd better start now. Irith ran into the bathroom, wet the soap and smeared it over the floor tiles in the bathroom doorway. Now she had to get Bragg to walk into the bathroom. She sat her bag on the bench by the hand basin, as if she had been packing there.

There wasn't anything in the room that looked remotely useful as a weapon. The lamps were too light, the drawers did not come all the way out and the chair was too big. She looked under the bed – nothing. There wasn't even a pencil to poke in his eye.

Irith rifled through the other drawers. Nothing but the underwear and the sex aids. She slammed the drawer then drew it open again, eyeing a massive black leather dildo, still in its plastic wrapping. It was a good forty centimetres long, five centimetres through the middle and double-headed. She couldn't imagine anyone gaining pleasure from such a thing.

Breaking the wrapper, she prodded the leather. It was hard. Her fingers closed around the shaft. The device was rigid and heavier than she had expected. She swung it experimentally through the air. A hard blow in the right place might well knock him unconscious. She took one of the dressing-gown cords to tie him up.

There was a noise outside the door. She thrust the dildo under the pillow, the cord in her jeans pocket. The door opened. Bragg stepped into the room. 'Ready?'

She stood up and collected the jacket. 'Where are you taking me?'

'There's no time for questions.' The sparkle was gone from his eyes; he seemed anxious.

Her heart was racing. Could she do this? He hadn't treated her badly, after all. She had to, for Jemma's sake. 'Where did I leave my bag?' Irith pretended to look for it.

Spotting it in the bathroom, Bragg hurried in. Irith slid the dildo out from under the pillow, held it behind her back and followed.

Bragg slipped on the soapy tiles, lost his balance and she thumped him on the back of the head. He fell hard, cracking his head against the edge of the tub.

Irith sprang, and was raising the dildo for a mighty whack when he groaned and turned his head, his grey eyes struggling to focus. He saw her upraised arm and flinched. She had hurt him badly, and her blow would smash across his nose and cheek, probably breaking bones.

She hesitated, then the chance was gone. She dropped the dildo. 'I suppose I'm a bloody fool, but I can't do it.'

He rubbed the back of his head and grimaced. 'Give me a hand.'

She helped him up. 'Are you all right?'

'I will be in a minute.' He staggered to the bed and sat down hard. 'I can't blame you.' His eyes fell on the dildo and a smile quirked the corners of his mouth. 'Put it away, and don't say a word about it.'

She fetched it, tossed it in the drawer and pushed it closed. 'Why not?'

The rueful smile warmed him to her. 'My reputation couldn't stand it. You won't try that again, will you?'

'No.' *I won't try* that *again.*

He took her arm, holding her so tightly that it hurt. 'Pull this over your head.' He handed her a stocking.

Irith did so. It felt uncomfortable and claustrophobic, but didn't impede her vision significantly.

He led her out and down. At the end of several flights of steps Bragg stopped at a security door and consulted a screen, which showed views of an extensive garden scattered with large trees, sloping in a series of terraces down to the bay. Another screen showed the street above, which presently was empty. He put his eye to an iris scanner. The door clicked and he jerked it open.

They followed a winding path through the upper garden, heading towards the street. In the distance Irith heard a double peal, as if an alarm had gone off, and thought she saw a small shadow fleeting through the trees to her left – Mikey. This was her chance.

Bragg swore and began to run, pulling her along. She propped, tore free and shoved him hard. Bragg fell sprawling.

Irith raced toward the place where she thought she had seen Mikey, but it was growing dark now and the shadows were deep between the trees. She ducked behind a massive white gum tree as someone ran through the garden to her left. Someone tall; not Mikey. Bragg?

Thinking that Mikey would head towards the water, she turned that way and made out a moving shape, twenty or thirty metres further down and to her right. 'Mikey?' she said softly.

The shape didn't answer, but it moved and she realised that it was too tall to be Mikey or Bragg. Fear curdled her stomach. Bragg must have called out the rest of the guards. The tall man was between her and the water, and Bragg somewhere behind her.

'Mikey?' she hissed. She was taking a risk, but not finding him was a bigger one.

'Irith,' he said. 'This way.'

He was down the slope to her left. As she turned, someone jumped her from behind, slamming her into the grass and knocking the breath out of her.

She gasped, 'Mikey, look out!'

A hand went over her mouth and her assailant pressed her into the ground. He felt bigger and heavier than Bragg. Irith struggled but he brought his knee up into her bruised back and the pain made her gasp. He tore off the stocking, twisted her head sideways and gave a grunt of satisfaction. Something shone on his collar. The most feared emblem in the country – a Security badge.

She kicked her legs. The officer cuffed her across the ear. 'Don't move. Don't speak.'

He lay on top of her, holding her down. The contact repulsed her. Shortly the boy appeared, creeping through the trees, his small head moving this way and that. Irith prayed he would turn the other way. He could do nothing to help her now.

Mikey turned her way. 'Irith?'

A click made the blood crystallise in her veins. Her captor braced his arm and light reflected off a large automatic pistol. She choked. Surely he wasn't going to shoot a kid?

She tried to call out but the officer pushed her face into the dirt. Despair gave her strength; Irith forced her right hand out from underneath and slammed her fist up hard into his groin.

The officer rolled off, emitting a muted groan. She sprang up, stamped between his legs and he shrieked. Irith looked for the fallen weapon but couldn't see it in the dark. The man rose to his hands and knees. She trod on a stick, grabbed it and thumped him on the back of the head. He fell down again.

Irith ran to Mikey, shaking. 'Why did you come back?' she hissed.

'You were kind to me,' he said simply. 'And I know what goes on in that house. And I . . . and I . . . '

'What is it?'

He was weeping. 'I was trying to find someone to help you. I must have led them to you. I'm sorry, Irith.'

'It's my fault. I should never have asked you.'

'I'm really sorry.'

'Which way?' she gasped.

He pointed downhill. 'We'll follow the fence around the point, to the boat.'

'I saw someone over that way a few minutes ago,' she said. 'What if we went right, through the bush, then down?'

'All right,' he said doubtfully.

Irith wasn't confident that her route was much better. And even if they got away, how, with not a cent to her name, was she going to survive?

They crept through the trees, which were denser here, growing between square outcrops of sandstone. It was almost dark, although garden lights had come on closer to the house, shedding a faint illumination into the trees. If there were any guards further out, she and Mikey would be silhouetted against the light.

Irith began to scramble down a steep ridge dotted with sandstone outcrops.

'Wrong way,' said Mikey, stopping above her. 'We should be going left from here.'

She kept going. 'I think we can get through further along.'

Irith was halfway down when a man stepped out from behind an outcrop and twisted her arm behind her back. She struggled to get away, using all the tricks she'd learned in her self-defence training, but he anticipated every move. He was also tall, but wiry and lithe, and very fast.

'Stop it!' he snapped, slamming the barrel of a gun into her side.

She went still and he did too, so still that she could hear her heart pounding. He was waiting for Mikey.

'Mikey!' she screamed. 'He's got me. Run!'

The man struck her on the side of the head. Irith watched dazedly, unable to cry out, as Mikey appeared from behind a tree. He crept down, only to stop halfway. He was staring at her captor.

'No, Mikey,' she gasped. 'You can't do anything.'

Mikey advanced. He had a stick in his hands and was swinging it back and forth. She struggled uselessly. The man raised his weapon, pointed it at the boy's chest and Irith froze in disbelief. He was going to shoot him, just like that.

She slammed her head up under the man's chin with all her strength. He reeled backwards; the gun went off and a dark patch appeared where Mikey's right earlobe had been. She pulled free, sprang and kicked the man in the belly with both feet. He fell backwards down the steep slope. She ran to Mikey and cradled him in her arms.

'I'm all right,' he said, staring at the blood on his fingers. 'I'm all right.'

Irith hugged him hard, then pushed him away. Another few centimetres and he would have died. 'Get going; I'll follow you.'

He ran but Irith didn't follow. She was almost throwing up with horror. The man would have killed Mikey for no reason at all, and she couldn't risk his life again – not even to save her mother.

'Don't move!' hissed Bragg.

He caught her by the arm and peered around the edge. She kept still, giving Mikey time to get away. The man down below fired, the bullet striking rock above their heads. Bragg pointed a gun and fired. She heard a grunt, then the sound of a body rolling down the slope.

'Quiet!' he hissed. She held her breath.

He pressed buttons on a remote in his other hand and all the lights went out. Bragg picked Irith up and, with a single glance around him, melted into the undergrowth.

He carried her a long way through trees, crossing fences and the shadowy parts of large backyards. Several times he stopped, listened, then retraced his steps. Once or twice he consulted a device on his wrist that displayed text messages. He also spoke into a phone, something about decoys and a new destination.

It must have been half an hour later when he crossed a main road where the streetlights were out. Bragg trotted down the street to a van parked on a corner. Someone opened the rear doors. He lifted Irith in, strapped her into a seat and sat beside her.

'Don't even breathe,' he said savagely. He tapped on the roof. The van moved smoothly away.

Irith closed her eyes. A man was dead, Mikey could have been killed, and it had all been for nothing.

CHAPTER EIGHT

Irith lost track of time after that, although she knew they had been travelling for ages. The driver said nothing, nor did the passenger beside him, or Bragg. She felt traumatised, yet numb. Her mind kept recycling what had happened, and it got worse each time. A man was dead and her reckless escape attempt could have resulted in an innocent boy's death.

A long time later they drew into the winding driveway of a house in bushland, and stopped. As Bragg opened the back door, cool air flowed in, so they must have been high up.

'Can you walk?' said Bragg, helping her out.

'Yes,' she snapped.

'Don't try to escape again.'

She said nothing.

He spun her around. 'Did you hear me, you little fool? A man died because of your stupidity, and the cover of the house has probably been blown. The man is no loss but if you think I wanted to kill him you're very much mistaken. So take one step away from me and I'll shoot you in your fat little arse.'

'It's not fat,' she said with a feeble attempt at dignity.

'That's all you care about, is it?'

'Mikey was my friend!' she hissed, 'and that man was going to kill him.' It was a nightmare.

'I sure hope I never become your friend,' he muttered.

'There's no chance of that.'

'Shut up and get inside.'

She neither argued nor tried to escape. Irith had nothing left. She just wanted the horrible day to end. She had vowed that she would do anything, even kill, to stay free so she could save Jemma. She'd had no idea what she was committing herself to, nor what the cost would be.

As she reached the door, Jolyen opened it.

'I didn't expect to see you here,' said Bragg.

'Who else could be trusted?' She inspected Irith mercilessly. 'You bloody little fool. And to think I paid good money to save you.'

'I'm not going to be a whore in your brothel,' snapped Irith. 'I'd rather die.'

'If Security catch us you may get your wish.'

Irith said no more. Better what Jolyen offered than Security, who would probably send her to the Woomera Rehabilitation Camp. No one escaped from there.

'Bring her through,' Jolyen went on. 'There will have to be a few . . . cosmetic changes before I send her on.'

'What cosmetic changes?' Irith cried. If she *was* unique, why did they need to change anything? 'Where are you sending me?'

No one replied. Jolyen led her up a flight of stairs into a room that resembled a dentist's surgery. A man waited there and he was gowned, capped and masked as if for an operation. A nurse stood beside him, similarly attired. Irith was pushed into the chair. Before she realised what was happening, the nurse slid a needle into her arm.

'What are you doing to me?' she cried.

They didn't answer. The doctor was counting under his breath. 'Ten, nine, eight . . .'

Before he reached three, Irith slid into unconsciousness.

Irith had fleeting moments of hallucination in which she was strapped to a bed while Bragg stood over her with a dildo-handled scalpel. Another time she dreamed that Jolyen was reshaping her body with liposuction, only she was pumping fat in, not taking it out. Her lips were swollen to the size of buttocks.

She slept and woke again. Her eyes hurt. She couldn't see, for her head was covered with a tight cap, bound over her eyes. Someone held her up in a shower, someone else washed her all over. She prayed that it wasn't Bragg. Irith felt so drained that she could not even move her fingers. Days seemed to have gone by, or weeks. Another prick in her arm and everything vanished.

Now she was in a car, driving down a winding road. With each corner her head flopped from side to side. She didn't have the strength to hold it up. She dozed.

A long time later, she was shaken awake. She opened her eyes and could see, though the light was painfully bright.

'Take this.' Bragg handed her a tablet and a glass of water. Irith swallowed it without question. Within minutes her head had cleared. She looked out the window. They were in a multi-storey parking station and she heard planes taking off and landing.

'Come on.' Bragg opened her door.

She lurched out. Her cheeks felt puffed up and her knees were wobbly. He collected two large suitcases, a small bag and a handbag, hung the handbag over her shoulder, the small bag over his, and picked up the suitcases.

'Walk beside me. Put your arm through mine. Don't look around. They're watching for Irith Hardey.'

Her wits were so dull she did not take that in. 'Where are we going?' Her voice sounded as if she had spent the night screaming.

'London.'

'*London?* Why?'

He leaned over and spoke in her ear. 'Australia is too hard to hide in these days. Britain has withdrawn from the Congress and is a pariah nation, but the resistance is stronger than ever. If there's anywhere on Earth you'll be safe, it's there. Don't ask any more questions. Your name is Hilarie Stamp, if anyone asks, and you've been ill.'

She felt ill. Every muscle ached and her thoughts laboured like a caterpillar through treacle. Why would a brothel owner ship her to London, in disguise? It made even less sense than the things Jolyen had said previously.

'But I'm not Hilarie Stamp,' she said. 'As soon as we go through immigration the scanners will pick me up.'

He squeezed her arm. 'You are Hilarie, now. You've been sick and you don't remember anything. Leave everything to me.'

Security was tight. All the luggage was scanned with 3-D X-ray machines and magnetic resonance imagers, which produced a listing of each bag's contents down to individual pills in a paper packet, compared every item to its database and signalled if anything looked suspicious. Most of the luggage was hand-searched as well. Sniffer dogs passed back and forth along the line. Samples of air from inside each bag were passed through a variety of analysers.

Irith shuffled along. The people ahead were removing their shoes and placing them on the moving belt. After the metal detectors, everyone was scanned with ion channel biohazard detectors. She stood in the line, trembling and sure they would be discovered. What would Security do to her? The line inched forward. She lost herself in her ponderous thoughts, only to be roused by shouting up ahead.

'Don't move!' a woman roared in a voice like a bullhorn. An alarm went off – *whoop-whoop-whoop* – followed by more shouting. A child screamed, then a man broke free and ran back down the line. He was short, overweight and balding, and so terrified that a whole trout could have been slid through his open mouth.

'Everyone, *down!*' roared Bullhorn Voice.

The people ahead of Irith dropped to the floor as if they had been drilled to it. Bragg pulled Irith down. The man kept running, his belly wobbling.

'Stop!' shouted the voice.

The man kept going. A security guard sprang over the line of crouching people and pointed a chunky device at the running man. Snap! Irith's hair stirred. He fell forwards, skidding along the polished floor on his face, and came to rest just a few steps away, vomit oozing from his mouth. His eyes were staring, his arms twitched, and a stain grew under his loins.

Officers converged from everywhere and slid him onto a stretcher. One of the officers noticed Irith's open-mouthed stare, her pallid face. He came up to her. 'He can't do any harm now, ma'am.' Touching his cap courteously, he turned away.

'Is he dead . . . ?' She broke off, realising she had been about to say 'too'.

'No,' said Bragg, once the officers had gone. 'That was a pulse-wave myotron, an up-market stun gun. Security likes to be able to question their victims.'

The line began to inch forward. Their bags moved through the machines. Bragg took off his shoes. Irith did the same. She looked down at her feet, which looked tiny and far away, and put her shoes on the belt.

Bragg went through the metal detector first. Irith waited until the Security officer beckoned, then walked through. He was staring fixedly at her. The machine beeped. Immediately two officers converged on her.

'Turn out your pockets please, ma'am.'

Irith did, but they were empty. They scanned her with four different kinds of hand scanners. As the metal detector passed over her chest, it beeped. Behind her, everyone in the line was staring. Ahead, Bragg was waiting with the bags. He looked worried.

'It's the bra,' said one of the officers, a stocky woman with pendulous jowls. 'It must have underwires. You'll have to take it off.'

'Here?' Irith said faintly.

'Of course not. Come with me, please.' The officer took Irith's arm and marched her in the direction of a door marked 'Security'. Inside, she began to unfasten Irith's blouse.

'I can do it.' Irith pushed her hands away and took the bra off.

The Security officer scanned her chest and back, and the bra, and took it outside. Irith followed, red-cheeked. She blushed easily and it was a constant embarrassment.

The bra, which was low-cut, transparent and lacy, unlike the utilitarian affairs she normally wore, went through the X-ray machine. The eyes of the whole line were on it. It came out the other end.

The officer at the console raised his thumb. The female officer picked up the bra, turning it over in her big hands. Her eyes were on Irith. Finally, she handed it back. 'Would you like to go back in to put it on?'

'No, thank you,' Irith said frostily, shoving it into a pocket.

'Well done,' said Bragg as she joined him.

Irith couldn't tell if he was being sarcastic, so she merely took the handbag and walked on. That had just been a practice run: the real test lay ahead, at immigration.

It took another hour to get that far, by which time she felt more panicky than ever. Already three people had been picked up by the iris scanner. Two had been escorted through an unmarked door, half an hour ago, and had not reappeared. A third had been seized, handcuffed and taken away in a portable cell that resembled an iron cage on a golf buggy.

She had no expectation of getting through. Her fake identity would be discovered at once and it was pointless trying to think of a story, since she had no idea who Hilarie Stamp was supposed to be or where she was going.

Bragg presented his documents. The officer scanned them, studied Bragg's face and checked his screen. He seemed to take a long time, but finally he motioned Bragg to proceed to the authenticam.

Bragg lowered his head, fitted his eyes to the eyepieces and stood still for the regulation thirty seconds. The machine buzzed: neither acceptance or rejection. Bragg looked questioningly at the immigration officer.

Irith admired his presence of mind. She was sure she would have screamed. The officer tapped several keys, frowned and then tapped them again. Another frown. He rose abruptly and came out of his cubicle. Irith held her breath. What was the matter? The officer pushed Bragg out of the way and put his own eyes to the scanner. Again that buzz.

He studied the machine, tapped gently on the eyepieces with his knuckles and put his eyes to the eyepieces again. This time the machine gave a sharp *ping*. With a nod to Bragg, he went back to his cubicle.

Bragg bent down, settled himself in place. *Ping*. The officer motioned him on. Irith shuffled forward. Her stomach felt like corrugated iron. She handed her passport card over without looking at it. He scanned it, tapped several keys, then more keys, frowned and looked up at her.

'Are you all right, Ms Stamp?'

She stared at him, then sluggishly realised that was supposed to be her name. 'Yes,' she said faintly. 'I've been ill.'

He looked down at the terminal. 'Are you sure you're okay to travel?'

'I just feel a bit faint. I've been standing up for a long time.'

'More trouble than usual today. Still, won't be long now.' He smiled as he handed back her card. 'Go through to the authenticam.'

'Thank you,' she said in a wisp of a voice. She took the six steps, bent over the device and fitted her eyes to it. A red line passed back and forth twice, there was an agonising wait, then *ping*.

Irith could hardly believe it. She stood back, staring at the iris scanner.

'Are you sure you're all right, Ms Stamp?' said the officer.

She shook her head and flashed him a weak smile. 'Yes.' She joined Bragg.

They continued on to the customs counter, presented their forms to the scanner and passed through. When they were well out on the concourse, and no one was nearby, Bragg said softly, 'Pull yourself together, Hilarie. We're not out of danger yet.'

Cameras could be watching them right now, microphones picking up every word they spoke. She did not speak until they had boarded the plane and were settled in their seats up on the top deck.

'First class,' she said. 'Why?'

'We're important people,' he whispered in her ear. 'Ask no questions until we get to London and are well outside the airport. This could still fall apart.'

Whatever 'this' was. She leaned back and closed her eyes.

She felt safer once they reached cruising altitude, although that was an illusion. For a fugitive from the Global Congress there was nowhere to hide. Even rebellious Britain swarmed with agents.

Once they were in the air she went to the toilet, caught sight of herself in the mirror, and gasped.

She was practically unrecognisable. Her fine, unmanageable hair had been cut short and dyed black. Her face looked rounder and her eyes were no longer brown but a deep and brilliant blue. How had they done that?

Bending close to the mirror, she brought her fingers up to her eye, but felt nothing except her eyeball. The scanners would not be fooled by contact lenses; the doctor must have given her iris implants. Irith wasn't aware that could be done, but what other explanation was there? Iris scanners were held to be foolproof and more diagnostic than fingerprints.

But the real question was, why? She couldn't make the jump from Mikey's squat to Jolyen's house of decadence, to here. It made no sense at all.

Irith slept through most of the flight, waking only an hour before landing. She still felt exhausted, no doubt from the injections, and wondered how long she had been drugged. It must have been days, for the slightest exertion, even walking to the toilet and back, exhausted her.

'What's the date today, Bragg?'

'March 17.'

She'd been sedated for four days. No wonder her legs felt like jelly.

'Australian?' said the man on the immigration counter. 'Cricket fan, I hope.' He chuckled nastily. 'That was the greatest Test series I've ever seen.'

Irith wasn't sure whether he was referring to the ritual humiliation of the Australian cricket team in the past few months, or the even more crippling defeat in England before that.

'Not our best performance,' Irith said uncomfortably. 'I'm sure we'll do better in the World Cup.'

'You could hardly do worse,' the officer said cheerfully, tapping at a battered keyboard. Everything in the terminal was shabby. 'Still, what can you expect? Once a penal colony, now a concentration camp.'

'I've always thought cricket was the stupidest of games,' said Bragg. 'Five days to play a match that half the time ends up in a draw. If you ask me –'

'Americans don't have the attention span for the noble game, sir,' the officer said. He found a condescending smile for Irith. 'There you are. Enjoy your visit, Ms Stamp. You're in a free country now.'

As they went out, a large sign said, 'Welcome to the Independent Republic of Great Britain – the Birthplace of FREEDOM'. On a piece of paper attached to the bottom, some wag had printed, 'Cast your shackles into the bin provided.'

The terminal was grimy, unheated and freezing, and most of the lights were out.

Bragg stood near the doorway, holding their bags and looking around anxiously.

'What's the matter?' said Irith, rubbing her aching fingers together.

'Someone was supposed to meet us,' he said out of the corner of his mouth.

'Can't you call them?'

'I have no details of the contact. It's safer that way. We'll go to the hotel and they can find us there.'

Outside it was raining, and Irith's depression grew as they waited for hours in a queue that didn't move. The cab, when it finally came, was as frigid as outside, the aged driver rugged up in a greatcoat, woollen scarf and knitted cap pulled down over her ears.

'Is it always this cold?' Irith asked through chattering teeth. 'What's happened to global warming?'

'Coldest winter I've ever known,' the old woman said with relish, her breath condensing in little puffs as she spoke. 'Thames froze over on December 11 and only thawed two weeks ago.'

'It doesn't seem to bother you.' Irith thrust her hands up her sleeves.

'We're a free country again, luvvie, even if the rest of the world is against us. I've never felt so good. After we beat you in the cricket, I had sex for the first time in twenty years.' The old woman's eyes glowed, for all that she would never see eighty again. 'No maiden overs that night, I can tell you.' She cackled wickedly.

'Can you turn the heater up, please?' said Irith.

'It is up, my dear. Been to London before?'

'No,' Irith said faintly. All she could think of was bed and blankets.

The first things she noticed when they alighted at their hotel were the smell and the sound. The smell was an all-pervading swampy reek, as if the city was rotting in brine.

The reverberating *thud-thud-thud* that came from every direction at once was the sound of the great pumps that forced the Thames around the dike, for with the sea level so high the river no longer flowed. Overlain on that rhythm was the *thump-thump* of the hundred thousand smaller pumps that sucked up the salty groundwater. But for them, London would have sunk into the mire years ago.

They checked into the hotel and walked upstairs, since the lift was out of service. Irith had to rest at every floor. Her room was little warmer than outside, and gloomy under its single, low-power light. She pulled the covers off the bed, wrapped them around herself and sank into a frayed chair. Her knees were trembling.

Bragg carried the bags inside, closed the door and locked it. Irith hadn't thought beyond this point. Now she was forced to.

'I'm not sharing a room with you,' she said limply.

He put a finger to his lips. 'You'll have to get used to it,' he said in a low voice. 'I'm not letting you out of my sight.'

Why? The question applied to everything in her life. 'What's going on, Bragg?'

He put a finger to his lips. 'Later.'

The light flickered and went out. 'All this must have cost a fortune,' Irith said in a low voice. 'Why did you bring me here? It doesn't make any sense.'

'Nor to me!' he said with feeling.

'What do you want me for?'

The light came on again, duller than before. 'I'm doing what I'm told,' he muttered. 'As far as I'm concerned, you're a stupid little fool who –'

'Then why dye my hair? Why change the –'

He threw his arms around her, pushing her onto the bed and covering her mouth.

'Don't say a word about your eyes,' he said, his breath tickling her ear.

Irith managed to get her mouth free. 'Get off me, you odious man.'

'I'm not joking. Your iris implants are a death warrant for us both, even here. The Congress has spies everywhere. Pretend we've just had a lovers' tiff, and now we're making up.'

She took the point, but it could not make up for all he'd done to her. 'I wouldn't spend a minute in your arms to save the planet.'

'The feeling is mutual!' he hissed. 'I think we're being watched.'

'Where's the camera?' said Irith.

'I don't know.'

Bragg palmed something from his pocket and brought it to her face, concealed in his cupped hand. The device resembled a small pen but it was vibrating an alert and writing scrolled along a one-line screen.

'All right,' she said. 'But don't take any liberties.'

'You don't have to worry,' Bragg muttered into her ear. 'I'd sooner sleep with a leper.'

CHAPTER NINE

The following afternoon they went walking in a park near the hotel, the only place where Bragg felt free to talk. It was windy and cold, and the air had a marshy reek. His contact had still not shown up.

Irith was starving, for the hotel breakfast had been two slices of bread with a distinctly grey tinge, artificial strawberry jam which tasted as though it had been made with parsnips and food dye, and tea the colour of urine.

'No point complaining,' Bragg had said. 'They'll just tell you that adversity is good for the soul.'

Irith had noticed that the people revelled in stoicism. The horrible food, intermittent power and general air of decay only served to make them stronger. Britain had survived, despite everything the Congress could throw at them, and people believed that it would soon would prosper again.

'Surely no one can snoop on us here?' She pulled the hood tight around her ears.

'I wouldn't think so.' He had thawed a little overnight.

She stopped, facing him. 'Then give me some answers.'

'Like what?'

'I was thrown out onto the street so Lindstrom could take revenge on Mum. Force her to read the President's Page, to humiliate her and turn her into a hypocrite. But why – when I was unanimously recommended for First Class Honours and the University Medal – did they fail me? Why were my scientific papers withdrawn?'

Bragg seemed to be looking at her in a new light. 'I didn't know they had.'

She told him about it while they walked among the trees. The wind grew stronger. Behind them, a branch was wrenched off and flung into a pond.

'It doesn't fit,' said Bragg. They continued in silence for half a mile, following the winding path until it brought them back to their starting point.

'Why am I here?' said Irith. 'I thought I was going to end up working in a brothel.'

'No one is forced. If they don't like what the house offers, they can go back where they came from.'

'That's not much of a choice.'

'It's not much of a world, Irith. People who want to work are looked after. Those that don't have to look out for themselves.'

I repeat, why am I here?'

He checked all around, then said quietly, 'The house is the perfect cover for Jolyen's real operation, which is picking up people with special skills, or are enemies of the Congress – often the same thing – and taking them to safety. It requires high-level contacts and lots of money. The house provides both.'

'But . . . it's disgusting,' she said.

He smiled as if she'd said something quaint. 'Had Jolyen not bought you, you would have been scavenged by some of the most bestial monsters in this world.' He shuddered, as if he'd had personal experience of them.

Again Irith wondered if he had. They walked some more. Now they were passing the pond again. 'So that's why you were so angry with me.'

'You caused the house a lot of problems. Security had tracked you down the harbour and must have suspected you were at Jolyen's place, but they didn't have the kind of proof required to raid a place with such high-level protection. I had my people lead their spies the other way, so I could get you out without them knowing. Then you ran and ruined everything.' He no longer sounded angry about it.

'How was I supposed to know? No one told me anything.'

'If you'd stayed quiet you would have been told.'

'And if it had been you?' she snapped. 'Would you have waited meekly?'

He turned away towards the pond, which was covered in leaves scattered by the wind. A scum of ice had formed around the edges.

'Bragg?'

He hunched down on the icy stone rim, looking as though he was trying to make himself small. 'You were once in the same position, weren't you? '

'Except that I was sold to someone else.' He stared directly ahead, looking more uncomfortable every second. 'Fortunately, I ended up with Jolyen before . . . too much damage was done.'

She felt for him. 'And you tried to escape?'

He didn't answer.

'You did! So why are you giving me such a hard time?'

'You could have ruined everything. And . . .'

She squatted and took his icy hand. 'The man you shot?'

'He was scum . . . but killing is no little thing. I won't ever forget it.'

'Nor I,' she said softly. 'I hope poor Mikey is all right.' She shivered and stood up; it was too cold here.

They paced along a squelching gravel path beside another pond, the rain blowing in their eyes. Irith looked up at his closed face. 'So if I'd done what you wanted, the man you killed would still be alive.'

'And the other man,' he said.

'You killed *two* men?' She spun around, staring at him.

'Not me; one of the house guards dealt with him after we left. It was a close thing – not even Jolyen's contacts could have saved the house from two dead Security agents on the lawn. Fortunately the guards got rid of them in time.'

She recoiled. 'Is that what you do for a living? Kill people?'

'No it isn't!' he snapped. 'Besides, he was trying to kill me. And he fired first.'

'He's still dead.' She thrust her freezing hands up her sleeves.

'You hit the other bloke over the head; that could have killed him. You might have killed me in the bathroom, for that matter.'

'But I wasn't trying . . .' She trailed off, confused.

'It's not as simple as it seems.'

'Why has Jolyen sent me here?'

'I don't know. I'm just a courier, charged with delivering you to London and handing you over.'

She had a feeling he wasn't telling the whole truth, but let it pass.

'And you'll be returning to Australia?'

'I hope to be going home.'

'Where's home?'

'Boston, these days. It's flooding too.'

'What's America like these days?'

He scowled, as if she'd reminded him of something he would sooner have forgotten. 'We never gave away our sovereignty the way most other countries did. We went into the Global Congress to control it and to maintain the American way of life.'

'But America never did control it.'

'The rest of the world joined to control America. Now the United States is more religious, more fundamentalist and more isolationist than it's been in two hundred years. It's trying to shut out the rest of the world.'

She changed the subject. 'What do they want me for? Whoever "they" are that you're delivering me to.'

'I imagine it has to do with your mother.'

'What do you mean?' said Irith.

'It would be a propaganda coup for the resistance to have the daughter of the woman who reads the President's Page on their side.'

'So I'm just a name? A figurehead?'

'So I assume.'

'I'm not sure that suits me,' said Irith.

He shrugged.

Bragg finally made contact that night. The following morning, they took a cab east along the river and Bragg pointed out the long-abandoned docks, the decrepit Millennium Dome, its fabric roof flapping in the wind, and the derelict Thames Barrier at Woolwich, a series of mud-stained curves just peeping above the water.

'What was that for?' said Irith.

'London's had a problem with surge tides for hundreds of years. The barrier used to stop the sea from flooding up the river.'

'Doesn't look much use now.'

'It cost billions, but the rising seas made it obsolete. They replaced it with a vast dike across the river at Thamesmead. We'll see it before long.'

Eventually the taxi stopped at the open gates of a rambling establishment of five or six storeys. A brass plaque read 'The Bruntling Institute'. The cab went up a boggy drive raised a metre above the surrounding lands, and drew up at the front door.

'There's the Thames Dike,' said Bragg.

A kilometre or two to their right, a vast curving wall ran across the river, like a reversed concrete dam. The open area between the dike and the institute was bog and mire, dotted with dead and dying trees. The dike could keep the sea out but it couldn't stop the water table from rising, and the water that came up was seawater, turning the parks and gardens of eastern London into salt marsh.

Irith got out, butterflies fluttering in her stomach. Bragg collected her suitcase and paid the cab driver.

'Come on.' He smiled reassuringly.

It didn't help. Her knees were trembling.

'It'll be all right.' He took her hand in his free hand. 'You'll be safe here.'

How would you know? she thought. *You've never been here.*

Irith gave him a weak smile. 'Thanks, Bragg. I do appreciate all you've done for me. And I don't even know your name. Is Bragg your first name?'

'It's my last. Here I stand, E. Power Bragg, at your service.'

'E?'

After some hesitation, he said, 'Stands for Eustace, but I'd prefer you didn't reveal that to anyone. Bragg does me nicely.'

'Eustace,' she murmured. 'Good grief.' A mischievous light came into her eyes. 'Another secret I'm expected to keep for nothing. What's my silence worth, Mr E. Power Bragg?'

He chuckled. 'A kiss.'

'You're supposed to be paying me.'

'I am.'

Irith supposed she owed him that. She kissed him on the mouth, which had more impact on her than she had expected, then pulled back hastily as the door opened, revealing a tiled foyer. A porter took charge of her suitcase. A security officer spoke into a phone.

Irith stood by awkwardly, her lips tingling. Bragg was regarding her thoughtfully. She glanced away and felt her cheeks colouring.

A woman appeared from a labyrinth of corridors. She was long-limbed and attractive in a robotic, catwalk-model kind of way. 'Irith Hardey?' She held out a hand.

Irith shook it and was surprised by the pulpy handshake, like a plastic bag full of chopped liver.

'I'm very pleased to meet you, Ms Hardey. This way, please.'

'What about Bragg?'

The woman curled her elegant but downy lip. 'He won't be required. Come along.'

Irith began to follow her, then turned back. Bragg was halfway out the door. 'Thanks again,' she said, rubbing her lips.

He raised a hand, and was gone. She felt more alone than ever.

Irith hurried after the woman. The place smelled of salty damp and the walls had a growth of mould for a metre or two above the skirting boards. They went up three flights, then along a corridor where the green carpet was worn, and passed through a large mahogany door. Across a large room, a white-haired man behind an antique desk looked up and smiled.

'Irith Hardey!' He rose, extending his hand before she had come through the door. 'I'm very pleased to meet you.'

She took his hand, which was as hard as a woodchopper's.

'I'm Greenhall Cliveden, the director of the Bruntling Institute, but you can call me Hall. Sit down. Would you like a sherry? Or perhaps you would prefer tea?'

Irith had never tasted sherry. 'Sherry would be fine, thank you . . . Hall.'

He led her to a long leather couch and gestured to the woman who had brought her here. She went to a cabinet and carried over a silver tray containing a silver-topped decanter and two crystal glasses.

Hall poured two sherries, just a fraction below the top of the glass. He passed one to her, took the other and pressed it to his lips, but didn't drink. Irith took a sip of her own. It tasted thinner than she had expected.

'Welcome, Irith.'

'Thank you,' she said. 'What . . . ?'

'Yes?'

'I've come all this way, passed from one hand to the other, but I have no idea what anyone wants of me.'

'You'll be a great asset to our work . . .'

'What is the institute's work, sir?'

'Hall, please. We carry out human-Earth systems modelling and simulation.'

'I'm not sure I understand what that means.'

Hall steepled his fingers and stared at her over the apex for a second before looking down at his sherry. He dipped a manicured finger in the pale liquid and ran it round the rim of the glass.

'We're engaged on the most ambitious research project ever attempted – to develop a computer model that completely describes planet Earth, its physical and biological environment, and the role of humanity in it from the smallest scale to the greatest. And then, to predict what is happening in that environment at any time, any place, any scale. What do you think of that?' He sat back with a self-satisfied smile.

Irith's scientific training told her that it couldn't be done even if every scientist on the planet were engaged in the task, and every supercomputer ever built worked full-time in processing the data.

'It, er, sounds like an ambitious project.'

'Many people have sneered at our work over the years. The world's top scientists have said it's beyond anyone. But people doubted Einstein too. Our sponsor has great faith in us and our models. We'll prove the doubters wrong, in time.'

'It must require a huge number of scientists, just collecting data.' And the moment it was collected, much of it would be out of date and would need to be collected again.

'Fewer people than you might think,' said Hall. 'After all, much of the work has already been done, and we use sophisticated algorithms to generate real-time environmental and sociological data that . . .'

They weren't even collecting real data, so how could their models ever produce anything of value? Garbage in, garbage out.

'I can see you're sceptical,' Hall went on. 'That's good. We must question everything, abandon approaches that aren't getting anywhere, and always seek out better ways.'

'For such a project you must have high-level support,' Irith began.

'We're privately funded. Not a penny of government money has gone into this project, and never will. It's better that way. It allows us to take the long-term view. For example, in calculating the disease epidemics of the future –'

'Epidemics?' she said curiously.

'Old diseases like the flu are constantly changing. Viruses swap genetic material all the time. Ahem!' He looked embarrassed. 'But of course you know all about it. And humanity has been tinkering with genetic engineering for fifty years. Defence scientists. Bio-warfare and all that. We're trying to forecast where new epidemics will occur, and when. How fast they'll spread; how many people will be affected. Mortality and so forth.'

Suddenly it all became clear to Irith. 'And that's why you want me? Because of my research on genome engineering?'

His lips twitched and she flushed with mortification. *You fool! Of course that's not why he wants you.*

'Not exactly ...' Hall looked away. 'Your mother and all that. What a coup!'

'I thought you wanted me for what I could do,' she said miserably.

'You can do more for us, as your mother's daughter, than all our scientists toiling day in and day out for a year.' He touched the glass to his lips again, then put it down. 'Thank you so much for coming.'

She rose and shook his hand. 'Thank you.' For nothing!

The tall woman escorted her to a room on the floor below. Her suitcase was already on the stand inside the door. Irith tried the doorhandle after the woman had gone. It opened.

The room was small and painted a drab brown. The ancient carpet was worn down to its backing, the plastic bed sagged in the middle and the light didn't work. Still, she hadn't expected luxury. She sat on the bed. What was she supposed to do? She looked out the window but could see only the grey wall of the Thames Dike and an expanse of marshland half covered in creeping water. It matched her mood.

She ate dinner by herself in the dining room. Everyone was friendly, although no one wanted to sit with her. Perhaps, being no more than a mascot, she was beneath them.

There was a set menu: one leathery chop, two small greenish potatoes, half a cup of diced carrots as tough as woodchips and a dollop of artificial gravy that looked like yellow snot. Irith was used to indifferent food but the meal plumbed new depths of unpleasantness.

'You didn't eat your dinner!' the aproned serving lady scolded when Irith took back her tray. 'And I made it especially nice for you.'

'Sorry,' Irith said mechanically. 'I guess I just wasn't hungry.'

'You'll fall away to a shadow, dearie. Still, it won't go to waste.' Dipping her finger in the gravy, she sucked at it with relish.

How did they stay so cheerful? Irith went for a walk in the sleety rain but soon had to turn back. Her nose felt as if it had frostbite.

Several weeks went by. She was introduced to hundreds of people, all of whom expressed delight at meeting her, though only because of her mother. They explained their research condescendingly, as if she were a moron. She was taken to dozens of meetings, where she sat in silent boredom for hours.

When she tried to speak she was waved to silence. No one was interested in what she had to say, just who she was.

Irith spent the rest of her time in the library, reading randomly, or the gym. She was determined to regain her fitness, mental and physical, and be ready for whatever happened next. This haven could not last.

The institute gave her an allowance of two hundred pounds a week but she soon discovered there was nothing to spend it on. The shops were empty of everything but essentials and the money sat in her account untouched.

CHAPTER TEN

'You stinking little hypocrite!'

Irith jumped. The speaker was a tall, attractive woman not much older than herself, dressed in green pants and a grey form-fitting blouse, and she was so furiously angry that Irith took a step backwards.

'How dare you set yourself up as a paragon, you Australian slag!' the woman hissed. 'You've sold out, just like your mother! Piss off back to your own country. You're not wanted here.'

'I didn't set myself up . . .' Irith began, but the other woman spun on her heel and stormed off down the corridor. She had a luscious figure that was rare in these days of dearth: broad hips that swayed as she walked, globular buttocks, a nipped-in waist and a statuesque bosom. Hair the colour of jet rippled halfway down her back.

Irith turned the other way and crashed into a hurrying man who was reading an ebook as he walked. A folder of documents scattered and the reader flew out of his hand to clatter across the floor. She held her breath, expecting the screen to smash.

Without a glance at her, he bent to gather up the papers. She reached for the reader but he snapped, 'Don't touch that!'

She stepped back. He was very tall, black-haired and extremely good looking. Running into him had been like hitting a wall, for his chest was twice the width of hers and his thighs were solid bands of muscle. Irith had always been attracted to big, muscular men, so different from herself. There was something familiar about his mouth. She stared at him, wondering if he was the brother of the woman.

He gathered his papers, giving her a glance of such ferocity that she quailed, then muttered, 'Quisling!' and stalked off. The muscles of his buttocks clenched with every step. She swallowed.

Hall came out through his door, holding a document case so slender it could only have accommodated a single sheet of paper. 'Good morning, Ms Hardey,' he said with that meaningless smile.

'Who are they?' Irith asked, looking after the pair.

'Thornton Arun and his twin sister, Gretel. Not the most pleasant of people, I'm afraid.' He gave a theatrical sigh.

'I haven't met them before. What do they do?'

'Thornton is Assistant Director of Security here. He's ex-SAS, and a champion triathlete. A brilliant mind too, though ...' Hall thought better of whatever he had been planning to say. 'Gretel is a senior systems engineer, one of our best. They've not been here long. Ah, Jim!' He waved at a short, balding man in a three-piece suit. 'You're back. Did you have a good trip?'

'Not particularly.' He inspected Irith. 'Hello, I'm James Barchitt.'

She shook the extended hand. Despite the cold, it was sweaty.

'Jim is Director of Security. Jim, Irith Hardey.'

'I'm very pleased to meet you,' said Jim, staring at Irith's bosom. 'Come down some time when you're free. I'd be happy to show you around my little domain.'

'I'd love to,' said Irith. Like hell.

'I'll see you at 11.30, Jim,' said Hall, and the two men went their separate ways.

Irith wondered why the twins, alone among the people here, were so hostile. She wanted to know more about them. Especially Thornton.

One day, after she'd been at the institute for nearly a month, Irith was reading in a vacant office when Gretel ran past the door.

'Thorn!' she hissed.

His voice came from a long way away. 'What is it?'

'We've got to talk, *now*.'

His footsteps approached. Irith slipped behind her door in case they looked in.

'Not out here,' said Gretel. 'Someone might see. This office is vacant.'

They went into the room adjacent to Irith's and closed the door. Irith put her ear to the wall. Gretel's voice carried through the thin partition.

'I've just heard from Vasey. The project's been pulled forward and we've got to do the job in two weeks.'

'Christ!' said Thornton. He must have walked away, for Irith heard no more until, 'I'm not sure I can get the explosives in time.'

Irith shivered. What were they up to?

'Vasey's taking care of that,' said Gretel.

'I hope so,' said Thornton. 'It's been a long time.'

'A week would be a long time in this shithole. I can't wait to see the end of it. We'd better go through the plan –'

'Not here. Let's go for a walk.' A chair scraped across the floor. 'Are you coming tonight?'

'I'll have to, now.'

The door closed and Irith went back to her desk. It seemed pretty clear what was going on. They were working for Congress Security and they had been sent here to destroy the institute.

If they did, she would be alone and friendless in a foreign country she'd entered illegally. Irith had to find out what they were up to, then go to Hall. He wouldn't listen to anything less than solid proof.

The twins left every night at 6 pm and sometimes, when they returned the next day, they looked as if they hadn't slept. Could they be tunnelling underground, to set their explosives?

Irith waited another minute, then followed, trying to look casual. The twins went out the front door of the institute but ran into Jim Barchitt, the Director of Security, and Thornton came back with him. Gretel returned soon after, scowling. Irith pretended to study the exhibits in the foyer.

Irith followed Gretel to the simulation division, then said hello to the people she knew and looked at the work on their screens. They were condescendingly friendly and she still felt like the team mascot.

She strolled across to Gretel's corner. A simulation was running in a corner of her screen but she was bent over a laptop. Edging around the wall, Irith caught a glimpse of its screen, which showed a map of an underground labyrinth or mine.

Irith looked away but Gretel must have sensed her presence, for she blanked the screen and spun around.

'What the fuck do you think you're doing?'

'I was just –' Irith began.

'Piss off! Don't come anywhere near me,' Gretel snapped.

Cheeks flaming, Irith hurried away.

A couple of hours later the twins went out again and headed around the side of the building. She hurried for the rear door of the institute and was behind an earth bank as they walked by.

'We'd better!' Gretel said vehemently. 'If this doesn't go perfectly there'll be bodies everywhere.'

'Most likely ours,' said Thornton. 'I think . . .'

They headed towards the river. Irith crouched in the icy wind, raindrops spotting her face. Bodies everywhere? Were they tunnelling under the institute to blow it up? If she got in the way, she would end up dead.

After borrowing an umbrella from the doorman, she took the path down towards the river. The wall of the Thames Dike loomed to her right and sea level was six metres higher on the other side. The dike had gates that opened to simulate an incoming tide and let water in to flush the river. Because of the difference in levels, the gates had to be closed and the outgoing tide pumped out. The pumps were thumping deafeningly, shaking the ground and making ripples on every puddle.

A muddy path wound through the bogs to the river. Gretel and Thornton were well ahead. Irith followed, half hidden by the umbrella, hoping they would stop and she could sneak up on them, but they walked out onto the end of a jetty and stood close together, talking.

She continued along the foreshore path to a bench and sat down. The wind brought tears to her eyes. She had read the history of the area. This stretch of the river had once been called Gallion's Reach. On the other side were the entrances to the former Royal Docks, and between them was the runway of London City Airport. A plane was just coming in to land. Up the river to her left she could see the obsolete Thames Barrier and, in the distance, the rusting masts of the Millennium Dome.

Irith turned back to the jetty but the twins had gone. They were halfway back to the institute and it was impossible to get close enough to overhear them. She would have to find another way to spy on them, though the only way she could think of required the assistance of the sleazy Director of Security.

She selected her clothing carefully – pants that were tight across the backside, a push-up bra, a blouse that nipped around her tiny waist and clung to her breasts, and slut-red lipstick. She looked like a cheap tart and felt bad about it. No, her own survival was at stake. She had to do whatever it took.

'Hel-lo,' James Barchitt said as she knocked on his open door.

'I've come to have a look around,' Irith said, 'if you've got the time.'

'I've always got time for you, Irith.' His eyes popped out on stalks and slid into her cleavage.

He showed her the offices, the monitoring screens and banks of recorders, and introduced her to the other members of his team. The women sneered and the men stirred uncomfortably in their chairs. Barchitt took her back to his office, sitting so close to her their knees touched.

'I ran into Thornton the other day,' she said casually. 'Literally.'

Barchitt's eyes oozed down her chest. 'I can't say I like the fellow much.'

'Oh?' said Irith.

'Not a team player, and his sister is worse.'

'Where did they come from?'

'I couldn't say. And I'm Director of Security. Ironic, isn't it?'

No, just incompetent. 'Jim?'

'Yes, my dear?' He plopped a meaty hand on her knee.

She wanted to vomit. Instead, she spoke in a naive, breathy voice. 'I've always wondered how 'bugs' work. Could you show me a few?'

He laughed condescendingly. 'We don't call them bugs. Come down the back and I'll show you. Bit of a squeeze, but I'm sure you won't mind.'

In the storeroom, he pulled down one tiny device after another, mostly listening devices or spycams. The shelves were close together and his chest rubbed against her breasts every time he passed, which was often.

'Now this is an interesting one.' He opened a small, grey plastic case which contained a tiny digital meter, smaller than a box of matches. 'The TrackMeister AA by Surveill Inc. It's absolutely top of the line.'

She put on the breathy voice again. 'What does it do, Jim?'

He was almost slobbering on her. 'It's a personal motion tracker. Tells you everywhere the target has been over a 24-hour period, to the metre. You can even tell which toilet cubicle they've been doing their dirty deeds in.'

Irith could have done without the insight into his mind. 'How does it work?'

'Er,' he frowned, 'I guess it continually records GPS data.'

'What's that?' said Irith, though she knew perfectly well.

'Global Positioning System. Or is it an inertia-based system? No, I'm sure it's GPS.'

'Isn't it a bit big to hide on someone?'

'Clever girl! This is the monitor. The sensor, or *bug* if you like, is tiny.' He opened the other side of the case, spilling out half a dozen tiny rods that resembled refillable pencil leads. 'It's brilliant technology – there are fifty million transistors in each of these. You can put one in the refill compartment of a pencil, inside a plastic paper clip, a thousand different places. Recover it afterwards, slip it in this little socket and you can read everywhere they've been.'

He moved in until his chest flattened her breasts.

'I've always been fascinated by bugs.' She looked into his eyes. 'Could I have a go of this one? Would that be all right, Jim?'

'Anything you want, Irith,' he said hoarsely. 'Anything at all.' There was a ridge nearly two inches long in his trousers. Just like a penis, only smaller, she was tempted to say.

Irith disengaged herself and took the motion tracker back to her room. There she prepared everything carefully. It had to work. She couldn't stomach that again.

That afternoon she walked past Gretel's bag when she had gone to the toilet. Irith slid a sensor rod in through a seam in the leather and kept going.

·· • ● • ··

For security, the TrackMeister did not transmit its data, so it was difficult to discover in a bug sweep. However, that meant it had to be recovered after use the following day, which was proving more difficult than Irith had imagined.

Gretel had spent the entire day at her workstation, not even stopping for lunch. Irith sat in the back of the office, surreptitiously studying her target. As usual, no one paid her any attention – not being taken seriously had its advantages. Thus far, Gretel hadn't been out of the room. And Thornton had been with her for the past hour. It was 5.30, so they'd be leaving soon.

She had to get them away from the bag. After filling a mug with synthetic coffee, which tasted like swamp water, Irith wandered across to Gretel's corner. Gretel was concentrating on a simulation on her screen. Thornton looked up and scowled.

The bag sat on the floor between the two workstations but there was no way she could get to it. She edged closer to Gretel's laptop, pretended to trip and spilled the cup of coffee on the keyboard.

'Shit!' she said. 'Sorry.' Irith dabbed at it with her sleeve.

Gretel shot out of her chair and turned the laptop upside down. Coffee dribbled out. 'You bloody fool!' She was trembling with rage.

'I'm really, really sorry. It was an accident.'

'Piss off, you little slag,' said Thornton.

Irith hurried out of the way.

Gretel disconnected the laptop, wiped it off and said, 'I'd better take it down to the workshop, just to be sure. Thorn, could you ...?'

'I'll give you a hand.' They went out.

As soon as they were gone, Irith retrieved the motion sensor embedded in the handle of Gretel's bag and went back to her office, but dared not check the TrackMeister in the institute. That evening she took a pencil torch and spare batteries and walked up Whinchat Road to a café.

It was empty apart from a thin little waitress sitting at a window table, reading a graphic novel..

'Hi,' said Irith. 'Could I have a black coffee, please?'

'Black coffee?'

She looked into the dessert stand. She had a hankering for something sweet, but the solitary wedge of pie looked so plastic she decided to go without. 'Do you have news readers here?' There were no printed newspapers any more.

'Of course,' said the girl, rubbing at a patch of eczema on her arm. 'That'll be eight pounds, please.'

Irith paid the money and the waitress set the news reader down, slipped its cable into the socket in the table and twisted until it locked in. The flat, flexible screen, the size of a printed atlas, lit up.

Irith read *The Times* until the coffee came. It was a purple-grey colour with a strange, bitter aroma. She took a sip. The taste was unbelievably horrible.

'Excuse me,' she called to the girl, 'where does the coffee come from?'

'Birmingham.'

That famous coffee-growing area. 'What's in it?'

The girl read the label. 'Roasted dandelion root, roasted barley and roasted acorns.'

'What about coffee beans?' Irith hated making a fuss but she had fixated on a decent cup of coffee, and thinking about it made it worse.

'You want *real* coffee?'

'Yes.'

'It would be twenty pounds a cup –'

'I don't care. I'll have one.'

'... if we could get it,' the girl finished. 'But we can't. Our regular customers don't seem to mind.' She hovered, somewhere between anxious and irritable.

'Never mind. I'll make do, thanks.'

Irith called up a street map of East London on the reader, then ran the motion tracker. Gretel had travelled quickly to Beckton last night, across the river north of the former Royal Docks, then spent the rest of the night moving about a small area to the east of the docks. There were a number of gaps in the record, though, and there was no way of telling where she'd been.

Was that where she and Thornton met their co-conspirators? What were they really up to? Irith took another sip of the gruesome coffee and tried to formulate a plan. Since Hall didn't take her seriously, she had to know where the twins had been before accusing them. But ... how could she hope to spy on a professional and get away with it?

One step at a time. She would go to Beckton, have a look around and decide what to do next.

She walked to Plumstead Station, caught a train to Greenwich and took the Docklands light rail to Gallion's Reach, the closest station to her destination. After checking the map, she set the motion tracker to trace out the path it had taken the previous night.

It took her north towards Beckton but after an hour she had not gone very far, for the TrackMeister proved rather less precise than its manufacturer's claims. The tracker was only accurate to within ten metres and there were long gaps in the record. It wasn't good enough to discover exactly where Gretel had gone, though it seemed she had not entered any of the houses there.

It was late April now but the weather was winter-cold with not a sign of spring, and doomsayers were saying that there would be no summer this year. Some climate models suggested they might be right.

Yellow fog wreathed between the buildings and Irith's footsteps echoed eerily on the pavement. There wasn't a single person on the streets and she wished she wasn't either. Even if she discovered where they'd gone, what good would it do?

Click! She checked over her shoulder, saw nothing, and pressed on toward a station not far ahead – Cyprus. She was almost back to her starting point.

She moved back against a wall to check the map and the tiny screen, and realised that there was a segment missing from Gretel's track. Furthermore, where it resumed, it went through a brick wall, but how could that be? The TrackMeister only showed movement in the horizontal plane, of course. Gretel must have gone below ground, and the tracker would not be able to detect any GPS signal.

The missing segment had been further east, near the river. The tracker led Irith east along Armada Way, around a couple of roundabouts and through a rusty chain-link fence into wasteland where the thump of drainage pumps shook the ground. Another gap appeared in the record. She wasn't far from the Thames Dike, but on the other side of the river from the institute.

She scrambled along the bank, feeling her way in the fog. A jetty appeared on her left. The track reappeared in the little screen. The cladding of the bank was broken here and she almost fell into a tangle of collapsed concrete slabs. As she crouched, the ground exhaled a gust of stale air. This had to be the entrance Gretel had taken.

Dare she go down? Irith took several deep breaths, then felt her way between the blocks. The cavity smelled vaguely chemical, which wasn't surprising. From what she'd read in the library, the area had been an industrial site for a couple of centuries and an enormous gasworks for half that time.

She worked her way down the bank. As she entered the hole, a brick slipped underfoot and her leg scraped across broken concrete, skinning her ankle. She moved in through the entrance, rubbed her throbbing ankle and turned on her torch.

She was in an old sewerage or drainage tunnel about two metres high. Judging by the brickwork, it went back to the nineteenth century. Water was seeping through the walls and covered the floor ahead. She would have to wade and dared not take off her boots; there could be anything below the water.

Irith rolled up her trousers. Her ankle was scratched but not bleeding. She moved forward until the cold water went over the tops of her boots. There was no sign that Gretel had been here. Was there any point in going further?

Fifty metres along, the tunnel met another and her vague feelings of claustrophobia eased. Irith decided to take a look around the corner and, if she didn't see anything, she would go back.

The junction had been bricked up long ago but a hole had been broken through the wall. She shone the torch in. The new tunnel was a square concrete conduit that ran straight as far as she could see in either direction. To her left lay a mound of rubble – reinforced concrete piles and other debris – where part of the roof had fallen in. It looked as if something had been built over the top, and the tunnel had subsequently collapsed under the additional weight. In the other direction, it was clear.

Irith consulted the TrackMeister but there was another gap in the record. Which way? This tunnel was also ankle-deep in water, so there were no tracks to follow. She waded down to the mound, inspecting it with the beam of the torch.

The grey concrete was threaded with little muddy trails – rats. She shivered. Rats carried disease, and plague had made a reappearance in the last few years. There were also less prominent markings, hand and boot prints, and one boot print was huge. Thornton's, she assumed. Few men would had feet as big as his.

Irith felt an uncomfortable sensation in the middle of her back and thought longingly of her room in the institute. *No, just a bit further.* She wasn't going to be a victim ever again.

The water was deeper on the other side of the rubble, almost up to her knees. She moved slowly through it, her feet freezing. The tunnel ran straight for a hundred metres before curving gently to the left. That seemed wrong, unless it had once run into the river.

She encountered another bricked-off wall but the motion tracker showed nothing. The track continued north-west of her present position, which was no help, since she couldn't see how to get there.

Irith ran her hand over the brickwork but it proved to be old and solid. She splashed back to the pile of rubble, climbed on top and shone her torch all around. Nothing but water and tunnel walls.

She shone the torch straight up, and saw that a long tear in the concrete was partly plugged by fallen slabs and pillars of the same material. Jagged, rusting iron rods protruded from broken edges. Could Gretel and Thornton have gone up there? It hardly seemed likely, although at one point the rods had been bent back on themselves. It could have occurred in the collapse, but Irith thought it looked artificial.

What were they doing in here anyway? Maybe their plans had nothing to do with the institute.

The hole was a good metre and a half above her outstretched arms. Presumably they had a rope, or let down a ladder. Irith climbed onto the highest point of the pile. A metre to go. She tested the stability of the rubble beneath her, wondering if she dared jump for the bars. She'd done gymnastics as a child, so it wasn't beyond her, but if she missed, she risked breaking an ankle.

Irith visualised the jump and thought she might just make it. She put the pencil torch between her teeth then sprang, straining upwards as far as she could stretch. She just caught the iron rods. He fingers slipped, she clenched them around the bars and hung at full stretch, the torch waggling in her mouth. She pulled herself up into the hole, where she managed to get her back to the concrete, her feet onto a reinforcing rod and was able to let go with one hand and use the torch.

It was hard to believe that this was the main way in – the cavity meandered through the wreckage and a big man like Thornton would have had trouble squeezing through. Irith managed it without too much difficulty, though the thought of the rubble shifting aroused fears of being crushed, trapped and taking days to die.

Finally she emerged into what appeared to be the basement of an abandoned building. To her left the concrete floor was intact, but on the right the broken slabs were tilted crazily. The far end of the room was heaped with rubble.

Irith stood up, shining the torch around, and thought she saw a movement in the rubble. As she turned to investigate, an arm went across her throat, another around her waist and she was lifted off the ground. She thrashed but could not break free.

'Stop struggling or I'll break your neck!' said Thornton.

CHAPTER ELEVEN

Irith tried to punch backwards but met only air. The torch flew from her hand and rolled across the floor. Thornton spun her around, then someone came up from the darkness and lashed out at her. Pain flared on her cheekbone. A torch came on, in her face.

'Don't try it!' said Gretel. She drew back her fist, Irith went still and Gretel bound her hands.

Thornton put Irith down. 'Don't move.'

She sat. Brother and sister exchanged glances. Gretel went through Irith's pockets and pulled out the motion tracker. 'You could die for this,' she said coldly. 'Who are you working for?'

'I'm not working for anyone,' said Irith, realising that if they were terrorists, this was the safest place in England to kill her.

Gretel struck her across the face. 'Don't lie to me, you little bitch!'

Thornton pulled Gretel away and they conferred in low voices, never taking their eyes off her. She hissed at him. He shook his head. She drew pointed fingers across her throat. He said, 'No!' low and urgent.

Irith went numb with terror. If Gretel convinced him, she was dead.

Thornton broke away. 'So that's why you were batting your eyes at Jim,' he said contemptuously, 'letting him feel you up in exchange for this tracker.'

'He wasn't feeling me up!' Irith said. 'W-what are you going to do to me?'

'Cut your throat and stuff you in a crack to rot,' said Gretel.

'I didn't mean any harm,' Irith quavered.

'Then start talking,' said Thornton. 'And don't leave anything out.'

'We can't afford this,' said Gretel. 'Just do the business, Thorn.'

He held up a hand. 'Wait a minute. There's something not right.'

'What do you mean?' said Gretel.

'If she was just a little tart she wouldn't have come anywhere near here.

But she's not Security, either. She's an amateur – so what the hell is she up to?'

Gretel hefted a lump of four by two with rusty nails sticking out of one end. 'Maybe you're right. Spill it, Irith or I'll smash your pretty face.'

She meant it, and Irith was no good at lying – she had to take a chance and tell the truth. She gasped out her story, and her mother's. At the end, the twins exchanged glances.

'Why are you spying on us?' said Thornton.

'I overheard you in the office the other day. You were talking about blowing up the institute.'

'The *institute*?' Thornton said incredulously.

Gretel nudged him in the ribs. 'Go on, Irith.'

'I . . . I thought you were spies for Security. If you destroyed the institute, what would happen to me? I had to find out what you were doing and try to stop it.'

Thornton laughed.

'Why the hell would we sabotage the institute?' said Gretel. 'It's a folly run by people who still believe in the tooth fairy.

'Then what are you planning to destroy?' said Irith. Could they be urban terrorists, trying to bring down the government?

'We're asking the questions.' Gretel exchanged glances with her brother.

'I believe she's telling the truth,' said Thornton.

'So do I but it doesn't solve our problem.'

'We'll have to take her with us.'

'Vasey will have a fit. Put her in some out-of-the-way hole until it's over.'

'And if we don't make it back?' said Thornton.

'We won't have to worry, will we?'

'I don't want to do that, Gretel.'

Gretel poked his chest with a stiff finger. 'I don't believe this, Thorn,' she cried. 'You want to get into her pants!'

'I don't,' he said coldly, but Thornton's lingering look gave the lie to that, and it had saved Irith's life. 'We're taking her with us. I'll handle Vasey.'

'I hope you can, little brother. If this fucks up because of her . . .'

'Let's not waste any more time, then.'

Gretel wound a piece of rag around Irith's eyes and tied it tightly at the back. She took her by the wrist and led her across the room. 'Crouch down here. Keep moving.'

It was a struggle to walk on the rubble-covered floor. Thornton put a big hand on the top of Irith's head and another in the middle of her back. 'Bend down.'

She went forward for about twenty feet.

'You can stand up now,' he said. 'Left here.'

The tunnel was narrow, for she kept bumping into the walls with one shoulder or the other, and the surface was irregular. She got a hand to the wall, which felt like chalk. They walked for a long time. Several times she heard the thud of doors being closed behind them. Once she smelled a bituminous odour; another time, old sewage. Further on, the ground had the smell of salt marsh.

Finally they stopped. A door was closed behind them and bolted. It was brighter here: light came through her blindfold and she heard the thump of a great pump. The air felt damp and had a mouldy smell, but her claustrophobia had been driven away by greater terrors.

'What the hell is this?' said a female voice in an accent that Irith thought might have been Swedish.

'This,' said Thornton with ironic emphasis, 'is the *famous* Irith Hardey.'

'She set off an alarm over by the jetty,' said Gretel. 'She was sneaking in through the collapsed area.'

'I thought that was blocked off last month.' A man's voice, authoritative but irritable.

'It must have collapsed again,' said Thornton. 'A hole goes all the way down.'

'Get someone to fix it,' said the man. 'And do the same for her.'

There was a long silence. Irith could feel the pounding of her heart. She wriggled her fingers but couldn't reach the knots.

'We might use her as a bargaining chip, Vasey,' said Thornton. 'Her mother —'

'Be buggered!' said Vasey. 'The operation's going ahead on Saturday night and we can't afford any more complications.'

'I thought we had another fortnight.'

'Things have changed! If we don't do it now the opportunity will be lost.'

'We can't put everything together in time. Something's bound to go wrong.'

'The other team has been given their orders and gone,' said Vasey. 'Most of your equipment's in place, so it's just a matter of following through the plan.'

'But we haven't rehearsed it,' said Gretel.

'I don't have any choice. Stick around, Thorn. I'll be giving the orders in a few minutes. Put her somewhere for the duration, then get rid of her.'

Gretel hissed something to her brother.

Thornton's big hand encircled Irith's wrist, pulling her away. 'Please give me a chance,' she whispered. 'I'm on your side.'

'Be quiet.' He dragged her backwards, then pushed her down. 'Gretel, can you come here for a minute?'

'I've just got to get a few things,' she muttered.

Irith heard Thornton moving away. She tore off the blindfold with her bound hands. She was in a cylindrical chamber, probably an abandoned underground storage tank. Through the opening she could see a large open space where three tunnels intersected. One was an ancient brick tunnel, several metres in diameter. The second was concrete, somewhat larger. The third tunnel was larger still. The centre of the intersection had been broken out to form a space ten metres across and it was crammed with desks, workstations, terminals and screens. Cables snaked across the floor. At least a dozen people sat at the desks. Others were gathered around a short, balding man with tufts of bristly hair sticking out above his ears, presumably Vasey.

He strode to a large screen and brought up a detailed map. It meant nothing to Irith. He gestured to a stout man in green overalls and began drawing on the screen with an electronic stylus, evidently giving him instructions. The stout man studied the diagram, nodded and stepped back. Vasey gestured to a little blonde woman, cleared the screen and drew on it anew.

Shortly it was Gretel's turn, followed by Thornton's. They received their instructions and came back to where Irith was waiting.

'This way,' said Thornton, drawing her into the smaller concrete tunnel.

'Where are you taking me?' whispered Irith, trembling uncontrollably. If he was going to kill her, then bound as she was there was nothing she could do to save herself.

There came a faint noise from down the old brick tunnel to Irith's left. *Tap-tap-tap.*

'What's that?' hissed Thornton.

Gretel, further along, didn't answer. Vasey stopped drawing, head cocked to one side. There was no further sound. He had just turned back to the screen when a muffled thud came from the brick tunnel and clouds of dust billowed out.

Irith first thought the tunnel had collapsed. Everyone in the room was staring at the entrance.

'We're under attack!' roared Vasey. 'To your positions!'

Crack-crack! A tall man on the edge of the group fell down, red patches flowering across his back. An automatic weapon chattered. Two more people fell, a man and the little blonde woman. Someone screamed. The white screen burst in a shower of glass and plastic, and everyone scattered.

'What is it?' cried Gretel, running towards them. She peered around the entrance at the brick tunnel, the dust and the bodies.

'We've been betrayed!' said Thornton, pulling her back. The defenders began to return fire.

'How?'

'The alarms didn't go off,' he said grimly. 'Someone let the bastards in.'

He sprang to a cabinet on the wall, tore it open and tossed a short, stubby assault rifle to his sister. He took another for himself and threw an ammunition box over his shoulder.

A woman shouted, 'Wipe the data! Then blow the machines!'

Half a dozen people were yelling at once. Across the room a man was moaning. A woman began to scream in terror. Irith could feel the tension. She tried fruitlessly to free her hands.

'Shut it!' roared Vasey. 'The plan, remember? Lights! Targets! Fire and withdraw. Then we blow –'

The lights went out, except for a single spotlight aimed at the brick tunnel. People began firing in that direction. A round object fizzed out of the tunnel, landed in the middle of the room and burst with a brilliant blue-white light. An automatic rifle opened up from inside the brick tunnel. As Irith watched in horror, five or six people fell, gorily dead. Bullets ricocheted around the room. Someone gasped, close by.

A group behind a row of workstations fired back. A man wailed. The rifle fired again, chewing chunks out of the plastic and toppling more of the defenders.

Irith realised she was standing in view of any gunman who might come out of the tunnel. She dropped to the floor and crawled under a table. She no longer knew what was right or what was wrong, but if she stayed here she only had minutes to live. For the moment that put her on the twins' side.

Vasey wriggled under the collapsed white screen and discharged a long burst of gunfire up the brick tunnel. The enemy gun fell silent. He scanned the room and, catching sight of Irith scrabbling across the floor, screamed, 'You led them here, you bitch.'

He swung his rifle at her but another burst came from the tunnel and he turned red all over. Irith wriggled behind a low bench. She could hear Gretel and Thornton whispering not far away.

'They're not taking any prisoners,' he said. 'We're not going to get out of here alive.'

Irith poked her head out. Gretel swung the rifle at her but Thornton threw out a hand.

'It wasn't her,' he snapped. 'This was an inside job. Who's not here tonight?'

Irith slipped up beside them. More shots echoed around the room, then came a pulpy thud and wetness spattered Irith's cheek. She put her hand up to her face and it came back red.

'Gretel?' cried Thornton. Gretel groaned. 'Are you all right?'

'I've been hit, Thorn.'

CHAPTER TWELVE

In the confined space, the firing was deafening. The flare burned luridly through the gun smoke, revealing soldiers at the entrance to the brick tunnel. Irith could see their outlines and their muzzle flashes. She ducked below the bench, furiously rasping her bonds against the edge of a concrete wall.

Gretel's blouse was soaked in blood from the left collarbone to her waist.

'Christ! It's bleeding bad.' Thornton tore her blouse open and studied the hole. 'A ricochet, and it's gone in under the collarbone. I'll have to get a bandage on it.'

'There isn't time, Thorn. Run while you can.' Gretel sagged against him. She was going into shock.

He tore the blouse into wide strips, folded one into a wad and pressed it against the wound. The blood soaked straight through it. He pressed another on top of it, then a third. 'Hold that, as tightly as you can.'

Gretel rallied a little. 'It's all over,' she whispered. 'We've lost.'

'Not yet! We're going to get out of here. We've got to.'

'It's too late. Blow the data centre and go.'

'I can't get to the switch.'

'Use a grenade,' Gretel said limply.

'I can't reach them either. We'll have to pray the data has been wiped.'

'We're fucked, Thorn.'

'Not while you and I are still alive.'

The intruders were fired upon from three or four places, but none went down, for they were wearing ballistic chest armour. They fired back. Another defender fell silent. An explosion behind the workstations sent pieces of sheet metal in all directions. A buckled computer chair landed next to Irith's foot. She continued rasping and the cords parted.

'Was that the databanks?' asked Thornton.

'Not a big enough explosion,' whispered Gretel.

'Is there another way out?' Irith hissed.

Thornton, packing another wad over the wound, did not answer. Irith picked up Gretel's weapon. 'Is there any special trick to using this?'

He looked doubtful. 'Not without –'

'I was in the rifle club at uni, for years.'

'Point and pull the trigger,' he said, 'but you can't –'

She crawled under the table. The attacking soldiers were just visible, sheltering in the brick tunnel entrance. Irith couldn't shoot them in cold blood, but she could scare them off. She pointed just above their heads and pulled the trigger. The weapon slammed back against her shoulder as the jacketed bullets chewed brick out of the tunnel roof. The soldiers ducked out of sight.

'Which way?' she hissed, crawling away in case they fired at her muzzle flash. Thornton tightened the bandage with quick jerks that drew winces from Gretel.

'Lead the way,' said Irith. 'I'll give you what cover I can.'

'Bring the ammo box.'

He slung his weapon over one shoulder, picked his sister up and ducked away. Irith kept watch on the brick tunnel. The soldiers were firing from inside now, picking off Vasey's people one by one. They couldn't shoot at Irith without coming out of the tunnel, but in a few seconds they would be able to.

A helmet appeared around the edge. She fired a short burst. The helmet disappeared in a cloud of dust. Irith hefted the ammunition box, which was incredibly heavy, and backed towards the gloom of the escape tunnel. Behind her, someone screamed. The last of the defenders?

The soldiers advanced warily from the brick tunnel. One was trying to call on his radio. She heard him say three times, 'Can you hear me?'

Irith fired. Bullets thudded into his chest armour, hurling him off his feet. The others threw themselves out of the way. She ducked into the concrete tunnel and stumbled after Thornton up a gentle slope.

He was at the far door, trying to open it with one hand. Gretel was propped against the wall, breathing shallowly, her eyes half closed. The bandage was soaked. Irith staggered up and slid the box across the floor. 'What can I do?'

'Don't touch the door!' he snapped. 'It's keyed to us. If you lay a finger on it, the security system will lock it and we'll be trapped. Guard my back.'

She pointed the weapon down the tunnel, which was so full of smoke and dust that she couldn't see the other end. Her eyes were stinging and she felt very afraid. Were Gretel and Thornton from Security . . . or were they terrorists? Who were these intruders who seemed bent on killing them all? The carnage made her stomach churn.

The door opened silently and Thornton was through with Gretel before Irith realised it.

'Come if you're coming!' he snapped.

She slid through. He pushed the door shut and pressed the locking device. It didn't lock. 'Fuck! What's the matter with it?' He pressed it again, with the same result.

'Where to?' said Irith.

'Go that way.' Thornton took her pencil torch from his pocket and pointed to the right. A stone's throw ahead, their tunnel met another at right angles. He tossed her the torch.

'And you?' said Irith.

'None of your business. I'm grateful for what you've done but you're not one of us.'

He shone his own torch on the wall. A number of conduits ran along it, power and communications for the covert operation within. Tearing a fire axe from its bracket, he smashed open a switchbox, bared wires with a rubber-handled knife and bridged them with the blade. Thunk. The lock slammed closed.

'Gretel,' he said urgently. 'Get off a warning code, *now*.'

She fumbled a mobile out of her pocket, pressed a sequence of keys, waited, pressed more keys then switched it off. 'The code for absolute bloody disaster,' she whispered.

Thornton was working on another switchbox, one with dozens of switches, panels and readouts.

'What are you doing?' Irith said.

'Sabotaging the place, otherwise they'll be through the door in minutes – and then nothing can save us. Bye.'

'How do I get out?' said Irith.

'You'll find a way.'

She took a few steps up the tunnel. 'What if I can't?'

The door was struck hard from the other side. Irith spun around, staring at the metal.

'Not my problem, Irith,' said Thornton. 'You've caused enough trouble as it is. Now run for your very life. If they catch you – Gretel, fill my pockets with ammo, please.'

Irith bolted up to the right-hand tunnel, which sloped toward the door, turned right and down a broad concrete tunnel. The floor was covered in a thin layer of clay, slippery to walk on, and the air smelled faintly of gas.

She had only gone a couple of hundred metres when the tunnel floor shuddered and she heard the scream of tormented metal. She stopped, head cocked to one side. Low rumbles echoed down the tunnel, and the sound of rubble falling in. A lot of rubble – it went on for the best part of a minute.

Then absolute silence fell. Even the groundwater pumps had stopped. Had Thornton cut the power? Or had the intruders?

How long would it take for seeping groundwater to fill this labyrinth? Days, surely? But if she couldn't find a way out she could be trapped in here for days, or even weeks, before she starved.

Irith continued down the tunnel, now noticing every thread of water that trickled down the walls, every water stain and calcareous concretion hanging from the roof. In the distance she heard a faint soughing, like wind around a ruined building. It was an odd noise to hear down here – unless she was close to an exit.

As she hurried forward, the sound grew. It was no longer a soughing but a sighing, and then a rush and tumble that grew ever louder. The sound wasn't wind, it was water! Her heart lurched. Thornton must have opened a floodgate into the river and a flood was racing towards her. Even had she been the best swimmer in the world, it was a death sentence here. If it didn't smash her against the wall, it would fill the tunnels and drown her.

Irith fought the panic and shone her torch forward. Ahead, the tunnel turned a corner. She ran down to it, hoping to see a shaft or riser that might indicate a way out, but ahead was nothing save blank concrete and the echoing roar of the water. A surge rushed toward her, calf-deep, and after that the level kept rising. She let out an involuntary cry and ran the other way.

Suddenly her ears popped – the air pressure had changed and the flood must be close. She splashed through water that dragged at her calves and her legs felt weak. Her scoured ankle began to throb.

As she approached the tunnel down to the command centre, Irith turned her torch off. The soldiers could be through the door by now and if they saw a light they'd shoot. She pushed through knee-deep water, trying to make as little noise as possible.

Lights flashed a long way ahead. Someone signalling? No, gunfire, an automatic weapon firing in bursts. Two weapons, directed away from her. The enemy must be firing at Thornton. She made out answering shots but saw no flash.

During a lull in the gunfire, a man cried out in pain. Not Thornton: his voice was deeper. More flashes had to be the enemy. She waded to the side of the tunnel, the better to see, tripped and dropped the torch. It clattered against the wall.

'What's that?' someone cried as she retrieved it. 'Jacques, behind us. Jacques?'

She dared not answer, but that was the wrong thing too. A shot ricocheted off the wall near her shoulder. Another plunged into the water not far away. They were trying to kill her.

Irith aimed at the muzzle flash, pulled the trigger and held it until her weapon stopped firing. The noise was deafening and, when it stopped suddenly, her shoulder felt battered black and blue. No one fired back. She pushed on hastily. There was no point in creeping now; if the enemy didn't get her, the flood would. With every step she expected bullets to tear into her.

Nothing happened. She passed the side passage that led to the door and shone her torch down it. The passage was empty, the door wide open, and water was pouring through. The chamber with the computers must be flooded already.

She kept going and at the next corner came upon a soldier, floating face down. The water was dark with his blood; her burst had caught him in the neck, above the ballistic vest. She edged by and turned the corner, shuddering and wanting to vomit. Only then did she realise that there could be more soldiers ahead and she was out of ammunition.

The soldier's gun was under the red water and probably useless. She waded to a second corner and ran into another body. One of Thornton's victims, presumably. The level of the water seemed to be rising, even though this tunnel led slightly uphill. Pushing through the water was exhausting.

In the distance, at the furthermost illumination of her torch, she glimpsed a steel door at the top of a ramp. Thornton must have taken Gretel through it. The water was moving up Irith's thighs, rising rapidly now. She prayed the door wouldn't be locked.

Something bumped into the back of her legs. Her flesh crawled and Irith whirled, flailing with the little torch. It was the man she had killed, now floating on his back, one arm outstretched as if reaching for her. She pushed him away with the barrel of her rifle but the rising water brought him back. His mouth was open and full of blood and his eyes seemed to be accusing her. The other corpse bobbed behind him.

She scooted up the ramp. At the door, the water was only knee-deep. She tried to turn the handle. It didn't budge. She banged on it with the butt of the gun.

'Help!' she yelled. 'Help, help, help!'

She was having to clear her ears continually. Only minutes left, if the water kept rising at this rate. The dead man prodded at her calf. Pushing him away, she pounded on the door until the stock of her rifle was warped. She let it fall, pushed the dead man off for the third time and slumped against the door, waiting for the inevitable.

Then, high up she saw a ragged, rusty hole, not much bigger than her thumb. She propped the rifle against the door, stepped up on it and, balanced precariously, screamed through the hole, 'Thornton. Help!'

After a long interval the door was thrust open, knocking her down into the water. She struggled to her feet, was caught by the collar and jerked through. The door was forced closed.

She collapsed on the wet floor, looking up. 'I didn't think you'd come back.'

With a thundering roar the flood hit the other side of the door, then water squirted underneath and all around, like leaks through the pressure hull of a submarine. A rod of solid water stung the back of her neck. Something thudded against the door.

'What's that?' he said.

'I imagine it's the soldier I shot.'

'That was *you*?'

'Yes.' She could not talk about such a horrible, final act.

'Then you saved our lives.'

Irith nodded curtly. 'Where's Gretel?'

'Up ahead. We'd better be going. Water pressure could tear those hinges out of the wall.' He headed up the tunnel, almost at a run.

Irith hobbled after him. 'What happened? With the water, I mean?'

Thornton broke stride for a second, then continued. 'We had a contingency plan in case they discovered our command centre, but the attack came so fast no one could get to the switches. The alarms had been disabled by whoever betrayed us. I cut off the pumps and opened a floodgate to flood the centre, but the water came the wrong way. Maybe their backup plan was to drown us all.'

'How is she?'

'In much pain, but she'll survive. She's the toughest person I know.'

'Where are we going?'

'We've got another hide-out . . . though it'll be difficult to get to now.'

He was giving nothing away. Thornton still didn't trust her and she could hardly blame him. She didn't trust him either. He could be a terrorist, and the men who had attacked could be legitimate authority, for all she knew.

Irith trudged after him, so overcome that it was a struggle to think. They were in a broad, square tunnel and the walls were cracked and oozing. Flakes of concrete had spalled off the roof, exposing iron-stained concrete and reinforcing rods rusted to nothing.

'What's all this for?'

He shrugged. 'Who knows? Second World War vintage, I'd say.'

They rounded a corner and the torch picked out Gretel, sitting up on a knob of concrete in pants and bra. A bloodstained bandage covered her shoulder. She looked very pale, although she was able to smile when she saw her brother.

'Irith saved us,' he said gruffly.

'Thank you,' Gretel whispered.

Thornton took his sister into his arms.

'I can walk,' she protested. 'I'm feeling better now. Put me down.'

'Save your strength. We've a long haul ahead.'

They trudged through a labyrinth of concrete and brick tunnels, conduits and shafts, sometimes intersecting, but more often linked to each other by lengths of tunnel excavated through the rock, or connected via underground structures such as storage tanks and disused bomb shelters.

At one point they crawled through a hole in a brick wall into a long-forgotten tar well that was half full of semi-solid tar. The surface was skinned like custard and quaked as they crawled across it. On the way out, Thornton packed bricks into the opening to conceal the hole. He had used a number of such concealments already.

An hour later they found themselves in what must have been a nineteenth-century pumping station. The pumps and fittings were gone, leaving an empty space set with grease-stained concrete mounting pads and their huge, rusting bolts.

After that they entered an oil storage tank, long abandoned and filled with rubble. A gap between the coarse material and the roof curved around the top of the tank. They exited through a pipe in a shallow tunnel cut through white chalk, which did Irith's claustrophobia no good at all.

'I hope you know where you're going,' she said after several hours had gone by. 'It feels like we've gone kilometres.'

'We have,' said Thornton, 'and there's more to go. I'm going to blindfold you now.'

'Why?'

'We've got to go outside and you can't know where we're headed.'

She submitted uncomfortably, prey to all sorts of terrors. He put masks over their faces, in case of surveillance cameras. After a short scramble across loose rubble that felt like broken brick, Thornton opened a well-oiled door, another scramble and they were out into the cold. The weather was unchanged – windy and spitting cold rain. It was still dark. Irith could smell the river.

'Sit here,' said Gretel. 'Thorn will be a while.'

Irith sat on wet timber, trying to work out where they were, but her mind had given up. She sank into a daze.

There was a thump beside her. 'Let's get cracking,' said Thornton. 'Take it easy down the steps, and try not to make any noise.'

He took Irith's cold hand. His was warm. 'Careful. The steps are icy here.'

They went down into a sheltered quay and she was handed over the side into a dinghy. She sat facing forward as Thornton rowed them for quite a distance. The breeze cleared her head. They were on the Thames, surely, not in one of the docks.

They rounded a bend and the wind blew in her face. It had been a westerly for days and presumably still was. They hadn't crossed the river, so they must be in the vicinity of North Woolwich, heading west towards the city.

Eventually the boat bumped against another jetty. Irith was helped out and after more scrambling they went underground again. Thornton removed the blindfold. Instantly her claustrophobia reappeared, worse than before. She took deep breaths, fighting back the urge to scream as they crept through more long tunnels, tanks, pits and buried chambers, more service corridors and ducts, more doors that they sealed behind them. One endless tunnel had an unexploded Second World War bomb sticking through the roof. Irith ducked low as she passed underneath.

Thornton was carrying Gretel again, panting with the effort. Finally, they clambered through a round metal hatch with a double circle of bolts around the rim. Beyond was a cramped room like a concrete bunker, where a series of plastic racks contained a variety of equipment.

Gretel lay on her back on the floor, her skin as white and waxy as a corpse's. Fresh blood seeped through the bandage. Irith took off her jacket and began to spread it over her, but Thornton shook his head.

'She's freezing,' Irith said.

'These days it's thought better that a trauma patient be kept cool, not warm.'

It must have been close to daybreak. She could not comprehend how Gretel had gone on so long, without a word of complaint. Irith could have slept standing up.

'You'd better get that bullet out,' she said to Thornton. 'She'll feel better –'

Gretel laughed hysterically.

'This is just a staging post,' Thornton rumbled. 'Prepared long ago in case of an emergency. We've got a way to go yet. The hardest part.'

'Get on with it, Thorn,' said Gretel. 'I'm on my last gasp.'

Thornton took down something electronic in a black box and plugged it into an outlet. The box said 'Pulsetron RVDS-3A' in white letters on each side. 'Better make sure everything we need is shielded,' Gretel whispered.

He went carefully through the equipment on the racks, collecting a number of electronic items which he placed in a metal meshed cage, then put their phones, and Irith's, in too. He twisted a dial on the black box, held it for a minute and released it.

'What's that for?' said Irith.

'It's a Remote Vehicle Disabling System. Basically, an electromagnetic pulse generator. Police and Security use them to disable the electronics of a fleeing vehicle. Our techs have tweaked it to burn out the chips in anything electronic within a few hundred metres. If they *have* followed us, they won't be able to report back where we've gone.'

'If it works,' Gretel said darkly.

'If it works,' Thornton agreed. 'Its effectiveness is questionable in this kind of environment, and the range limited. Still, better than nothing. Now comes the difficult bit. Have you ever done any scuba diving, Irith?'

'No. I suffer from claustrophobia.'

'That's a pity. Tunnel diving is hazardous, even for experienced divers.'

Water *and* tunnels. She could think of nothing worse. 'Where are we going?'

'A refuge built for just this eventuality,' he said. 'We have to go down through a series of old tunnels that have been flooded for decades.'

'How did they get here?'

'We're under part of the old London docklands. There was industry here for a couple of hundred years, torn down and reconstructed many times, and they built as much below ground as above. When the area was redeveloped at the end of the twentieth century, they concreted over everything.'

Many of the old underground basements, wells, conduits, pipes, sewers and tunnels are still here,' added Gretel. 'We mapped them out, knocked through the walls to connect them, and found a way through the lower, flooded ones. It's as good a hide as can be found anywhere in London. Is there something the matter?'

Irith was shaking. 'Just being in here makes me want to scream. You've got to take me up.'

'You'd be found within minutes,' said Gretel. 'We can't let you go.'

'But surely, after that long trek . . .'

'Security doesn't *ever* give up,' said Thornton. 'Somewhere, cameras will have picked up the boat, and once the tapes are checked they'll know roughly where we've gone. You have to come with us, and we've got to go somewhere they don't know about.'

'And that is?'

'A place that's always been flooded and has no obvious entrance.' Thornton had been walking along the racks and now came back with a small wetsuit and hood. 'Put this on.'

Irith had never liked tight-fitting clothes, and the idea of wearing a wetsuit made her feel panicky. 'Can't I go without?'

'You'd be dead of hypothermia in ten minutes. Be quick!' He lugged up an air tank in either hand, checked that the backpacks were tightly fastened and fitted a regulator to each.

Gretel was already undressing, one-handed. Every movement made her wince, and there was a film of sweat on her brow, although she gave no complaint.

Irith self-consciously stripped down to her knickers and bra as Thornton came and went. The wetsuit overalls proved surprisingly hard to pull up her legs. She fitted the straps over her shoulders and reached for the jacket.

'Here,' said Thornton, holding it out behind her. 'Reach back with your arms.'

She did so and he pulled the jacket on, adjusted it around the neck, spun her around, pulled the crutch flap up tight between her legs and twisted the fasteners. The process felt disturbingly intimate, though his manner was professional. He smoothed out the inner flap and pulled the zipper all the way up.

Irith felt like a plump little pixie and found walking difficult in the thick rubber. 'I don't see how I'm going to swim in this. I can hardly move.'

'Once you're in the water it'll be different. Put these on.' He tossed her the hood, a pair of booties and a large plastic bag. 'Pack your clothes into the bag, fold it over carefully several times and tape it down. There's nothing worse than putting on wet clothes at the other end.'

Her clothes were still damp anyway. She put the booties on, which were too large for her small feet, but left the hood where it lay. She couldn't bear the thought of stretching it over her head. Gretel was struggling with her wetsuit overalls. Her face had gone grey and threads of blood were trickling down her side from beneath the bandage.

Irith helped her pull up the suit. 'Are you all right?'

'I just want to lie down and die,' she said faintly.

'You're not . . . ?'

'It didn't strike anything vital, and I haven't lost that much blood. It just hurts like all fuck!'

'I'm worried about the wound getting infected. Can I –?'

'We haven't time. Help me with the jacket.'

By the time Gretel was dressed, Thornton had all the gear ready and was sliding the wetsuit up his long, muscular frame.

Irith watched him out of the corner of her eye. She had never met a man quite like him. He caught her eye and grinned unselfconsciously. Irith turned away, blushing. She felt like a schoolgirl caught spying.

Somewhere in the distance there was a clang. Thornton spun around, staring at the door.

'What was that?' said Gretel.

'I'd say,' he said slowly, 'that they're after us.'

'Could they know who we are?' said Irith.

He shrugged. 'Who knows?' He carried two tanks to the far end of the room, then came back for the rest of his gear. Irith's bag of clothes went into his chest pack.

Irith gathered her flippers, mask and snorkel, and weight belt. 'Do I really need all this?' she said, trying to lift the tank in her free hand. She could barely get it off the ground.

'The wetsuit is buoyant. Without the weights you won't get under the water. Go through the far door. I'll bring the tank.'

Another door, beyond the shelves, concealed a drop into a water-filled tunnel.

'Listen carefully, Irith,' said Thornton, with one eye on Gretel. 'Scuba diving is dangerous unless you're properly trained, and there's no time to train you. There's one thing you absolutely must remember, because if you don't, it will kill you.'

'What's that?' she said in a whisper. She was already sweating and felt sure she was going to faint as soon as she went into the water.

'When you're underwater, you're breathing compressed air, and the deeper you go the higher the pressure has to be, to stop your lungs collapsing. Whatever happens, *never* hold your breath.' He put the rubber mouthpiece of the regulator into her mouth. 'Breathe normally.'

She breathed in and out, in and out. The rushing air was surprisingly noisy and she did not like the feeling of the huge piece of rubber in her mouth. She felt that she was going to gag. She took the regulator out.

'What happens if I *do* hold my breath?'

'If you're going up, it can burst your lungs, they'll collapse and you'll probably die. Or you could get a gas embolism – air in the bloodstream –

which can be fatal in a number of unpleasant ways.'

'We've got to go,' said Gretel. 'They're coming!'

'Do we have to dive a long way?' Irith asked.

'It's not that far. How are you feeling, Gretel?'

She moved her left arm and shuddered. 'I think I can manage it.'

'I'll be right beside you. Ready?' he said to Irith, as if he doubted her capacity.

'Yes,' said Irith, thinking, *I can't do this. I'm going to drown at the bottom of some stinking, festering pit. They'll leave my body there and Mum will never know what happened to me.*

'Where's your hood?' said Thornton.

'I couldn't bear the thought of wearing it.'

'You lose half your body heat through your head and neck. Get the fucking thing!'

When she handed him the hood he pulled it over her head so hard that it hurt. Irith put on her flippers and weight belt as he bolted the door behind them. Ahead, the old brick tunnel sloped down into the water. They spat in their masks, rubbed the spit around and put them on. Thornton lifted the tank onto Gretel's back and did up the straps. She sagged under the weight. He passed her an underwater torch. She turned it on, put the mouthpiece in her mouth, then shuffled forward and slid into the water.

He did the same for Irith. The tank was so heavy that she could barely stand up.

'Here's your torch,' he said. 'This is how you turn it on and off.'

She pressed the rubber button. The torch came on.

He put the regulator in her hand. 'You all right?'

'Yes,' she gasped. Her eyes must have looked like saucers.

'I'll be right behind you. Don't hold your breath.'

She nodded, put the mouthpiece in and waded forward. The water was like icy needles as it crept up her crutch, belly and back. Irith let go, pushed forward and tried to swim the way Gretel had.

She sank straight to the bottom, stirring up a cloud of silt that swirled around in front of her and obscuring the beam of the torch. Irith tried to swim forward but her belly struck the rough floor and the straps and buckles caught on unseen obstacles. The mouthpiece was a thick, choking lump that made her gag. The water was black; she couldn't tell down from up. She forced herself to her knees, pushed off and thrashed. When her head broke the surface she tore the regulator out of her mouth and immediately sank again.

She groped around but couldn't find it. She opened her mouth to scream and water rushed in. This was it. She was going to drown.

Suddenly two big hands lifted her bodily out of the water. She choked, spat out water and sucked in a gasping breath.

'What's the matter now?' said Thornton.

'I sank straight to the bottom,' she gasped. 'The mouthpiece makes me gag and in the dark I feel really claustrophobic. I can't do it.'

'You can,' he said, calmly, 'because you don't have any option.' He ferried her back to the edge. 'You just need a little more buoyancy.' He showed her how to inflate the buoyancy vest attached to her tank to compensate for the weight belt, and how to let out the surplus air. 'The deeper you go, the more air you need in your vest. And the converse as you come back up.'

Gretel's head popped up at the far end of the tunnel. 'Problem?'

'Irith needs a diving lesson.'

Gretel inflated her vest and floated. 'Make it a quick one.'

'All right,' said Thornton. 'We'll swim out to Gretel, then go down and sit on the bottom until you feel comfortable. Remember, you don't need to use your arms to swim. And don't thrash your legs. Just scissor them, gently. You've got flippers on the end of your feet, remember?'

But he hadn't told her any of that before. Irith gulped, crammed the mouthpiece in and sucked hard. She gagged and had to spit it out before she threw up. 'I can't do it!'

He took her hand. 'Of course you can. Gently now. You do everything gently underwater. Don't clench your teeth, you're not trying to bite the mouthpiece off.'

'Why are you taking the trouble?' she said hoarsely. She'd always felt in control before. Now, suddenly, she was singularly useless.

'You saved our lives. You're one of us now.'

One of us. That was a change from a few hours ago.

He slipped the mouthpiece in, easing it back and forth, and massaged the taut muscles of her jaw. It felt surprisingly intimate. 'Is that better?'

She nodded.

'Good.' He sank into the water, turned so he was facing her and pulled her in after him. 'Breathe.'

She drew on the regulator and went in beside him. This time she didn't go under at all – the vest held her up. He turned on his back, kicking gently, and watched her. She managed to follow him to where Gretel was floating.

'Now we'll go down and sit on the bottom for a minute. All right?'

Irith jerked her head, already feeling the panic rising at the thought of the black water. She tried to go down but bobbed up again.

'Let some air out of your vest, just until you start to sink.'

She scratched around for the ribbed hose and the release button, but could not find it. Everything felt so awkward in the wetsuit. She found it hard to move her arms and the mask cut off most of her vision.

Thornton found the vest hose and put it in her hand. Irith went down slowly, trailing bubbles. He was beside her, the weight of his hand on her shoulder. It felt comforting, and when the panic rose again she was able to fight it. She knew she was safe with him beside her.

They drifted gently to the bottom and settled there. Irith concentrated on her breathing, in and out, afraid to hold it for a second in case her lungs exploded. Realistically, she could only be in danger when rising through the water, but she could not overcome her irrational fears.

Thornton and Gretel made hand signals to each other, though Irith couldn't read them. The panic faded. Touching him on the shoulder, she gave the thumbs-up signal. He squeezed her arm and pointed with a finger towards the deeper water. Gretel headed that way, her flippers moving lazily. Irith followed, trying to emulate her. She couldn't see Thornton but the light from his torch made a beam through the water below her.

They swam a long way before going down into what must have been some kind of sump. At the bottom, a ragged hole led into a lower tunnel of ancient brickwork. It was hard work getting around the corner into it. Irith was afraid she would damage her tank or tear the air hose.

They got through safely and continued on their way via a labyrinth of shafts, tunnels and linking passages, before finally coming up to the surface in a tunnel that looked identical to the one they'd first taken. Its roof rose gently out of the water.

'I think we're safe now,' said Thornton. 'There's little chance of anyone following us through all that. Safe for the moment, anyway.'

Walking backwards out of the water, he took off his tank and lay it down on its backpack. 'How are you doing, Gretel? Gretel?'

She was swaying at the water's edge then just toppled backwards. Irith managed to grab her as she went under, though she dropped the torch.

Thornton was there in an instant. 'It's all right, I've got her.' He hauled his sister out, lay her on the dusty floor and checked her pulse, her eyes, and listened at her chest. When he rose again, his eyes were grave.

'She needs attention badly, and she's not going to get it.'

'Is there anything that can be done here?'

He helped Irith off with her tank. 'Not much.' Thornton looked haggard. 'Better get that torch.'

Irith felt for it. 'Will she die without help?'

'She might if the wound gets infected. There could be every kind of germ imaginable in this place.' He shook his head. 'I don't know what to do.'

'Can't you go and get help?'

'Our cover is blown. If they got into our computers, they'll know our names. And . . .'

'What, Thornton?'

'We haven't given up hope of carrying out the operation.'

'Can't it be put off?'

'It's now or never, and never would be very bad.'

'Why, Thornton? What is this all about?'

'I can't tell you.'

'I think I deserve some kind of explanation. You don't have to tell me any secrets. For all I know, you could be criminals, or terrorists.'

'I dare say Security thinks we are. All right, I can tell you this much. We have reason to believe the Global Congress is working on a project that could have very unpleasant consequences. We're trying to stop it.'

'What kind of a project?'

'We're still trying to find out. That's why we're here.'

'So this is a spying operation?'

'If you like. And that's all I can say.'

It was better than nothing. Her moral dilemma eased a fraction. Assuming he was telling the truth, of course. 'And to succeed in your mission, whatever it is, you have to risk your sister's life?'

'That's about the size of it.'

CHAPTER THIRTEEN

Thornton carried his sister up the tunnel, through an ancient cast-iron door that was almost rusted out, and into a cramped little room that looked like the basement of a metal-working factory of yesteryear.

The walls were oil-stained brick, oozing with damp. The place was crammed with antiquated equipment: lathes, milling machines, drills, presses and grinders, all rusted into immobility. They appeared to date back to the dawn of the electrical age. A small space on the far side of the room contained a bench, two decaying chairs and a pair of computer keyboards, each with a small screen.

Irith wondered how many such refuges they had, and how many people were involved. She didn't bother to ask.

Thornton lay Gretel on the floor and began stripping off her wetsuit. 'Get the gear, Irith.'

She put her bag, torch, mask and flippers down and went back for the tanks. She tried to carry one in each hand, as Thornton did for balance, but they were too heavy. She had to make three trips, and another two for the weight belts.

He had Gretel's jacket off and was unravelling the bandages. Her eyes were closed and her breathing shallow. The ragged wound below her collarbone was a livid red and purple against her pale skin.

His hand shook and suddenly his self-control collapsed. 'The bullet's in deep. I'm afraid, Irith.' His face had gone pale, though the skin around his eyes was as dark as bruises. 'I don't know what to do. Gretel's everything to me.'

'I've done a bit of first aid,' said Irith. As it happened, she had done a lot, part of her mother's obsessive training for every kind of contingency – except diving through underground drains.

'Is there a first-aid kit?'

'I imagine so.' He looked around distractedly.

'Are we in any immediate danger?'

'Depends on what you call immediate. Over the next hour or so, probably not. The next five or six, very probably. They'll have a lot of people on the ground, searching with the best equipment money can buy, and we've only one advantage.'

'What's that?' she said listlessly.

'Congress Security can't act openly in Britain. That's not saying it doesn't have support in this country – it does, and friends in high places – but they have to be circumspect about what they do. It gives us a chance.'

'So we're being hunted by *Congress* Security?'

'Yes,' he said, amazed that she hadn't realised. 'Who the hell did you think they were?'

'At first, I thought *you* were Security. Since the attack, I didn't know whether they were police, British security, or someone else. How could I know?'

'And you still helped us?'

'They were shooting at me. You weren't.' Irith did not have the energy to discuss it. 'I'm freezing. Is there any chance of a cup of tea?'

'There's a kettle and gas burner here somewhere. I'll find the first-aid kit.'

The tea tasted vaguely of mould but she drank it scalding with five spoons of sugar, and felt better for it. As she was spooning sweet tea into Gretel, Thornton came back with the first-aid kit.

It was basic: scissors, tweezers, needle and thread, antiseptic and disinfectant, antibiotic powder, various painkillers, burn cream and a variety of bandages. Irith gave Gretel the maximum dose of strong painkillers and put the rest in her pack for later, along with the antibiotic and the bandages.

The tweezers were tiny and useless for probing such a deep wound. Irith gripped the scissor handles with her shirt then held the blades in the flame of the burner to sterilise them. Once they had cooled, she probed the wound.

Gretel writhed. Irith put one knee on her chest but couldn't keep her still. 'Thornton,' she yelled. 'You'll have to hold her.'

He did so, looking away. Irith felt in the wound with one blade of the scissors and struck something that grated. It wasn't bone, down there, so it had to be the bullet. She tried to get the scissors in behind it. Gretel screamed in agony.

The sound went right through Irith. 'It's in between the top of the top rib and the clavicle,' she said to Thornton. 'I don't know how I'm going to get it out. It keeps sliding off the blade. What if you had a go?'

'No!'

She sat back on her haunches, staring at the wound. Thornton wiped his sister's brow. He looked haunted.

'Have you got any wire?' Irith said suddenly.

'There's wire everywhere. What sort do you want?'

'Some copper wire I can make a loop out of, then sterilise. Not too thin. It needs to be stiff but a little bit flexible.'

He jumped up and began to pull apart the electrical cord of one of the computers. After stripping the copper wires out of the insulation, he braided them together and made a loop at the end, the diameter of a small coin. 'How does that look?'

'Not bad,' said Irith. 'Make the loop a bit smaller, then sterilise it.'

He did so and handed it to her. Irith waved it about until it had cooled, and slid it into the wound, feeling carefully until she touched the bullet. She pushed the loop into the torn flesh beside the ragged projectile, wiggled it until the back of the loop passed behind, then tried to ease the bullet out.

Gretel moaned. Thornton clutched her hand. Irith eased the wire loop a little more but it slipped off. She tried again and again, with the same result each time. Even after her loop caught the bullet, it took twenty minutes of the most careful work before she got the bullet to the opening. It had been deformed in ricocheting off the wall, and the jagged edges continually caught on flesh and sinew.

She eased the bullet out, feeling nearly as shaky as Gretel, whose screams had unnerved her. She looked up at Thornton. 'I wouldn't like to have that in me.'

'It wouldn't have healed.' He placed the ragged piece of metal on the desk, staring at it.

Irith checked there were no fragments left in the wound, cleaned it with boiled water, shook antibiotic powder all over it, stitched it and bound it tightly, then made a sling. The arm would be too painful to move and, if Gretel did, she risked tearing the wound open again. Thornton dressed her in dry clothes and Irith folded the wetsuit under her head for a pillow.

Thornton got busy with a shielded laptop into which he had plugged a variety of sensors. 'I'm trying to see how close they are,' he said when Irith came up. 'They're giving off as much EM as a radio station.'

'Good news or bad?'

'I think they've lost us, unless they're being really clever. Get some sleep. We've got some time now. We'll stay here for the next twenty-four hours. It'll give Gretel a chance to recover.'

'What about you?'

'I'll keep watch. I couldn't sleep, anyway.'

Irith slept the sleep of exhaustion, curled up in a corner of the room among the rusting lathes. Some hours later, a nightmare woke her. She was in a tunnel filled with bloody water, chained to a man she had killed days ago but who seemed to have come alive again. She could hear his soggy breathing, his clotted moans, and smell his decaying blood and maggoty flesh. The stench clung to the insides of her nostrils.

She took a shuddering breath and opened her eyes. The room was pitch-dark. She put her fingers to the tip of her nose and couldn't see them. On the far side of the room, Gretel moaned. The sound made Irith's scalp crawl. She was on her hands and knees when she heard Thornton's voice, soothing his sister.

Silence resumed, apart from the low thudding of groundwater pumps, just on the edge of hearing. She closed her eyes but claustrophobia surged to the surface. She felt for the torch and turned it on. The feeling of confinement retreated, but now she noticed how stale the air was, how mouldy, how thick and humid and salty. How still.

What had Thornton meant by, *a project that could have rather unpleasant consequences*? For whom? And could she trust anything he said? Her greatest fear returned – what if Gretel and Thornton were terrorists, and she was helping them?

When she woke again around midnight, the room was lit by a tiny bulb and Gretel was whispering to Thornton. Irith rose, combing her short hair with her fingers. She missed that long, heavy tangle.

'Are you feeling better?' she said sleepily.

Gretel pushed herself upright with her good arm. It took an effort and she had to lean back against the wall. 'A little. I just need to rest a bit, then I'll be ready . . . ' She trailed off with a glance at her brother.

'We can't do it, Gretel.'

'We must,' Gretel said stubbornly. 'Failure is unthinkable.'

'The mission required six and everyone else is dead.'

'This is our only chance, Thorn. Once Security recovers our data, they'll know everything.'

'How long will that take?' Irith asked.

'Depends,' said Gretel. 'If the explosion destroyed our computers, the data should be irrecoverable. But if, as I suspect, the computers weren't destroyed, just wiped, Security will have the data in days. They'll have our names, our finances and our future plans, and the resistance will soon be erased. That's why we've got to go ahead.'

'Even if you weren't injured, the two of us couldn't do it,' said Thornton.

'The clock's ticking, Thorn.'

'What are you suggesting?'

'That we ask Irith to help us.'

No way, Irith thought.

'Don't be ridiculous,' said Thornton. 'We need a trained clearance diver at the very least. Someone big, strong, fast and combat experienced.'

'I think she can do it. She's proven herself.'

'No, I haven't,' said Irith. 'I'm little and weak, and diving scares me shitless.'

'We can teach you the essentials,' Gretel went on inexorably.

'In a few hours?' Thornton cried.

Gretel whispered in his ear. Thornton rubbed a hand along his bristly cheek then looked thoughtfully at Irith.

'No,' she cried.

'It could work,' said Thornton.

'I've had enough,' said Irith. 'I'm going back to the institute.'

'You can't go back, Irith.'

'Why not?'

'You know too much. You're one of us now.'

'I don't want to be one of you,' Irith said desperately.

'We can't let you go,' said Thornton. 'Besides, you've killed at least one Security officer, and maybe more. They never forget.'

'They don't know it was me. No one does but you and Gretel.'

'Cameras may have picked you up, going underground.'

'I'll take that chance.'

'But we can't take a chance on you,' said Gretel. 'If you went back and were caught, and you would be, you'd blow our cover.'

'I won't talk, I promise.'

'Under truth drugs?' said Thornton. 'Under torture? When they threaten your mother?'

Of course she would talk. Irith knew it.

'Well?' said Thornton.

'How do you know you can trust me?'

He smiled.

'You might be using me,' said Irith. 'And planning to kill me afterwards.'

The twins exchanged glances. 'You'll have to trust us, Irith,' said Thornton. 'That's the deal.'

'It's a crap deal.'

'Yes it is,' said Thornton, 'but it's all we're offering.'

'What are you trying to break into?' said Irith.

Neither answered. 'That's dangerous knowledge,' he said after a lengthy pause.

'We have to give her something,' said Gretel. 'Since we're asking her to trust us, we should do the same.'

'All right,' said Thornton. 'There's a Congress data centre not far from here, which is why we chose this place in the beginning. We've been trying to hack into its computers for a year but they're not on any network – they're completely isolated. It has to be a physical break-in but the place is well protected, and the centre has embassy status, so the British government can't do anything about it.

'However, it does have a weakness no one realised when the data centre was moved there. The building wasn't purpose-built and a lot of the old underground structures in the area were simply filled in, or slabbed over. That was back in the early noughties, before the emergency that gave rise to the Global Congress.'

'Are you saying that there's an old tunnel underneath the building?' said Irith.

'Not underneath. If there had been, they would have dug it out to construct the foundations. But a deep underground tunnel does run within two metres of a basement corner, and it wasn't much of a dig from there to the wall.'

'Surely they have vibration detectors that will pick us up when we try to get in?'

'They do,' said Thornton, 'but another team is going to do something that will render the detectors useless.'

'Like what?'

'Let's just say that if the whole docklands area is shaking, the signals from their vibration detectors will be meaningless.'

'What do you want me to do?' said Irith.

Again that exchange of glances. The twins often communicated that way. 'We lost four of our team of six yesterday,' said Gretel. 'We had two divers trained in zero visibility clearance diving, to scan the area for traps and defend us in case of counterattack, and another team of two to use the special equipment that would get us in through the wall. They're all dead. There's only Thorn left, and me. He's the weapons and demolition expert, but he can't do it on his own.'

'And Gretel has to run the systems and pull some data out of their computer,' said Thornton.

'Get to the point,' said Irith.

'You'll be our extra pair of hands. A carrier. A scout. A guard,' he said.

'You still haven't told me why you're breaking in.'

'Haven't you seen enough with your own eyes?' said Gretel, wiping her forehead. Despite the cold, she was sweating.

'I was brought up to believe in the rule of law,' said Irith. 'I'm not a revolutionary and if you ...'

'What?' Thornton said dangerously.

'I'd sooner die than become one,' she said simply. 'I mean it. I would sooner die.'

'The highest duty of a government is to protect its citizens, wouldn't you agree?'

'Of course,' said Irith. 'But I don't see –'

'The Global Congress, as led by Per Lindstrom, does not have the best interests of the world at heart. He's engaged in a monstrous plot against humanity.'

'I don't go much on conspiracy theories. You could be the terrorists and Security the good guys, for all I know. Words mean nothing.'

'Then there's nothing I can say that will make a difference,' said Thornton. 'You'll have to make that judgment and you'd better make it quickly, or none of us will survive.'

For all Irith knew, there could have been a legitimate reason for the attack on their command centre, and even for Jemma's arrest and the confiscation of her property. Everything that had ever been blamed on the Congress might have been done with full justification.

Irith had never been a rebel. Neither did she want to sacrifice herself for her convictions. She wanted to live, to work, to love. But she would make the sacrifice, if put to the choice.

Then, in a flash she realised that she did have evidence of the Congress's corruption. She had done nothing wrong, yet she had been thrown out of her home, her honours mark had been changed to a fail and her money confiscated. None of that was legal, and it had all been done on orders from the highest authority.

'All right,' she said. 'I believe you. What do you want me to do?'

They did not tell Irith the details of their plan in case she was caught, but she did have an hour's practice in tunnel diving. It wasn't near enough. As Thornton said, they needed two divers with years of experience. Unfortunately, they only had three spare air tanks and no compressor, so one tank – one hour's diving – was all the training they could afford. After that, Irith practised with an assault rifle and a pistol, though not firing them. Sound travelled a long way through water and they dared not take the risk.

While Gretel rested, Thornton spent the rest of the morning cleaning and preparing weapons, programming a variety of equipment, calibrating meters and packing their gear into waterproof cases whose enormous O-rings had to be rubbed with silicone grease then checked minutely for the least speck of grit that might break the seal and let water in. The pile was daunting.

He stopped every hour to check his sensors. 'Nothing,' he said after waking Gretel for lunch. 'And that worries me. It's too quiet. They're up to something.'

'How close are they?' said Gretel.

He looked tormented. His instruments had failed him. 'I can't tell. They could be just around the corner.'

'What if we were to move the mission forward?' said Gretel.

'We can't. The other team has to make the diversion and we can't contact them until they're in place. I don't see how we can do it.'

'We'll have to make two trips,' said Gretel.

'That doubles the chance of detection,' said Thornton. 'Or of something going wrong.'

'The number of trips is the same,' Gretel said. 'We just have to do two each.'

'Therefore it'll take twice the time, with twice the risk of being discovered. I don't like it.'

'Nor do I, Thorn, but there isn't any choice.'

CHAPTER FOURTEEN

They put their heads down in the afternoon, though no one got much sleep, and were up again by 6 pm. Irith rose the moment Thornton stirred, for the diving lesson had undermined her confidence. It had taught her how little she knew and how much could go wrong. When working underwater, everything was ten times as hard, and even in the wetsuit she was always cold. Irith couldn't remember being warm since she came to this country.

'Do you want me to use the pulse generator again?' said Gretel.

'Better not,' Thornton replied distractedly. 'They might get a fix on it.'

By the time Irith had eaten, Thornton had ferried everything down to the water. She pulled on her wetsuit, which smelled of foul water and things long decaying.

'I don't know where I got the idea that diving was romantic,' Irith grumbled as she sat down to pull on her booties.

Thornton pressed his fingers against his temples and winced. A dense growth of black beard had aged him at least a decade.

'Do you think Gretel is up to it?' she said softly.

'I do not. Nor you.' He stared at her with those intense eyes. Before she could take offence, he added, 'Nor I. None of us are up to it and I can see only one ending. We're all going to die.'

Irith felt a sharp pain in her belly. The recent bloody encounters had not numbed her terror; they had heightened it.

'And that's the good alternative.' He went on. 'It's more likely that one or all of us will be caught. If they look like catching you, jump into the water with your weight belt on. Don't bother to take the tank.'

'They can't be that bad,' she murmured, although she knew he was serious.

'Security plays for keeps. It's a pity, Irith.' His eyes swept up and down her. Irith didn't think she cut much of a figure in a wetsuit, but there was something in his eyes . . .

'What?' she said.

'Oh, nothing.'

'If I'm going to die you have to tell me.'

He gave a brief half-smile. 'I would have liked to get to know you better.'

Irith had little skill at that game but she eyed him off. The wetsuit made the most of him. She liked what she saw, very much.

The initial dive proved uneventful, although it was long, tiring, cold and claustrophobic in the dark water and the confined spaces. The way back would be worse, since the water would be full of the silt they had stirred up. Irith was surprised at how exhausting diving was. By the time she reached the other end and had deposited her towed burden on a cramped rock ledge between two rust-streaked concrete columns, she could barely hold her head up.

Groundwater pumps thumped in the background. Thornton was kneeling on the ledge by a stack of instrument cases, staring at his sister. Gretel sat with her back against the rock wall, almost as pale as she had been when they removed the bullet, and shivering violently.

The space was a couple of metres high, about the same wide, and three metres deep. It resembled a cave picked out of soft green sandstone, at the back of which was a concrete wall.

'Is that the building?' whispered Irith.

'It is,' said Gretel.

'How far below ground are we?'

'About sixteen metres. This basement is four floors below the surface.'

'A wonder it's not flooded.'

'It would be, if not for the pumps.' Thornton was shaking his head as Irith took off her flippers, tossed them up, then dragged herself out of the water. 'It's no good, Gretel. You can't go back.'

Gretel pursed her blue lips. 'I've got to, otherwise –'

'You won't make it. Irith will have to do it.'

Irith felt an instant of panic, although she managed to cover it up. It was the only solution. Thornton couldn't go, since he was the only one who could break into the building and it required a lot of preparation. And once inside, Gretel's skills were vital to cracking into the computer in the basement and stealing the data.

'I'd better go.' Irith tried not to think about swimming underwater all that way, by herself. If she thought it through, she would never find the courage.

Thornton took her arm. 'Get your breath back. It's not that urgent.'

'I'd sooner go right away.' She did not meet his eye, afraid he would read her mind. Something occurred to her. 'What about decompression and all that? Am I likely to get the bends?' That had not been covered in the lesson.

'Only if you're diving deeper than ten metres, and there's no water that deep in here.'

'Good. I'll bring back everything I can.'

'Take it easy,' he said soothingly. 'There's enough time.'

He did not think she could do it. That was fair enough. Irith had no confidence in herself either.

She got ready and slipped under the water. Instantly, her claustrophobia was back, plus the gagging reflex – the big mouthpiece made her stomach heave.

She imagined what it would be like to throw up underwater. Not good at all; it might clog the mouthpiece. She concentrated on controlling her fears as she went down. *Take deep, slow breaths. Don't dwell on problems. Concentrate on the route you have to follow and the job you've got to do.*

The first couple of minutes were easy: a slow descent to the concrete floor of the tunnel then a gentle swim along to its end. A right-angle turn took her into a narrow, tall space, after which she had to get through a broken opening in a double wall of brick. She managed that all right. Her tank scraped along the irregular upper surface, which shocked her momentarily. Sounds were louder underwater and she could not tell which direction they came from.

On the other side, she settled to the bottom to get her bearings. The directions were hard to work out; everything looked different coming the other way. And the creeping cold was getting to her.

Irith swam across an enormous concrete storage tank, then an empty basement, and wriggled through a circular hole in its wall. After that it was a narrow squeeze along what appeared to be an old, corroded cast-iron pipe, with her head bumping on the roof and the tank scraping all the way.

As she was halfway to the destination, she realised that Thornton had forgotten to do an EM sweep before they'd left. She stopped. Her throat felt unusually dry, although that would be from the compressed air. She continued on and, with every stroke, expected the enemy to appear.

At the end of the pipe she came out into a cylindrical sump, cloudy with suspended sediment that formed ghostly shapes in the light of her torch. She had to swim up through the phantom clouds for three or four metres, then search for a narrow conduit that led off to the left. Or was it her right? It was hard to remember, and that was another thing about working underwater – her thought processes were amazingly sluggish.

She kicked slowly upwards, rotating in the water as she searched for the opening. A bipedal shape of silt swirled towards her and for a few horrified seconds Irith thought it was the enemy. She batted her hands feebly in front of her, kicked out of the way and the menace smeared out into a dirty cloud.

'Fuck!' she said to herself. 'Fuck, fuck, fuck!'

It was a measure of how uncomfortable she felt, because she never swore. She swam to the brickwork and turned around in a full circle, trailing her hand across the slimy surface. The wall was solid all the way. She must be too low. She swam up a metre and did it again, only to realise that she was now too high.

Above her the sump had a concrete cap with fissures so deep she could have squeezed into them. One side of the brickwork, just below the cap, had collapsed and the cavity was choked with rubble. Below that, a section of the curved brick wall was tilted inwards.

Down she swam and found the exit, near the bottom. The black, tarry opening looked much smaller than when she had come through it behind Thornton. Why had she thought it was up high? Was she lost?

No, Irith remembered a long pipe just ahead. She swam on, finally reaching the pipe, and knew she wasn't far from her destination. As soon as she entered the conduit, which was narrower than the last, her claustrophobia returned. Her breathing went up, she began to kick wildly and she felt a powerful urge to tear the regulator out of her mouth. Panic overcame her, she thrashed wildly and cracked her head on the rough, corroded surface.

The impact really hurt. Shocked at how easily she'd panicked, and feeling dazed, she settled to the bed of the pipe and lay unmoving, listening to the rushing of the air in and out of her regulator. Her silvery bubbles, which in the light of the torch looked like globules of mercury, trickled along the roof of the pipe.

She must have lain there for five minutes, trying to calm herself, before realising that the time was ebbing away, not to mention the air in her tank. Irith pulled herself out of the pipe and ascended carefully, not using her torch in case Security had tracked them here.

In the original plan, two of Thornton's team of six would have guarded this point to make sure the others couldn't be taken by surprise. A third and maybe a fourth person would have patrolled underwater and checked for mines, traps and divers who might have come in another way.

Her head broke the surface without a ripple. A dim light still burned down the dry section of the tunnel. She saw no sign of intruders, although that didn't mean much. They could be hiding well back, their assault rifles trained on her head right now. If they fired, would she even know it? Would her death, like all the others', be instantaneous?

She was almost paralysed by terror, but nothing happened. Irith rose higher in the water but saw nothing except the gear they'd left on the ledge. She checked her pressure gauge. The tank was over half full; ample for the return journey. She would have to come back – there was too much gear for one trip. She eyed the pair of tanks at the water's edge. One was a spare but she would need the other next time.

After collecting three of the five waterproof cases, Irith set off for the long trip back. She felt more in control now and made it without incident. Gretel seemed a little better. She was sitting up, her back resting against the concrete column, while her brother monitored the wall. Irith heaved the first of the cases onto the excavated floor. The twins turned at the sound.

'I was getting worried,' said Thornton. 'Is everything all right?'

'Yes.' She slid the other cases beside the first and turned away before they could say anything.

As she approached the other end again, Irith turned off her torch. The luminous dial of the pressure gauge told her that the tank was three-quarters empty. She would have to change it for a fresh one. She rehearsed in her mind how to do that. Climb out, remove the backpack and buoyancy vest, turn off the valve and hold down the button on the regulator until all the air was gone from the hoses. Take the regulator off, being careful in case residual air blew out the O-ring, and put the regulator on the other tank. Tighten the regulator securely over the high-pressure valve. *If you don't, Thornton had told her, and it comes off when you've got the air turned on, it'll smash through the back of your head.* Finally, open the high-pressure valve.

Irith drifted through the opening and surfaced as quietly as an otter, taking pleasure in her control. She looked across the water to the ledge and the spare tanks. They weren't there. Her heart gave a great leap. Someone had been here. *Was* here! She scanned the small platform but could see no one. They must be further back, in the shadows. Or in the water!

Irith slipped under the water again, holding her breath to listen for the rattle of bubbles from other divers. She heard nothing, although they could be using military re-breathing equipment that didn't produce bubbles.

Never hold your breath, Thornton had said. Could it be a risk this close to the surface? Irith didn't know. She dribbled the air out and came up. What if they'd seen the light of her torch? She had turned it off while still in the pipe, well underwater, but the glow would have been visible for some distance. But then, if they had night-vision gear, or motion detectors, they might already have picked her up.

Was it an ambush, or did they plan to follow her, to catch the others? Irith would have turned back – the air in her tank might just be enough, if she stayed calm and kept her breathing low – but these last two cases could be vital.

Her heart was leaping in her chest. She had to save every bit of air she could. Irith spat out the regulator, took several deep breaths and swam underwater to the ledge. There, out of sight, she drained the air from her vest so she could dive quickly if she had to.

She surfaced in the shadow of the ledge and took more calming breaths. The cases were across to the right. Irith edged along, sure she was going to be killed. It was the bravest thing she had ever done.

She couldn't see anything but the vague outline of the cases. They were standing up, and too wide to grip by the ends, so she would have to come head and shoulders out of the water to grab the handles.

The cases were just to her right now. Irith rose in the shadows and went hand over hand along the ledge. If they fired when she was behind the cases, they could hardly miss.

Sheltering below the ledge, she reached up at an angle and managed to get hold of a handle. The case came up too easily – it was empty.

Floodlights went on, an automatic weapon snarled and the case was torn to shreds. A chunk of plastic slammed into the heel of her hand; she snatched it out of the way and pushed herself beneath the water as bullets plucked at the surface. She expelled all the air in her lungs and went down as fast as she could. Spent bullets fell past her.

At the bottom she panicked when she couldn't find her dangling regulator. There it was. She crammed it into her mouth and fled for the entrance to the pipe. If she could get a bit of a lead, further on the flooded passages went three ways and she might be able to get away.

Pain speared through her sinuses. She had gone down too quickly. Holding her nose with one hand, she blew hard. The pressure eased, although the pain didn't entirely go away.

Irith flashed the torch a couple of times to find the opening and shot into the corroded pipe, kicking hard and pulling herself along with her fingertips. She had the advantage here, because the pipe was barely wider than her shoulders. Gretel had had trouble getting through, while Thornton had been forced to take his tank off and push it ahead of him.

Thump. Thump – two divers hitting the water behind her. She prayed they were big men who would have the same problem as Thornton.

Her buoyancy vest caught on a piece of corroded metal. Irith had to stop to free it. Her heart was hammering so hard that she could hear it in her ears, and she was gasping at the air. Calm down, she thought, you don't have any to waste. The harder she worked, the more air she would use, and once the tank was empty, that was it.

Light flooded the tunnel from the divers' torches. She worked the vest free and looked back. A wriggling shape partly blocked the other end of the pipe. They were having trouble getting in.

Irith heaved forward. Ahead of her the pipe curved, which might cause them more trouble. Not far now. She felt that she might make it after all. Then there came a sharp thudding noise that hurt her ears, like a gun being fired underwater. Behind her, something whirred up one side of the tunnel, caught on the decaying metal and slammed into the other side between her feet. Irith screamed into her mouthpiece. A multi-pronged, barbed spear from a speargun, it would have made a horrific wound.

She swam as fast as she could, assisted by streaks of torchlight that shone past her. What was the range of the speargun? She had no idea. Irith felt so vulnerable. Any sort of a decent shot would hit her feet, her backside, or the tank. How strong was a scuba tank? Could it resist that kind of impact? What if they used an exploding powerhead, as were used to kill sharks? If that didn't tear her to shreds, or the shockwave cave her chest in, the subsequent rupturing of the air tank would do the job.

She came to the bend and eased around it. It would provide some protection. She kicked out but tore her suit, and her wrist, on a projecting piece of metal. She chanced a quick flash of the torch. Her blood was black in the water. As she moved, the air hose snagged and for one awful moment she feared it would tear, but it proved to be made of tough material.

The injury was minor. Irith kept going and shortly saw the circular end of the pipe. Pulling herself out into the basement, she looked around. Openings went three ways and the middle way was the right one. She swam into the other two and stirred up the silt, hoping that would buy her a little time.

The middle way, of egg-shaped brickwork, was a long-abandoned nineteenth-century sewerage tunnel. Irith checked her pressure gauge. The level wasn't far from the red zone. She turned her torch off and swam steadily, concentrating on her breathing, on using as little air as possible.

She was only a short way along this lengthy section when she saw a light behind her. They were through already. How could they have negotiated that narrow pipe so quickly? They must be professional divers. And professional killers. She wasn't even halfway, and every second she expected a barbed spear to plunge into her. Why didn't they fire? Perhaps the range was too great. They would catch her within minutes anyway. There hardly seemed any point to going on.

It's the ones who give up that are doomed, her mother had told her every time a terrorist abduction was featured on the news. Jemma had been obsessed about that. If you never give up, you'll find a way.

What nonsense, Irith had thought, and was thinking now. *Some people might survive, but most wouldn't, for the simple reason that their attackers were professionals. They knew what to do in any situation.*

She reached the end of the brickwork tunnel. Just ahead was the circular brick sump, seven or eight metres across and maybe eight metres deep. Its bottom was full of mud and rubble.

She swam around the elbow, felt her way out into the sump, kicked above the exit and flashed her torch. A section of one wall had tilted inwards. Above that, the deeply fissured capping slab offered a number of meagre hiding places.

Irith dived to the bottom, feeling in the silty sludge and rubble until she found a clump of bricks cemented together. It was the best weapon she would get. Holding it in both hands, she swam round and round, kicking furiously. A cloud of brown sludge rose from the bottom, reducing visibility to zero. She spiralled up, carrying the cloud with her, then edged into the largest of the crevices. Adding air to the buoyancy vest to hold her there, Irith turned off the torch and waited.

They weren't long in coming. She saw their lights as bright smears in the brown water six metres below. Bubbles rose in wobbling spheres. The lights circled the sump, then one disappeared. She prayed he had gone into the other tunnel.

If he had simply turned his torch out, intending to sneak up on her from one side while the second fellow came at her the other way, she had no chance.

The light came upwards, moving slowly. The water wasn't so silty here; she would see him when he came within a metre. It wouldn't be easy for him to make her out in the dark crevice, but soon he must.

Was it her imagination, or was it harder to breathe than before? Normally she simply drew breath and the regulator gave her air, but now she had to suck at it. Irith didn't dare check the pressure gauge. She knew what it would say. She had a couple of minutes' air left and that was not nearly enough to get her to Gretel and Thornton.

She held her breath so the diver would not hear her bubbles. Surely it was OK to do that, here since she was not rising? He rose slowly through the murk, rotating as he did, so his view swept through a circle. He had a long knife in one hand and a speargun in the other, armed with another five-pronged spear. Even discounting for the magnification underwater, he was almost as big as Thornton.

She looked at him sideways so his torch wouldn't reflect off her mask. He had swept around the walls and was moving in her direction. Irith clutched her lump of brick and concrete in both hands. In the air, a blow on the head from such a mass could have killed. Here, the resistance of the water meant she couldn't swing it nearly as hard. Whereas he, with the knife and speargun, could do all the damage he wanted.

CHAPTER FIFTEEN

The diver snaked to one side, following a chasm that zigzagged through the concrete. He was going to pass beneath Irith. It was the only chance she would get. She pressed her feet against the back of the crevice, tensing her leg muscles ready to spring, and squeezing the bricks so hard that her fingers hurt.

As the diver passed beneath her some sixth sense must have alerted him. When she moved, he twisted his body sideways. The speargun was in the wrong position but he thrust the knife at her face.

She snapped her legs straight and swung the bricks at his head. He ducked sideways, slashing at her regulator hose. The knife caught it, not hard enough to sever the reinforced rubber, but enough to nick it. Bubbles ovulated out.

Reflexes got his head out of the way but her clump of bricks, with all the force that water resistance would allow, came down hard against the high-pressure valve of the tank. It made a muffled clang, then a metal-tearing scream, and compressed air exploded from the side of the valve.

The diver spun around in the water, eyes staring. He jerked at the tank harness, trying to see what was going on. Before he managed it, the valve blew out of the tank and slammed into the side of the crevice near Irith's hand, tearing the regulator out of his mouth and the hose from his vest.

He shot the other way, driven by jet propulsion as the tank, at a pressure of five thousand pounds per square inch, voided its contents in a few seconds. The water became opaque with bubbles. The diver was driven knees first into the wall and, even above the roar of escaping air, Irith heard the gruesome sound of his leg bones breaking. He screamed into the water, shot past her and crashed head-first into the other side of the sump, before sinking into the silty clouds. The knife followed, then the speargun, falling more slowly and rolling over and over in the water.

Irith sucked a meagre breath and went after it. If the diver was not dead already he soon would be, since he had no air left. She snatched the speargun up before it disappeared. Bubbles still streamed out of her hose; she put a finger over the nick. That she could hold it against the pressure showed how low the tank was.

The top third of the sump was now full of air. Irith went to the surface, breathing until she had calmed herself. She kept a close watch in case the diver had the same idea, but he didn't appear. After a few minutes she knew he had to be dead. She swam down, trying not to look, but couldn't avoid the flippered feet hanging over the rubble, or the blood clouding the water. Her stomach heaved and she vomited into her mouthpiece.

She waggled it through the water to clean it out, then crushed the emotions into oblivion. She couldn't afford to feel just now. Could she possibly get back to Gretel and Thornton? She had to try. Irith headed for the other tunnel, studying the speargun as she went. Just aim and pull the trigger. Simple enough. She made it to the end of the tunnel without incident, by which time she was having to suck really hard to get a breath, and her head was throbbing.

She kept going, but as she emerged from the basement into the great concrete tank, Irith saw the other diver pulling himself in through the hole on the far side, maybe ten metres away. He saw her at the same instant and raised a stubby, five-barrelled pistol. The other hand held a knife. She had the speargun by her side and perhaps he had not seen it.

Irith sucked at her regulator and got nothing. Her air tank was empty. She pointed the speargun at the diver's chest but, before she could fire, that strange pistol went off with an ear-tearing thump and for a second he was obscured by bubbles. The bullet clinked off the side of the concrete tank, practically spent. He darted sideways in case she fired. A true professional. She did the same. He turned the torch off and fired again.

The shot missed; the range was too long and she had gone in a different direction. Irith was now fighting for air. She could go without breathing for another thirty seconds, at most.

The vest! She'd added air to maintain buoyancy. Irith put the end of the hose in her mouth and pressed the button. Blessed air streamed out.

Then she realised that her opponent had made a mistake. He shouldn't have turned the torch off. Once he turned it on again, she would have the advantage for a few brief seconds. Irith could hear his breathing but she could not tell where it was coming from. At least he couldn't hear hers.

She swam down slowly, praying he wasn't doing the same. He might be planning to take her by feel. An experienced diver would be good at that.

She took another breath from the vest. Not much left this time. She had to do something. Irith put the loop of her torch around her left wrist, held it as far from her body as she could reach, and flashed it for a split second. *Thump!* This time she saw the muzzle flash and the bubble track of the bullet. He was above her and to the right. She aimed the speargun and flashed the torch again. He was coming straight for her, the knife out in front as if he intended to tear her belly open.

As he swung the pistol at her, she steadied the speargun and pulled the trigger. The gun must have been gas- or explosive-powered, for it went off with a concussive thud. She kicked out of the way in case she'd done no damage, since he had been moving so quickly that he would be on her in seconds. She fumbled for the dangling torch and turned it on.

The diver hung upside down in the water, arms and legs spread like a spider climbing a web. The regulator had fallen out of his mouth, which gaped open, dribbling air. Air was also leaking out of the hole at the base of his throat. The spear had gone vertically through his chest. He was already dead and surrounded by a spreading cloud of bloody water.

Irith dropped the speargun and stared at the mess she had made of another living man. He would have done the same to her, had tried to, but even so . . .

Her diaphragm spasmed. She sucked a few molecules from the vest before realising that the diver had air. He was drifting, neutrally buoyant, the dangling regulator bubbling gently. She swam the three strokes to it, spat out her mouthpiece and crammed his in. Then she went around behind him; the front view was too horrible. Irith caught hold of the valve on the top of his tank and they drifted slowly down.

At the bottom she pulled the release and shrugged out of her tank harness. The empty tank drifted upwards. She was amazed at her calmness. She should have been a quivering, claustrophobic wreck, but she was as methodical as a machine. She thought how to go about it.

After turning the dead man onto his back, she undid the buckles, took off his tank and put it on herself without ever taking his regulator out of her mouth. She couldn't shorten the straps enough to tighten them, so she simply knotted the ends around her waist. Then she swam towards the next obstacle, never looking back.

'What happened?' said Thornton, offering her a hand out of the water. He helped her off with the tank then, to her surprise, embraced her. 'We were sure you were dead.' He was staring at the tank, which was smaller than hers had been and painted matt black. 'That's not one of ours.'

Irith couldn't respond to his embrace, nor Gretel's. A part of her was thinking, *Then why didn't you come after me?* But she knew they had no option. They had to go ahead.

'They were waiting,' she said. 'Two of them. Divers. Armed.'

'And you got away?' he said incredulously. 'What happened?'

'I killed them.' She dropped her weight belt.

Thornton snatched it out of the air. 'Careful. That could be enough to set off the vibration detectors.'

'Irith?' Gretel said urgently.

'I don't want to talk about it.'

'We have to know,' said Thornton. 'I never thought they would be that close. How many were there?'

'I only saw the two divers, but there could have been others. '

Irith told them what had happened. She felt numb and, although she could remember everything perfectly, it did not feel real at all.

'The underwater pistol would be a Hechler and Kock P11,' said Thornton. 'It's designed for use against divers, although sometimes it's used on covert operations, because it's powerful and almost silent. You have to get close though, underwater.'

'How are you getting on?' she said dully, once the story had been told, retold and marvelled over. 'I'm sorry I couldn't bring back the last two cases. They'd already been emptied.'

'We may be able to do without them,' said Thornton. We'll have to. We're not doing too badly. Everything has gone to plan so far, but . . . '

'What?' said Irith. She felt so cold now. She closed her eyes and saw dead men.

'We can't contact the other team,' said Gretel. 'We've no idea whether they're in position or not, or whether they're even alive. And without the diversion they're supposed to be making, we'll be detected the instant we break in.'

'How long until they're supposed to act?'

'One hour and thirty-five minutes.'

'Well, since it's so close, you might explain what they're supposed to be doing.'

It sounded arrogant but Irith didn't care. After what she'd been through, the last thing she was worried about was their feelings.

Gretel and Thornton exchanged glances. 'We owe you that much.' He got out a map printed on plastic. 'Not as convenient as a map on a reader, but this close to the target we don't dare any kind of electromagnetic emissions. The whole area is scanned constantly.'

'So we can't call the other team with a mobile phone, either,' said Gretel.

He spread the map out on the uneven concrete and traced the path of the Thames with a fingertip.

'There's the city, west of here. Stepney, Greenwich. The old Thames Barrier. Here are the Royal Docks – Victoria, Albert and King George V. The runway of City Airport is here, between the Albert and KGV docks.' His finger moved east along the river for a few kilometres. 'There's the new Thames Dike, immediately upstream of the sewerage works. It was raised to seven metres last year, and if the sea keeps rising, it'll have to be raised again in a decade.

'Where you originally found us was here, east of Beckton.' He pointed south of the sewerage works. 'The area was once the greatest gasworks in Europe, which is why there's such a labyrinth of underground structures. It's the last place anyone would have looked for us, or so we thought. We rowed down to a point between North Woolwich Pier and Silvertown, where we went underground again, deeper this time. This whole area has been industrial since the Industrial Revolution, hence the underground labyrinth here. We wandered back and forth underground and we're now under North Woolwich.'

'Whereabouts?' said Irith.

Again that exchange of glances. 'South of the King George V dock.'

'And the diversion?'

'That takes a bit of explaining,' said Thornton. 'The river is low at the moment, and the water level in the Royal Docks is more than three metres higher. That level has to be maintained because the walls are in poor condition and, if the docks are ever drained to river level, the walls are likely to collapse. There's a fail-safe system on the lock-gates to the King George V dock to make sure that can never happen.'

'And?' said Irith.

'The other team has hacked into the program that controls the lock-gates, and inserted a bug that will lock the gates open. They were also going to override the alarms and damage the mechanism, so the gates couldn't be closed manually.'

'The plan seems unnecessarily complicated,' said Irith. 'Won't that look suspicious?'

'It's designed to look like a series of accidents due to poor maintenance. And the beauty of it is, the collapses will create a series of shocks over a long period. Just what we need to disguise our break-in. Everything relies on that.'

'And even if they suspect saboteurs,' said Gretel, 'there are plenty of targets in this area. The City Airport, for example. If we can just get in undetected, we'll be gone before they realise we're there.'

'We have to,' said Thornton. 'Or we'll never get away.'

'The water should start draining out of the docks pretty soon,' said Thornton. 'If the other team has been able to do their work.'

'Won't it take rather a long time?' Irith asked.

'Hours, at least.'

'I don't know much about engineering,' said Irith, 'but surely it'll take ages before groundwater pressure starts to push the walls over. How can you possibly predict when it's going to occur?'

'Some parts are in really poor condition. The KGV dock is more than a hundred years old, the Albert a hundred and sixty, the Victoria dock a hundred and ninety. I wouldn't think it'd take long at all. Remember, we don't need the docks to collapse. Any section of wall moving will be enough to set off the vibration detectors. Then we go in, at once.'

'I still think it's a cumbersome plan,' said Irith.

'It seems so now, since everything's gone wrong. The original plan was to get in, get out undiscovered, and flee the country before anyone realised there'd been a break-in. That's still our best chance, although Security will be on high alert now. Especially since their divers haven't come back. And the gear they found back there may arouse suspicions.'

'What was in the last two cases?'

'A variety of sensors, some Powerbricks and the medical kit, among other items.'

'How will you know when the vibration detectors have gone off?'

'My instruments will tell me.'

'Don't they emit electromagnetic radiation?'

'They're shielded.'

'Then why can't you ...? Sorry, stupid question. You can't shield a mobile.'

'There is another way, if we can get it to work. An old-style telephone that sends a signal down a wire.' He pulled it out of his bag.

'Can't that be detected too?'

'Only if you know which wire to check.'

Irith thought about that for a moment. 'All right. Suppose we do all this and it works. How do we get out again, and where do we go?'

'I can't tell you. If we get away, but you're caught, they'd have that out of you in an hour.'

It was the sensible approach, but inwardly Irith was fuming. After all she'd done, they still didn't trust her. Would they put themselves out to save her, the way she'd done for them? She felt she knew the answer to that question, too.

And afterwards? Did she already know too much?

She slumped against a column. The diving, and the fighting, had exhausted her physically, mentally and emotionally. She tried to nap but her mind would not switch off. Four hours had gone by. Security must have found the dead divers by now. How long before they traced a path through the labyrinth of tunnels to here?

Thornton had a black laptop set up in a metal shielding-cage. An array of sensors was connected to it while he listened to the walls with something that resembled a stethoscope. A shielded lead ran from it to a port on the computer. He marked out a square on the wall with a black marker.

'Okay,' he said. 'The basement's empty and locked for the night.'

'Ready to check our vibration sensors?' said Gretel. She seemed better now.

He nodded. She went as far away as she could get and slapped the rock with her open palm. He checked the monitor.

'The up–down and east–west sensors picked it up, but I got nothing from the north–south sensor. Check the lead.'

Gretel took it out of the computer, blew out the socket with a pressure can and plugged the sensor back in. She walked away and slapped the rock.

'That's better,' he said. 'All the instruments are set. Now to get inside.'

'How are you going to break through?' Irith said.

'Only the supporting members are thick, reinforced concrete. The walls are just four inches of concrete, with an inner layer of rubberised waterproofing. My shaped charges will cut right through it.'

'Won't the explosions have a characteristic vibration signature, quite different from a collapsing dock wall?' said Irith.

'Well, yes,' said Thornton. 'But I'm using small amounts of explosive, and timing them to coincide with a collapse, so we should get away with it.'

Irith said nothing. Presumably, they'd thought it through. 'They'll be after us by now,' she said tonelessly.

'Things can go wrong for them too.'

'Can they find this little tunnel from above ground?'

'Theoretically, yes,' said Thornton. 'There are a swag of methods they could use, such as ground-penetrating radar. In practice, that kind of operation requires specialised equipment that can't be used in secret, especially not right next to an airport. My biggest worry is more divers.'

'Then I'd better keep watch,' said Irith. 'Have you any way of telling if divers are coming?'

'My hydrophones were in one of the lost cases, unfortunately,' said Thornton.

'Do I just wait for them to come up, then shoot?'

'That's it. If they're well equipped, they'll look first with a snorkelscope and fire a grenade from underwater. At least, that's what I'd do.'

'Very comforting.'

'They may not have an underwater grenade launcher,' Gretel remarked.

'Even more comforting,' said Irith.

Gretel had connected the phone to a wire she'd bared from a bundle that snaked along the roof. She checked the battery was charged, picked the handset up and pressed a series of numbers. She looked up at her brother, then after a long wait, frowned.

'Nothing?' he said.

'Not a thing.' Gretel's long fingers stroked the keypad.

'Are you sure this is the right bundle, the right wire?'

'I checked twice.'

'Then either the other team isn't listening or they've already been taken.'

'Or your plans are wrong and it isn't the right wire at all,' said Irith.

'That's possible,' Gretel replied, 'but I don't have any way of testing it and I daren't try any of the other wires.'

'Keep trying,' said Thornton. 'If we can't get confirmation, we'll have to take the risk and go ahead anyway.'

'Confirmation of what?' said Irith.

'That the lock-gates have been jammed open and the docks are emptying,' said Gretel.

She tried the phone for another few minutes, with no result. Holding it away from her ear, she raised an eyebrow to her brother. 'Still nothing.'

'Well,' he said heavily, 'it looks like we're on our own. I —'

The phone emitted a faint squawk. She slapped it to her ear then as abruptly threw it down and ripped the connectors off the wire.

'What was that?' cried Thornton.

'A digital squeal. They're onto us, Thorn.'

'Right!' he said. 'Do we try it anyway, which is suicide, or try to get away?'

'I vote for trying to get away,' said Irith, sure they would ignore her.

Gretel popped four strong painkillers from their foil and swallowed them dry. She grimaced.

'I agree with Irith,' said Thornton. He looked up at his sister. 'But if you say we go in, then we go in.'

The concrete beneath them shook, very slightly. Thornton sprang to the computer and tapped a single key.

'That's it! They've done it.' He studied the screen, which showed a map of the docks area. Calculations were running in a small window. A pale green line began to blink along one section of the docks. 'That collapse was a part of the Royal Victoria dock wall, up by Connaught Bridge.'

Gretel pushed herself to her knees and stood up. 'Let's go.'

Thornton had a small pile of equipment to one side, covered in a cloth. Gretel moved to her own pile. 'Put this on,' she said, pulling out a bulky vest of grey material which she passed to Irith.

'What is it?'

'It's bulletproof,' said Thornton. 'Well, at least to pistol fire.'

'Unless they use armour-piercing rounds,' said Gretel.

'Or a knife,' said Thornton.

'Then what's the point?' Irith snapped. She hated the way they talked, and their casual assumptions about violence to come.

'Ever been shot?' Thornton said.

'Of course not.'

'I have. Put the bloody vest on and stop whining.'

Irith jerked it over her head and settled it around her chest. Gretel raised the rigid collar, which gave partial protection to her neck, though it wasn't comfortable. Irith pulled the groin protector up through her legs and fastened it at the front. The vest wasn't heavy, but it was relatively inflexible. There was a large pocket on the front.

'What's this for?' said Irith with an attempt at humour. 'My lunch?'

Thornton didn't even smile. 'It takes a Kevlar plate, for protection against AP rounds, but we didn't bring them. Can't carry everything. Now this.'

He handed her a hood, of similar material, although thinner, rather like a diving hood in shape but semi-rigid. Irith didn't like it either.

'This'll only protect you from a glancing shot,' said Thornton. 'If a bullet hits it straight on, concussion will kill you even if it doesn't go through. But it's better than nothing.'

The vest was too big. Irith tightened it as much as possible, uncomfortably aware of all it didn't protect. Thornton and Gretel donned their own gear.

He handed around gasmasks. 'Hang this around your neck. If you have to use it, make sure it seals completely around your mouth and nose. Wish I'd thought to shave.'

Gretel drew lightweight assault rifles from cylindrical tubes and slid a long magazine into each. 'Do you know what to do with this?' she asked, passing a rifle to Irith.

'Aim and pull the trigger.'

'It's much the same as the one you used before,' said Thornton.

'What do you want me to do?'

'As soon as we get in, help Gretel to secure the door. This room is meant to be lockable from the inside. They'll get through it pretty quickly, though, should they realise we're there. Once the door's locked, you and I are on guard duty. We've got to make time for Gretel to do her work.'

'Which is?'

'To extract data from a mainframe that's not connected to any network. That's why we have to physically break in. Ready?'

Irith adjusted her hood and nodded. Thornton was busy at the keyboard. A couple of minutes later the ground shook, more strongly. He tapped away, then stood up.

'The vibration alarms have gone off inside the building. They're false alarms due to the dock collapse, of course, so they'll reset them, and when it happens again, maybe they won't look so closely. My firing program is running. The next time a shock exceeds the set threshold, the charges will be set off in the middle of the vibration curve. Ready?'

Irith nodded.

'Now we wait.'

They moved out of the cave onto the shelf above the water-filled tunnel. Irith eyed the black water anxiously. The wait proved so long that she began to think there wasn't going to be another collapse. Gretel and Thornton were giving each other worried glances.

'If they've identified the location of that call,' whispered Gretel, 'they'll be on their way by now.'

He muttered an oath, so Irith assumed that was a possibility.

The floor shook gently. Irith held her breath. One, two, three, four, five. There was no explosion. They all turned and stared at the wall.

'Too gentle,' said Thornton. 'Turn away.'

The floor shook again, more strongly. There was a roar in Irith's ears and dust exploded out of the wall. Gravel rained into the water. A vertical section of wall wobbled, hanging by a few fragments. Thornton ran and pulled it outwards.

'In!' he hissed at Irith, who was just standing there, dazed by the violence of the explosion. Taking a box of gear in each hand, he pushed through the hole.

Gretel followed swiftly, despite her shoulder injury. Irith went next, her weapon out. By the time she had climbed through, Thornton was on the far side of the room, racing up the stairs. He pressed a red button on the wall and the locking bars slid closed.

'What about surveillance cameras?' said Irith.

'Too great a risk of them picking up what's on the computer screens. This place is ultra-top-secret.'

Irith panted up to him. Her legs ached. 'Can the door be unlocked from the outside?'

'I dare say there's an override code somewhere in the building, but just to be sure we'll secure it manually. Come on.'

Thornton injected a quick-setting epoxy into the lock to prevent it from being used. Gretel was slumped in front of the squat black cube in the centre of the room, already tapping at the terminal keys.

'The system seems to be connected to something.' She dropped to her knees, wrenching open the lower doors. 'Should I unplug it, Thorn?'

'Will that tell them we're here?'

'Probably, but so will using the system while it's connected to upstairs.'

He cursed. 'Pull the plug.'

'I thought you said it was completely isolated,' said Irith.

'It is, normally,' said Thornton, 'but they have to upload and download data at times. When doing that, they would disconnect the entire building from the net so no one could gain access.'

Gretel twisted a connector the diameter of a water hose and jerked out the cable. 'That's it! We're in business.'

She connected the laptop to the mainframe, raced through a series of hierarchical menus and set a series of programs to run. While that was going on she continued to work at the keyboard. A minute later all the lights went out; so did the mainframe's monitors. The room was lit only by the glow from the laptop screen.

'They've cut the power,' said Irith.

'They know we're here, bugger it! Thorn?'

He opened one of her cases, drawing out an object roughly the size of a car battery, though it was relatively light.

'It's a programmable Powerbrick,' said Gretel. 'Not sure how long it'll run this computer, though. It uses a hell of a lot of power.'

Thornton connected the Powerbrick to the mainframe. The screens came back up. Gretel switched all but one off and continued to work.

'It's sucking the juice right out!' she said a minute later. 'We'll never do it.'

'There must be an emergency low-power setting,' Thornton called.

'You'd think so, but I'm stuffed if I can find it.'

Something slammed into the steel door so hard that it boomed. Then again, and again.

'What do we do?' Irith cried.

'Pray that it holds them long enough,' Thornton said laconically. 'The door is designed to keep out a determined attack.'

The banging and crashing continued without interruption. Gretel worked furiously. She swore. 'Another Powerbrick, Thorn.'

'How's it going?' he said as he changed it over.

'Not well. The system has layer upon layer of protection. I've eight separate programs running, trying to crack it, but as soon as one wall goes down a new one appears that I haven't seen before.'

A couple of minutes went by. The crashing against the door continued. 'I've found the power saver, but it still uses a lot of power. More than I expected.'

A few minutes later Thornton changed the second Powerbrick for a third.

'That's the last,' said Gretel. 'If this doesn't do it, we're sunk.'

'I thought we had six,' said Thornton.

'The others were in one of the cases we lost.'

'What if we ripped out the hard discs?' said Irith.

'They're in a steel box that we'd need a forklift to move.'

Gretel looked over her shoulder at the door. 'They won't get through it like that.'

Irith cocked her head, listening. 'The banging seems just a little too regular.'

'It may be a decoy while they try to get in some other way,' Gretel yelled above the din.

'Keep a sharp lookout, Irith,' said Thornton. 'They'll probably blow small holes in the wall and toss in gas grenades. They won't want to damage this set-up. If they do use gas, fire single shots through the hole to deter them. It's all we can do. We'd better check the walls.'

He went one way and Irith the other, pressing her ear to the wall at intervals. She heard nothing except the banging on the door and, once, a lengthy shudder that was probably another of the dock walls collapsing.

'I'm in!' Gretel shouted. Then she added, 'At least, I think I'm in.' Her long fingers worked furiously. Colours, patterns and text flashed on the screen.

Irith kept moving, scanning the walls, but she saw and heard nothing. It took a couple of minutes before she met Thornton halfway. They both turned to Gretel. She looked wan.

'How's your shoulder?'

'Hurts like hell,' she said with a twisted smile. 'Cuts my typing speed somewhat.'

The banging continued on the door. Gretel put her head down on the desk. 'Hey,' Thornton called. 'If anyone should be having a rest, it's me.'

Gretel didn't answer.

'Shit!' Thornton exclaimed. 'Gretel?' He practically flew across to the console.

She raised her head sluggishly, trying to smile. 'What is it, Thorn?'

'Get up!' He dragged her bodily off the chair, pulling her backwards across the room.

'What's the matter?' said Irith.

Thornton dropped his sister on the floor and pulled up her gasmask. 'Put yours on, Irith, and have a look under the console.'

For what? Irith fitted the mask and went down on her hands and knees. There was nothing underneath but flat panels and a thick power cable that ran through a hole in the floor. Tendrils of vapour were oozing out. Her head spun.

'They're pumping gas through the power conduit,' she said.

Thornton had the gasmask on Gretel, who was now sitting up, and another on himself. He gestured. Irith came over.

His speech was difficult to understand through the mask. '. . . can't do anything . . . about that. Masks won't . . . work . . . long.'

Gretel checked the main console. 'Last Powerbrick . . . running down.'

The big screen faded to black.

CHAPTER SIXTEEN

'What if we connect the Powerbricks together?' yelled Thornton. 'There might just be enough power.'

'Yes!' Gretel staggered back to her laptop. Thornton connected the Powerbricks and the main screen came up.

Gretel battered the keyboard and a dozen windows collapsed on themselves. 'We've got something!' she shrieked. Words flashed across the screen of the laptop. 'The Terminator Project.'

'That's it!' cried Thornton over her shoulder. 'Get the data.'

'I'll do the checks in case it's a dummy, if you don't mind.' Gretel tapped away, windows opening across her laptop screen and graphic simulations running in each. She looked over her shoulder and her eyes were alive. She checked the windows, her lips moving. 'I think it's the one, Thorn. The stats are showing really good matches. Yes! My simulations match: twenty out of twenty. This is it!'

'Have you broken the download protection?'

'Just finishing now.'

'Then dump the fucking data, quick!'

She kept tapping. More graphic simulations exploded on the screen. 'There are fifty-six thousand files. Hundreds of terabytes. It'll take a couple of minutes.'

'Do the big ones first. It'll be a large file.'

'Or a series of little ones.'

'Then pray there's enough juice left.'

Gretel consulted the power monitor. 'Not good.'

The download proceeded. Outside, the banging had stopped.

'That's a bad sign. Let's go,' Thornton said.

'Another minute. I'm not going while there's any power left. We might be leaving behind the one file we came for.'

Boom! A small hole appeared to the right of the door. Dust billowed out, carrying chips of concrete. Irith aimed and fired. The bullet kicked up dust from the side of the hole. She adjusted her aim and fired again, and again.

Out of the corner of her eye she saw Thornton desperately rummaging through his pack. A hand appeared at the hole. She fired again but the gas grenade was already through. She watched it curve toward them.

'Turn away!' he roared, leaping to one side.

The grenade struck the floor, bursting with a dull thud. Something hit her in the middle of the back, although her vest absorbed the impact.

Clouds of gas clung to Thornton as he moved. Irith checked the hole and saw movement behind it. Another hand appeared. She fired. There was an explosion of white vapour on the other side.

'That'll give them something to think about,' she said with satisfaction.

'Out!' roared Thornton, staggering about. The gas must have been getting in under his mask. 'Now.'

She scrambled through the wall aperture, knocking her mask half off. An acrid whiff made her choke. Tear gas? She looked around. Thornton was already outside, bent over and gasping.

'Where's Gretel?' Irith yelled.

He was too overcome to answer. Gretel was still inside! Irith turned back, adjusting her gasmask as she went. The room was full of white fumes and she could not see the console. 'Gretel?'

She had collapsed on the floor, the laptop clutched in her left hand. Her eyes were flooding.

'Come on.' Irith tried to lift the much larger woman.

'Take the computer,' Gretel mumbled.

Bugger the computer, Irith thought, but she snatched it from Gretel's hand and dropped it through to Thornton, then took Gretel under the arms. She must have had twenty kilograms on Irith, but with desperate heaves she got Gretel to her knees, then on her feet, and they fell through the wall together.

Thornton pulled them the rest of the way. Behind them, Irith heard a series of pops, which she took to be more grenades exploding, then a dull crump! accompanied by a red flare. She felt a blast of heat on her exposed cheek. Gas whirled out at them.

'Now where?' said Irith. 'We don't have to go underwater again, do we?'

'I'm afraid we do,' said Thornton, 'though not very far. Get your gear, quick! Forget the wetsuits – they'll be through that door in minutes. You won't need the weight belt either.'

Irith heaved on her flippers, tank and mask. Gretel did the same, while Thornton packed essential equipment.

'Where's the MemoStick, with the data?' he said suddenly.

'It's safe,' Gretel replied.

'Where?' he persisted.

'I've got it.'

'Did you finish downloading the data?'

'Not quite. There were about four thousand files to go.'

'So we might not have what we came for?' said Thornton.

'It's possible,' said Gretel.

'Shit!'

'Can't do anything about it. I'm ready.'

'So am I,' said Irith, not looking forward to going in the water again. 'What about other divers?' She couldn't stop thinking about the ones she had killed. She kept seeing their mangled bodies and tortured faces.

'Good point.' Thornton withdrew a small rectangular grenade from his pack. 'Put your hands over your ears and turn away.' He activated the grenade and threw it in the water.

On the count of five the water erupted at them. It was like standing under a freezing waterfall.

'Water is incompressible,' Thornton said casually after the deluge had ceased. 'The shockwave will be magnified up the tunnels and it'll take care of anyone within a hundred metres or so.'

'What does he mean by "take care of"?' Irith whispered.

Gretel did not reply.

Irith stared at Thornton. He revelled in violence and destruction, and suddenly he did not seem at all attractive.

'Bring that case, Irith,' he said. 'Gretel, can you . . . ?'

'I'll manage.'

'I'll carry these two. Follow me. It's not far.'

The water was petrifyingly cold. Irith felt it close around her, like a frosty fist trying to squeeze the breath out of her.

The swim was no more than a hundred metres but it felt like kilometres.

With every stroke the cold seeped further into her, like ink through a stick of chalk. She wondered how long her unprotected body could stand it. Her muscles seemed to be freezing up. Irith took no notice of anything except Gretel's flippers moving up and down in front of her, and when they finally reached the exit she could not have told a single detail of their route.

'This way,' said Thornton, pulling off his flippers.

They squeezed through a narrow hole. He packed rubble into it until it was blocked behind them. Irith tried to press the water out of her clothes, without success. She couldn't stop her teeth from chattering.

'Put on the ballistic vest,' he said. 'It'll be better than nothing.'

Shuddering with the cold and her shoes squelching as she walked, Irith followed the twins down the tunnel.

Thornton, supporting Gretel, wasn't even shivering. He seemed indestructible. He called over his shoulder, with an attempt at a grin, 'Bring the bloody computer, would you, since we've gone to all the trouble.'

Irith went back for it, tucked it into the front pocket of her bulletproof vest, set her rifle to *burst*, and followed. 'What was that last explosion? Did the gas grenades set something off?'

Gretel took off her face mask and dropped it on the ground. Her lips were blistered and her eyes red. 'I set off a thermal grenade inside the console, hoping to wipe out all traces of what I did, and what I got from their computer. If anything,' she said bitterly.

'Where are we going now?' asked Irith.

'You ask a hell of a lot of questions,' Thornton said wearily.

'If you ever volunteered any information I wouldn't have to.'

'Got to get out of the country,' said Gretel. 'But since everything has gone wrong so far, our network has probably been blown. In which case, we're stuffed.'

Some distance on, they came to a T-junction. Thornton turned left.

'Think I can manage now,' said Gretel. She pushed back her hood and ran her fingers through her dark hair, which stood out in curly tendrils.

Irith was so exhausted that she could barely shuffle. 'Can I take my vest off?'

'They'll be after us by now.'

'Any chance of losing them?'

'Not much.'

They followed a labyrinthine path, Gretel leading them through rusting pipes, ancient basements and storage tanks, old sewerage tunnels and other conduits whose purpose Irith could not fathom. Several times they passed along tunnels that looked recent, cut through chalk and other kinds of rock.

'This looks freshly excavated,' Irith said as they trudged through a section of white chalk.

'Our people dug it out over the past few years, to connect the existing passages,' said Thornton. 'This job has been long in the planning.'

'How do you know your way around?'

Gretel answered. 'I've spent months of nights underground in the last couple of years, getting ready for this day.'

They wound their tortuous way through the maze. Irith could not imagine how Gretel found the way, but she never faltered.

Several hours later, in another recently constructed tunnel in green sandstone with pebbles of flint, Gretel sat down and wrenched off her vest. Despite the cold, there were drops of sweat on her brow.

'You all right?' Thornton said.

'I'm sick and my shoulder hurts like hell.'

He took the dressing off. The wound had torn open and the area around the bullet hole was inflamed and swollen.

'It needs medical attention – in a hospital.'

Gretel looked down. 'It's not going to get it in this country. See what you can do.'

'All I can do is bandage it up. The medical kit was in one of those lost cases.'

'Do it then and let's get on,' she snarled, swallowing more painkillers.

'Is there anything to eat?' Irith said when Thornton had crusted the wound with antibiotic powder and put on a fresh dressing.

He passed her a bar of chocolate. 'You want anything, Gretel?'

'No!' she snapped.

'You need to keep your strength up.'

'Piss off and leave me alone.'

Thornton merely grinned and gave her a hug, keeping well away from the injured shoulder. She pushed him off but the anger was gone as quickly as it had come. 'Perhaps a few squares,' she said softly. 'I'm really not hungry.'

He broke off four squares of chocolate and handed them over. Gretel put them all in her mouth at once. 'Water?'

He passed her a flask. She took a small sip and handed it to Irith. 'Is this all we have?' Irith said.

'There's another, and we can get more.'

Irith finished the flask, only a few mouthfuls, and looked around. The tunnel looked vaguely familiar. 'Have we been through here before?'

'Day before yesterday.'

Irith walked up the tunnel, sweeping it with the beam of her torch. Not far along, the green rock changed to a purple-grey clay marked by a network of fissures. Water trickled out and in places the clay had collapsed into wet heaps. Shallow pools of water lay here and there.

She caught a trickle in one hand and put it to her mouth, then thought better of it. 'Can we drink this?' she said, walking back.

'I wouldn't recommend it,' he said dryly. 'Most of the pollution was buried when the docklands were redeveloped.'

She wiped her hand vigorously on her trousers. 'Wasn't that kind of irresponsible?'

'There was nowhere else to put it.'

'We'd better be going,' said Gretel, rising painfully. 'Thorn? What's the matter?'

He was staring at a monitor in his hand, no larger than the screen on a mobile. 'I think we're being followed.'

'But I've used every trick in the book,' said Gretel.

'And I've been a bloody fool!' Thornton took the laptop from the pocket of Irith's bulletproof vest, opened it and touched a key. The screen sprang to life. 'After Irith dragged you out of the basement, I forgot to make sure the damn thing was off.' He switched it off.

'They've tracked it by its electromagnetic signature?' asked Irith.

'Yes. How could I have been so stupid?'

'You're not superman, no matter how much you like to think so,' said Gretel acidly. 'And I didn't turn it off either.'

'We're still a good way from our destination,' he said with a glance at Irith, 'and not heading towards it, so it hasn't given that away. But security can travel faster than we can, and get other teams down here to block any routes they know about. Since they discovered our command centre ... When was that, exactly?'

'Two days ago,' said Gretel.

'Really? Feels like twenty years. Anyway, they'll be furiously mapping the labyrinth, now they know it exists.'

'They won't do that in a couple of days.'

'But they can give us plenty of trouble. We'd better move.'

They hurried on. The tunnel wound around, going back into the green rock and then, briefly, into chalk again. They slid sideways behind a wall built to conceal an opening, through a narrow gap and into a clean box-section concrete tunnel with knee-deep water running along it.

'Lucky it's been dry lately,' he said, 'or we'd need a canoe here.'

'It's rained every second day since I came to London,' Irith murmured.

'You Aussies!' He ruffled her hair. 'That's just drizzle.'

Twenty metres along, they took a side passage too low to stand up in. The concrete was slimy and the flow strong enough to cause them trouble. Irith pressed her hands against the sides to prevent it from sweeping her off her feet.

They continued in this way for what seemed like hours. Every so often they stopped while Gretel and Thornton crouched over his monitor, conferring in whispers. Then they would move on, in a different direction as soon as the labyrinth offered one. Irith felt that they were doubling back and forth. Surely in a straight line they would have crossed out of the docklands long ago?

'I haven't got the faintest idea where we are,' she panted, squatting down for a moment's rest.

'Unfortunately our pursuers do,' said Gretel, consulting the monitor again. 'They're closing fast.'

'Which way are they coming from?'

'Behind us.' Thornton jerked a thumb over his shoulder.

'How are they tracking us?'

'No idea, but if we can't shake them off, this has all been a waste of time.'

'Time for desperate measures then,' said Gretel. 'Which is why I brought us this way.'

She didn't elaborate and they continued as before, though off at an angle. On rounding a corner ten minutes later, Irith looked up. 'We've definitely been here before.' Just ahead was the roof with the rusting bomb embedded in it.

Thornton stood under it, scratching his bristly chin.

'Is that from the Second World War?' Irith wondered.

'Yep. Docklands was one of the most heavily bombed places in Britain. It's not uncommon to find unexploded ordnance here, even after all this time.'

'Is it still dangerous?'

'Could be. A couple of hundred kilograms of TNT, I'd say. If it went off, it'd blow out a crater you could fit a mansion in.'

'What's above us?' said Irith.

'Open space in an industrial estate, south of the Royal Victoria Dock.'

'Is there any way of setting it off, safely?'

'The air blast would be worse than a hurricane in these confined spaces. Even if we were a couple of hundred metres away, it'd splatter us against the nearest wall like a bag of tomatoes. Not to mention a firestorm sucking all the air out and burning us to a crisp.'

'The same goes for our enemies,' said Gretel. 'At least we'd have time to prepare for it.'

'How would you set it off?' said Irith.

'Got some plastic explosive left,' said Thornton. 'That's not the problem.'

'What is?'

'I left my electronic detonation system behind. Didn't think I'd need it anymore.'

'So there's no way of setting off the plastic explosive?' said Irith.

'I've a tiny bit of detonating fuse.'

'How tiny?' said Gretel.

He went through his pack. 'About a minute's worth.'

Gretel measured the tunnel with her eyes. 'It's seventy metres to the corner, then, if my memory's correct, another hundred and ten to the side tunnel off that. Get into that and there's a solid steel door we can slide –'

'In sixty seconds I might just possibly ignite it, drop to the ground, get up and run like buggery in the dark, and make it past the corner,' he replied. 'I may even get to the door, but we'll never close it in time. And even if we did, the air blast would probably blow it off and squash us like cockroaches under a toilet seat.'

'If you wore the bulletproof gear . . .' began Irith.

'I wouldn't even make it to the corner. Anyway, it's not designed to protect from that kind of impact, or those temperatures. Fucking big bomb.'

They considered the bomb. Irith shuddered. 'What can I do?' She looked for crevices she might be able to take refuge in.

'You've done enough already,' said Thornton. 'Keep your eyes open and your finger on the trigger. They won't be long.'

'What if I take your vest?' said Gretel. 'When you reach us you can wrap it around your head and chest. There's a recess we can shelter in, beyond the door.'

'All right. ' He measured the cord. 'It's a bit longer than I thought. May just be enough.'

The lower end of the bomb was half a metre above his upstretched fingers. They gathered fallen rocks into a pile and he climbed up to inspect it.

'The nose was crushed by the impact,' said Thornton. 'It came through a few metres of earth and soft rock, yet it didn't explode. There's a chance my explosive won't set it off either.'

'Can't be any worse off than we are now,' said Gretel. The monitor let out a tinny buzz. 'They're coming! Can you do it in the dark?' She turned off the torch.

'I'll have to,' he muttered.

There came a chatter of gunfire and Irith was struck in the chest so hard that she was thrown off her feet. Something smashed – the computer. Beside her she heard Gretel grunt in pain, but she managed to fire back.

Irith rolled over, gasping. She felt as if she'd been hit by a brick. 'You all right, Gretel?'

'Banged my shoulder on the wall,' she said. 'Shit it hurts.'

Irith pointed her weapon down the tunnel, fired a short burst and rolled out of the way.

'Thorn?' cried Gretel. Her voice rasped like rags being torn in a high wind.

'I was imagining what would happen if the plastic explosive was hit.' He chuckled. 'I almost hope it will be. Give them another burst.'

Irith fired and moved. As soon as she stopped, Gretel fired three times, waited a couple of seconds, then moved and fired again.

'It's nearly ready,' said Thorn shortly. 'Get moving.'

'We'll wait . . . ' Gretel began.

'Be buggered!' he snapped. 'After you get around the corner, keep running and put your hands over your ears. You've got ninety seconds. Piss off, *now*!'

Gretel fired another burst and they ran, Irith counting the seconds. Twenty-two had passed before they rounded the corner. Gretel flashed the torch for a second. Irith saw nothing but unmarked tunnel.

'Where's the side tunnel?' she cried. 'I can't see any door.'

'Shut up and run!'

Fuck you too, Irith thought. 'Wish I'd left the bloody vest behind,' she gasped.

Despite her injury Gretel had been running faster than Irith and now accelerated away. Suddenly a red light flashed in the distance, far ahead, and a small red spot appeared on Irith's chest – a laser sight. If they were using armour-piercing rounds, she was dead.

She sidestepped on the run. A bullet caught at the edge of the vest, spinning her around and knocking her off her feet. She landed flat on her back and her rifle went flying.

Gretel fired a long burst from the hip and kept going. She probably didn't know Irith was down. There came a distant scream. Her footsteps disappeared down the tunnel.

Irith staggered to her feet. The back of her head hurt and she had no breath left. Both palms were bleeding. Her mental clock was still running: fifty-four, fifty-five, fifty-six. She felt for her rifle but couldn't find it.

Someone slammed into her from behind. Irith cracked her knee on the rough floor and stifled a cry. Thornton picked her up. Sixty-three, sixty-four . . .

'I can't find the rifle,' she cried in a panic.

'Forget the fucking rifle!' He found her hand, gripped it like a vice and ran, dragging her along behind.

Her heart felt like a time bomb inside her chest, her lungs were burning and her legs melting down to cooked meat. The back of her head felt as if it had been struck with a mallet. Every stride sent a shock of pain through her. She could run no further.

She staggered, fell down and didn't have the strength to get up. Thornton scooped her into his arms and seemed to run even faster, though surely that wasn't possible.

The torch flashed on in front of them, illuminating the door. 'Hurry!' Gretel screamed.

Seventy-nine, eighty. They were through. Thornton dropped Irith on the floor and helped Gretel slam the door across. They banged the bar into its socket.

Eighty-one. 'Get away from the door,' he roared. 'Cover your head, your eyes and ears.'

Thornton picked Irith up and heaved her into a niche ten metres past the door. He piled in after. Gretel came last. Throwing herself on top of them, she spread Thornton's vest over their heads and chests. Irith pulled his head down against her breasts and wrapped the leaves of the coat over them both.

Ninety-two, ninety-three, ninety-four. No explosion.

'Shit,' said Irith. 'It hasn't gone off. Now what do we –?'

The whole world shuddered, then the roaring, thundering blast was so violent and terrifying that she was deafened, even with her hands tightly pressed to her ears. She screamed and clutched Thornton to her.

Pieces of rock pounded the steel door. With a shriek of rent metal, the door was torn off and bowled down the tunnel like a sheet of paper in the wind. Something stung Irith all along her exposed right thigh – the shockwave. It felt as though she had been whipped from buttock to knee.

A hail of particles thudded into the bulletproof gear. Tongues of flame licked around them. Behind her eyelids Irith saw an internal explosion of colours and sounds and something slammed into the pile. Thornton grunted.

The heat was terrible, and she could smell something burning – Thornton's hair. She beat it out. The air sucked back the other way, carrying more hail-like grit and choking dust. There was a long, rumbling crash from some distance away, then another, and a roar that shook the rock around them and seemed to go on forever. Again the wind rushed past, not so strong this time but even hotter.

Rubble continued to fall, thankfully none too close. They waited for it to stop.

'Gretel?' said Irith.

She groaned. 'I feel as if I've been beaten all over and cooked like a turkey. But I'm all right. What about you, Thorn?'

'My arse feels as though it's got a half-brick jammed up it.' He withdrew his bead from Irith's bosom and ruffled her dusty hair. 'But if I did have to die, I can't think of a better way to go.'

Irith didn't even flush. She was too emotionally drained. 'Now what?'

'I don't imagine our hunters could have survived that,' said Gretel, 'but it's probably created a collapse hole up to the surface and the area will be crawling with people before long. That might inhibit our surviving friends from pursuing us too aggressively.'

'I wouldn't count on it,' said Thornton. He was moving gingerly, shining the torch around the tunnel.

Irith saw only swirling dust. Her thigh was throbbing.

Gretel covered her face with her sleeve and walked back to where the door had been, disappearing within a few steps. A couple of minutes later she reappeared.

'The tunnel's blocked fifty metres along. They won't find us coming from that direction.'

'Let's pray this tunnel isn't also blocked,' said Thornton ominously. 'If it is . . .'

Irith stood up and broken glass tinkled in her vest pocket. She withdrew the smashed laptop. The first bullet had gone through the outer layer of the vest, the case and the screen, and was embedded under the keyboard.

'It saved my life.'

'The case is solid titanium,' said Thornton. 'That bullet would have gone right through the vest, any ordinary computer, and you.' He took out the hard disc and put the computer back in her vest pocket. 'Next time we come to a hole full of water, drop it in.'

Irith pulled her pants down. Modesty seemed irrelevant here. The shockwave had given her a bruise along her buttock and thigh the size of a loaf of bread.

She limped away. The floor was littered with rubble and about fifty metres further along they came upon the steel door, twisted over on itself and jammed in a narrow section of the tunnel. They crawled under it and continued.

'Surely they'll think we were killed in the explosion,' Irith said hopefully.

'Our hunters aren't wishful thinkers. They'll believe we're dead when they identify our burnt, bloody and dismembered corpses.'

'Do you have to be so graphic?' said Irith.

'I don't want you to have any illusions.'

'I don't! Where are we going?' Irith felt shaky, empty and ravenously hungry.

'We follow this tunnel along for a few hundred metres, then see which way we can get through.'

'To where?'

'Tell you when we get there.'

They took several doglegs and negotiated a variety of passages similar to those Irith had previously experienced in the underground. An interminable time later, when she had given up hope of ever getting out, she heard waves lapping on a hard surface.

'We must be near the river.'

'We're coming up against the south-western end of the King George V dock,' said Gretel. 'But we shouldn't be able to hear the water from here . . .'

'Unless this part of the dock wall has collapsed,' said Thornton.

'Is that bad?'

'I dare say we can get out, but can we do it unseen? This is a secure area.'

'Because of the building we broke into?'

'No,' he said as if she were an idiot. 'Because we're just across the dock from the London City Airport.'

They reached a point where the tunnel was broken and half full of water. Daylight grew in front of them, the first Irith had seen for days. Ahead, a great stretch of the dock wall, at least a hundred metres, had been pushed outwards and now leaned into the dock. Parts of the wall had crumbled away and disappeared under the brown water.

Thornton crept to the edge and peered out through a gap. It was late in the afternoon of another miserable April day, though it could have been December. Ice coated the sides of the wall.

'Winter still hasn't broken,' said Irith.

'I don't think it will,' said Gretel, who looked ready to collapse. She lay on the concrete and closed her eyes.

A squall swept sleety rain down the length of the dock. They could see the airport runway just beyond. Part of the dock wall had fallen there too, and engineers in white hardhats were perched on the edge, looking down. There were police everywhere.

Thornton stood well back. 'We've got to get across to the airport,' said Thornton, 'and I've no idea how we're going to do it.'

'Better find a way,' said Gretel. 'Once they discover that we've survived, Congress will pressure the government to close the airport.'

'Can they do that?' said Irith. 'The UK is independent.'

'Doesn't mean it's immune from pressure. If they close the airport, we're rooted. Any ideas?'

'If we wait till dark,' said Irith, 'we might scramble along the gap where the wall has collapsed and get to the airport from the other side.'

'There's sophisticated surveillance there at the best of times, and it'll be supplemented with patrols now.'

'But when you planned this mission, you must have had a way through.'

'We didn't expect to blow up half of Docklands and knock down the rest. We expected to have a full team. And I expected to have some explosive left, to create false alarms while we got in another way.'

'Aren't there any tunnels under the airport?'

'None that we know of,' Gretel said in a cobwebby voice.

'What are we going to do?' The enemy was probably moving into position for the kill. Irith moved back into the tunnel, to the dark that was slightly more welcoming than daylight.

'Just have to wait,' said Thornton. 'Have some chocolate.' He offered a squashed and battered bar.

'I don't want any bloody chocolate,' Irith snapped. 'I just want to go home to my mother.' But that thought was unbearable.

Brother and sister exchanged glances. 'I don't understand how you can bear to utter her name,' Gretel said coolly.

'Only one thing could have forced Mum to help them,' Irith cried. 'A threat to my life.'

'I don't think we'll discuss that any further,' said Thornton. 'And now, since there's nothing we can do till after dark, I'm having a nap.'

CHAPTER SEVENTEEN

Irith closed her eyes and settled back against the wall. Her mind was racing and she could not have slept at any price. She was freezing and the vest made no difference.

Dark fell in an instant. Lights appeared along the airport perimeter, and extra floodlights where the wall had collapsed on the other side of the dock. The hours crept by: seven o'clock, eight. Thornton woke up.

'Ten minutes,' said Gretel. 'Get ready.'

He sprang across the water gap where the dock wall had tilted, climbed the tilted section, slipping on the ice, and carefully raised himself above the edge. A minute later he returned, got out what looked like a pencil-thin torch and mounted it on the barrel of his rifle. He mounted a telescopic sight behind it, squinted through the sight and made a number of adjustments to both torch and sight. 'That'll do.' He laid the weapon on his coat.

'It's a laser signalling torch,' he said before Irith could ask. 'It makes a spot only a centimetre across at a distance of a kilometre. It works in the UV, so it doesn't make a visible beam, and the message can only be read from the point where the beam ends up. That makes it secure and almost undetectable.'

'Why the rifle, Thorn?'

'Helps to line the torch up. Could also be a broomstick, as long as it had a telescopic sight.'

'So someone's watching at the other end.'

'They will be, at precisely ten past eight, though for only a minute. If we miss it, we have to wait till 9.16, and then 10.49. Random intervals, in case you're wondering.'

'And then they'll send a signal back?'

'A pair of numbers. The first is the correct confirmation for the day; the second, agreement to a specific plan.'

'That you've already worked out?'

'Of course.'

'Three minutes,' croaked Gretel from the floor. She could barely raise her head. Thornton climbed onto the wall and Irith lost sight of him. Five minutes later he was back. 'No answer.'

'Is that bad?' said Irith.

He shrugged.

At 9.16 he tried again, and again there was no response. Gretel roused. 'I don't like it. He's very reliable. Something must have gone wrong.'

'Maybe he doesn't dare risk revealing himself.' Thornton didn't sound convincing.

Time dragged. Irith was so exhausted that she had begun to have hallucinations. Gretel moaned. Irith gave her the last of the painkillers and checked the wound, which was inflamed in a ragged circle the size of a cricket ball. She shook on more antibiotic powder, re-bandaged it and slumped against the wall, too exhausted to care about anything.

'It's a quarter to eleven,' Thornton said suddenly. 'I'll go.'

Irith was glad it wasn't her job; she couldn't have held the rifle straight. She closed her eyes and drifted.

Splash! Thornton's wet hand touched her face. 'He's there,' he said in a low voice. 'He'll be on his way at 11.45, on site eight minutes later. Plan five. Gretel?'

She moaned.

'Gretel?'

'One minute I'm freezing,' she said hoarsely, 'the next I'm burning up.'

'We've got to go. We don't have any spare time.'

'Go where?' Her words were slurred.

'Plan five,' he repeated.

'What's . . . that?' She sounded like a record running down.

'Stay with me. I can't do this by myself.' But Gretel slumped sideways, breathing raggedly. 'Irith?' said Thornton.

'Yes?' Was anything ever going to go right?

'We're in trouble. Keep watch. Take her rifle and prepare to use it . . . though if you do we'll never get away.'

'What are you doing?'

'I'll carry her up. It's going to be a bastard of a climb. Then we've got to get to the pick-up point without being seen, and that's going to be difficult. Come on.'

It took him thirty minutes to get Gretel up onto the dock. This wasn't a high-security area, for the docks had been closed down decades ago and there were now houses and offices to the south.

Once up top, they lay on the pavement with their grey vests over them, trying to look like concrete. That proved not as hard as they had imagined; some of the lights along the dock wall had failed in the collapse and others were off because of the energy crisis. The rain made haloes around those few that remained.

Irith felt cold sweat pool in the middle of her back. The plan seemed rather weak.

'Gretel?' Thornton said hoarsely. She didn't answer. 'Gretel? Please answer me.'

Irith felt her hand. 'She's slipped into –'

'Oh God!' His voice went shrill. 'She's going to die, isn't she?'

'Of course she's not,' said Irith, having no idea. 'It's for the best, Thornton. She was in a lot of pain.'

'I can't do it without her. She's been my prop all my life. I –' Thornton, who had been their rock for days, sounded as if he was going to break down. Irith couldn't allow that. She checked her watch: 11.35.

'We've only got eighteen minutes!' she hissed. 'If we aren't in position in time, she *will* die. Pull yourself together.'

'I – can't – do – it.'

It was freezing cold on the concrete, with the rain blowing in their faces, and the wind was almost a gale. If the weather got any worse the airport might close, and that would doom them.

'Thornton!' She slapped him across the face. 'Seventeen minutes now.' He didn't move. She stood up. 'Fuck you, you self-indulgent prick. Do what you want. I'm going my own way.' She threw the gun on the ground and stalked across the road.

He sat up, blinking frozen tears off his lashes. 'Come back.'

She kept walking until he grabbed her by the shoulder and spun her around. 'You bloody little fool. This whole area is within range of the airport cameras.'

'Fifteen minutes!'

With a visible effort, he pulled himself together. 'We've got to get across the road and down behind that row of offices. Then we wait.'

The streetlights went out further down the row, came on again, then sparks fountained from the side of a substation. The last overhead lights faded.

'That's for us. Come on.'

He heaved Gretel over his shoulder. She cried out. He put his hand over her mouth and staggered into the darkness. Irith darted after him. As they reached the perimeter road, a vehicle screamed out from a side road behind them. She slid behind a phone box, readying her weapon, but the vehicle turned the other way and raced towards the substation, which was still sparking. Two other vehicles followed – police and ambulance.

Thornton and Irith slipped into the darkness under a row of street trees. There were few lights in the offices, though any number of people might have been inside the houses, looking out. They made it around the corner, where Thornton had to put his burden down. 'She's a big girl,' he said, wiping his brow.

'Heard that,' Gretel slurred. 'Rude bastard.'

'Hush!' He stroked the hair off her brow. 'I meant big and beautiful.'

'Sooner be little and cute, like Irith.'

'Cute?' Irith cried.

'Appears that's a mortal insult in Australia,' Thornton chuckled.

'Too bloody right, mate.'

'Come on.' Thornton hefted Gretel again.

'Want me to take that bag?' said Irith. He passed it to her. 'Come on. We've only five minutes.'

'Not far to go,' said Thornton. 'Just around the corner.'

They turned the corner and went along the street for fifty metres, as far as Irith could judge in the darkness. The back of the row of offices was a blank wall. He walked onto the street and lay Gretel down.

'Where to now?' said Irith.

'Right here.'

'In the middle of the street?'

'That's right. Our ride should be here in a minute. Lie down. It'll come right over us and stop. We pull ourselves up into a purpose-built cage and it takes us into the airport. It's the only way to get where we're going.'

'Where are we going?'

'The airfreight section,' said Thornton. 'It's the only way. Iris implants won't do it this time.'

Now how did he know about that?

Lights appeared in the distance, turning their way. Irith lay on the road, unable to believe this could work. Suddenly a truck came roaring towards them. It looked as if it was going to run right over them.

'Stay down,' Thornton hissed, 'or it'll knock your bloody head off.'

She lowered her head, sure those huge tyres would crush her skull like a road-roller. The truck sped towards them, slowed at the last minute and, just as she was about to scream, stopped above them.

The driver's door opened and a man jumped out, flashing a torch as if checking one of the tyres. He bent down. The torch passed over the three of them.

'Get into the cage, quick,' said a voice that would have been familiar had Irith not been so desperately tired.

'It'll take a minute or two,' said Thornton. 'Gretel's been shot; she's not in real good shape.'

'I can't help you, in case a distant camera swings onto the truck. I'll walk around a couple of times and check under the bonnet as if something's wrong. That's all I can do. It's been a shit of a day. I'm lucky to be here at all.'

Fortunately Thornton knew what he was doing, because Irith had no idea. He pulled down a cage, rolled Gretel into it, then crawled in next to her. 'Get in, Irith.'

She crawled in. The only space left was on top of him. She huddled there. He worked another lever, jacking the cage into place, and locked it. 'Ready,' he called.

The driver kicked his tyres again then returned to the cab and drove off, more slowly this time. He did a circuit past the substation, waved to the police and technicians there, and rumbled away.

Shortly they stopped at the airport gates. 'Where have you been?' said a tired guard on the gate. 'You just went out.'

'I'm bored shitless,' the familiar voice said. 'Went down to see what that fuss was at the substation.'

'What was it?'

'Buggered if I know, but it's going to take a while to fix. Thanks.'

He drove off. After several minutes he turned into the freight terminal and drove down the back, where it was gloomy. The lights didn't seem to be working.

'Get out of the cage,' the driver said, 'but stay under the truck.'

He walked off, whistling. Irith crawled out and lay on the floor. Thornton heaved Gretel beside her. The man came back. 'You can come out now. Walk straight down the back in the darkness and get into airfreight container ALJ6772XBB. Go up the front. A space has been made for you there. It's reinforced, in case the freight moves. There's food and drink but I wouldn't advise you take too much. It could be a long trip and there's no toilet.'

'Is there one we can use now?' said Thornton.

'Just behind the containers. Be quick!'

'How long have we got?'

'Ten minutes. Or maybe ten hours. You know what airports are like.'

'Any chance of getting a broad-spectrum antibiotic? Gretel's pretty crook. And painkillers.'

'See what I can do.'

Thornton took Gretel to the toilet, then Irith went, and joined him in the container. Near the front a steel grille had been fixed across its width, with a door on one side. Crates were stacked behind the grille. Thornton was sitting with his back to the front wall, his arm around his sister.

'It'd be a laugh if he was working for Security,' he said. 'After all the trouble we've gone to.'

'Hilarious,' said Irith.

She was slumped in a daze when the man returned. He was inside the container before they realised he was there. He put down a small box, squatted in front of Gretel and shook his head. He stood up slowly.

'How are you, Irith?'

She started, rubbed her eyes and looked up. 'Bragg!' she whispered, pleased to see a familiar face.

'Is this what you call keeping out of trouble?' He gripped her hands, sending a shiver of memory up her back. 'It'll be a long trip, I'm afraid. Or rather, a series of short trips with long waits in between. We're sealing the container up in a minute. Try not to move or talk loudly, just in case.'

He left. More crates were loaded until the container was full. The rear door was closed and locked. Thornton turned on his torch, which now gave only the weakest of glimmers, and opened the box. Inside was a variety of medical supplies, including four packets labelled 'Tamoximycin – Emergency Use Only'.

'Why is it for emergency use only?' Irith said blearily.

'It's for germs resistant to all other antibiotics.' Thornton opened one of the packets, read the instructions and gave Gretel two of the small jelly capsules with a few sips of water.

She opened her eyes. 'Where are we?'

'In a shipping container at the airport. Go back to sleep now.'

She shuddered.

'Are you still in pain?'

'Of course I'm in pain, you moron.'

He went through the box. 'There's Maxidol here, and morphine.'

'It's not *that* bad. Give me a couple of Maxidols and turn the bloody light out.'

Gretel swallowed the painkillers, pillowed her head on the bulletproof vest and closed her eyes. Irith did the same. Thornton remained where he was.

The container lurched, swayed and settled with a thud. She jerked awake. 'What's happening?'

He was snoring in the other corner. 'Gretel?' She didn't answer. Irith checked her watch: 5.05, but was it morning or night? She still felt tired.

The container was swaying, vibrating too, and she heard the faint sound of an engine. She presumed they were on a forklift. Shortly, the container was settled down again. The next time she looked at her watch it said 9.12. Thornton had stopped snoring, although she could still hear his heavy breathing. She reached over to Gretel. Her hand was cold.

Irith scrambled up, feeling for her throat and a pulse. Gretel knocked her hand away. 'What the bloody hell are you doing?'

'You were so cold. I thought you were . . .'

'Dead? I wish I was.'

'Do you want another Maxidol?'

'I got it myself while you were snoring.'

'I don't snore,' Irith muttered.

'It sounded like you were bringing up your intestines.' Gretel chuckled nastily.

Irith's mouth tasted like a sumo wrestler's jockstrap. She pulled her coat around her. 'It's freezing. Where are we?'

'Out in the yard, I'd say.'

'Still in London?' Her voice rose. 'You mean we haven't left the airport yet?'

'Afraid not.'

Every minute they remained here increased the risk of inspection and inevitable discovery. 'What do you think is happening?'

'I've no bloody idea. The airport might be closed due to the weather, or for security reasons. They might be searching all the containers with sniffer dogs.'

'Wouldn't need dogs to smell us,' Thornton muttered.

'Speak for yourself!' Gretel said curtly. 'I don't have BO.'

'You do now.'

He sounded offensively cheerful. 'I don't see what there is to joke about,' said Irith. 'I'm really scared.'

'Nothing we can do any more. What will be, will be.'

'That's extraordinarily uncomforting.'

'Best I can do.' Minutes later he began to snore.

'Are you feeling better now?' Irith said to Gretel.

'It's not as bad as before. The antibiotics must be working. Want some breakfast?'

'Thanks. What have we got?'

Gretel flicked the torch. 'Bread. Apples. Tins of sardines. Cheese. At least, I think it's cheese, though it's a funny colour. Water.'

Irith ate some bread, cheese and an apple, and drank a mug of water. The torch was turned off and it became utterly black. She lay back on the coat, staring up at the invisible roof.

'How did you get into this, Gretel?'

'Even as a kid I never believed the propaganda.'

'What propaganda?' said Irith.

'That we needed the Global Congress to protect us from unstoppable climate change. The Congress had far too much power and it was driven by ideology. I was growing up when the debate about secession was going on, and I guess it radicalised me. We'd given up our rights for the common good, and got precious little good out of it.'

'I felt we were working together for the benefit of humanity,' said Irith.

'Sounds like your mother talking.'

'She's a good person,' Irith said stoutly. 'Mum's thought a lot about the issues.'

'Her generation felt so guilty about their lifestyle that they overreacted and gave up our freedoms. Did you know that the first works of the Congress were labour camps? It was unaccountable and soon became corrupt, and the President answers to no one. The only solution is to tear it down and go back to real democracy.'

'So you're just a revolutionary!' Irith said bitterly.

'I believe in personal freedom, human dignity and the worth of the individual – and the right of every person to work hard and improve their lot. I –'

'Well, so do I.'

'But have you had it?' said Gretel. 'The old system may have been decadent and corrupt, but your mother could never have had her property confiscated without proper compensation. You couldn't have had your honours project failed without recourse. You couldn't . . .'

Irith scuffled her feet on the metal floor and Gretel broke off.

'I . . . This is hard for me, Gretel. I hear what you're saying, but it goes against my entire upbringing.'

'I'm not going to replace their propaganda with my own. Work it out for yourself.'

Irith lay in the darkness, trying to think things through. She believed in the rights of the individual, but she also believed in the duty of the state to protect the world from climate change, and everything she'd done over the past few days was an attack on legitimate authority. In her own eyes, she *was* a criminal.

The container was jerked into the air, carried some distance and set down again. It bumped and vibrated every so often, as if moving on a conveyor, thumped into something and finally settled. The silence resumed, though once or twice she felt other bumps, as if it had been placed in a stack and others stacked around it.

Sometime later there was a gentle vibration, then the roar of jet engines. The floor tilted and levelled again. Bitter cold penetrated the container. Gretel wrapped herself in her coat and began to snore gently. Irith pulled the vest about her but it made no difference.

She flicked the torch on and Thornton was sitting up, blinking at her. 'I'm bloody freezing,' she said. He held out his arms. She hesitated for a second, then crawled across. He opened his coat. She pressed herself against the warm length of him and he pulled the coat over her back.

'You're lovely and warm,' she murmured.

'You're not.'

'Sorry.'

She turned on her side but he held her. 'I wasn't complaining, Irith.'

'Oh.'

His warm hand slid across her back, reached in under the coat and under her shirt, to rest in the small of her back.

'That's like having my own personal radiator,' she said with a sigh.

Time drifted languorously. It could have been hours before either of them moved. Irith felt vaguely aroused, probably because there was no possibility of doing anything about it. He moved his hand across her back, down and up and onto the back of her neck. 'Are you giving me the cold shoulder?' He chuckled at his paltry wit.

She pulled the coat around her neck. 'Actually, it's not my shoulders that are cold. It's my bottom.'

His hand curled around her left shoulder and lay there.

'My bum is freezing,' she said, disappointed that he hadn't taken the hint.

'Really?' he said in her ear. 'Would you like me to warm it up?'

'That would be nice.'

The hand slid down inside her knickers, clutching one cheek and then the other. 'It really is freezing!' he exclaimed.

'Did you think I was joking?'

'No, I thought ... Oh, never mind.'

The feeling of his hand was lovely. She wished he had both down there. It gave her a warm, achy feeling.

'Thornton?'

'Yes?' he said thickly.

'Is that a gun in your pocket?'

His hand caressed back and forth. 'Not the kind you're thinking of.'

She moved and her thigh pressed against his groin. He drew a deep breath and slid his hand out and up to caress the sides of her breast. Then he took his hand away.

'More,' she said, emboldened by the dark and her recent near-death experiences. What did she have to lose? She wriggled around so as to give him better access.

'Still cold?' he murmured, his lips so close that his warm breath tickled her ear.

'Getting warmer.'

His fingers crept back, tapping out a little dance around her nipple that made her want to shriek with frustration. They went away, came back, went away again.

Irith couldn't stand it. The next time his fingers approached she grabbed them and thrust them hard against her nipple. She arched her back and kicked her legs, and the feeling was so intense that she almost cried out.

'You all right?' He was rubbing her nipple between finger and thumb, back and forth, back and forth.

Irith couldn't speak. It was nothing like the lonely, mechanical self-pleasuring she had indulged herself with whenever she couldn't stand the frustration any longer.

He took his hand away. 'Don't stop!' she cried.

'Shh! You'll wake Gretel.'

'Bugger Gretel! Just get on with it.'

His mouth closed around the nipple and sucked gently while his tongue flicked back and forth across the very tip. Irith thrashed her hips and squeezed her thighs together, and was on the very brink when he pulled away.

'What's that?' he said. The note of the engines had changed and the floor tilted down. 'We must be landing.'

CHAPTER EIGHTEEN

He sat up and it was over. Irith felt a cold waft on her breast and hurriedly covered it. There was an achy congestion in her groin and she felt disappointed and irritable. 'I wonder where we are?'

'It's only an hour and a quarter since we took off, so we haven't gone very far.'

'Scotland?' said Gretel from somewhere to her left.

Though they were in complete darkness, Irith pulled out of Thornton's grasp and moved away. Her cheeks grew hot. How long had Gretel been awake? What must she be thinking?

The container was unloaded, loaded onto another plane and flown somewhere else, though again it was only a short trip. Thornton had gone to sleep. Irith hunched up in the corner, cold and cranky, and brooding about the dead she was, in one way or another, responsible for: the men in the garden in Sydney, the dead guards in the water, the divers ... She'd managed to repress them before, but they clamoured for her attention now.

After landing, they sat motionless for hours. 'How long will the air last in one of these things?' she said suddenly. It seemed thicker than before, which reminded her of the last moments of that fateful dive.

'A good while, I should say,' said Thornton sleepily.

'How long?'

He turned on the torch and shone it around the container. 'This thing is about six metres by two by two, so that's twenty-four cubic metres of air. If we don't move, we'd each breathe about fifteen cubic metres in a day, so –'

'So it'll only last half a day!' Irith cried. 'We've been in here that long now.'

'Air contains twenty-one per cent oxygen and you only use a fifth of that in each breath. Most is breathed out again. We can actually breathe all the air in here two or three times before we reduce it to the level where we lose consciousness. We don't have to worry for a while yet.'

'But the container's half full of boxes, so the air will only last half as long.'

'I was hoping you wouldn't mention that. And the bad part is –'

'Yes?' she cried.

'I'm bursting for a pee.'

·· • ● • ··

After several more flights, which Irith mostly slept through, the container was put on a truck and driven somewhere. By this time the air was really thick; Irith had a splitting headache and was wondering if they would get out alive. The truck stopped, the container was unloaded and the door cracked open, letting in air as cold as the inside of a freezer.

'At last!' said Gretel, who had perked up as the antibiotics took effect.

'Where the bloody hell are we? Siberia?' said Thornton to the figure at the door. After so long in darkness, the light was blinding.

'In a refrigerated warehouse outside Minneapolis, Minnesota,' said Bragg. 'Come out, and be quick.'

Minnesota? One of the central states, flat and cold and full of lakes. That was all she knew about it.

'What the fuck are we doing in America?' said Thornton.

Irith might have echoed that. Never having been religious, she had no understanding of how a country could be so dominated by faith.

'Put these on,' said Bragg, handing Thornton an armload of dark blue robes.

He picked out the smallest and tossed it to Irith. She pulled it over her head. The garment was too long and she had to hold the hem up off the floor. Bragg flipped the shapeless hood up. She could have been anyone – well, anyone small.

Bragg put on his own robe. 'Listen up,' he said in a low voice. 'America is really run by the Christian militia and there are checkpoints everywhere. They take religion seriously, especially hereabouts. The only way for us to travel safely is as members of a registered faith. We've got the documents to prove it.'

'What happens when we go through a checkpoint?' said Irith. 'I don't know anything about –'

'We're members of the Church of the Doomsday Mutes,' said Bragg. 'We don't say anything.'

Thornton roared with laughter. 'You've got to be joking!'

'It's a registered religious order, been around for at least a decade. It's small but wealthy and it gives freely to the militia.'

'I don't –' said Irith.

'Pipe down and let me finish. Every member of our church has taken a vow of silence until the Day of Judgment.'

'That's just silly,' said Gretel.

'Maybe, but such vows are respected in this country, and no one will force you to talk. I've got your papers here.' He handed each of them a smart card. 'If anyone questions you, hand them the card, press your right thumb to the reader or your right eye to the scanner, and say nothing.'

'It can't be that simple,' said Gretel. 'We're illegal aliens, for God's sake.'

'It is that simple, with the right papers. Silence won't blow your cover, no matter who questions you, but saying a single word in public will destroy us all. There are cameras everywhere.'

'What about in the car?'

'As long as you speak without moving your lips. Come on.'

They stepped out, moving stiffly. 'Where are we going this time?' asked Irith.

'Somewhere a bit warmer, I hope.' Bragg blew in his cupped hands to warm them.

'Any chance of a shower first?' said Gretel. 'I can't remember when –'

'Into the van and be quick about it!' said Bragg. 'You can't imagine what it's taken to get you here.'

'You could be a bit more civil,' Irith said. They had parted friends six weeks ago, but this man was a stranger.

'I haven't slept for two and a half days and I won't be getting any today. They were onto us after we landed in Lyon. We had the very devil of a job to get you out and cover your tracks. Levi had to disrupt the entire air traffic of northern Europe to do it. They're still trying to sort out the chaos.'

'Levi?' said Irith. 'Do you mean Levi Seth?'

'Yes. He's a genius with computers and networks. Without him you'd all be dead, *or wishing you were*. How do you know him?'

'He was a friend of my mother's.'

'Ah,' said Bragg. 'That explains a few things.'

'I thought he was dead.'

'Death is an excellent way to cover your tracks. Unfortunately he's blown his cover now. Into the van.'

They piled in through the rear door. The van had no side windows and the rear glass was curtained. Irith fastened her seatbelt. Bragg got in the left-hand side and started the engine. A small bald man was sitting in the passenger's seat with a computer on his lap. He turned and said hello, rather distractedly. It was Levi. A woman sat in the middle. She was blonde, suntanned and pretty in a Californian sort of way. They both wore robes.

'Hi,' she said. 'I'm Siah.'

'Hello.' Irith held out her hand.

Siah shook it. She had a grip like a pipe wrench.

They followed the back roads. The countryside was flat, farmland for the most part. Irith soon lost interest in the monotonous scenery. What was Levi doing so far from home? Where were they being taken?

A few kilometres down the road they came to a mobile checkpoint manned by half a dozen men dressed in black uniforms. Levi turned around in his seat, gesturing for everyone to get out. He drew a finger across his throat. Irith cleared hers nervously and he scowled. Weren't they allowed to make any sound at all?

She followed the others out of the van, thinking, *I'm an impostor and an illegal alien, to add to my other crimes. What happens when they find out?*

They formed a line, identity cards at the ready. Irith fumbled under her robes for hers, terrified that any little thing could give her away. The line inched forward. Thornton blocked her view and her heart was thumping wildly. As the others passed the checkpoint, they stood to one side rather than going back to the van. That bothered her too.

Thornton passed through. The black-shirted officer motioned Irith forward.

'Name?' he said, staring at her face.

She held out her ID. He looked annoyed. What was the matter? She should have passed it through the scanner. She did so. He looked at his screen.

'Thumbprint!' he said coldly.

Irith froze, unable to remember whether the left thumb was required or the right. The wrong one would be highly suspicious. She looked up, stricken.

'Thumbprint!' the officer said furiously. Perhaps he wasn't a true believer.

Irith glanced at the others. Bragg was rubbing his lips with his right thumb. Heart now leaping in her chest, she pressed her right thumb to the scanner.

After an agonising wait, the officer handed Irith her ID. 'Have a nice day,' he said mechanically, gesturing her away and calling the occupants of the next vehicle forward.

They got back in the van. Irith's knees were trembling. No one said anything as they drove off.

Once they'd rounded the corner, Irith said quietly, 'If there's anything else I need to know, you'd better tell me now.'

'And you'd better pay attention when we do,' said Bragg. 'That could have done for the lot of us.'

They went through other checkpoints at random intervals, and there was no further trouble, but Irith never got over her fear of them.

CHAPTER NINETEEN

After a few hours, Siah took the wheel and turned west. Thornton spoke in a low voice to Levi. Irith dozed. That afternoon they changed vehicles and directions, heading north until after dark, when they drew up at an isolated house that appeared to have been empty for some time, judging by the state of the garden. Though it was the end of April, it was cold here too. Frost was already settling on the grass.

'Don't speak until we're inside,' Bragg warned before they got out of the vehicle.

The power was off. They sat in the kitchen around a portable gas burner and ate dinner out of cans. No one spoke more than a few words and as soon as the meal was over, Bragg disappeared into one of the bedrooms. Levi boiled a pot of water and brewed real coffee. It tasted glorious.

Siah, who was moderately tall and willow-slender, also retired early. Gretel drifted off after Irith changed her dressings. Thornton followed, leaving just Irith and Levi at the table.

'Bragg said you saved our lives.'

'It's been quite a week.' His tired brown eyes met hers. 'There were days when I despaired of ever finding a way to get you all out.'

'Days? What do you mean?'

'Gretel got out a message that the rest of the team was dead but she and Thorn had escaped into the underground with an intruder. I've been working on it ever since.'

'What did you do?'

'Countless things. Jamming their communications while they hunted you. Causing random breakdowns and failures, including the lock-gates. Sending false alarms all over the city to distract undercover operatives. I also leaked false messages, between members of Congress Security, to the British government, purporting to reveal that they were behind the dock collapses and the explosion. Dozens of Security operatives were arrested.'

'How did you manage that?'

'Ah, well. You know.' He grinned boyishly. 'The diplomatic situation between the British government and the Global Congress is, as they say, fraught. I also changed the codes in the airport security system so Bragg could get out to pick you up, and get in again without being searched. And I inserted false X-ray scans of the container at several places.'

'I had no idea. I thought . . .'

'That you escaped on your own? You three did incredible things, Irith, but it could never have been enough. An army of covert operatives was hunting you and my job was to frustrate them and send them in the wrong directions. I still can't believe we managed it.'

'An army? '

'More than three hundred people were involved in the hunt, at the end.'

'The data Gretel got from their computers must be pretty important.'

'I hope so.'

'Have you any idea what it is?'

'I know what we were looking for . . .'

'And you can't tell me what that is,' she finished.

'It might be better if you got some sleep. We've a long day ahead of us tomorrow.'

Something else had been preying on her mind all day. 'Levi?'

'Yes?'

'I can't help thinking about all the coincidences I've experienced lately.'

'What do you mean?'

'Meeting you. Then Jolyen buying me and sending me to London with Bragg. Then meeting the twins. Now being rescued by you and Bragg. Did you orchestrate all that too?'

'No. After we met the first time, I had to disappear fast, and I didn't think you were in danger then. I had nothing to do with getting you out of Australia, although Jolyen did liaise with me. We go back a long way.

'I thought you'd be safe at the Bruntling Institute. It didn't occur to me that you'd start spying on my two operatives there, though after you disappeared I worked out that you were the intruder the twins had found underground. I did my best for you after that.'

'Thank you,' she said softly. 'How come they didn't know about me? They acted as though they hated my guts.'

'They didn't need to know about you, or Bragg. Safer that way. '

'Who's behind you, Levi? Behind all this?'

'I can't answer questions like that.'

'What are we doing in America? It's the last place I'd –'

'It was the only place I could get you to that was safe from Congress Security. Well, probably safe.'

'But America's a member of the Congress.'

'Yet staunchly isolationist, prickly about its sovereignty and powerful enough to defy Lindstrom when it so chooses.'

'Why would it?'

'His policies are loathed in America, which is one reason why the country has gone the other way. '

'Then why doesn't America withdraw?'

'Then it would have no control at all. As long as we can maintain our cover, we should be okay..'

'How long will we be here?'

Levi shrugged.

'What's going to happen to me?' said Irith.

'You got yourself into our affairs and I can't see how to get you out. You're stuck with us for the time being.'

'What about Jemma?'

'She's in good health. That's all I know.'

'It's enough.'

Irith's skin was still salty from the diving, and very itchy. She was desperate for a shower but the water was freezing and there was neither soap nor towels. She washed her face and hands and slept in the kitchen, wrapped in her coat. It was the only warm place in the house. She dreamed about bloody violence and dead men coming at her with spearguns.

The following day they drove north through St Cloud, Brainerd and Duluth, then north-east up US61 along the western edge of Lake Superior. Up here the checkpoints were less frequent, but just as alarming. Halfway to the Canadian border they turned north-west into the hills, driving for kilometres along winding forest roads, and then through a windswept, empty land. The farms looked to have been abandoned.

Late in the afternoon they turned up a rutted track, climbed a series of round hills and went down into a wooded valley scattered with little lakes. They passed through an electronically keyed gate in a high fence, drove up a long driveway and drew up outside a large timber house by a pretty crescent-shaped lake. Irith could smell the pines.

'You can talk here,' said Siah. 'With any luck we'll be staying for a while. If Levi finds what he's looking for, it may soon be over.'

'What do you mean, *over*?' said Irith.

'Hopefully the Global Congress, and President Lindstrom, will be so discredited that the Congress will collapse.'

The idea was laughable. But if it could happen, what would take its place? 'And with no luck at all?'

'We'll be on the run again tomorrow,' interjected Bragg.

'We've covered our tracks well,' said Levi. 'But we could still be discovered through sheer bad luck. Everyone must stay inside the fence and Siah will do all the shopping, at a different place each time.'

'Any precautions we need to take?' said Gretel.

'Keep to the area inside the ring of hills.' Levi swept his arm around the horizon. 'And always wear robes when you're outside. '

They went up broad timber steps onto a deck set with a wooden table and chairs weathered to silver, and into a wide hall floored with flagstones of blue schist. The walls were pine, stained the colour of dark honey. Beyond was a large rectangular living area with a steepled ceiling, also timbered. Leather chairs and sofas, all well-worn, were set around a hexagonal, glass-walled wood heater whose flue went up through the roof. The walls bore a number of framed prints of mountain and valley scenes; they looked like enlarged photographs from ancient *National Geographic* magazines.

'Can I have a room with a view?' Irith said. 'I've never –'

Siah laughed. 'They all have views, Irith. The end room is best.' She pointed. 'Go and claim it; it has its own bathroom.'

Irith scooted across the room like a schoolgirl, through the door and down another wide hall. Rooms opened off to either side. She opened the door of the end room and let out a little sigh.

It was nearly the size of her mother's old flat, with a bed big enough to sleep in crossways. The side window looked over forest to the hills beyond, while the main window framed the view of the lake. The bathroom, tiled in green schist from floor to ceiling, was beautiful.

She found towels and a bathrobe, locked her door and turned on the water. Within a minute steaming hot water came out, so strongly that the needles stung her outstretched hand. Having not had a shower in a week, and that a lukewarm, dribbling, rationed English affair, nothing could have been more blissful.

Irith scrubbed until all the grime was gone and her skin glowed pink. Then, mindful that hot water would be limited, she got out and towelled herself vigorously as she looked out the little window. Here, for now, she could put the horrors of the past days and weeks out of mind. She could almost forget that she was an illegal alien in an intolerant society where, on her own, she would be discovered within minutes.

She wrapped herself in the robe, lay on the bed, gazing out at the lake, and fell asleep.

Someone knocked at the door. 'Come in,' Irith said drowsily.

It was the ever-smiling Levi. 'Dinner's ready.'

'Already?'

'It's seven o'clock. You've been asleep for hours. You must have been exhausted.'

'Yes, but I haven't any clean clothes. I don't even have a comb.'

'There's probably one in the bathroom. Come as you are. I dare say we can find you something to wear later on.'

Everyone was at the table when Irith arrived, her scalp stinging from a hundred strokes with a stiff-bristled brush she'd found in the bathroom cupboard. Gretel and Thornton were also wearing robes. His exposed most of a broad, muscular and very hairy chest. Irith stared at it in fascination. Rising sea level had submerged the beaches when she was a child, and she wasn't keen on swimming pools, so men's chests were a novelty to her.

Thornton was looking at her just as appreciatively. Her robe had fallen open, exposing part of one blue-veined breast. Pulling the robe together, she looked away, discomfited. It was all right for her to stare, but not for him.

Levi and Siah came out of the kitchen with platters, one covered in grilled steaks as big as pumpkin leaves, the other in baked potatoes, carrots and onions. Placing them in the middle of the table, they went back for more: a bowl of minted green peas with a chunk of butter melting on top, a jug of gravy and a fresh loaf with another enormous slab of butter. Irith had never, in all her life, seen anything like it.

'Are we expecting visitors?' she said.

'You could call this a political statement,' Gretel said out of the corner of her mouth.

'Tuck in,' said Levi. 'The dog gets the leftovers and I don't want to spoil him.'

Having been brought up to waste nothing and take no more than she needed, Irith scraped butter over a slice of bread, took a small helping of vegetables and waited for the plate of steaks. When it came she cut off a piece the size of a matchbox and put it on her plate.

'Is that all you're having?' said Thornton.

'It's all the protein I need,' she said primly.

'No wonder you're so little. You don't eat any more than a sparrow.'

Irith was hurt by the personal remark, after all they'd been through together. 'I have small genes. Anyway, it's immoral to consume more than you need.'

'Spare me!' He turned to Siah, who was tucking into a steak that hung off either side of her plate.

Irith carved small pieces from her baked potato. It was delicious. The other vegetables were just as good, the buttery peas sheer bliss. She shaved an edge off the steak and slipped it into her mouth. She'd not eaten steak more than a dozen times in her life, and then it had been old, tough and usually overcooked. This was so tender that it practically dissolved on the tongue, yet richly flavourful. She took another piece.

'Good?' said Levi, who was on her right.

'Wonderful. Did Siah cook it?'

'No, I did.'

They ate in silence. When her plate was empty, Irith wanted more, despite the persistent voice in her head warning about greed and over-consumption. 'Oh, to hell with it!'

'I beg your pardon?' said Levi.

'Sorry. Thinking aloud.'

Levi smiled. 'Good for you.' He tapped his glass with a spoon. 'We'll be here for some time while Gretel and I decrypt the files . . . assuming we can.'

'And then what?' said Siah.

'Depends what we find,' said Gretel.

'We know from other intelligence,' said Levi, 'that it's almost time for a major Congress plan to come into effect. One we've been working for years to stop. We believe the evidence of it is in the files Gretel got from their computer.'

'What kind of project?' said Irith.

'One targeted at humanity itself,' he said direly.

Though it was the first of May, the house was high in the hills and at these northern latitudes the night was chilly. Bragg lit a fire. Someone opened a bottle of red wine, and after that, another. Irith hadn't touched alcohol in years. She tried a glass, found she liked it and drank it sip by sip. A couple of hours later she accepted a second glass, and then a third. They sat around the fire well into the evening, talking about everyday things as though they were ordinary people. It was a wonderful night. She wanted it to go on forever.

Around midnight, people drifted off to bed until only Thornton was left, sitting across from her on the other sofa. Her eyes kept drifting to his chest. She was fascinated, and a little repelled, by all that black hair. His body was so different from hers.

Her robe had fallen open again, revealing more than before, but after all the wine she no longer cared. The way he stared at her was thrilling and it reminded her of the time in the container. His hand on her bottom. His mouth on her breast. She wanted more but did not know how to go about getting it.

She stretched her toes out to the fire and the robe slid up her thighs. Thornton leaned forward, staring at her thighs as if willing the robe to dissolve. He looked like a man who knew what he wanted and how to get it. A little afraid, she pulled the robe down.

In a swift movement he was beside her. He grinned and it wasn't the shared smile of days ago, when they had been fighting for their lives. This smile had a hint of the predator. He was used to getting his way with women.

Had she been experienced and sober it would have put her off instantly, but Irith was aroused, curious, and it was time.

Thornton's eyes flicked to her breast, then away. He was no crude starer. He extended his hand, palm up. She looked at his chest, his mouth, his eyes, then let her hand fall into his.

He drew circles on the tips of her fingers and goose pimples rose up her arms. He raised her hand to his face, looking all the way up her slender arm to her armpit. For some reason, it made her shudder with desire. She crossed her legs and uncrossed them.

He touched her fingertip with the tip of his tongue, just for a second. Irith could tell that it was a much practised routine and, had it not been for the drink, she wouldn't have gone along with it. But she wanted it badly.

'Shall we go to your room?' he said softly.

They went up the hall, hand in hand. All her senses were exquisitely alive. Her feet on the cold tiles felt sensuous. As she went by, the door two down from Irith's opened a crack and Gretel's pale face, framed by that dark hair, appeared in the gap. She scowled and banged her door. Irith felt a chill on the back of her neck.

Thornton eased her through her door and closed it. Irith stood by, wondering how to get from here to the bed, and then to the act itself?

Thornton turned off the light, leaving the room lit only by the glow of a deck light coming through the bathroom window. 'Has anyone carried you to bed before?' he said with a teasing smile.

'Not since I was little.'

He was so big. Her head didn't reach his shoulders. So muscular. He swept her effortlessly into his arms.

Thornton looked down. 'Your robe has come undone, Irith Hardey.'

'Oh!' she said, and left it to him.

He bent his head and kissed her on the lips, and she luxuriated in the explosion of feeling that ran all the way down her belly. Her robe came all the way open and he carried her to the bed.

'Are you safe?' he said hoarsely.

'I have a ten-year implant.' Every woman did. Another Congress policy.

He threw his robe over a chair piled with folded clothes, standing proud and spread-legged so she could admire what she was getting. She felt a momentary irritation, but it passed as he went to work on her breasts, her belly and then, an unexpectedly erotic shock, her armpit. It made her toes curl up. Irith closed her eyes while he explored her in ways expected and unexpected.

He was very experienced, another faint irritation. A little experience would have pleased her – one of them had to have it. But Thornton played her as if he were playing the harp, and it began to feel like a performance. She couldn't connect with him emotionally, either. It was a letdown after all their experiences underground. And she also felt that he had pleasured many women yet bonded to none.

But those niggles were forgotten once he began the last movement of his symphony. She'd heard that most women didn't enjoy their first time but, before Thornton finished, Irith let out a shriek that rattled the windows in their wooden frames.

She lay back, panting. He was holding his weight above her with his arms, which was more than gentlemanly. She pulled him down and put her arms around him. She wanted to feel the weight of him on her. It felt good for a minute, but after that he was too heavy. His weight was crushing her ribs, giving her that awful feeling she'd had on the dive and in the freight container – that she was suffocating.

She heaved. He didn't move. Irith tapped him on the shoulder. He gave a gentle snore and that irritated her too. She was feeling all warm and satisfied and loving and she'd wanted to share the moment with him.

Struggling out from under him, she went to the bathroom, showered and crawled in between the sheets. She went to sleep at once. In the night she woke and his hand was busy between her legs. It felt good, though not as good as before. She was too tired to participate, though she didn't mind him doing it. It took longer this time and when he was finished she had only just become aroused. She tried to communicate that to Thornton but he was asleep again and she couldn't wake him.

Irith lay awake for hours, feeling more and more frustrated, and when not long before dawn his hand slipped across her breast she'd had enough.

'No!' she snapped. 'Go away and leave me alone.'

He froze, then slid out of bed, pulled on the robe and was out of the room in an instant. The door closed quietly, but Irith knew it was over and he would never come back. Did she want him to? Yes, she did. He had woken her and she wanted more of it. Why was life so hard?

CHAPTER TWENTY

That morning was not the best of Irith's life. It hurt just to walk to the bathroom. Thornton rose from the breakfast table as soon as she appeared, scraped his heaped plate into the waste and went outside.

Gretel stood up, glaring at Irith, and suddenly all their shared experiences meant nothing. 'You fucking bitch! 'She followed her brother out onto the deck.

Levi, who was at the sink, frowned but said not a word. Siah attacked her plate as if nothing had happened. Bragg looked up from his PortaBook reader, flashed Irith a curious glance then bent his head again.

Irith replayed the events of the night. Had she been wrong about Thornton? He had been everything she could have wanted in a lover, apart from the too-polished performance. And except, she now realised, for the complete lack of intimacy afterwards. Not a cuddle, not a caress nor even a fond word. The act had been the end of it.

Had she been unbearably rude? Hardly. His ego must indeed be fragile.

Levi slid a mug of coffee in front of her. Irith looked up. The others were gone.

'Care to tell me what that was all about?'

'Not really.'

'I've got to make this team work, Irith, and this isn't a happy beginning.'

'What if I don't want to be on your team?'

'That would cause certain difficulties,' he said with a grimace.

'You mean you'd have to kill me so I couldn't be made to talk?'

Irith said it matter-of-factly. Her life had been so emotionally over-exposed for so long that everything had gone flat.

He reared back, deeply hurt. 'Do you truly think so little of me?'

'I don't know what to think. I . . . Thornton and Gretel threatened me repeatedly when we met underground. Thornton said I knew too much and

I thought . . . I just thought . . .'

'Bloody Thornton!' he said savagely. 'If he wasn't the best there is, I wouldn't have touched him, nor his precious sister. He's a machine, Irith, an emotional retard, and she's no better. Together they're brilliant, but they aren't running the show. I am.' His soulful brown eyes were on her. 'If you want out, say so and I'll do my very best to place you somewhere safe until all this is over . . . one way or the other.'

She wanted out. Irith wanted to go back to her old life in Jemma's little flat, so why, why was she saying, 'I want to be on your team. Just tell me what you want me to do.'

There was something about him that inspired loyalty and trust. He gave off such an aura of calmness and confidence that she didn't want to let him down. And if *he* couldn't help her get Jemma back, no one could.

'What about you and Thorn?' said Levi.

Levi was also a gentle and sensitive man. She told him everything, including her lack of experience, her feelings and Thornton's performance.

He listened in silence until she had finished. Resting his cheek on his arms, he looked at her sideways. He resembled a bald pixie.

'You remind me of your mother,' he said at last.

'What do you mean?'

'Oh, something about the way you talk, and think.' He sighed. 'Thornton is a clever man and an essential member of the team. It would take pages to list all his good qualities. Unfortunately, forming meaningful relationships is not one of them. Neither is what he would see as rejection.'

'I was tired and irritable. That's all it was.'

'I can see that, but he's a control freak. He expects people to do what they're told.'

'Should I apologise and try to make up?'

He shook his head. 'As far as he's concerned, the rejection is irrevocable.'

'If that's the pathetic kind of man he is,' she snapped, 'I don't want him.' Her words were just bravado. She looked at Levi mournfully. 'What am I supposed to do?'

'I'm hardly qualified to give advice in matters of the heart. Pretend it never happened and he'll get over it. Thornton isn't one to hold grudges – unlike his sister.'

'Gretel holds grudges?' she said hoarsely.

'She resents his lovers and, once the inevitable breakup occurs, nurtures ill-feelings against them. How dare you reject her wonderful, *perfect* brother? She'll be thinking that you cold-bloodedly set out to hurt him.'

Irith looked around for a spoon, didn't see one and stirred the coffee with her finger. She licked it, took a sip and looked at him over the rim of the mug. 'Can I take my toys and go home?'

He smiled to show he understood. 'I imagine it'll blow over, in time.'

'How much time do we have, Levi?'

The smile disappeared. He looked old and troubled. 'I don't know, but not long. I'm really worried.'

'Why?'

'The Terminator Project, whatever that is, has to be stopped and only we can do it. And hopefully, free Jemma too.'

'Then I definitely want to be part of the team.'

'And I'm very pleased to have you.' He looked at his watch. 'Better get to work.'

'Is there anything I can do?'

'We'll all take a hand at cooking, cleaning and keeping the place in good order.'

'I meant, with the real work.'

'Not at the moment. Your specialty is genome engineering, isn't it?'

'It was, before they failed me!'

'I may have something for you in that line, once the files are deciphered.'

'I'll look forward to it.'

'Thorn is going to set up a training course to keep us in shape. I think he has me in mind.' Levi chuckled. 'In the meantime, relax, go for walks and do whatever you want to do. There's a good library here. Not real books, of course – everything is digital. But even so . . . ' Levi had a faraway look in his eye. 'Despite everything you've heard, they *were* the good old days. I loved the feel of a real, printed book in my hand.'

Irith had grown up with ebooks but she knew what he meant. She looked out the window. The sun was shining. 'I think I'll go for a walk.'

She put on her Doomsday Mutes robes, pulled the hood over her head and took a winding path that led to the lake. It was a hundred metres across and three times that in length, and curved like a banana. A boatshed sat at the middle of the curve, built of rough-sawn timber. A jetty, supported on three pairs of piles, ran a few metres into the water. A dinghy was tied to one of the end piles.

She sat on the end of the jetty and reached down to the water. It wasn't as cold as she'd expected.

'Don't be fooled,' said Siah's voice behind her. 'It's only warm down the length of an arm. Below that it's just a few degrees above freezing. Fancy a swim?'

'I've had enough cold for one lifetime,' said Irith, resting her back against the pile.

Siah sat against the other, pulling her robes up to her knees. Underneath she wore tight-fitting jeans that ended just below the knee, revealing the taut, lightly tanned calves of a runner. Her toenails were painted, which was unusual these days. Her fingernails were long and well-shaped. Irith examined her own battered, broken nails and her scratched and scored fingers. 'What do you do, Siah?'

'Logistics. I organise things and make sure they run smoothly.'

'Sounds complicated.'

'Right now it's only buying groceries and paying the bills. And finding you some decent clothes.'

'It hardly matters, since I've got to wear these wretched robes.' Irith was uncomfortable with the idea of other people spending money on her. 'Besides, I can't pay.'

'You lost everything you owned helping us. The least we can do is buy you a few new outfits.'

'Thanks,' said Irith. 'How did you find this place?'

'I own it. It was my grandfather's.'

'You don't have a Minnesota accent.' Irith had learned that much on the way here.

'I grew up on the west coast. In Seattle.'

'What's it like there?'

Siah laughed. 'What's it like in Sydney?'

'Sorry. Stupid question.'

'I imagine our experiences have been much the same: the sea ever rising, evacuation of low-lying areas, the flooding of homes, farmland, railways and towns. Sky-high taxes to resettle everyone and rebuild. It's the same everywhere.'

'I heard Venice has been abandoned,' said Irith. 'I would have liked to see it.'

'There's not much to see. Only the empty buildings are left and you can see six metres less of them than you used to. But personally, I think it's good to lose some of the treasures of the past.'

The remark was so heretical that Irith gaped at her. 'Why do you say that?'

'There's too damn much of it. We're obsessed with the past when we should be thinking about the future.'

'But . . .' Irith couldn't think of a suitable rebuttal.

'Want to talk about this morning?' said Siah.

'It's too embarrassing.'

'Why?' Siah looked puzzled.

Irith wanted to run away and be by herself, but after all, bridges needed to be built.

'It was my first time,' she said abruptly. 'And my second. And later on, Thornton was feeling me up when I was asleep and I snapped at him. That's all.'

'Did he treat you badly?'

Irith smiled. 'Not at all. It just felt . . . as if I was an instrument he was playing for the joy of the performance, rather than someone he cared about.'

'What did you do for him?'

'I beg your pardon?'

'You talk as though the act was entirely for your gratification.'

'I . . . Oh! Do you think so?' That hadn't occurred to Irith.

'Well, as you say, it was your first time. And he is obsessed with performance. He has to win at everything he does.'

They spent the morning together and Irith discovered that she liked Siah. She was everything Irith was not, and refreshingly uncomplicated and friendly. What's more, she answered Irith's questions without hedging her answers.

'What would you have done last night?' she said as they climbed the hill.

Siah laughed and linked her arm through Irith's. 'I'd never have been in that position.'

'Why not?'

'I can tell his type from a mile away, and he knows mine. He wouldn't come near me.'

'Why not? You're a beautiful woman.'

'Um,' Siah said with a wry little grimace, as though the compliment was distasteful to her, 'but that's not what he's looking for.'

'What is he looking for?'

'Women he can dominate physically, and control because of their youth, their inexperience or their desire for him. I'd control him and it would drive him insane. Assuming I found him attractive, that is.'

Irith couldn't believe that she didn't. 'He's so tall, handsome, strong and clever.'

'But is he thoughtful, generous, caring and kind? Is he good-humoured, stable, trustworthy?'

Irith thought about that as they walked. 'What about Bragg, then?'

'He doesn't turn me on either, although he's a better man than Thorn. There's something cold inside Bragg; broken, perhaps. If I were choosing a man from this lot, and I don't intend to, it'd be Levi.'

'But he's an old man!'

'He's fifty-two and I'm thirty-one. Levi is secure in himself. He's kind, generous and sensitive, and he has nothing to prove, which seems the greatest virtue of all. But that's academic; I'm not that keen on men, sexually.'

Irith stopped walking. 'You like *women?*' She let go of Siah's arm.

'I do.'

'Me?' she squeaked and was embarrassed at the childish reaction that she couldn't prevent. 'Do you fancy *me?*'

Siah sighed and sat on a convenient rock. 'We'd better talk this through. Sit here, Irith.'

Irith sat, anxious now.

'I've lost count of the number of times women have asked me that question,' said Siah. Irith got the impression she was choosing her words carefully. 'I'm not a predator, Irith, nor am I promiscuous. There have been times when I've got to know another woman, and there's been a deep friendship as well as a ... mutual desire, and we've become lovers. There haven't been many, and none in the last year. I like you but I don't know you, so the question doesn't arise. Does that help?'

'Sorry, I've had a sheltered life.'

'You're lucky. I've seen more of it than I care to. Shall we go up?'

At the house, Bragg was sitting on the deck in the shade, his nose still in his reader.

'What's that you're reading?' Siah said cheerfully.

'*War and Peace*.'

'I never thought of you as a man for the classics.'

'Shows how little you know about me.'

'I guess it does.' Siah went inside.

Irith sat in one of the chairs.

'Good walk?' Bragg set the reader down.

'It's a pretty place.'

'This is the best time of year for it. Winter in these hills is about five months long, and the wind blows all the way from the North Pole.'

'Summer must be nice, though.'

'Apart from the mosquitoes, which swarm in such clouds that they blot out the sun.'

'You're exaggerating,' said Irith.

'If we're still here in a month you'll see for yourself.'

'What a cheerful fellow you are, E. Power Bragg.'

'I say it how it is. Getting on well with Siah, are you?'

'She's nice.'

'Not the word I would have chosen.'

'What word would you have chosen?' she said acidly.

'Oh, it doesn't matter. Let's all try to live together. We could be here for months.'

'Months?' she said in alarm.

'It appears there's a problem with the files.'

'Is Levi around?'

'He's working in his room.'

'Which one is that?'

'The first on the left.'

She hurried inside and knocked on Levi's door, which was half open.

'Come in,' said Levi. 'Ah, Irith. Have a chair.'

She took the wicker chair offered. It was so old that some of the cane was unravelling. 'Bragg said –'

'It's nothing to worry about. We always have teething troubles with a new code.'

'What if you can't break it?'

'I'm pretty sure we'll be able to. I've been breaking codes all my adult life. It always seems impossible, at first.'

But everything depends on deciphering those files, Irith thought. *What if it is impossible?*

CHAPTER TWENTY-ONE

'Let's see what's going on in the real world,' said Siah several days later, turning the screen on.

Irith usually avoided the late news because it was followed by the President's Page, which was still read by Jemma. She had watched it on the second night here, just to know that her mother was still alive, but she could not bear to hear what Jemma was reading, nor stomach Gretel's and Thornton's comments afterward.

The Global Congress was threatening to tighten sanctions on Britain for 'harbouring terrorists and subversives'. There was the usual trouble in the Middle East. Climate forecasters predicted that the next six months would have more extreme weather than ever, and more disasters and deaths. And there was religious turmoil, too.

In Rome this morning, Pope Joan created a furore by announcing two measures aimed at preventing the bankruptcy of the European Catholic Church. Church assets including the Vatican are to be sold to a property developer, although key parts will still be occupied by the church on a ninety-nine-year lease. Equally controversially, Michelangelo's Pieta, the last remaining treasure of the Church, is to be auctioned by Sotheby's in July, and the proceeds used to fight poverty worldwide.

'The scourging of the temple is finally complete,' said Pope Joan today. 'Out of the fire we shall be renewed. Henceforth, the Church will devote its efforts to serving the poor and the needy. We shall build no more gilded empires or ostentatious bishops' palaces.'

'Whoa!' said Bragg. 'The American Popes won't stand for that.'

'American Popes?' said Irith. 'You're joking, I assume?'

'In the Schism of 2022, the American Catholic Church broke away to form the Catholics Under God. The American cardinals elected a pope, but the Catholics Under God subsequently split into Western, Southern and Eastern churches, each choosing their own pope, and each claiming to be the one true faith. Hold on . . .' He turned the sound up.

> The American Popes, after an emergency meeting, denounced recent developments in the Vatican and announced that their churches would henceforth work together to serve the purpose of God on Earth. As a symbol of unity, they will jointly bid for the Pieta at the forthcoming Sotheby's auction. Observers say, however, that should they succeed in purchasing the masterpiece, it will be difficult to reach agreement on where to keep it.

··•●•··

A few days later, Levi said at breakfast, 'Thorn has put together a training program and we're all going to follow it, except where we're busy with other work. In my case, I regret to announce,' he chuckled, 'that will be most of the time. Thorn?'

Thornton rose. 'The program is divided into five parts and we'll begin the first today. It's basic fitness training: gym workouts, running with and without a pack, rope climbing, swimming and so forth. The aim, over the next six weeks, is to bring everyone to their personal peak of fitness, and then to maintain it for as long as we remain here – so we're ready when the time comes. Today is 5 May. By 20 June, you'll all be athletes.'

Thornton took a breath. 'Part two I call stealth. You'll be learning the basics of covert operations: moving without being seen, using surveillance equipment, lock picking, computer hacking, data extraction, destruction and recovery. You'll probably never use any of that, unless you take up a life of crime later on.' He paused but didn't smile. 'But if the worst happens and we lose a critical member of the team, everyone must be able to fill in for them.

'Part three is self-defence and unarmed combat, with emphasis on the quick and the dirty. You're aiming to disable your opponent within seconds – if there's a long fight, the amateur will always lose. I won't be wasting time on the formal schools of unarmed combat, because they take years to master. You'll be learning to attack your opponent with whatever is to hand – a pen to the eyeball, a knee to the balls, an instep-crushing blow with your heel. Your best chance is to look innocent, like little Irith, then act so violently that they're taken by surprise.'

Irith flushed but he didn't glance in her direction.

'Part four will be armed combat with a variety of weapons, target practice and special methods for special situations: such as when the enemy is wearing body armour. You'll learn to recognise all kinds of weapons, armour and equipment, their characteristics, strengths and weaknesses, and how best to combat them. '

'Do I have to do this?' Irith said to Levi. 'I'm already having nightmares about my dead.'

'We all do,' said Levi. 'Sorry.'

'Part five,' Thornton went on, 'will be a basic course in sabotage, mayhem and destruction. You'll learn the use of explosives of various kinds, large and small, from cracking doors and safes to the demolition of buildings.'

'Why do we need to learn that kind of stuff?' said Irith.

'I hope you never have to use it. If there's any time left when you've mastered it all,' he gave a mirthless laugh, 'we'll go over escape and survival.'

'What if there isn't time?' said Irith.

Giving her a cold stare, Thornton said, 'You'll have to improvise on the run. Let's get started. After today, we'll be beginning at dawn.'

Irith had considered herself to be reasonably fit but soon discovered how wrong she was. Thornton was a slavedriver who expected as much of everyone else, including her and Levi, as he did of himself, and he could run, jump, climb and swim all day. He made no allowances for fitness, ability or motivation.

At the end of the first day Irith went to bed without dinner because she was too exhausted to sit at the table, and the following morning her muscles were so sore that she could barely walk. Thornton made her run. He drove her harder than anyone else.

May passed into June, June into July. Levi and Gretel had been working solidly on the decryption for two months. It wasn't going well.

Irith had attained levels of fitness she could never have dreamed of, although in every exercise she was last and slowest – she simply did not have an athlete's body.

She also had problems with armed combat, though not for want of skill. She knew what was to be done and how to do it, but every time she took up a lethal weapon Irith saw the faces of her dead – the faces that still haunted her nightmares – and knew she could not go through that again.

Nonetheless, she was an exceptionally fine shot, better even than Thornton. But no matter how many targets she hit dead centre, she took no pleasure from it. He didn't intend to use her talent on inanimate objects.

'I'm too exhausted to sit up,' she said one night in the second week of July. After two months of training, she was still at the point of collapse every night.

'Take a few days off,' said Levi. 'All of you.'

'Excellent idea,' said Bragg. 'I've been thinking about going for a hike.'

'Where to?' said Siah.

'The top of Eagle Mountain. It's not far. Any problem with that, Levi?'

'I don't see why not,' said Levi. 'The Doomsday Mutes are keen hikers. Just be careful not to attract attention.'

Bragg, Irith and Siah drove up into the hills, left the car and set off on a muddy trail strewn with granite boulders. The going was hard and mosquitoes, the biggest Irith had ever seen, were everywhere. The sandy soil was gritty underfoot. In the afternoon, they wove up a steep hill covered in pine, oak and aspen. The smell of the pines was sweet in her nostrils.

Siah was in the lead, walking so quickly that Irith struggled to keep up. After a while Bragg fell back.

'Beautiful day,' he said.

'Can we talk here?'

'Yes.'

Irith brushed sweat out of her eyes with her blue hood. 'I'm tired already.'

'Take it easy.' He slowed his pace.

Irith matched him. 'We'll fall behind.'

'I love these mountains too much to hurry through them.'

At the top of the hill, a rocky outcrop bare of trees, they found Siah sitting on a round boulder. 'Sorry,' she said. 'Was I going too fast?'

'A little,' said Bragg. 'Irith didn't have time to see what we came here for.'

She climbed a club-shaped outcrop to stare down over the forest. A low mountain chain protruded up to the south, a rounded range of hills to the north. Even the rocks were smoothly curved by the ice sheets that had ground this country down. Lakes glittered everywhere among the trees.

'This is the only boreal forest in the continental United States,' said Siah. 'Isn't it beautiful?'

'Is there much wildlife here?' Irith asked.

'Apart from bears and wolves, you mean?'

'Bears?' Her voice went squeaky.

Bragg chuckled. 'You're in a lot less trouble in my country than I would be in yours. Even the jellyfish are deadly, Down Under. We probably won't see any bears or wolves, but there's plenty of other wildlife here.'

They camped in a wooded valley where she learned the difference between red pine and white, red oak and pin oak, and was taught to recognise aspen, fir, spruce and hazel. They dined on fish from the stream and wild raspberries, drank coffee brewed over the campfire as the sun was going down, then slathered themselves in mosquito repellent and headed up to the top of another rocky hill to look at the stars. As darkness fell, a faint green glow lingered on the northern horizon. The night was mild and it quickly grew dark. There was no moon.

'This'll do,' said Siah, perching on a rock.

They sat for ages, not talking, just staring up at the stars. Irith lay back against the rock, closed her eyes and fell asleep.

In her dreams she was distantly aware of Siah and Bragg talking quietly. He had been speaking for some time before she realised that he was telling Siah about his life in Sydney, before he'd come to Jolyen's house.

'They took everything,' he was saying. 'Left me destitute; an alien. It was impossible to get work, a place to live, or to go home – I simply didn't exist. I'd never known despair before. I'm a strong, capable man and I was starving to death in a rich country. Sometimes I wish I had.'

Irith sat up. Siah said nothing.

'I was taken by the same kind of vermin that caught Irith,' he continued. 'In olden times they would have been called slavers. They sweep up the friendless and destitute, and *recycle* them.'

Siah let out a little cry.

'It goes on in this country, too,' Bragg went on. 'Some people are sold as slave workers of one kind or another. The lowest, those good for nothing else, go to the organ strippers.'

'And in your case?' she said in a hoarse voice.

'To Gentle George's brothel as a sex slave. I spent a year there, and it was ... pretty bad.'

Siah lay a hand on his arm. 'Oh, Bragg.'

'I tried to hang myself a couple of times but they cut me down real quick. Finally, after some months, I broke out of my despair and realised that I was just one of dozens there. Most were young women, weaker and less skilled than me, but suffering equal degradation and surviving it better. They looked after me and it gave me heart. I'll never forget them. That's what drives me now – to destroy a system that so abuses people who've fallen through the cracks. To see them free, and the millions like them throughout the world.'

'How did you escape?' said Siah.

'I didn't. Jolyen bought out my contract; she saw the value in me and I'll not forget it either. It taught me to live for the moment, while it lasts. Life holds few fears for me any longer. Nor death.'

'I'm sorry,' said Siah. 'And to think I thought of you –'.

'As a cold, stand-offish jerk?' Bragg chuckled. 'Sometimes I am. It's better than getting too close to people, then losing them.'

'You're braver than I'll ever be,' said Siah. 'At heart, I know I'm a coward.'

'It's not bravery unless you're scared shitless. The bravest person I've ever met lived a thousand terrors in Gentle George's, yet she overcame them all. Anyway, that's not why we came up here.'

Bands of green light, with touches of blue and red, were wavering across the sky like banners in a slow-motion wind.

'The northern lights,' Irith said. 'They're beautiful.'

The night was enchanting. Not a light could be seen, not a vehicle heard. There was no sound but the breeze sighing through the tips of the pines. Even the mosquitoes had disappeared.

'I do feel rejuvenated,' Irith said as they stood up to go down to the camp.

Siah and Bragg exchanged glances and she knew what they were thinking. This was just the calm before the holocaust.

CHAPTER TWENTY-TWO

A few days after the hike, Irith was in the living room, talking to Siah, when Bragg said, 'Shh!' and turned the volume up.

> After a furious bidding war, Michelangelo's Pieta has just been sold by Sotheby's for a world-record $1.88 billion. The winning bidders were the consortium of American Popes, who are already at loggerheads over where the masterpiece will be housed, in Houston, Boston or Seattle.

Siah flicked to a story about a yellow fever epidemic in the Deep South.

> After a month of the epidemic, it is estimated that as many as 120 000 people may be infected. The US Institute of Medicine puts the projected death toll as high as 150 000 before seasonal factors bring the epidemic to a temporary end.

Irith rubbed the welts on her arm. 'I hope the mozzies around here aren't carriers?'

'Wrong species,' said Bragg. 'It's a horrible death, yellow fever. Fever, haemorrhages, black vomit.'

'Thanks for telling me.' The screen showed images of wasted people with staring eyes and yellowed skin.

> ... as with most viral diseases, there is still no effective treatment available. People most at risk are being vaccinated but there is not enough vaccine available to treat everyone who could come in contact with the disease. Because of its high cost ...

'That's bullshit!' Siah said furiously. 'The vaccine's less than thirty dollars a shot.'

'How do you know?' said Irith.

Siah hesitated. 'I've just bought enough to inoculate us all.'

'Are we going south?'

She shrugged. 'Levi wants us vaccinated for a variety of diseases – typhoid, cholera, dengue fever, yellow fever, bubonic plague, Ebola. You name it, I'll be pricking you for it.'

'So why isn't the government doing vaccinations?' said Irith.

'It's costing trillions to resettle people each time the sea level rises a bit more. Cheaper to let them die,' Bragg said cynically. 'It's mainly the poor and they don't contribute much anyway.'

'But the American Popes can afford $1.88 billion for a statue!' said Irith.

'I'm an atheist,' said Bragg, 'but not even I would describe the *Pieta* as *just a statue*. It's one of the masterpieces of western culture.'

'And worth more than thousands of human lives,' snapped Irith.

'Dinner's ready,' said Levi. 'We're eating outside tonight, since it's so hot.' He attempted a smile but it didn't reach his eyes. His work was still going badly.

'Only a month and a half to the test,' he said, carrying his plate outside. 'I know the date now – 27 August.'

Irith put down the insect repellent. It tainted everything she ate and still didn't keep away the swarming mosquitoes – Minnesota's state bird, as Bragg called them. 'What is this "test"?'

'I believe it's the day Lindstrom implements the Terminator Project, whatever that is.'

'Hopefully not a robot from the future coming to wipe us out,' said Bragg, who had his mouth full.

'And we don't even know what it is, or where it's going to take place,' Thornton said. 'What a bloody fiasco.'

Levi turned those mild brown eyes on him. His ears looked particularly droopy today. 'I think they've used a quantum encryption scheme, and that's generally held to be unbreakable.'

'I didn't think any code could be truly unbreakable,' said Irith.

'Well, let's just say that all the computers on Earth, linked together, would take more than the life of the universe to crack this code,' said Levi heavily. 'I'm sorry.'

'I don't see that it's your fault,' said Irith.

Gretel glared at her as if she'd done the damage herself.

'It's nobody's fault,' said Levi.

Irith had to say something in his defence. 'If this was pure maths, some genius would simply invent a new branch of mathematics where it was possible to solve such problems, and use it to break the code.'

'And if magic was possible,' sneered Thornton, 'Levi could wave his magic wand and read the files.'

'Wait a minute,' said Levi, staring at Irith as if she'd just said something profound. He rose from the table, leaving his heaped plate behind, and went inside. His door slammed.

'What the hell was that about?' said Thornton.

'I have no idea,' his sister replied. 'I'm going for a quick swim. Coming?'

After they had gone, Irith sat at the table with Siah, who seemed immune to the mosquitoes. Irith kept waving them away but, gorged on her blood, they barely moved. She slapped, leaving three more bloody splatters on her arm. Her skin was covered in red welts.

'I never studied the sciences,' said Siah. 'Were you being serious?'

'Yes and no,' said Irith, still puzzling over Levi's reaction. 'Sometimes, when mathematicians can't solve a problem with the tools they have, they invent a new branch of mathematics that has the tools they need. Newton did it to work out his theory of gravitation. So did Riemann, in the nineteenth century, by creating a new kind of geometry where it was impossible for any two lines to be parallel.'

'But . . .'

'I don't understand it either, but I wasn't brilliant at maths. What's the point of Riemann geometry, you might well ask, since it's obviously impossible?'

Siah's eyes had begun to glaze over. 'What is the point?'

'Fifty years later, Einstein realised that Riemann's curved space described the shape of our universe as it really is. In fact, Euclid was wrong – two lines in our universe can never be parallel. We just think they are because –'

'Don't say any more,' said Siah. 'My head is hurting. I'm allergic to higher maths.' She grinned. 'Where does that leave us?'

'I don't know.'

'Let's go and talk to Levi.'

Siah had to knock three times before he answered, and then with a curt, 'What is it?'

She smiled in that disarming way of hers. 'We were wondering what you had in mind.'

He ran his fingers over his bald head. 'In the mathematical apocrypha there are works that have never been fully understood. I'm thinking of the lost notebooks of the tragic Indian mathematician Ramanujan, some of the unpublished work of Paul Erdos and the staggeringly esoteric theorems of Fritjulf Vaiha in the early part of this century. Some weren't comprehensible to Vaiha himself, when he re-read them after his brain surgery. But there are nuggets that bear on number theory and quantum cryptography.'

'Sounds pretty desperate to me,' Irith said quietly.

'I am desperate,' said Levi, 'but Vaiha is still alive, and he was never a friend of the establishment. So if you could give me a while . . .'

They took the hint. Gretel and Thornton were on the way up from the lake, and the atmosphere could be hostile in the living room when she was in one of her moods, so they sat in Irith's room, drinking tea and talking until late that night. They were still at it when Levi came in.

'I was hoping I'd find you up,' he said to Siah. 'I need you to organise something for me.'

'You've found Vaiha?'

'In Finland.'

'It's not a Finnish name.'

Levi shrugged. 'He was born in Romania, but only because his parents were passing through. I don't know what his ancestry is. I need you to get him here, post-haste and in the utmost secrecy.'

'What if he doesn't want to come?' said Irith.

'Siah is very good at her job.'

Irith barely saw either of them after that, for they spent day and night at their terminals. Siah was planning how to bring the mathematician in secret, and making all the arrangements. Levi was just as busy setting up false trails and smokescreens, should anyone become suspicious, and untraceably manipulating a dozen security systems to ensure that Vaiha's passage left no trail that could lead Security to them. He also had to obtain – or create – documentation that he was a follower of one of the acceptable faiths.

On 18 July, Siah left to do the shopping and collect the great man from a distant airport. They weren't told which one, though Irith suspected it was

O'Hare in Chicago. Siah planned to be away for three days, but four days later she still hadn't returned and Levi was beside himself.

'Has she been picked up, or just been delayed?' he said to Irith that afternoon. They were taking a break, walking down to the lake in their blue robes.

'It's not uncommon for her to be delayed. I wouldn't start worrying yet.'

'This is our last chance, Irith, and our time is running out. Should I go looking for her?'

'Can you do as much on the road as you could here?'

'No.'

Siah turned up at dawn the following day. Levi ran down to the van in his pyjamas. Irith followed.

'Sorry about the delay,' Siah said, jumping out and hurrying towards them. 'I had some difficulties. He . . . doesn't fit very well.'

'Fit into what?' said Levi.

'Anything. And I had to procure certain items that he requires.'

'Where is he?' There was no one in the passenger seat.

'In the back. He's not comfortable with people. The trip must have been a nightmare for him.'

Levi opened the sliding door and held out his hand. 'Good day, Dr Vaiha.'

Crouched against the far side of the van was a short, skinny man with a paper grocery bag over his head. He wore a long black coat, so moth-eaten that it might have been found on a rubbish tip, baggy brown shorts in desperate need of washing and thick leather sandals held together by brass rings. His thin legs revealed every detail of bone and sinew. He was mumbling under his breath, but whether it was some Eastern European language, higher mathematics or mere gibberish, Irith couldn't tell.

'He doesn't like to shake hands, or any form of contact,' Siah said.

The man pulled the bag up far enough that his eyes were visible. Long grey hair framed a pallid and cadaverous face. Grey stubble speckled his chin and sprouted in random clumps on his cheeks. A yellow moustache, the hairs twisted into felt at the ends, framed a shrunken, blue-lipped mouth. His nose was bladed although the nostrils flared like miniature trumpets. Were it not for his eyes, which shone as though coated in glycerine, he would have looked like a man on his deathbed.

Levi let his hand fall to his side. 'I'm Dr Levi Seth. I asked you to come because –'

Vaiha let the bag fall over his face. 'I fill go to fork at fonce.' His voice was like a saw struggling to cut through hardwood. 'Take me to woom.' He scuttled out of the car, walking on the spot, his sandals slapping on the paving, while Levi went around the back for his bags.

'He doesn't have any luggage,' said Siah.

'No wonder he's upset.'

'No, he carries only what he can fit into his pockets.'

'Well, I dare say he's happy that way. Will you come this way, Dr Vaiha?'

'Go! I follow,' the great man said from under his sack.

Levi glanced at Siah, who grinned and jerked her thumb at the house. Levi went and the mathematician followed, evidently finding his way by Levi's footsteps.

'What is it with this fellow?' Irith asked Siah.

'He's off the planet. You have no idea what I've gone through to get him here, and not the least of it was procuring drugs.'

'What?' Levi spun around.

'He can only function, mathematically speaking, after taking a particular kind of amphetamine that is rather difficult to obtain legally, and not much easier illegally. Still, that's what I'm here for.'

'But he was a child prodigy,' said Levi.

'He had a great trauma ten or fifteen years ago, a brain tumour I think, and lost his ability to do mathematics. It drove him certifiably mad. Since then, he's discovered that small doses of this particular amphetamine give him back the talent without which he's utterly lost.'

They went into Levi's room. The mathematician had taken the paper bag off and was sitting in Levi's chair, grinning idiotically at the computer screen. The text of an encrypted file was scrolling so rapidly that the words were a blur. Surely he couldn't be reading it?

Irith went outside. When she returned a couple of hours later, the file was still scrolling as quickly as before.

'Do you think this is going to work?' she said quietly to Levi.

'I very much doubt it,' he whispered. 'The man's a bloody lunatic and he's going to cause us trouble.'

An hour later, Vaiha came to the end of the file. He got up, blundered into the wall, then snapped at Levi, 'Wamanujan's lost notebook. Get.'

Irith was sitting quietly up the back, afraid to breathe in case it upset the genius.

'Which one?' Levi consulted his screen. 'The one found in Trinity College in the 1970s?'

'Later. Much later.' Vaiha twisted his moustache ends furiously.

'I didn't know there was a later one.' Levi tapped at his terminal. 'Ah, here's something. The Madras Fragments, discovered in the archives of the former Madras Engineering College a decade ago. The fragments cover work done in 1920, the last year of Ramanujan's life, after he returned to India. Hmm. There doesn't seem to be a version online.'

'Mikwofiche!' yelled Vaiha.

'Why would it have been microfilmed a decade ago?' Levi said to himself. 'Everything was digital long before then.'

Irith moved up silently beside him, watching the screen as Levi searched the databases.

'Here we are,' said Levi. 'It was microfilmed in the 1970s, but no one knew what it was at the time. It wasn't until someone recognised his handwriting that its importance was understood.' He read from the screen. 'The Madras Fragments contain fifty-six priceless theorems. At least, it's supposed that they're priceless, although most are incomprehensible to other mathematicians.'

'And all fithout pwoofs,' growled Vaiha. 'Fool of a man – no technique. Kvick, kvick!'

'There's no digital copy,' said Levi. 'Just scans of the microfiches. Here we are. It's a pretty poor image.' He turned to the mathematician. 'Are you sure?'

'Pwint! Pwint!'

Levi cleaned up the images, enhanced the resolution and sent them to the laser printer. Five minutes later Vaiha had the precious ninety-six pages, snatching each out of the printer the instant it appeared. Without a word he went out, his sandals slap-slapping down the hall. The door of his room slammed.

Irith and Levi looked at one another. 'It's out of my hands,' said Levi. 'Care for a glass of wine?'

Irith hadn't touched a drop since that fateful first night. 'But it's not even lunchtime.'

'I don't care. Come and join me.'

·· • ● • ··

Irith couldn't believe that one man could cause so much trouble. Vaiha kept to his room, except for a series of demands screamed down the hall at any time of the day or night. He would never eat the same thing twice, and his tastes were exotic, even bizarre. One day's requests included pig's ovaries, prawn eyestalk soup and lasagne made with sheets of dried Tasmanian kelp layered with krill. When Siah was unable to supply any of those delicacies, Vaiha did as he always did when he couldn't get what he wanted. He sulked, loudly and tediously.

He had other, less endearing tendencies. On the first night, Irith was washing her hair in the shower when she had the uncomfortable feeling that she was being watched. She rinsed the shampoo out of her eyes and discovered Vaiha standing only an arm's length away, leering at her. She screamed and threw water on him, whereupon he vanished and had one of his sulks, so loudly that no one in the house got any sleep.

After that the women locked their doors but it made no difference; he could defeat any lock in the house within minutes. The following morning it was Siah's turn to have a visit in the shower, though she handed it with rather more *savoir faire*. She stepped out, dripping wet, picked the little man up in her arms and carried him back to his room. Putting him on the bed, she said, 'Don't come into my room, please.'

He never did, although he followed her around like a puppy afterwards. Siah, of all people, could get him to do whatever was needed, when even Levi could obtain nothing from him.

That evening Vaiha appeared outside Bragg's shower, though Bragg didn't realise it until the mathematician gave him a playful tug on the penis. 'Fuck off, Vaiha,' Bragg said without rancour. Vaiha went away.

There were no intrusions the following day but the morning after that Irith was woken at dawn by a short scream, a thud and Gretel screeching herself into a fit.

'If you ever come near me again, you disgusting little pervert, I'll tear your eyeballs out and shove them so far up your arse you'll choke on them.'

Irith pulled on a robe and ran out. Gretel had punched the little mathematician in the face. Blood poured from his trumpet-shaped nostrils and dripped from his blue-tinted lips. He lurched blindly up the hall, weeping, for he truly didn't know what he had done wrong. Gretel followed him, screeching insults.

Siah curbed Gretel with a few quiet words, then carried Vaiha carried into her room. Oddly, he did not mind her touching him. Levi went in soon afterwards and there was a long muttered conversation, punctuated by wailing and sobbing, after which Vaiha took to his bed.

Siah joined Irith on the deck soon after. Bragg sat with them. Gretel and her brother were over the far side, talking between themselves.

'I never thought you'd be the one to suck up to the little shit,' Gretel sniffed loudly. 'After what he did to you.'

'He didn't do anything to me,' said Siah, 'and I'm not sure I know what you mean by the innuendo.'

'I don't understand how a man-hating dyke like you –'

'I can name a dozen men I'm close friends with,' Siah said quietly, the only sign of agitation a flush of colour at her throat. 'I just don't want to sleep with them. How many friends can you name, Gretel? Of either sex?' She stood up to walk to the other table, then thought better of it. 'I pity Vaiha, who is a greatly troubled man, but doing violence to him doesn't help our cause.' She sat down again.

Bragg, not normally the most sensitive of men, reached across the table and gripped her hand. 'You handled that well. As you always do.'

Siah gave him a wan smile. 'It didn't upset you, him watching you in the shower?'

'He's harmless.'

Vaiha emerged from his room two days later and closeted himself with Levi for the morning. At noon, Irith heard shouting and Levi's door burst open.

'Not kvantum,' Vaiha screamed, running down the hall wearing only his pyjama top. 'Not kvantum at all.'

Levi followed, trying to placate him. 'My dear Fritjulf.'

'Dr Vaiha to you, asshole! False pretences you bring me here. Big pwoblem, you say; kvantum enkwyption. No one else can solve. Not kvantum at all.'

'I'm sorry,' Levi pleaded. 'I thought –'

'Vaiha world's gweatest genius. Not demean genius on pissy factowisation enkwyption. Going home.'

His door slammed so hard that it rocked the building.

CHAPTER TWENTY-THREE

Levi came back, haunted about the eyes. He opened his office door but closed it again without going in. 'I don't know what to do,' he said to Irith.

'Cup of tea?'

'Thanks. That'd be lovely.'

'What exactly is the problem?' she said over her shoulder as she rinsed the tea-leaves out of the pot.

'Vaiha fancies that he can break quantum encryption. He was bitterly disappointed to discover that this wasn't one.'

'How could he tell?'

'I haven't got the faintest idea.'

'Then how *are* the files encrypted?'

'In the normal way, according to Vaiha, but with an exceptionally large key – a number with hundreds of digits. It's unbreakable by any method I know. I have the encryption and decryption algorithms, of course.'

'How did you get them?'

'They're in the public domain. Security of the code doesn't depend on the algorithms, nor on the public key to them, but only on the private key.'

'Levi, I haven't got the faintest idea what you're talking about.'

'The principle is like a safe with two keys,' he explained. 'Everyone has a public key to put their message in and lock the safe, but only the person to whom the message is sent has the private key that will unlock the safe and release their message.'

'And there's no way to get hold of the private key?' said Irith.

'In theory, it can be calculated from the public key because they're mathematically related. In practice that's not possible. Security relies on the fact that some mathematical operations, such as factoring large numbers, can be done easily but are extremely difficult to undo. For a very large number, such as a key with a hundred digits, the time taken to undo the operation with a supercomputer is considerably greater than the age of the universe.'

'So we're stuffed.'

'I refuse to give up. Ah, Siah, have you got a minute?'

Siah sat down and poured herself a cup of tea. 'I heard what happened. You want me to talk to Vaiha?'

'If anyone can convince him to stay, you can. He's got to help us.'

'But the encryption is unbreakable,' said Irith.

'By normal methods.'

'Meaning?'

'Vaiha keeps sneering at the "pissy encryption methods" he's had to look at. I think he knows more than he's letting on.'

'Then why doesn't he say so?'

'He wants us to cajole it out of him,' said Siah. 'After we tell him how clever he is.' Her eyes met Levi's across the table.

'Offer him whatever he wants,' Levi said wearily. 'Though I'll bet it's another of his games.'

Siah spent several hours in Vaiha's room. Late that afternoon he emerged, bouncing as if there were springs in his toes. He flew into Levi's office and jerked on the back of the chair till he got out.

Vaiha sprang over the back of the chair into the seat, cleared the screen with a keystroke and began typing so fast that his fingers were just a blur on the keyboard. Irith stood behind him. It was a subroutine for a computer program, but full of mathematical symbols that meant nothing to her.

He typed for two hours without stopping, then abruptly propelled himself out of his chair and bounced away.

Levi was staring at the screen. 'What the bloody hell am I supposed to do with this?'

Vaiha stopped with his stubby fingers on the doorknob. 'Is Vaiha–Wamanujan factowing algowithm,' he said, speaking word by word as if to an idiot. 'You put into dekwyption pwogwam.'

The door closed. Levi scrolled through the screen. Irith slipped into the chair behind him.

'Will it work, Levi?'

'I don't see how. The maths is incomprehensible. I've never seen anything like it. Oh well. Nothing ventured and all that.'

He saved the file, copied it and pasted it into his decryption engine in place of a pre-existing slab of code. 'I'll say this for the little bugger, he's the best programmer I've ever come across. This fits perfectly and he's only seen the program once. I'll try it on one of the smaller files.'

He tapped keys and hit the return. The screen showed an error message. Levi cursed. 'Can you get him back, please?'

Irith knocked on Vaiha's door. He wasn't there. She eventually found him out below the deck, studying a trail of ants walking up one of the piers.

'Could you come back to the office please, Dr Vaiha? There's a problem with the file.'

Vaiha's eyes glittered with vindicated malice. He had been expecting the summons; perhaps had planned it. 'Pwogwammer's pwoblem.'

'Well, would you please come anyway?'

Pushing by her, he bounced inside. Irith followed and was just in time to hear him say, 'Can't find pwoblem, Seth?'

'No,' said Levi.

'You vewy stupid man.'

'I must be.'

'Fwitjulf Vaiha is gweatest genius world has ever seen.'

'If this works, I'll heartily agree.'

Vaiha's look was somewhere between a sneer and a leer. He jerked at the back of the chair until Levi got out. The little man scrolled through his subroutine and in the middle of thousands of lines of code, tapped a single key, a colon. Turning to Levi, Vaiha raised an eyebrow.

'You are the greatest genius the world has ever seen, Dr Vaiha,' said Levi.

Vaiha still glared at him.

'And I'm the biggest dunce,' Levi went on.

Vaiha chortled with glee. 'I am; you are. Going home.' He went out.

'Hey, aren't you going to see if it works?'

Vaiha did not deign to answer. Irith lay a hand on Levi's shoulder. 'What an obnoxious little bastard.'

'If he's right, he can afford to be. Let's try this again.' Levi hit the keys and stood up. 'Let's go to dinner. Even if it works, we won't see anything for days.'

Irith was just following him through the door when the computer chimed. 'There's another error, Levi.'

'That's not an error message,' he said, looking puzzled. 'It's the completion tone.' He ran back to the computer. 'I don't believe it! It's not possible!'

As they watched, the gibberish of the file slowly changed to text.

'It's broken the code,' said Irith.

Levi had to sit down. 'A hundred-digit key and his factoring algorithm cracked it in under a minute. He'll get the Nobel Prize for this.'

'There isn't a Nobel Prize for mathematics.'

'For a discovery like this, they'd give him a special one. We've done it, Irith!' He hugged her. 'In my heart I never thought we would.'

'So we've won. What do we do now?'

'We haven't won. This is just another step and the crucial documents may not be among the files Gretel stole from the data centre. And even if they are, I've got to get the message out to the world without Security stopping it. That's not easy, these days. But if I can do all that, and it works, it may just bring down Lindstrom and the Congress, and we might all end up heroes.'

'What if it doesn't work?'

'There will be nowhere on Earth to hide.'

The following morning Vaiha was gone, with Siah. She did not return for two days, by which time Levi had batch-decoded all fifty-two thousand documents recovered from the Terminator Project file. The team was about to go through them, a monumental task even after Levi had run a keyword scan and sorted the 'probably relevant' files from the 'unlikely to be useful' ones.

Irith had put together a briefing report. 'This is what we have –' She broke off as Siah appeared at the door.

'Siah! Thank heavens you're back. Is everything all right?' She looked pale.

'Congress Security is onto us. There was a watch at the airport. And certain other signs.'

'What did you do with Vaiha?'

'I had to bring him back. He's not happy.'

'That'll be the understatement of the decade,' said Bragg.

'Sorry, Levi,' Siah continued. 'I couldn't risk Security interrogating him.'

'You did the right thing,' said Levi. 'I don't know what I was thinking, letting him go.'

'Doesn't solve the problem of what to do with him,' said Bragg.

'I know what I'd like to do.' Gretel cracked her knuckles.

'That doesn't help,' said Levi. 'We'll have to keep him here, uncomfortable as that's going to be. Irith, go on with your briefing. I'll do a security check and see how long we've got.' He ran out of the room.

'We've narrowed the search down to 7108 files,' said Irith. 'All contain one or more of the trigger keywords or phrases. We'll have to read every document, or at least scan them. Since they average thirty pages each, plus associated data, that's going to take some doing.'

They each sat down to a terminal and began to work.

'Irith,' said Levi, late the following evening. 'Come in here and tell me what you make of this.' He drew her into his room, closed the door and locked it. He looked haggard. It was 1 August and time was running out.

'Surely you don't suspect the loyalty of the team?'

'I certainly don't suspect you, since every emotion shows on your lovely face. Don't ever take up the noble game of poker. As for the other members of the team, what people don't know, they can't be made to tell.'

He scrubbed at his bald head, fretfully. 'I've got something to show you.' He led her to his terminal, put his eye to the iris scanner and the computer gave him access. A file opened to a window displaying a long string of letters, consisting only of A, C, G and T. 'What do you make of it?'

'It's part of a sequences of bases, letters if you like, that make up the description of a gene. Genomes are written in three-letter words, using those four letters, which stand for the bases adenine, cytosine, guanine and thymine.'

'Is it from the human genome?'

'I can't tell from such a small sample,' said Irith. 'We have most of our genes in common with other organisms, even such lowly creatures as earthworms and bacteria.'

'What if I gave you the complete file?'

'I could identify it, with the right tools. The human genome contains three billion bases, arranged into a billion words. I'd need a suite of computer programs but I can get them off the net.'

'You can use that computer.' He indicated a small black one on a table by itself. 'It's a secure connection.'

'It'll take a while.'

'That's all right.'

'I'll need passwords, account details and so forth, to get access.'

'Just put in the addresses. The system will do all that for you.'

She turned around. 'All right,' she said doubtfully. 'But they're restricted sites.'

'I can get you in.'

Irith had the programs within an hour, but it took another day to set them up and format the data so she could use it. She set the master program to give her graphical representations of the data, and then to search for similarities with its library of genome sequences.

The graphic came up quickly, long before the library search was finished. Irith frowned at the first image on the screen.

'What is it?' said Levi, coming across.

'It's not the human genome; it's far too small. In fact, it just looks like a virus.'

'Whatever we find in these files, there will be no "just" about it. Have another look.'

She spent a day running the comparisons with her library. 'It's a virus all right,' she said to Levi, 'similar to one associated with mild, flu-like symptoms in humans. Nothing unusual about that – dozens of viruses have similar effects. But this one is almost certainly an engineered virus and . . . some of the sequences aren't characteristic of viruses at all.'

Levi did not seem surprised. 'What are they characteristic of?'

'I'll have to do more work.'

His eyes drifted to the date at the top of the screen: 3 August. Twenty-four days left and they knew practically nothing.

Irith felt panicky. Clearly, this was high-level genome engineering and she was just a failed honours student. What if she couldn't work it out?

'I'm not going to bed until I've solved it,' she said rashly. She didn't want to let Levi down.

'No. Don't risk making a mistake. Get it right, check it then tell me what it is.'

That took several days, but well before the end Irith was in no doubt. The virus would be extremely contagious, and few people would have immunity to it. And it had been carefully tailored. But for what? She checked again. To affect the sex chromosomes. That was easier done in the male, because the female was born with all her eggs formed.

She looked out the window at the rain but found no inspiration.

Irith first thought the virus was intended to be some kind of male contraceptive, though why would anyone create a male contraceptive this way? She checked the library again and it struck her. This wasn't a contraceptive at all. Rather, it resembled a terminator gene, one designed to render males sterile. Plant-breeding companies had once inserted terminator genes in new varieties of grain to make sure they didn't form viable seed. The gene ensured farmers had to buy fresh seed for each new season's crop, rather than saving seed from the harvest.

This appeared to be a human terminator gene, and on a virus so carefully tailored to sneak through human immunities, it could only be designed for one purpose: to sterilise large numbers of people. Could it be a racial weapon? A super form of ethnic cleansing? Or was it intended for bio-warfare?

Again Levi was not surprised, and she wondered to what extent she was merely confirming his suspicions.

'Is that really all there is to it?' she asked.

He thought for some time before answering. 'It appears to be an adaptation of earlier work designed to wipe out pest animals and plants. In the first two decades of this century, a great variety of terminator genes were developed to eliminate different pest organisms. As I recall, the work was abandoned because of the danger of the terminator segments crossing the species barrier and sterilising other organisms, which could have caused an ecological collapse, or a crop failure.'

'So why is it being developed here?'

'I don't know.' He rubbed his eyes. 'It could be exactly what it appears – a better form of sterilisation, to reduce the population explosion. Or . . .'

'Or what?'

'It might also be to wipe out troublesome nations or ethnic groups. Vaccinate one's own people and then release the virus.'

Irith caught her breath. 'But surely . . .'

'Probably not,' said Levi. 'Lindstrom's not a racist. And then again, it could be a red herring.'

'How can we find out? You must have other sources, Levi. How did you discover the date?'

'What date?'

'The critical one – 27 August?'

An even longer hesitation. 'I have a mole in the President's office.'

'Can't you ask him to find out what the Terminator Project really is?' said Irith.

'I've tried, but security is tighter than ever.'

'I have really bad news,' Levi said at dinner. He looked ghastly. From ecstasy to agony in a few days.

'I rather suspected that.' Bragg was eating heartily. Nothing put him off his food. 'You haven't found what you're looking for.'

'I have, more or less, but it's not enough. The secret project appears to be the creation of a human terminator gene. I say appears to be, because there's got to be more than what we're seeing. I don't yet know its purpose, but you can bet it's unpleasant. Unfortunately, there's no proof that Lindstrom, or the Congress, are responsible for it.'

'How can you be sure?' said Gretel, 'in all those documents –'

'The evidence I'm looking for isn't there. The proof might have been in the four thousand documents you didn't recover from the data centre. Or it might not have been there at all.'

'So he's beaten us,' said Bragg, cramming in a baked potato the size of a tennis ball.

'No, but we'll have to go to Plan B – which is far more dangerous.'

'What's Plan B?' said Irith.

'To destroy the facility where the terminator gene virus is being produced,' said Levi.

'Where's that?'

'Somewhere in the US. I should know by tonight.'

'The *suicide mission*,' said Siah. 'All along I thought it'd come to this.'

'Suicide mission?' cried Irith.

'The facility will be closely guarded,' said Levi. 'Moreover, even if we can get in, and destroy the virus and the equipment it's replicated with, it won't stop Lindstrom from trying again. And he'll hunt us ruthlessly. We won't have the chance to put our side to the world. He'll close down the net before he allows that.'

'I didn't think you *could* close down the net,' said Irith.

'You can if you've got server-busting computer viruses already prepared, and you control the lines and satellite connections,' said Gretel.

'We won't be heroes,' Levi continued, 'but reviled terrorists. Revolutionaries under a death sentence. We'll be hunted down, tried in secret and executed. Lindstrom will be stronger than ever and we'll have achieved nothing.'

'Then why are we doing it?'

'To give the future a chance. Someone else may seize it.'

'I really hope so,' Bragg muttered. 'I've never been that keen on self-sacrifice.'

CHAPTER TWENTY-FOUR

It was three o'clock in the morning and Irith was still awake, listening to the pouring rain and trying to understand why the terminator virus had been such a letdown, when Levi banged on her door.

'Get up!' he roared. 'Emergency evacuation.'

Everyone scrambled out of bed, except Vaiha, whose door was bolted on the outside. They could tell he was still there from the banging and screaming.

'What's wrong now?' said Bragg.

'Security's onto us. I don't think they know who we are, where we're hiding or what we're up to, but that won't take long. We've got to be well gone before they find this place.'

'How long do we have?' asked Gretel.

'No way of telling. Drop every vital file on a MemoStick and put it in the DataDump in case we have to destroy it if they catch us on the road. Everything else – every scrap of paper, and every storage disc except the one in my laptop – has to go in the high-temperature incinerator, *now*. Before we leave, the residue must be smashed to powder and dumped. We can't leave a single trace. Not even our DNA.'

Siah cried out, as if in pain. 'Levi,' she said urgently. 'Please . . .'

'I'm sorry, Siah. I know what this place means to you, but we've got no choice.'

They watched the flames spring up inside the beautiful house. Siah's cheeks were wet. 'Most of the happy memories of my life have been here,' she said to Irith. She wiped her face and climbed into the van.

Thornton carried Vaiha out, bound and gagged. His eyes were like a hyena's. Irith had to look away. *I did everything you asked of me,* they said, *and this is how you repay me.*

'Can't we do something for Vaiha?' Irith said quietly to Levi. 'I feel so guilty.'

'It's a squalid betrayal,' said Levi, 'but what else can I do? He knows too much to be let go; he wouldn't keep his mouth shut for a second.'

'Where are we going?' said Bragg, sliding behind the wheel.

'Tell you when we get there. Head south-west on the back roads towards Grand Rapids, then west on US2.'

'It sounds like you don't trust us,' Gretel interjected.

'Levi is treating us the way you and Thornton treated me,' said Irith.

'We've proven our loyalty. You were a blow-in with a treacherous bitch of a mother who —'

'No one can ever *prove* their loyalty,' Irith retorted. 'To disprove it, on the other hand, takes but one negative incident.'

'Thank you!' Levi said coldly. 'I'm not telling anyone where we're going because I'm still not sure myself. I'll be working it out on the way.'

He passed a black cube the size of a soccer ball over the seat to Irith. 'This is the DataDump. If we're searched, unlock the red button on top and press it right down, past *two* points of resistance.'

'What does it do?' said Irith.

'It gets very hot,' said Bragg. 'Don't hold it in your lap — I hate the smell of roasted pubes before breakfast.'

'Charming,' said Siah.

'Eleven hundred degrees Celsius,' said Levi. 'Which will irretrievably destroy the data in any object inside. Keep a sharp lookout — if you thought we were in danger before, think again. '

'Who's hunting us?' said Irith.

'Congress Security,' Levi replied.

'What about the US authorities?'

'Unlikely, since relations are rather frayed at the moment. That's the only advantage we've got. Get moving, Bragg.' Levi was already typing into his computer. 'And remember your vows of silence.'

Irith cast one last look out the window at the flames and wiped away a tear of her own. She had been happy here, but she would never return. Chances were, none of them would.

They continued as far west as Church's Ferry, North Dakota, where they diverted from the town centre to avoid a checkpoint. It was still raining heavily and houses in the path of rising floodwaters from the lake were being demolished.

They stopped to refuel. Vaiha had to be sedated. As soon as they had taken the gag out he began to kick, scream and bite. Just out of town they were pulled over by the religious militia. Irith held her breath but Levi indicated, with gestures, that Vaiha was sick. The officers scanned his card, took his thumbprint and waved them on.

They turned onto US281 and drove south through Jamestown to Aberdeen, South Dakota. There they stopped for hamburgers and fries, which they ate on Captain Hook's Ship in the Storybook Land theme park. Even the Doomsday Mutes acted as tourists, occasionally.

They changed vans and continued, passing through many towns that Irith missed because she had fallen asleep. When she woke the following morning they were in Osceola, Iowa, a town that seemed to have an inordinate number of parks. They ate a silent breakfast in Grade Lake Park, watching rain teem down on the water. After that, they stretched their legs at the Clarke County Fair and were just in time to see the Grand Champion banner awarded in the steer show. The beast was the size of a small hippopotamus.

As soon as they were back in the van, Levi resumed his typing. Bragg continued east. A horrible stench grew down the back.

'What the hell's that?' said Bragg, sniffing. 'Smells like the great man has shat himself.'

Siah checked. 'He has,' she said grimly. 'Any volunteers?'

They all stared stolidly forward. Irith felt ashamed of herself, but it was beyond her. Siah did the business and they stopped at a public convenience at Chariton, so she could clean up afterwards.

'Do you think he crapped his pants deliberately?' said Bragg once they were back on the road and it was safe to talk.

'Of course he did,' said Siah, who had gone off the little man.

'Maybe it's a protest against the way we've treated him,' Irith said quietly. She could identify with that.

She sedated Vaiha again. It was inhumane, but Irith was relieved to be free of those raw, desperate eyes. They went south and west, then south and east, then north and west again. Levi understood the mathematics of patterns and made sure he left none behind. By now they could have been anywhere in America; Irith had tuned out of her surroundings long ago.

On the third night, on a dark road from nowhere to nowhere, Siah vaccinated them all in the van.

'What's this for?' Thornton said suspiciously.

'Yellow fever, among other things.'

'So we're going south.'

'That's not the only place that has yellow fever.'

It's the most likely place, Irith thought. *Something else to worry about.*

They turned into a drive-in church by an anonymous highway in an unknown state, then sat for an hour in silence, watching the flickering display in the driving rain, before heading east again.

Siah and Bragg drove in turns while Levi spent day and night at his laptop, monitoring the net, setting out false leads, covering their tracks and doing who knew what else.

They stopped in a backwoods motel for two days and didn't go out at all, then got in the van and drove due south, and every hour it grew hotter and more humid.

'Chattanooga,' said Bragg, sometime after dusk. Later, 'Birmingham, Alabama.' Levi took the wheel. The van sped on. 'Meridian, Mississippi. We're heading for New Orleans.'

'Good guess,' Levi said dryly. 'But it's only a guess.'

A couple of hours after that, he said, 'Take off your blue gear and pack it away. And give me all your IDs.' He passed back another set.

'Why the change, Levi?' said Irith.

'People in robes and hoods don't go down too well in this part of the world.'

'Why not?'

'Reminds them of the Klan, Irith,' said Bragg.

Around five in the morning they passed over the vast causeway across Lake Pontchartrain and Irith knew, unless it was another of Levi's diversions, that they were indeed heading for the city on the delta.

'A quick briefing,' said Levi. 'New Orleans is the poorest city in America, and one of the most violent, so we must be careful. It used to lie about a hundred kilometres upriver from the Gulf, but almost all the Mississippi delta has gone underwater and the sea is now lapping at the eastern suburbs.

'New Orleans is different from every other city in America. It has a tradition of tolerance which may work to our advantage. It's also a sinful place where the religious militia tread carefully, if at all. They've got no checkpoints here.'

They crossed off the causeway just as it was getting light. There was water everywhere. Almost immediately they were waved to the side of the road.

'Christ!' said Bragg. 'Robes, everyone!'

'Don't panic,' said Levi. 'It's not that kind of checkpoint.'

'You'd better be right,' said Thornton.

It turned out to be a health station and they were allowed through after Siah produced yellow fever vaccination records. Mosquitoes swarmed in through the window. As Irith slapped at them, she was grateful for the injection.

'Baton Rouge is that-a way,' said Bragg, pointing up to the right. 'It's an industrial complex for a hundred miles up the Mississippi.'

'Cancer Alley, we call it,' said Siah.

'Never mind Baton Rouge,' said Levi, turning onto the Veterans' Memorial Highway. 'We're here. New Orleans has nearly drowned several times in the past, and with sea level up six metres it's on the very brink of catastrophe. Even before the seas started rising, the city centre lay below sea level. Unlike London, which could be protected by a piddling little dike on the Thames, New Orleans is threatened from all sides. The lake forms the northern boundary, the Mississippi runs through the city to the south, while the advancing sea has covered most of the delta and is now only a few kilometres east. Should the levees break, or the water come over the top, New Orleans will disappear like Atlantis.'

'Spare us the geography lesson,' said Thornton, irritable after days on the road and constantly being told what to do. 'It's time for answers, Levi.'

Irith pulled herself down in her seat, swatting at her neck. Why had they been brought to this mosquito-ridden hellhole?

Levi drove in silence, turning left up West End Boulevard towards Lake Pontchartrain. Near the marina and yacht harbour he took the road along the top of a massive earth levee, seven metres high, that kept the lake from overflowing into the city. After a kilometre or two he pulled off the road, stopped the van and wound the window down. Though only eight in the morning, the air was so humid it was stifling. The thermometer on the dashboard said eighty-eight degrees Fahrenheit.

'It's going to be a stinker of a day,' said Levi.

'The south had its hottest summer on record last year,' said Siah. 'It was half a degree hotter than the summer before, and that was a record too. They say this one is even hotter.'

'What's that smell?' said Irith. A sweet, rank odour, like sweaty decay, permeated everything.

'The whole world decomposing,' said Bragg. 'When the delta went underwater, salt killed the freshwater marshes and the cypress swamps. Now they're rotting away. The stench hangs over New Orleans all summer.'

'The city is eleven metres below the normal level of the Mississippi, and seven below the lake,' Siah said quietly. 'When it rains, they have to pump the water out.'

'Every year the US Army Corps of Engineers raises the levees higher,' said Levi. 'And every year the city installs more pumps. The cost is already unsustainable and the sea is still rising. One day the waters will take New Orleans for good, and that'll be a tragedy. For all its faults, I love this city.'

He fell silent. Irith stared out the window. On one side of them, the lake stood only a metre below the top of the levee. On the other there was a long fall to street level. Parkland extended to east and west, inside the levee. 'That's the university campus, beyond the bayous,' said Levi, 'and in the distance you can see the Lakefront Airport. They have to keep building up the runways.'

Irith could just make them out, extending into the lake. Beyond an enormous park framed by canals, she saw the towers of the central business district.

'City Park,' said Levi. 'Don't go there at night. Or Lakeshore Park, for that matter.'

'Don't go *anywhere* at night, on foot,' said Siah.

'Hold on,' Levi said, as Irith pulled the handle of the sliding door. 'There it is, Thorn. The Pontchartrain Viral Research facility. Our target.'

Off to their right, in the middle of a suburb of derelict mansions, was a square compound. Ten or fifteen hectares in extent, it was surrounded by walls topped with spirals of razor wire. A trio of buildings, eight or nine storeys high and faced with black stone, were clustered in the centre, a good hundred metres from the perimeter walls. Built in the Neo-Brutal style, the buildings looked as solid as a quarry full of basalt. The crashproof, bombproof gates would have done justice to a US embassy in the Middle East, and guards could be seen moving behind bulletproof screens.

'What do they do there?' said Bragg.

'What the name says,' said Levi. 'It was established a couple of decades ago, funded by a private foundation. According to my informer, it's where the terminator gene virus was created and is being produced. The test date is 27 August and today is the seventeenth. We've got ten days to find a way in there – and destroy it.'

'Any idea how we're going to get inside?'

'Give me a break! I only discovered the location yesterday. There's not much information available about the place. That's our first task, after we set up.'

'How can you be so sure about the date?' said Thornton.

After a considerable hesitation, Levi said, 'A high-level contact, sympathetic to our cause, has taken an enormous risk to find out. I'll take no more questions on that topic.'

'Where are we setting up?'

'Those apartment towers straight ahead.'

A cluster of white towers, twelve storeys high, sprouted up near the eastern side of City Park. Levi drove into the underground car park and stopped next to the lift. He handed the keys to Siah and got out. She slid across to the driver's seat.

'Bragg, Thorn,' said Levi. 'Stand close while I work the lift. Shield me in case there's a security camera.'

Levi swiftly popped the lift control panel and plugged in a device similar to a remote control. 'Wait till the doors open,' he said to the others, 'in case it's got passengers.'

The lift was empty. Thornton and Bragg carried the suitcases in, including a large one that shook violently. Levi sent the lift non-stop to the top floor, the twelfth. They followed him along the hall to an apartment at the end. He slid an electronic key into the door and it opened. They went in and he locked the door behind them.

'The rest of this floor is vacant,' said Levi. 'The reason I picked it.'

'That was lucky,' said Thornton.

'Not really. New Orleans has the highest vacancy rate in the country. The population has gone down by a third over the past decade.'

'Rats leaving the sinking city,' said Gretel.

'You really don't like humanity much, do you?' Irith muttered.

'Where's Siah going?' Bragg said hastily.

'She's getting rid of the van, just in case.'

'What do you mean, "just in case"? If it could have been tracked here –'

'All vehicles are tracked in cities and on main highways,' said Levi. 'I've taken precautions. I changed the plates last night, as well as the van's inbuilt ID beacon and the locator chip they don't tell anyone about. Even so, it was time to get rid of it.'

'I suggest you freshen up, have something to eat and a nap. We'll get together at noon. That's two hours and forty minutes.'

Irith's room was small and undecorated. Everything was grey, including the carpet and the mould. She hung up her clean clothes, put the dirty ones in a plastic bag, showered and washed her hair, then lay on the bed. The next she knew, someone was knocking on the door.

'Irith? The meeting!' It was Levi, already looking harried.

'What's that banging noise?' she said, sliding off the bed.

'Vaiha, trying to break his door down. I had to lock him in.'

'Poor man. What are you going to do about him?'

'I've no idea. Be quick.'

'Levi?' she said.

'Yes?'

'Have you heard anything from your mole in the President's office?'

'No. I'm afraid to make contact again, with Security on such alert.'

'Isn't that going to make things difficult?'

'More than you know.'

CHAPTER TWENTY-FIVE

The others were sitting around a long table in the main room when Irith got there, barefoot and her hair unbrushed. Gretel gave her a cold stare. Siah, looking freshly scrubbed, slid a plate of sandwiches towards her.

Irith took one and sat back. Levi spread a large-scale map on the table. It showed the research facility, the surrounding streets and an arc of the lake. 'We know where we have to go. Here! And what to do – destroy the virus and all the equipment used to make it. We just have to determine the trivial matter of how to do it.'

'A tactical nuclear missile would come in real handy right now.' Bragg grinned.

'Very helpful,' said Gretel. 'As usual.'

'I don't think a little light-hearted humour does any harm,' said Levi. 'Certainly less than sniping and backbiting. First of all, we need good intelligence about the facility. Some will be easy to obtain, some extremely difficult. There's a reasonable view from my window, including the gates. That's another reason why I chose this apartment. I'll set video equipment up. Irith, I'd like you to monitor the tapes and prepare a report for tomorrow, this time.'

Irith nodded and he went on. 'I've already done a preliminary search for the technical details of the site: building plans, sewerage, drainage, communications conduits and so forth. They're proving difficult to obtain –'

'I thought you could crack into any computer on the planet?' said Thornton.

'Even if I could, every time I hacked into a secure system I'd be taking a risk. They could have someone watching whose skills are the equal to my own, or greater. Now we've got this close, I'm avoiding all unnecessary risks. On the other hand, the facility was built before the Global Congress was formed, so the information we're looking for could be found in a hundred databases: for example, in old engineering conference proceedings, consultants' archives, local government files, college dissertations and real estate guides. We'll have to be creative.

'Gretel, track down the service details and the building plans. Report back to us tomorrow at midday.'

She saluted with one finger.

'Siah,' said Levi, 'you'll walk around the facility, secretly filming it from across the street. Use an EM-shielded camera. You won't see much, except through the gates, but you never know what may be useful.

'Thorn, look into the flood situation for the whole area from the West End yacht harbour to Lakefront Airport. Concentrate on the location and heights of levees, floodgates, canals and bayous, pumping stations and locks. Get the current river and lake heights, height predictions based on rainfall in the upstream catchment, tides, historical flood heights, storm surges and so And get the weather forecasts for the next two weeks.'

'What do you want all that for?' said Thornton.

'I don't want to spend a week planning an attack, only to discover we can't do it for some reason we should have identified at the beginning.

'Bragg, you'll work with me on this one. We need to identify all military and law enforcement facilities within four hours' drive, or one hour by helicopter, from the centre of the city. Religious militias, too. Plus the hospitals, ambulance and fire stations, emergency services, airports and heliports, and so on.'

'Shouldn't take long,' said Bragg. 'I know the area well.'

'Good, because I've plenty more for you. Get a radio frequency scanner and log all the communications frequencies used at the facility: phones, walkie-talkies, microwave and infrared networks, and so forth. We'll need the details so we can jam them, later. All right, everyone? We'll meet again this time tomorrow and I'll have a five-minute verbal report from each of you, plus all the backup details in spreadsheets and on maps. Let's get stuck into it.'

'We'd better do something about the great man,' said Siah. Vaiha was still banging on his door.

'What did you have in mind?' asked Bragg.

'Removing all communications devices from his room, and all methods of signalling or breaking out.'

'I did that before we put him inside,' said Levi.

'Then sedate him again and put a bolt on the outside.'

'Poor bastard,' said Bragg.

'All right,' said Levi at noon the following day, 18 August. 'What do we have? Gretel?'

She stood up. 'I looked carefully at the underground services, since we're used to breaking into facilities that way. No luck. The water table is less than a metre below the surface in that part of town, and only maintained at that level by constant pumping. Therefore, everything below a metre is saturated.'

She tapped her keyboard and a map flashed up on the wall screen. 'This is a composite plan. Any tunnels, conduits or pipes that ran under the facility grounds have been plugged or rerouted, and the water and sewerage lines aren't big enough to crawl through.' She traced them out, one by one, with a yellow laser pointer. 'Even if we cared to swim through shit. There's no way in from underground.'

'A pity,' said Levi, 'though not unexpected. We'll take a more detailed look later on. What about stormwater drainage?'

'Open channels, visible to the patrolling guards. They pass through the perimeter walls here and here, and into the city's stormwater pumping system. The wall passages have gratings that couldn't be pulled out with a dozer, and they're alarmed and inspected hourly.'

'Thanks, Gretel. Irith?'

Irith played the video she had cut down from Levi's recordings. 'The three buildings of the facility, called Buildings One, Two and Three, lie on an arc in the centre of the compound. Building Three is closest to the levee, Building One is in the middle and Building Two furthest away. They're thirty or forty metres apart, but connected at the third floor by aerial walkways that run from Building Three to Building One, and Building One to Building Two. There's no direct connection between Buildings Two and Three.'

She pointed out the heavily reinforced front and rear gates, the defences of the three buildings and the solidity of the walls.

'This barracks, beside the rear gate, sleeps at least two dozen guards. Ten are on duty at any time, patrolling inside the walls in random patterns. The roofs of the three buildings are flat and surrounded by walls a metre high. Each has structures for air-conditioning, cooling towers and so forth. Building Three also has a communications tower with a number of antennae mounted on it, as well as microwave and satellite dishes. These objects here, on the roof walls, are surveillance cameras watching the perimeter walls and grounds.'

'Okay,' said Levi. 'The basements are probably connected underground as well, but that doesn't help us if we can't get in.'

'What about employee movements, visitors, deliveries and shipments?' asked Bragg.

'There weren't many deliveries or shipments. Three delivery trucks came during the day but they weren't allowed inside. Everything was unloaded in this covered embayment at the rear gate.'

'Do you know anything about that, Siah?' said Levi.

'Everything that comes in is scanned, then loaded onto a guarded underground conveyor. Inside the wall it discharges to another conveyor, which takes the deliveries underground for distribution to the three buildings.'

'We'll come back to that,' said Levi. 'Go on, Irith.'

'Five other vehicles, all passenger cars, went in and out, but all were thoroughly searched, including bug sweeps.'

'What about the workers?'

'I didn't get the precise number but it's about three hundred and seventy. They all go through security checkpoints.'

'Siah?' said Levi.

'Very thorough,' said Siah. 'Bug sweeps, strip search, scanners, rectal probes – the lot!'

'What, every day?'

'Yes.'

'They *are* serious,' said Bragg.

'Anything else, Irith?' said Levi.

'No.'

'Thank you. Siah?'

'The facility has a three-layer wall, almost certainly steel reinforced, topped with razor wire. We identified a variety of security and alarm systems to detect break-ins. There could be others.'

She ran her perimeter video, fast-forwarding along the first wall section to the front gate, and froze it there. 'As Irith indicated, the front and rear gates are strongly reinforced. A tank might break through if it could get past the crash barriers, but nothing else would – not even a heavily laden truck.'

They studied the image. 'What do you think, Thorn?' said Levi.

'Even if we could crash through, we can't fight a gun battle to get inside.'

'Go on, Siah.'

She restarted the tape. 'We can't tell the strength of the wall from here, but –'

'I came across some images of the construction phase,' said Gretel. 'It's heavily reinforced. You couldn't crash through it, either.'

'Okay, we can't break in,' said Levi. 'I didn't expect to.'

'What about flying in with rocket packs or gyrocopters?' said Bragg.

'The motion detectors would pick us up, and the guards would slaughter us in the air.'

'The same goes for sneaking over the razor wire with protective matting, I suppose,' said Bragg.

'There are at least three separate wall security systems,' said Levi. 'There's a Maxi-Fence Electronic Taut Wire intrusion detection system, combined with electric barbed tape that gives a non-lethal shock and sets off an alarm, and a multi-zone smart-sensing motion detector set-up. I believe they aren't linked into the network, so there's nothing we can do to sabotage the systems from outside. I don't see how they can be bypassed with the resources we have, though I'll be devoting more effort to that. Let's have a look at that conveyor system, Siah.'

'You can't see much.' She brought up the wall embayment, running the video back and forwards until she found the best angle.

Bragg leaned forward. 'There are two guards, in addition to the security personnel. And another in that booth behind the glass. See the shadow there? And the booth is bound to be armoured.'

'Everything passes through a variety of scanners,' said Siah. 'Anything that's the least bit suspicious is opened right there.'

'And I understand,' said Levi, 'that a large percentage of the packages are opened randomly. We can't get in that way either.'

'If we had a helicopter gunship . . .' Bragg said wistfully.

'Boys' toys,' sneered Gretel.

Thornton gave her a rare black look. 'It's a bloody good idea. I'd be prepared –'

'We're not going to start a war,' said Levi. 'Even if we could steal a Blackhawk or two, and pilots, we couldn't do it without alerting the military. Besides, the facility probably has anti-aircraft defences. Let's have a look at your video again, Irith.'

Levi zoomed in on two locations inside the walls. One turned out to be an equipment storeroom, or possibly an armoury, but the other contained a compact air-defence missile system consisting of a bunker-like control centre and a pair of launchers.

Taking the laser pointer, Thornton drew light circles around the bunker. 'It's a Strela-10M6 air-defence missile system. Russian built – cheap but reliable. They've been around for decades, and they can bring down their targets in all kinds of jamming environments, optical and thermal. They're not so accurate at night, though, unless they're fed radar data.'

'There's no radar here,' said Bragg.

'Doesn't mean they don't have a feed from somewhere else,' Thornton retorted. 'This is going to cause us problems, Levi. A strange chopper approaching the facility would end up a ball of flame in the lake before it got within a couple of kilometres.'

'Unless the visibility was really poor,' said Bragg. 'Like in a storm.'

'You're talking crap!' said Siah. 'Even if it is restricted airspace over the facility –'

'Which it is,' said Bragg.

'. . . America isn't *quite* a police state yet. They can't just shoot down a helicopter that happens to stray into their airspace.'

'But should an unauthorised chopper attempt to land on top of one of the buildings,' said Levi, 'it'd be different.'

'But we *can* approach it,' said Bragg. 'And maybe, if the weather's bad enough, we might get down and off again.'

'*Might* isn't good enough,' said Levi. 'We'd better find out more about the missile defences.'

'All right,' said Thornton. 'We can't sneak in underneath, or through the conveyor, or over the walls. A direct attack on the gates and the walls is out, and so is an assault from the air unless we can neutralise the missile defences first, which seems unlikely. The only thing left is to break the security systems and go in with false identities.'

'I can't break them,' said Levi. 'I told you, they're isolated from the network. You can't crack into a system if there's no way to connect to it.'

'What about a radio connection, or infrared, or –' Irith began.

'That still requires the correct receiver or sensor at the other end. If it's not there, and as far as I can tell none is linked to the security system, it's still not possible to get in. The same applies to tapping into the communication cables running into the facility. The security system, as far as I can determine, is designed to be completely separate. And there are manual overrides. If, say, I managed to hack in and turn off the security system along a portion of the wall, it would set off alarms which can only be reset manually. The officer on duty would turn the system back on and a patrol would go to check. No one can beat that kind of set-up from outside, except with overwhelming force.'

'You seem to have eliminated every possibility of getting in,' said Siah. 'Is there another way, or are we just wasting time? Time that we have little of.'

'I have an idea,' said Levi. 'It's . . . pretty radical.'

'If it involves huge explosions, you'll get Thorn's vote,' Siah said caustically.

'Er, it does, actually.' Levi looked sheepish.

'Great!' said Siah.

'Under the present situation,' said Levi, 'there doesn't seem any feasible way for us to get in.'

'No,' said Bragg.

'But if the situation were to change,' Levi continued, 'due to some external force, the possibilities readjust themselves in our favour.'

'Don't talk in riddles,' snapped Thornton. 'Just tell us what you have in mind.'

'Thorn, show us your map of the facility and the nearby lake.'

He did so. 'This is the US Army Corps of Engineers' hurricane protection map sheet 2–35,' he said. 'The Corps is responsible for flood and hurricane protection, as well as dredging and maintaining the waterways of the Mississippi and delta. The area in blue is the lake. Who's got the laser pointer?'

Siah tossed it to him.

'Here's the Mississippi,' Thornton went on. 'The city lies between it and the lake. The facility is here, at Lake Vista.' He circled it with the pointer. 'These floodwalls are designed to stop the Mississippi from entering New Orleans from the south, even in normal flow. Likewise, this levee system stops Lake Pontchartrain, which with sea level rise is now a marine bay, from flooding the city from the north. The high-water mark is just 1.3 metres below the top of the lake levee, so under certain wind conditions the levee can overtop, causing minor flooding of this part of the city.'

'Very good,' said Levi. 'Enlarge the map so we can see just the facility, the streets around it and the edge of the lake.'

The new image came up. They stared at it in silence.

'What's the levee made from, Thorn?' said Levi.

'Compacted earth or clay, for the most part. Some sections have a facing of rock, geotextile fabric or interlocking concrete slabs, to prevent erosion. This section, between Lakeview and the Lakefront Airport, is faced with rock but some of it is eroding. Small gullies have begun to form on the lake side in several places, including here, opposite the facility. Repairs are scheduled for September.'

'Thanks, Thorn,' said Levi. 'All right, everyone, here's my proposal. We attack the levee by boat at night, here and here.' He marked two points opposite the facility. 'We blow holes right through it. If we do it properly, a tidal wave of lake water will tear the perimeter walls of the facility out of the ground and wash the guard posts away. While they're trying to deal with that we go in, by boat or in a hired chopper, do the job in a few minutes and get out again.'

There was a deafening silence.

'It'd have to be one hell of a hole,' said Bragg.

'It doesn't have to wash all the walls away,' said Levi. 'If we do it in the middle of the night, the flood would create total confusion. Our opportunity.'

'But . . . the lake could flood into the city,' said Irith.

'That would take hours,' said Levi. 'And the emergency response here is first-class. They've been living with the threat for decades.'

'This is madness, Levi,' said Siah. 'What if the whole levee gives way?'

'It won't. It'll just be a small break – the Corps will deal with it in half an hour.'

'What if there's a major collapse?' said Siah. 'The current would be incredible. It'd cut through the core of the levee like an axe through cheese and nothing could stop it. You could drown a hundred thousand people.'

CHAPTER TWENTY-SIX

'There are contingency plans for levee breaks,' said Levi.

'They're not designed for holes the size of a building!' said Siah.

'I'm aware of that,' he said testily. 'I don't like it either but it's the only idea I can come up with that has a chance of success. If anyone has a better idea, I'd love to hear it, because we've only got eight days left.'

'The idea is insane,' said Irith.

'And the damage would run into billions,' said Siah.

'We're trying to stop a lunatic and you're worried about money!' Gretel shouted. 'I don't believe I'm hearing this.'

'The livelihoods of tens of thousands will be ruined. That's no trivial thing.'

'We're prepared to lay down our lives – all they'll lose is a few lousy bucks!'

'The idea stinks, and if you actually gave a shit for humanity you'd realise it.'

'Calm down, everyone,' said Levi. 'Go on, Siah.'

'I'd want to see a lot better planning, and realistic chances of success, before I could agree to it.'

'I feel the same way,' said Irith. 'We don't know enough about the virus. Is it really that bad that it's worth risking all those lives?'

'Breaking the levee isn't a plan,' said Levi. 'It's just an idea. If we decided to go with it, we'd calculate the flow needed and design the break in the levee to be the smallest that would do the job. Ideally during bad weather and at night.'

'We're in the stormy season,' said Bragg. 'With luck we'd have a couple of bad weather nights in the next week.'

'It'll take at least two more days to plan and organise and plan everything, which only leaves a window of six days. What's the medium-range forecast?'

'Much the same for the next three days – hot and humid. After that, unsettled for a few days with a good possibility of rain and thunderstorms, then back to hot and humid around 26 August.'

'We can't leave it to the last minute,' said Levi. 'Our best chance is to plan the attack for the stormy days, say the twenty-second to the twenty-fifth.'

'What about getting out again after the job is done?' said Irith.

'I . . .' Levi looked down at the table, which gave him no inspiration at all. 'I'm not sure we will be able to get away. Once we blow the levee, it'll be seen as terrorism on a September 11 scale, and even if we use a chopper the chance of escaping will be remote.'

'You're so sure the virus has to be destroyed,' said Siah, 'yet you haven't told us why. What do you know that we don't?'

Levi twisted his fingers together. 'It came from my high-level contact in Lindstrom's office. Someone I know and trust absolutely.'

'Who?' said Thornton.

'I can't say. If there's even a hint of a mole, he'll purge everyone in his office.'

'What did your contact tell you?' Irith asked.

'That the terminator project was targeted at certain races or nations and had to be destroyed at any cost.'

'And what *is* the virus?'

'That was our job, but the answer must have been in the files we didn't recover.'

'You'd better go back to your contact and find out,' said Siah.

'I daren't take the risk.'

'Yet you're asking us to risk our lives, and the lives of innocent people. It's not good enough.'

'I'm with Siah,' said Bragg.

Levi looked around the table. 'Thorn? Gretel?'

'Yes,' they said.

Levi bowed his head. 'I'll go back to my contact, though I suspect . . . No matter. Let's get together at five o'clock.' He rose and trudged off to his room.

When everyone re-assembled, he was already at the end of the table, and his face was a yellowy shade of grey. 'I think I've just killed my contact,' he said bleakly.

'What happened?' cried Irith.

'I received the acknowledgment code but the message immediately cut off and a Security program was already backtracking the source. I had to do an emergency escape and I'm not sure it worked in time.'

'What are you saying, Levi?' said Bragg.

'I may have blown our cover.'

'What do we do?'

'We either pull out completely, abandon the job, or sit tight and pray.'

He looked up, directly into Irith's eyes. In spite of the heat, she shivered. He looked like a man who had unwittingly betrayed his best friend.

'What are you going to do?' she said softly.

'I'm going on. How can I do otherwise?' He looked around the circle, not begging, just showing his own resolve. 'I'll do everything in my power to hide us.'

'That's good enough for me,' said Bragg. 'I'm with you.'

One by one the others agreed. Levi's eyes touched Irith's, questioningly.

'As long as you can find a way to do it without risking a city,' she said.

They sat down again at dinner, a gumbo proudly manufactured by Bragg. The dish wasn't a success, being so mucilaginous it could have been used as a personal lubricant.

'Guess I went a bit overboard on the okra,' Bragg said apologetically.

'Told you so,' said Siah. 'You just won't listen, big boy.'

Levi rapped on the table. 'Shall we get on? Irith, you had something to say, I believe.'

'If we were to go with this plan, what can be done about making it safer?'

'Minimal design,' said Levi. 'Bragg's the engineer; he'll work on that. And we'll anonymously notify the authorities of the break as soon as it occurs, so they can implement their emergency response plan.'

'How long do we have to think of alternatives?'

'Until tomorrow. I'll start preliminary planning on this option right away. Whatever we decide, the go-ahead can be no later than midday tomorrow. So those of you who don't like this idea, and I'm one of them, get working on alternatives.' Levi picked up his laptop and his notes, nodded curtly and went to his room.

'He isn't happy,' said Bragg.

Neither was Vaiha. In the end room, he was screaming and kicking at the door. Irith felt guilty, yet helpless.

'I like the plan,' said Gretel. 'If we don't do anything, a lot more people are condemned to die than the few at risk here.'

'I'm with you,' said Thornton.

No surprise there, thought Irith. It was rare for the twins to disagree. 'Isn't the "good cause" argument the one Lindstrom uses to justify his policies?'

'I take it you're against breaking the levee?' said Gretel.

'I hate the idea.'

'Bragg?' said Siah.

'I'm a simple man,' he said. 'Let's get on with it.'

'You like it because it involves whacking big explosions,' said Siah pointedly. 'You're just a big boy, Bragg.'

'I admit it.'

'It's you and me then,' said Irith.

'The lesbian and dyke show,' sneered Gretel as she got up.

'If speaking sharply to your precious brother makes me a lesbian,' said Irith, 'I'm sure I'm in good company.'

'When this is over, Gretel,' Siah said with a smile, and only Irith knew how hard it was for her to pretend that she wasn't hurt, 'we're going to have a private chat. In the meantime,' she went on with cold ferocity, 'if you make one more allusion about my friend Irith, I'll bite your nipples off. Do I make myself clear?'

The bigger woman took an involuntary step backwards. 'I . . .'

Thornton came storming around the table, his face as red as cordial. 'Lay a finger on my sister and –'

'I can fight my own battles, Thorn,' said Gretel. 'It's nothing.' She linked her arm through his and drew him away.

'Thank you, Siah,' said Irith. 'But I can also fight –'

'I don't know what came over me. It's so hot here.'

Irith and Siah went to Irith's room and spent the rest of the evening going through scheme after scheme, possibility after possibility, but soon dismissed all as impracticable or unachievable. Their numbers were too few, they had too little time, and the facility was too well protected.

Siah threw herself on the bed. 'I can't think! See if there's anything mindless we can watch.'

Irith turned on the screen. 'I'll just check the weather first.'

The report showed hot and sticky weather for the next three days, with a band of storms moving in after that. Unsettled weather was then forecast through to 27 August. Siah reached for the remote.

Irith said, 'Hang on just a minute.'

Tropical storm watchers are keeping a close eye on a tropical depression that formed two days ago in the vicinity of the Cape Verde Islands, off the west coast of Africa. The system has been tracking steadily west ever since. Presently located some 500 nautical miles east of the Lesser Antilles, the depression is moving towards Martinique.

'That's a long way from here,' said Siah. 'Turn it over.'

They watched a soap opera so forgettable that Irith couldn't remember the names of any of the characters. Before it finished, Siah leapt up. 'I'm going to bed.'

She had a strange expression on her face. For an instant Irith thought Siah was going to break down.

Irith caught her by the hand. 'What's the matter?'

'My sister lives here, with her partner and their twin boys. My grandmother too.' She went out. The door closed behind her without a sound.

Levi called them to the meeting at noon. 'Where's Siah?' The outside door opened and she came in. 'Ah, there you are,' he said cheerily. 'Where have you been?'

'I went to see my sister, my little nephews and my grandmother,' she said. 'Possibly for the last time.'

There was a long silence.

'That's a blatant breach of security,' said Gretel. 'Levi . . .'

Levi waved her to silence. 'I didn't realise you had family here,' he said heavily. 'Even so, you should have asked first.'

'I had to go, whatever you said, so I thought I'd save you the angst.'

'Well, it's done now. Let's get on. Has anyone come up with a more workable method of attack than the one we discussed yesterday?'

No one replied.

'Anyone?' said Levi, looking in turn at the faces around the table.

'No,' said Irith.

'Neither have I. So now it comes down to it. Do we go ahead with the plan, or do we sneak away and let them win?'

'We go ahead,' said Gretel, and Thornton nodded his agreement.

'What about a cruise missile?' said Bragg. 'We could put it through any window you name.'

'I can't get hold of military hardware, Bragg,' said Levi patiently, 'and even if I could, I don't plan to do something that would necessarily kill hundreds of people in the facility.'

'Is there no alternative to going in?' said Irith.

'No. Before we destroy the virus, we've got to make absolutely sure we're in the right part of the facility, and we can only do that from inside.'

'All right,' said Bragg. 'We proceed with your plan, Levi. I'm sorry, Siah.'

'Siah?' said Levi.

'What can I say?' she said. 'My sister Mia lives here, her partner Jack, their twin boys Niki and Charli. And my grandmother.'

'Everyone in New Orleans is related to someone,' said Gretel. 'Vote! Either for it or against it.'

'What if they were given advance warning?' said Irith.

'We can't give advance warning,' said Levi. 'The reasons are obvious. Do they live near the facility?'

'No. They're south-west, at Jefferson Heights.'

'That's miles away,' said Bragg. 'They're not in much danger.'

'Can they be warned at the same time as emergency services?' begged Irith. 'Please.'

'I dare say that can be managed,' said Levi. 'Siah?'

'All right,' she said. 'It's wrong but I'll vote for it, since the alternative is worse.'

'Irith?'

'I'll go along with it, for the moment.' Her conscience was even less clear on the matter than she imagined Siah's to be, but Irith would have to come to terms with that. Or not, if the unimaginable did happen.

'Good. Let's get to it.'

CHAPTER TWENTY-SEVEN

Two days later, on 21 August, Irith sat in on the planning meetings for breaking the levee. Bragg had calculated that a breach some sixteen metres long, and down to three metres below lake level, would release enough water to overwhelm the closest walls of the facility.

'The flood will dam against the side and southern walls,' said Bragg, indicating them with the laser pointer, 'inundating the gates, the barracks and pouring into the entrances of the three facility buildings. With a bit of clever design the flood might also overwhelm the anti-aircraft defences.'

'Where does the water go then?' asked Irith.

'It'll either push the walls over, flow round them or over the top. Some will flood west into the Orleans Outfall Canal, some east into Bayou St John. Most should spread south, over or under Robert E. Lee Boulevard, then spill east and west into the same waterways. Stormwater from these points is pumped into the lake, but the pumps won't be able to cope with this kind of flow. Even so, it'll be at least twenty minutes before a measurable amount floods into the city. Time enough for people nearby to get to safety.'

'What about the people of Lake Vista? They won't have any warning.'

'Most of the old mansions are derelict; there's only a few squatters there,' said Levi. 'I'll do what I can.'

'We'll need two boats,' said Thornton, the explosives expert. 'If we used only one, I'd take too much explosive and there might be unplanned effects.'

'What does that mean?' said Irith.

'An uncontrollable ten-metre-deep hole, or even total collapse of part of the levee,' said Bragg.

'The boats will come into shore simultaneously,' Thornton went on, 'here where the levee armouring has eroded.' Taking the laser pointer, he marked the locations. 'They'll be scuttled and sink to a depth of three metres, lying against the levee, and then we'll set . . .'

Irith had to leave the room. The cold, clinical planning of such destruction was too horrible. When she returned half an hour later, the three men had agreed on the details and were planning the assault on the facility.

'I haven't been able to learn as much as I'd hoped about the building interior layouts,' said Levi. 'Management, administration, record-keeping, the library, canteen, first-aid centre and other communal facilities appear to be in Building One. That's the one in the centre. Building Two may be involved in the project: it mainly does virus research and design. According to my information, which I hope is correct, Building Three is where they did the terminator gene research, and where they culture a whole variety of gene-tailored viruses, mostly for legitimate medical purposes.'

'So we've got to get into Building Three, and maybe across to Two as well. That makes it complicated,' said Thornton.

'If we can get better intelligence,' said Levi, 'we may be able to eliminate Building Two.'

'Why not destroy all three buildings, just to be sure? They may keep backup stocks of the virus.'

'Totally destroying the contents of three buildings is too big an ask,' said Levi. 'Okay, how to get in?'

'There'll be so much wild water and so much debris in it,' said Bragg, 'that using boats isn't an option. It's got to be a chopper – or two.'

'I'm having trouble getting the right kind, but you can leave that to me and Siah,' said Levi.

'I've had an idea about the anti-aircraft facility.'

'What's that?'

'Have a look at this topographic map.' Bragg brought it up on screen. 'The ground slopes across the site towards the corner where the missile defences are. If we could shape the cut in the levee this way – I'll do a quick-and-dirty flow model to see if it's feasible – we might be able to wash the missile defences down into Bayou St John.'

'That would certainly take the pressure off,' said Levi. 'Though, it has to be said, boats filled with explosive form a very blunt instrument. Now, assuming that the guards and missile defences are out of action, how do we get into Building Three?'

'From the roof, by chopper,' said Thornton. 'In all the chaos, and on a dark, stormy night, they might not realise we're there.'

'What if the roof doors lock automatically, or there are high-security areas?' said Irith.

'Thorn will take care of that,' said Levi.

'Hacking in could take a lot of time,' said Irith.

'I'll be using my own hacking system,' said Thornton. 'High explosives. Blow the shitter out of it and *bam*! Instant access!' He chuckled.

The hairs rose on the back of Irith's neck. Thornton enjoyed his work too much. How could she ever have admired him? Slept with him? What the hell went on behind those beautiful eyes of his?

Levi gave Thornton one of those mildly inscrutable glances he was so famous for. Irith could read it by now. Levi appreciated Thornton's skills, but did not like him.

'For once I agree with you,' Levi said. 'We blow our way in.'

'And when we are in?' said Irith.

'That's your department. You've got to do four things: find out where they did the research, where they keep the stock and where they culture the virus.'

'What's the fourth?' said Irith, overwhelmed.

'If there's time, try to find documents linking the project to Lindstrom and the Congress – solid evidence of a conspiracy. It's the only thing that can save us after the job's done.'

'What if people refuse to talk?'

'The documents will be in their computers,' said Levi. 'Once we're inside, access won't be a problem.'

'Time will be,' said Thornton. 'We'll only have a few minutes. So we take a couple of hostages and threaten to blow their brains out unless someone tells us exactly where the virus is.'

'What if they won't talk?' said Irith, her skin crawling.

'It won't come to that,' Levi said. 'Threaten ten people and two or three will talk, no matter how top-secret it is. We'll grill them separately and compare their stories.'

'Just remember who we're dealing with here, Irith,' Thornton said coldly. 'We don't have time for the niceties. Here's how I'd do it,' he said to Levi. 'We land and blow the roof door – two minutes. We find the terminator virus floors – ten minutes. We set out the incendiaries while Irith and Gretel look for evidence – another ten minutes. Whether we find it or not, we piss off back to the roof and fire the incendiaries remotely from the chopper – five minutes. Elapsed time, twenty-seven minutes, and even that's too long if we hope to get away.'

Every time he opened his mouth, Irith felt more uncomfortable.

'And if we knew exactly where to go,' said Levi, 'that's how we'd do it. Unfortunately we don't, and any number of things could go wrong . . .'

'So flexibility is essential,' said Bragg. 'About getting away. They'll be after us in minutes; they'll shoot us down.'

'What about we go out the back door into a jet boat,' said Thornton, 'and have a chopper pick us up from the other side of town?'

'How are we going to get a jet boat there?' said Levi.

'Siah can park it across the street on a trailer. When the flood hits, she cruises in through the broken walls and picks us up.'

'If the wall doesn't collapse,' said Bragg, 'we're stuffed.'

'We take the chopper,' said Thornton.

'It's too cumbersome,' said Levi. 'And there are too many ways it can go wrong.'

'Not if it's planned properly.'

'All right. Put a plan together and we'll go through it. If it's too risky, we take the chopper from the roof. Just make sure the boat is reliable. We'll look a prize pack of fools if the engine won't start.'

'We don't make those kinds of mistakes,' said Thornton. 'We'll have a backup, in any case.'

'How do we stop Security tracking us if we do get away?' said Bragg.

'We jam their communications,' said Thornton.

Levi shook his head. 'I can't jam military communications.'

Thornton looked irritated. 'You're a survivor, Levi. You've always got a way out, so spill it.'

'This operation will engender the biggest manhunt since September 11,' said Levi. 'They'll close every airport, highway, waterway and back road for 500 kilometres around New Orleans. There'll be no fooling around with fake identities or iris transplants. The only thing that could save us is new faces on new bodies and all the papers to go with them. Or evidence that directly implicates Lindstrom or his Congress.'

Thornton was sweating now. 'But . . . I thought you'd have a way out.'

'Cold feet, Thorn? It's a bit late to back out now.'

'I gave my word and I'll be there to the bloody end.' He went out.

'What about you, Bragg?' said Levi. 'If you've got misgivings, now's the time to tell me about them.'

'I'm in this because I believe what we're doing is right,' said Bragg.

'Irith? You look as if there's something you want to tell me.'

She flushed and had to avoid his eye. 'I don't know what to believe, or who to believe in.'

'But you're pretty sure what you don't believe in,' Levi said shrewdly.

'I know that horrible things sometimes have to be done for the greater good, but I can't agree to breaking the levee. I'm really sorry.'

'I feared as much,' Levi said heavily. 'I admire your principles, Irith, but I've got no choice but to lock you up until it's over.'

'Like poor Vaiha.' She had been expecting it.

Bragg was studying her. Irith couldn't read his expression, though surely he was thinking that her problem was not a moral objection, but cowardice. Somehow, that mattered.

She went to her room and lay down on the bed with her eyes closed. The thought of what was coming made her want to vomit.

CHAPTER TWENTY-EIGHT

Irith had been locked in her sweatbox of a room for two days and already she felt like clawing at the walls. She felt a flood of empathy for Vaiha, although they no longer had to sedate him; he now spent twenty-one hours a day at a desk, writing furiously. Levi wouldn't allow him any kind of computer, in case he pulled it apart and fashioned a radio transmitter, but Vaiha had already filled three paper writing pads with mathematical calculations.

It was 23 August and the weather continued unrelentingly hot and humid. Sooty mould had begun to grow on the walls, the curtains and the leather of Irith's boots, but the longed-for storms had not come. The weather forecasts promised more of the same until 25 or 26 August, when there was some possibility of relief.

She spent most of her time obsessively studying the weather channels, as if she could single-handedly will storms upon the city. Not that it would help her moral dilemma. She wanted Levi to succeed, but not this way.

The tropical depression of a few days ago had turned into a hurricane, which had passed through the Lesser Antilles, causing minor flooding on Martinique, St Luca, Barbados and St Vincent, and was now drifting across the Caribbean towards Jamaica, gathering strength as it moved. On its present track it would have no effect on the United States. Irith prayed the hurricane would turn north; the wilder the weather the better. Nothing else could save them from this awful folly.

Sometime after midnight, she was woken by the click of the door and the light flicked on.

Irith shot up in bed. 'Who's there?'

'Don't panic,' said Levi.

She rubbed her eyes. 'What is it?'

'I've got something.' He had a strip of paper in his hand.

'What?' She had no idea what he was talking about.

'Something's come through from my mole in the President's office.'

'So he's not dead?' Irith still felt guilty about pressuring Levi.

'I don't know. The message was sent just after my initial contact and it's come by a very roundabout route.' He handed her the strip of paper.

Irith smoothed it out. It contained only four words: *IT'S IN THE CAG–*. 'What's that supposed to mean? Could it be, "It's in the cage"?'

'Who knows?' Levi called up a dictionary on the laptop that never left his side.

'If it is "cage",' said Irith, 'what kind of cage? A birdcage, a lift cage, gun cage, prison cage? It could have any number of special meanings.'

'Or the clue might be cryptic,' said Levi. 'A reference to John Cage, the avant-garde composer, perhaps.'

Irith consulted the dictionary. 'There are lots of places that begin with c-a-g. Cagliari, Sardinia; Caguas, Puerto Rico. But if that was the case, why does the message say "*the* cag–"?'

'Or a James Cagney gangster film,' said Levi, 'or a caguole, a lightweight anorak or monk's hood. It could be anything. I'll see you in the morning.'

Irith kept on with the puzzle but could make nothing out of it. Levi brought her breakfast the following morning, 24 August. She was reading the local news in the online *Times-Picayune*. There had been 627 murders in the city already this year – a record.

'Any luck with the message?' he asked.

'No.'

'I don't suppose you've changed your mind about working with us?'

'I can't, but . . .'

'Yes?'

'Can I come out for a while? I'm going spare in this room.'

'As long as I have your word that you won't attempt to communicate, in any way, any aspect of our plans to anyone outside this apartment.'

'I give you my word,' she said.

There was some muttering from Gretel and Thornton when she appeared, but Levi stilled it at once. Then Vaiha began to bang furiously on his door. 'Go and see what the matter is, Siah.'

'He wants more of that amphetamine. He says he can't work without it.'

'Christ, what a loser!' said Gretel. 'Can't we get rid of him? He's driving me insane.'

'In case you're forgetting,' Levi snapped, 'we wouldn't be here at all without him. We owe Vaiha, and I'm disgusted with myself for treating him the way we have.'

'I hope you're not asking me to buy more drugs for him,' said Siah.

'I don't dare take any unnecessary risks. He'll have to go without for a couple of days. He'll be all right, won't he?'

'I'm sure a few days won't make any difference.'

'If we survive this, I'll buy him a crate of the stuff,' said Levi.

When Siah gave the mathematician the news, he began to shriek and wail and bang on the door again, though it soon stopped. Siah checked through the spyhole and he was back at his desk, writing more furiously than before.

'Let's get on,' said Levi. 'The weather forecast is not looking good. Or rather, it's looking too good. There's little likelihood of storms today or tomorrow. It's possible in the early morning of the twenty-sixth, and slightly more possible that night, the last night before the test date. I didn't want to leave the attack to the last night – it makes our attack predictable if there's been any kind of leak – but the chances of success are so much greater if the weather is bad that it's worth the risk. How are the preparations going, Siah?'

'I've got everything organised except the choppers. They should come together today.'

'Thorn?' said Levi.

'The boats are ready, and the explosive. The detonators and ancillaries were a little harder to come by, but I have them too. Everything's ready for the levee-breaching operation.'

'Glad to hear it. What about the plastic explosive to break into the facility?'

'It's on its way,' said Thornton.

'And the incendiaries to destroy the virus?'

'I'm thinking I might use petrol, in jerry cans.'

Levi frowned. 'It's too dangerous. Any spark –'

'I wasn't planning to tip it out!' Thornton said sarcastically. 'I'm going to blow the jerry cans, two or three to each floor.'

'All right, but make sure there's enough. This virus is so contagious that once it gets out there's not a hope of stopping it. Gretel, have you completed analysis of my snoop data yet?'

'Nearly. Assuming we can believe the data, everything related to the Terminator Project is in Building Three, the building closest to the levee. It's a lucky break. If we can rely on the information, we won't have to go into the other buildings at all. Here's the file, if you want to look at it.' Gretel swung her laptop around.

'What makes you think we can rely on the data?' said Bragg quietly.

'It's consistent with what we know from independent sources,' Levi replied.

'But how independent are they? These people studied deceit at their mother's breast. All internal data must be regarded as suspect, unless proven otherwise.'

'I agree,' said Levi, 'but in this case, security of the terminator virus, and what they plan to do with it, would be paramount. It's logical to assume that everything would be kept in a dedicated centre.'

Irith sat back in her chair. Why would a terminator virus need such security, since it would affect all people equally? Was it targeted at a particular nation or ethnic group? But how could it be?

'Irith?' said Levi.

'Sorry. Did you ask me a question?'

'I asked you to have a look at Gretel's file. Which floors are we to target?'

Did Levi think she was back on the team? She wasn't. But, she rationalised, if they were going ahead with the levee-breaking plan anyway, surely they should have the correct information? Irith stared at the computer screen, not seeing it, consumed by her conflict.

'Irith?' he said irritably.

She started, then checked the file. 'According to this, the research laboratories are on floors three, four and five of Building Three, while the culturing laboratory is on floor six. If we can rely on this information, those are the only floors involved.'

'What else is there? I've got a feeling we've forgotten something.'

'Weapons,' said Bragg. 'We've got equipment for six people, including ammunition and body armour. The only thing we haven't been able to obtain is anti-personnel gas. I can get any amount of the latest capsicum mist, though.'

'That'll be no bloody good in a gun battle,' Thornton said sourly.

'But it'll do nicely in hand-to-hand fighting,' said Levi. 'Quick knockdown and quick dispersal. Get it.'

'What about the escape boat?' said Thornton.

Siah answered. 'No luck on a jet boat but I've got a sixteen-foot inflatable with twin outboards, all checked and fuelled up.'

'Splendid. You and Thorn are going to drive the other boats into the levee, right?'

'Yes. We'll arm the charges, pull the bottoms out, go nose-in to the levee and jump off as the boats go down.'

'Won't that be risky?' said Irith.

'The charges are triggered remotely,' said Thornton. 'We'll run along the levee for a couple of hundred metres, I'll blow the charges and immediately signal the chopper, which will be hanging in the air, hopefully in a storm. It'll pick me up. Once the flood takes out the facility wall, or overtops it, the chopper will carry everyone but Siah to Building Three. Hopefully the anti-aircraft gear will be out of action by then, or unmanned. If it's not, *boom*! Our troubles are over.'

'What if the flood doesn't take out the wall?' said Levi. 'What if the explosives don't even blow a hole through the levee?'

'They will, though what happens then is another matter. I can't predict exactly how big the break will be, or precisely where the flood will go. We'll have to decide whether to go in, or whether to abort.'

'If we blow the levee,' said Levi, 'we go in no matter what. I can't justify it to myself, otherwise. Hell, I can't justify it anyway.'

'Okay,' said Thornton.

'Top of the building, or bottom?'

'Top. The front or back doors are too risky. The floodlights are waterproof and may still be working, and one man with an automatic weapon could take out the lot of us.'

'Entry to the top of the building is solidly reinforced.'

'We can do it,' said Thornton.

'How do we get to the escape boat?'

'Before I blow the charges, Siah runs down the levee and gets the inflatable going. As soon as the flood comes by, she takes to the water and hides in the darkness. When we signal, she picks us up from the rear of Building Three.'

'It's too risky,' said Levi. 'What if she can't get through the broken wall? What if she's spotted, or attacked, or her props hit debris in the water?'

'If she doesn't answer the signal, we take off from the roof and try to outrun our pursuers.'

'What about Siah?' cried Irith.

She had been sitting quietly. 'I wasn't coming with you anyway. Security don't know my face – at least, I hope they don't. I'm staying behind to look after my family.'

'I hope you make it,' said Irith.

'I've a better chance than you all have.'

'That's not saying much,' said Bragg.

CHAPTER TWENTY-NINE

Hurricane Jemma, which has been upgraded to Category Three, has caused widespread damage and torrential rain in southern Jamaica and is now tracking towards Mocche on the Yucatan Peninsula. Present computer models predict that it will move south-west and weaken into a rain depression, causing widespread flooding between Coatzacoalcos and Ciudad Madero in eastern Mexico. There is, however, a chance that Jemma will move north-west towards the coast of Texas. The National Weather Service has issued a Hurricane Watch for the Texas coast from Galveston through Brownsville.

'I was vaguely hoping it would come this way,' said Irith, 'and give you the cover you need to get away.'

'Don't you hope any such thing!' Siah said incredulously. 'If a major hurricane hits New Orleans, they'd need a freighter to carry away the dead!'

'Sorry, wasn't thinking.'

'It had some terrifying near misses in the last century,' said Siah. 'And that was before the sea rose six metres. One day, a hurricane is going to wipe it out.'

'How?' said Irith.

'Storm surge. The city was below sea level even before the sea rose, and the levees have barely kept pace with it. But an approaching hurricane, a big one, can cause a storm surge of three, four or even five metres. It would pour over the levees from one end to the other and nothing the Corps of Engineers could do would make the slightest difference. Every road out of the city crosses water, and the surge could come in so fast that the roads would be flooded. The only way out would be in a body bag.'

Irith couldn't think of anything to say. She walked over to the window, looking out at the lake in the darkness, and the lights of ships at anchor, awaiting their berths. There were dozens of them.

Siah selected *Hurricane Update*. 'Hurricane Jemma? Named after your mother, perhaps?'

'I suppose it's Lindstrom's idea of a joke.'

'You miss her.'

'All my life it was just her and me. My father died only days after I was born.'

'It must have been hard for you both.'

'It was harder for her – I never had him. I thought about him all the time, and compared him to other fathers I knew, but he was just an abstract.' Irith did not like talking about family matters to outsiders. 'How's Vaiha? I haven't heard a peep out of him lately.'

'Still working furiously.'

'I hope he's not dropping notes out the windows.'

'They're unbreakable. I feel so guilty. He trusted me. I hate this. I just *hate* it.' Siah's voice cracked. She sprang up and ran to the window.

Irith came up beside her. 'What is it?'

'I'm an organiser, not a damned marine! I hate guns, and the idea of going over there, armed and ready to kill . . . I can't take it, Irith.'

The next day, 25 August, dawned hotter, more humid and more unpleasant than the previous ones had been, if that was possible. The power had been off for most of the night and, even with the windows open and no clothes on, Irith sweltered in her bed. She was still locked in at night. Condensation ran down the bedroom walls and by 6.30 am it was so hot that she could not bear to lie on the sheets.

She checked the weather. There was no sign of the longed-for storm. Hurricane Jemma had, however, unexpectedly turned north-west in the night, wreaking havoc on Pinar del Rio, at the eastern tip of Cuba, before roaring towards Corpus Christie, Texas, at more than twenty knots. It had been upgraded again and now was Category Four, with a central pressure of 935 millibars and winds in the eyewall of 120 knots, 220 kilometres per hour. There was a Hurricane Warning for the entire coast of Texas and Hurricane Watches for the remainder of the Gulf Coast.

'Is tonight going to be the night?' she said to Levi at breakfast.

He shook his head. 'There's something going on at the facility. People are running around the grounds everywhere. It looks like they're preparing for an official visit.'

'Perhaps they are,' said Irith. 'Maybe there's going to be some kind of ceremony on the twenty-seventh.'

'I . . . shit, I should have thought of that!' Levi punched his right fist into his left hand. 'We should have planned it for tonight, no matter what the weather. Tomorrow will be worse. Too late now.'

'Why too late?'

'We need a day's notice so everything can be checked, and all the equipment tested and calibrated. If we don't do it, something will go wrong when it's too late to do anything about it.'

Irith was perversely glad. Anything was better than deliberately breaking the levee and she prayed something would happen to make the mission impossible. She felt disloyal, but it was better than feeling like a terrorist.

At lunchtime, Bragg pushed Irith's door open. 'Ready?'

She sat up and turned the screen off. 'For what?'

'We're going out. Didn't Levi tell you?'

'No.'

'Must've slipped his mind. Come on. Bring a hat.'

She pulled on sandals and found a hat. 'Where are we going?'

'I'm taking you for a quick look at the city.'

'Thanks, Bragg! What's on in New Orleans today?'

'Precious little. August is the month all the smart people leave town. But the food's as good as ever.'

'What do I do if we're stopped?'

'We shouldn't be, except by panhandlers.'

They went out into the heat and humidity, and strolled along Bayou St John, past the grand old homes, many of them now abandoned and falling into ruin. Bragg gave Irith a running commentary of the city's history as they walked.

'This way,' he said, turning into City Park. They went by the Duelling Oaks, although Irith saw only one, and past the Museum of Art, but didn't go inside. She wanted to see the city, not paintings. They meandered through the park and down to Lake Vista, keeping well clear of the facility, then west along Lakeshore Park inside the monstrous levee, where the humidity was out of control and there wasn't a breath of air, to West End.

'It's so hot!' Irith wiped perspiration off her brow. 'Are we going much further?'

'Not on foot,' he said. 'I wanted you to see a bit of the city from the ground. You get a better feel for a place once you've walked it. Let's get something to eat.'

They had lunch at a restaurant outside the levee, overlooking the yacht harbour. Irith had a cup of gumbo followed by blackened redfish, Bragg the soft-shell crab and a jambalaya so hot he couldn't speak for ten minutes afterwards. It was pleasant sitting outside, in the shade and with a cooling breeze off the lake. They didn't talk, just enjoyed the moment. It would be the last good moment either of them would ever have, but she put that firmly out of mind..

They caught a cab to the Quarter, where they walked about, looking at the architecture, until she began to feel faint from the heat. They sat in an almost empty Cafe du Monde, near the river, and had iced coffee with chicory and beignets.

'Thanks, Bragg,' she said, picking up the crumbs with a damp finger.

'What for?'

'For giving me one last look at the real world.'

'It's not that bad.'

'I've been having feelings of doom for months now. I don't think any of us are going to survive.'

'I don't worry too much about the future any more,' he said. 'I used to, until I was taught to live for the day.'

'Then why are you here?'

'I didn't say I don't care. I said I don't worry.'

'I'm anxious about Siah. She's not coping,' Irith said.

'She's got a lot to think about.' Bragg signalled for the bill. 'We'd better get back.'

That night Hurricane Jemma changed direction again, turning abruptly northeast in the centre of the Gulf of Mexico and heading towards Tallahassee, Florida. The hurricane no longer posed a threat to Texas, however, Hurricane

Warnings were issued for the coasts of Louisiana, Mississippi, Alabama and Florida. An evacuation order was issued for coastal areas near the projected landfall. Then Jemma began to weaken, dropping to a Category Three.

'Is it usual for hurricanes to be as changeable as this?' Irith said to Siah at breakfast the next morning, 26 August.

'Perfectly normal. They can last for weeks, loop around in circles, die down and re-form, die down and re-form again. And their courses can't always be predicted, even with the best computer models available.'

'Category Three isn't so bad, though?'

'It's still a severe hurricane.'

'All right,' said Levi, banging on a cup with his teaspoon. 'Tonight is the night. The weather isn't going to offer as much concealment as I'd hoped, but that's the way it is.

'We'll stay in the apartment until after dark, then move to our respective stations. The levee breaking is timed for tomorrow morning, at 2 am precisely. Synchronise your watches, and the clocks in your gear, to the second. Irith, you'll be locked in your room while we do it. Siah will let you out afterwards.'

'What if you don't come back?' she said.

'Better pray we do,' said Bragg.

She spent the morning monitoring the National Weather Service bulletins, afraid for her friends and herself. At 10 am, when Hurricane Jemma was 500 kilometres east-south-east of New Orleans, it abruptly changed direction again, heading towards Pascagoula, only 150 kilometres to the east.

By 11 am, Jemma had intensified back to a Category Four hurricane, slowed and turned west-north-west, directly for Biloxi, 120 kilometres east of New Orleans. Shortly after that, a bulletin flashed onto Irith's screen.

HURRICANE JEMMA LOCAL ACTION STATEMENT
NATIONAL WEATHER SERVICE
NEW ORLEANS LA 11.30 AM CDT 26 AUG

Hurricane Jemma poses a major threat to life and property in south-east Louisiana and south Mississippi.

A hurricane warning is now in effect for south-east Louisiana and coastal Mississippi.

CRITICAL INFORMATION SUMMARY

LOCATION

At 10 am cdt, Hurricane Jemma was located near latitude 28.4 north, longitude 85.5 west, or about 320 miles south-east of New Orleans.

Jemma was moving west-north-west near 20 mph during the morning and is forecast to continue on that heading, slowing as it approaches the coast.

INTENSITY

Maximum sustained wind 145 mph with higher gusts. Jemma is currently a category 4 hurricane on the Saffir-Simpson Scale. Strengthening to category five is possible during the next 12 hours.

WINDS

Hurricane force winds, 74 mph or greater, will spread into coastal south-east Louisiana this afternoon and evening, then spread north-east across much of south-east Louisiana and south-west Mississippi during the night.

TIDES

Tides are already 2 feet above normal. They will increase to 3 to 4 feet above normal later this afternoon. Coastal flooding may cut off lower evacuation routes by 5 pm today. A storm surge of 10 to 14 feet is expected in many areas tonight and tomorrow. Local areas, including the tidal lakes pontchartrain and maurepas, may experience storm surge of 15 to 20 feet.

RAINFALL

No significant rainfall is expected this afternoon. Rainfall will increase tonight with up to 10 to 15 inches likely, higher amounts possible.

EVACUATIONS

Many parishes along the louisiana and mississippi coasts are ordering evacuations in coastal area. Shelters will be open at 3 pm today.

All roads out of the city of new orleans are closed until further notice. Those living inside the hurricane protection levees should complete all preparations before 4 pm today.

The hurricane continued to deepen; by the early afternoon, the central pressure had dropped to 912 millibars. Jemma was now Category Five, the strongest of all. Maximum sustained winds in excess of 160 knots were expected in the eyewall, nearly 300 kilometres per hour.

The wind, which had just been a breeze when Irith slid off her rancid sheets that morning, grew stronger every minute. The sky was covered in black cloud but it refused to rain. The temperature was as hot as ever and the humidity rose until her clothes began to drip.

The power went off. Used to blackouts by now, she pulled the curtains and looked out. The wind wailed around the corners of the building.

'I'm afraid,' she said to Siah, who had come in with a cup of peppermint tea.

'So am I.' Siah had been subdued since her outburst, as if she regretted revealing her vulnerability.

'I don't see how you can go ahead with the mission.'

'Nor I. Let's go and talk to Levi.'

'Am I allowed out now?'

'As far as I'm concerned.'

Levi, studying the weather channel on his laptop, looked like death. 'I knew I shouldn't have left it to the last day.' He trudged to the window, but the sky only reflected his torment. 'We're stuffed.'

Thank God, Irith thought. But, in the next breath, *So Lindstrom's going to get away with the Terminator Project after all. Whatever it really is. There had to be more to it than a sterilisation virus.*

'The hurricane's still heading for Biloxi,' said Siah.

Levi put his shiny head in his hands. 'But the storm surge, even from that distance, will probably overtop the levee. I can't break it now; it's too dangerous. Three years this mission has been in the planning. Three bloody years!'

'You don't have to cancel yet,' said Irith. 'The hurricane could turn away.'

'The weather forecasters think otherwise.'

They remained glued to their seats. The power came back on, briefly, then went out again. Jemma continued her stately march north towards Biloxi then, at four in the afternoon, veered gently north-west in the direction of Lake Pontchartrain. As far as New Orleans was concerned, that was the worst possible direction, since it would drive the storm surge directly up the lake.

Bragg put his head around the door. 'What's the latest?'

'There's a general evacuation order for coastal Louisiana and Mississippi,' said Levi. 'That's millions of people, and with many of the roads already flooded they probably can't get everyone out in time. The hurricane's moving too quickly.'

'What about inside the levees?' said Bragg.

'All roads are closed,' said Siah. 'Because full-scale evacuation of the city would take too long and there'd be a monumental gridlock. The airports and the port are closed too. Residents have been ordered to remain in their homes or offices and batten down.'

'The storm surge is already close to a metre and rising fast,' said Levi. His screen showed airborne views of the most critical levees. 'Waves are breaking over the levees near the University of New Orleans and at Pontchartrain Shores.'

'This is the one we've been dreading,' said Siah. 'When the hurricane hits, the storm surge will go three metres over the levee.'

'Pray it washes the facility into the sea, and the virus with it,' said Irith.

It's too contagious,' Levi said gloomily. 'Half the people in the city will get it without even knowing, and they'll give it to others. It'll spread across the planet within months.'

'What about a vaccine?' said Siah.

'It takes up to a year to develop a new one,' Irith replied. 'Even with the latest genetic engineering techniques. And it wouldn't reverse any damage the virus had already done.'

She went to the window. The sky was a threatening purplish-black. Irith turned away. The screen was comparing Hurricane Jemma to other hurricanes in the Gulf over the past decades.

Hurricane Jemma will be one of the most intense hurricanes ever to make landfall on the Gulf Coast. Only the monster Hurricane Camille, which struck Mississippi in 1969, was stronger. Camille, with a central pressure of 909 millibars and winds up to 165 knots, caused the highest storm surge on record: twenty-four feet. Hurricane Jemma is, however, a relatively small diameter hurricane, being only a hundred miles across with an eye of ten miles, so the damage, while severe, is expected to be more localised.

'That's something,' said Irith. She was getting an idea.

'The size won't affect the storm surge much,' said Levi.

'But it *will* affect the winds on the edge of the hurricane. And the surge comes ahead, doesn't it?'

'That's correct, and it's highest to the right-front of the eye. We're left-front on its present heading. The storm surge is like a great dome of water. It takes some time to rise, and to fall again afterwards.'

'What's the maximum wind speed it's safe to fly a chopper in, Levi?'

'Depends on the chopper. Little commercial models, only thirty or forty knots. Some of the big new search-and-rescue models can fly in winds of up to seventy or eighty knots, as long as they're not too gusty. Military ones can do better but we don't have access to them. Besides, the wind speeds in the eyewall will be 150 knots plus. Even if we had the best chopper in the world, it couldn't fly in that.'

'But it's not coming at us. The hurricane's heading towards the north side of the lake, thirty or forty kilometres away. We're in the left-front quadrant, so the winds here will be slower.'

'Not much!' He called up the latest wind simulation. 'If Jemma keeps to its present path, which we can't rely on, winds near the facility are forecast to increase to 100 to 125 knots, with gusts up to 140 knots. That's way too strong.'

'But the hurricane may move away, or may weaken. It may take a long time to get here. Anything can happen.'

'What are you saying, Irith? Are you back on the team?'

The words tumbled out of her. 'Of course I am! This is our chance, Levi. The water's already coming over the levee, so we're not risking anyone's lives except our own. And in the chaos of the hurricane, if we can get in and torch Building Three, we might even get away with it.

'Don't you see, Levi?' Irith clutched at his brown hands. 'We might be able to get in and out without anyone knowing. And tomorrow, no one will have the time to investigate one disaster among thousands. We can escape before anyone realises what we've done. It's perfect!'

'Except for one thing,' he growled. 'The choppers I'd organised are grounded and they aren't safe to fly in the conditions we're expecting by the time we could be ready.'

'What about your original plan?' said Bragg.

'It's too late to organise it,' he snapped. 'What's Vaiha up to?'

'There hasn't been a peep out of him this morning, although he was banging on the wall late last night.'

'Who took him his breakfast?' said Levi.

'I think Gretel was going to,' said Siah. 'I'd better check.' She was back a few minutes later. 'Seems Gretel thought I was doing it. I feel awful. I'll take him in a tray now.'

A few minutes later, they heard Siah scream. They ran into Vaiha's room. He was hanging by the neck from a piece of bared electric cord tied around one of the ceiling lights. His eyes were out of their sockets and his tongue touched the tip of his chin. Siah was on her knees on the floor. Her mouth was open but she made no sound.

They stood there in silence. 'Poor bastard,' said Bragg. 'He must have been dead since last night. Help me get him down, Thorn.'

They cut Vaiha down, laid him on the bed and covered him with a sheet. His body made such a little shape beneath it.

Levi sat on the bed, head in hands. Irith looked through the stack of writing pads. 'Take a look at this,' she said.

Vaiha had covered hundreds of pages with mathematical formulae and workings that were beyond her ability to comprehend, though they looked perfectly coherent. Then, halfway through the fourth writing pad, he began to repeat one algorithm over and over, about forty times on the page. The next twenty-two pages contained endless repetitions of the same formula. On the twenty-third page, midway through the formula, it changed to carefully drawn squiggles. The identical squiggles were repeated for another seventy-seven pages to the end of the pad, and that was all.

'He was right,' Siah said brokenly. 'He did go mad without the drug. He lost his talent and the torment was so unbearable that he took the only way out. We killed him, Levi. After all he did for us.' She began to weep.

'Well, he's dead,' said Thornton. 'We'd better get rid of the body before it stinks up the apartment.'

Siah threw herself at Thorn, pummelling him with her fists. Thornton fell backwards. 'What did I say?'

Bragg separated them, took Siah into his arms, and she wept as though the whole world had been destroyed. They left the room and closed the door behind them.

Levi sat down at the table. 'What a terrible day. And tomorrow's going to be worse.'

CHAPTER THIRTY

At 5 pm, Irith came in from the kitchen with tea, coffee and a tray full of mugs. Siah was standing by the window, staring at the sky. A shattered cup lay on the floor at her feet and she had bitten her fingernails to the quick. She kept shaking her head, over and over. Irith suspected she was having a breakdown and had no idea what to do about it.

Bragg was reading *A Confederacy of Dunces*. The choice seemed peculiarly appropriate. Thornton and Gretel were at the other end of the conference table, checking items off on a long list. Levi sat in the middle, making calculations on a pad.

'What was the original plan?' Irith asked. Levi looked up absently, then bent his head to his work again.

'Levi has an old friend near here,' said Bragg. 'An ex-military chopper pilot who does search-and-rescue work all along the Gulf, pulling people off collapsing deepwater oil platforms and so forth. He flew in one of the wars in Afghanistan decades ago, didn't he, Levi?'

'Yes.' Levi's voice was dead.

'What *original* plan?' Irith repeated.

'Jack's absolutely the best in a crisis, and has the best machine. But . . . if we'd broken the levee he would have been risking life and livelihood, and I couldn't ask that of him. '

'But now we're just taking advantage of the hurricane. How good is his chopper?'

Levi turned around. 'Damn good! It can fly in winds up to eighty knots, I believe. It might do, if he can beat the hurricane here. *If* the chopper's still available.'

He half rose from his chair, consulted his screen again, then abruptly stood up. 'The hurricane's 250 kilometres east of New Orleans now. It's still moving in the same direction at thirty kilometres per hour, so it'll hit land in about eight hours. Wind speeds here could reach eighty knots within five hours. It'll be touch and go, but we might just do it. I'll call him.'

'What if he won't do it?' Irith said.

'He'll do it if he's not already committed. That's not the problem.'

'What is?'

'He's based a couple of hours away and he'll have to fly across the path of the hurricane to get here.'

'So even if he can get here in four hours, we might only have an hour to do the job and get out?' said Bragg.

'That's right.'

'That's really putting the pressure on.'

'It's our only chance,' said Levi.

He sat at the keyboard, typed a number and hit the return. He waited for a couple of minutes, then typed another number. 'That's it. Now we wait.'

'That's all?' Irith said incredulously, walking around to see his screen. 'How can he answer that?'

'He already has.'

The screen showed a single number, three, the reply, one, and the confirmation, zero.

'You didn't think I was going to call him on the phone, did you? Everything is monitored and decrypted. This message goes a roundabout way and the source computer can't be identified. And we agreed on the code a week ago. No one else knows it,' said Levi.

'How long till Jack gets here?'

'Depends where he is now and how long it takes to prepare. Assuming he needs a couple of hours to fuel up, do all the safety checks and so forth, and another two to fly here, I wouldn't expect him here before nine-thirty.'

'He'll call on approach?' said Irith.

'When he's half an hour away.'

'So we just wait.'

'If all your preparations are complete,' said Levi.

'I can be ready in ten minutes.' Though, emotionally, she would never be ready. She wasn't planning on taking a gun. No more killing!

'Then do so.' Levi looked around distractedly. 'Better get my own gear organised.'

Irith went to her room and looked out the window. A police vehicle was moving slowly along the street, loudspeakers blaring, although she could not hear the message. Below and to her right was a tiny park: just grass, a few trees and a couple of benches. Water had pooled in low-lying areas. It must have rained in the night.

There was no one on the sidewalks and no other vehicles moved along the streets. Most of the windows were shuttered and New Orleans looked like a city at war. The air was full of debris: whirling pieces of paper and cardboard, plastic bags, the red-stained corpse of a seabird.

To the east, in the direction of the hurricane, the sky was darker than ever, the bloody purple of a bruise. She turned away, gathered everything she would need, checked her list and went back to the main room.

'Any news?' she said to Levi.

'Jemma continues as before. Same path, same speed, same category.'

'What about the storm surge?'

He gestured. The power was back on and the big screen showed a series of views of the levees, some from fixed cameras on the tops of buildings, others from wildly gyrating helicopters. In most places the water was just below the levee; in others, waves were breaking over the top.

'The surge is moving up the lake. That's why some of the levees are doing okay – the ones further upstream. The water level will rise for hours yet.'

Irith moved closer, studying the breakers foaming over one of the levees. 'Where's that?' She pointed.

'Between Lakefront Airport and the University of New Orleans. That levee is one of the critical ones.'

'Where are the others?'

'For the moment, the eastern side of the airport, and here at Lakeshore East, not far from the facility. You can see it out of the window. Also the Mississippi floodwall near the French Quarter.' He marked them on the map. 'But another metre of storm surge and they'll all be critical.'

'What's it going to be like at its peak?'

'I don't even want to think.'

'You haven't heard from Jack?'

'No,' he snapped, 'and I don't expect to for another few hours, as I've already told you.'

'Sorry,' she muttered, and went over to the window.

'Levi,' said Siah quietly, moving close, 'do I have to come with you? I don't think I can take it.'

'I really need you, Siah. Please don't let me down now.'

She closed her eyes as if in pain and walked out of the room, moving as silently as a nun.

'What's the estimated time of landfall?' said Bragg, who had come in from the kitchen with a dripping muffuletta sandwich the size of a cake tin.

'Depends on what you call land,' said Levi. 'There's not much left in Chandaleur Sound; most went underwater years ago when Lakes Borgne, Pontchartrain and Maurepas amalgamated to form an inlet 120 kilometres long. If the hurricane should track all the way up the sound, it wouldn't hit land until sometime tomorrow: maybe as late as midday. If it wobbles south towards the city, landfall could be as early as midnight. If it turns north towards Gulfport, roughly the same time. We should hope it does turn north. That's our best chance.

'Anyway, landfall isn't what we have to worry about. The storm surge will be four metres plus along the southern side of the lake, and it comes ahead of the hurricane. The worst will be between nine o'clock tonight and eleven in the morning. If the forecast's correct, there'll be a wall of water three metres high going over the levees, and three-to-five metre waves on top of that.'

'Causing massive erosion of levees and seawalls,' said Bragg, licking at a line of olive relish running down his arm. 'A lot of people are going to die tonight.'

'And we're right at the top of the list,' said Irith.

'The danger depends on how long it goes on,' said Levi. 'If the city ends up with a few metres of water in it, it won't be too bad. Everyone's trained for that. People can take refuge in taller buildings and upper floors. But if there's, say, five metres or more, the deaths will be in the thousands. New Orleans is like a bathtub floating in a pond. The water will come in from all sides and once it's there, the only way to get it out is to pump it. That can't be done if all the pumps are under water.'

'We should be using Jack's chopper to rescue people,' Irith said.

'If this works, we'll save more lives tonight than the emergency services will.'

Again Irith felt a tiny niggle, that there was more to the terminator virus than they'd discovered. She went over the message Levi's mole had sent:

'IT'S IN THE CAG–'. What could it mean?

Levi began to go through his checklists again. Irith turned back to the big screen. Bragg, Thornton and Gretel were carrying boxes and bags of gear up the stairs to the roof.

The time crept by with agonising slowness. By 7 pm, water was roaring over the levee from one end to the other. There were also breaches in the Mississippi floodwalls at the Chalmette National Military Cemetery and, more dangerously, upstream near the warehouse district and Audubon Park.

By 9 pm, the streets of New Orleans had become canals and the body count stood at thirty-seven, though the true total must have been far higher, since the weather was poor for counting dead. The water level in the lowest area, south of the University of New Orleans, was already more than two metres and rising rapidly. All the pumps in the city made not a jot of difference.

Irith wished she could look out the window but the mechanically operated shutters had been closed. From time to time, over the shrieking of the wind, heavy objects crashed against them. Conversation was almost impossible. Water had begun to drip through the ceiling, and the power went on and off intermittently.

Levi came running into the room, holding a mobile to his ear. 'What?' he bellowed.

'I thought using phones was dangerous,' Irith shouted to Siah.

'I don't think anyone will be keeping too sharp a lookout right now.'

'What's going on?'

'We're getting ready to move.'

'The chopper is on its way, then?'

'That's Jack now,' said Siah.

'How long is he going to be?'

'Ten minutes.'

Irith felt a great internal thud, as if a bowling ball had dropped into her stomach. 'Already?' she whispered.

'What?' Siah yelled.

'I wasn't expecting him for another half-hour,' Irith shouted over the noise of wind. 'It's too soon. I don't feel ready.'

'Neither do I.' Siah's voice cracked. 'Where's the bulletproof gear?' She was white-faced but deadly calm, trying to hide her terror under a mask of efficiency.

'It's here.' Irith indicated a box with her foot.

Siah opened the box and took things out. 'Where are the chest plates?'

'I haven't seen any.'

Siah went through the box. 'Fuck! They're not here. Why didn't I double-check?' The mask cracked. She tore at her bloody fingernails with her teeth.

'You've been frantic. Can't we do without them?' asked Irith.

'Sure, if all we're going to face is low-velocity handgun slugs. Assault rifle bullets will go straight through a standard bulletproof vest.' Siah picked out a small vest. Her hand shook. 'Put this on under your shirt. It's a lightweight vest. You can put a thicker one over the top.'

'It's too bloody hot as it is,' said Irith. 'Why do I need two?'

'I just told you!' Siah yelled. 'Put the damn thing on, Irith. I wish we had the chest plates. Even if the vest stops the bullet, the impact can kill you.'

Irith took off her shirt and put the lightweight vest on. 'I didn't know that.'

'You should have!' Siah screeched. 'Thorn told us up in Minnesota. Put on the main vest. Got your helmet? We're going.'

Levi was gesticulating furiously at them from the door. 'Jack's here. Up the stairs. Wait just inside the fire-escape door.'

Irith gathered her waterproof coat, pack, mobile and all the other gear she needed. It was as much as she could carry and she was almost fainting in the heat. She had a last look around. Her room was clean and nothing incriminating, apart from her DNA, had been left behind. And Vaiha's body, of course, but they couldn't do anything about that.

The rest of the apartment was the same, except for Levi's room. He was still tapping at his terminal. Bragg was packing gear under his direction.

Although the other apartments on the top floor were vacant, and Levi had checked for hidden cameras, Irith made sure there was no one about before she went out. She was unmistakably prepared for war.

Siah slipped in beside her. Her fingertips were bleeding. 'I can't do this, Irith. I'm going out of my mind.'

Irith set down her gear and took Siah's hand. 'I feel just the same. You'll be all right once it starts.'

'What if I'm not?' Siah said shrilly.

'You will be.'

'It's all right for you, Irith. You proved yourself in London.'

'I'm not sure that makes it any easier.'

'I'll crack and run at the worst possible time.'

This was so unlike the ever-competent Siah.

Someone yelled from upstairs. 'Come on!' said Irith.

Panting up the stairs, she encountered Thornton and Gretel by a pile of bags and sealed containers. Bragg and Levi appeared, Levi with packs over both shoulders and shouting into his phone.

'We've got no chest plates for the vests, Levi,' said Siah, breathing hard. 'They weren't packed with the order and I missed it when I went through the list. I'm sorry.'

'Buggery-shit!' said Thornton, glancing at his sister. 'Why didn't you check properly?'

'There's one in *my* vest pocket,' said Gretel. 'It was there when I unwrapped it.'

'Lucky you,' said Bragg. 'Make sure you wear it so you can come to our funerals.'

'Can't do anything about it,' said Levi. He looked around at the group. 'Ready? Jack's just coming in. We'll run to the chopper, two at a time, with the gear. Stay back till last, Irith. The wind would blow you away.'

Irith moved to the rear, feeling like a kid who wasn't old enough to go to the party. Some party! Sweat trickled down her front and back. She put the helmet on. Although made of titanium, and therefore light, it was sweaty and confining. The air was so humid it was hard to breathe. She felt her claustrophobia stirring.

'Have we got everything?' Levi asked Bragg.

'All but the drums of gasoline for the big barbecue. We'll pick them up on the way to the facility.'

'Jack's already got them. Stick your head out the door and see if he's down.'

Bragg forced the door open a fraction. The wind blew it closed, but not before a blast peppered them with stinging drops.

'Shit!' said Bragg. 'We need diving gear in this.'

'Is he down?' snapped Levi.

'Just settling.'

'All right, you and Thorn, get going. Gretel, hold the door.'

Bragg forced the door open and Gretel put her back to it while the two big men heaved up the largest of the containers.

'Where the fuck is the chopper?' screamed Thornton. 'I can't see a fucking thing.'

Bragg pointed to the left. A light blinked. They staggered in that direction, disappearing into the darkness.

Irith turned her back to the wind and the sheeting horizontal rain; the raindrops whacked through her pants like the ends of a bundle of wires. Why didn't Gretel shut the door?

In a rush the men were back, water pouring off them.

'It's like a nostril full of black snot out there,' roared Bragg. 'The whole world is blowing its nose on us.' Taking a large wooden case in both hands, he forced his way out into the storm.

Thornton picked up the other box, slung a pack over his shoulder and followed.

'All right,' said Levi. 'Siah and Gretel, get your gear and be ready to run.' He put his head out the door, waiting for the signal. 'Go!'

They went. Levi held the door open with his back. It kept trying to slam closed under his slight weight. His knees flexed and straightened, flexed and straightened.

'Pack your bags, Irith,' he said. 'Ready?'

Irith didn't think she would ever be ready. 'Yes!'

'Go! Keep your head down.'

Irith ran, or at least tried to, but the wind was so strong, and the rain so violent, that she made little progress. She wasn't even sure she was going in the right direction. The rain struck at her eyes, the wind whirled her around and she didn't have the faintest idea where she was going.

She pulled her visor down, which didn't help. It needed wipers. She turned around and around. Levi must have closed the door, for the rooftop was inky and there wasn't the faintest shadow to indicate the chopper. The wind thrust her towards the edge of the building and her legs weren't strong enough to push against it.

Irith imagined a gust lifting her in the air, over the edge and hurling her thirteen floors to her death. Or worse, she might be about to walk into the rotor of the helicopter. In this wind, she wouldn't hear it. The thought froze her to the spot. She opened her mouth to scream.

Someone caught her around the chest and pressed her down. 'Take my hand,' Bragg roared in her ear. 'Don't let go.'

She clutched his thick wrist. Holding her tightly, he forced his way against the wind. They took a winding path across the roof. Lightning flashed, revealing the dark shape of the chopper nearby. How had she not seen it? How had she missed the tail rotor?

Now they were in behind the chopper, slightly sheltered from the wind. A tiny light flicked on, then off; a door was highlighted. Bragg dragged her towards it, heaving her up the steps with one hand on her bottom. The steps were jerking up and down, the whole frame of the chopper shuddering in the wind.

'Air-Sea Rescue Inc' was painted on the side in large, reflective letters, and below that a picture of a long-legged bird with a bandage around one knee, and the words *Grus americana*. As she reached the top of the steps, Levi jerked her inside. He had beaten her there. Bragg came up the steps in a rush and slid the door closed. A light came on.

Irith clung to him for a moment. How easy it would have been to walk into the rotor and splatter her brains across the roof. 'Thanks.'

He squeezed her shoulder. 'You can do the same for me some day.'

Levi climbed into the front seat next to a wizened little gnome of a man, nothing like the beefy, cigar-smoking Texan Irith had imagined. He turned around in his seat. His teeth were very white in his tanned face and he wore a gold cross on a chain around his neck. His grey hair was wavy and cropped short. His ears were small, his nose enormous and his eyes blue and twinkling.

His voice came out of a speaker just above her. 'I'm Jack. Glad to have you aboard in one piece, Irith. Next time you go walkabout, keep away from the rotor. Put your harnesses on, everyone, and the headsets.'

Irith took off the helmet, fitted the headphones over her ears and the roar of the wind lessened.

'Welcome to the Whooping Crane,' said Jack. 'An endangered species, like me. A quick briefing before we go. This baby is tough but she can't fly through a hurricane. The maximum wind speed she can fly in is eighty-five knots. That's about 155 kilometres per hour for you metric folks. If the wind approaches that, we're outta here. If it gets too gusty, we're outta here. She can hover in winds of sixty knots, though there wouldn't be much point because we couldn't do anything.'

'How long have we got to get the job done?' said Bragg.

'Wind speed is forty-five knots and rising fast. That's at 150 feet. It's less at ground level, but gustier. The wind could reach our maximum in an hour. If you're still inside then, I'll have to leave you behind.'

'How much fuel have you got, Jack?' Levi said quietly.

'With the reserve tank, about four hours' worth. I've just refuelled.'

The engine screamed, the chopper shook and they lifted off, the gale tossing them like a shuttlecock in a wind tunnel. The apartment building, a dark shape illuminated by occasional flashes of lightning, fell away beneath them. The chopper rotated on its axis, jerked sideways then headed towards the lake.

The trip took only a couple of minutes. Irith looked out towards the south-east, hoping to catch the kind of glimpse of the hurricane that one saw on the news. She saw nothing but rain, lightning and black whirling clouds with no shape at all. The streets she had looked down on only hours ago were submerged.

Levi's voice crackled in the headphones, barely audible over the din. 'Go over the lake levee so we can get an idea what we're dealing with. Keep away from the facility.'

They curved around over the levee. All the streetlights were out and, as Irith looked down, in the lightning flashes she saw that the lake was covered in huge waves, blown into spindrift and streaky foam. The levee was underwater for as far as she could see, the lake roaring over it like water over the spillway of a dam.

The flood had undermined most of the northern wall of the Pontchartrain facility and long sections had disappeared. The north-eastern corner still stood but the water had banked up inside the remaining walls, metres deep. A section of the southern wall had collapsed and water was pouring through it. The three buildings of the facility looked like islands in a muddy, storm-tossed sea. The rear gatehouse wasn't there at all, while the barracks had been reduced to wall framing and a section of iron roof that threatened to go any minute.

'There are still people in the main gatehouse,' came Jack's crackly voice, 'although I don't imagine it'll last long. There goes another section of the southern wall. Water pressure is pushing it over.'

'What about the facility buildings?' said Siah.

'Their foundations go down a long way,' said Levi. 'But if –' He broke off as the chopper lurched violently.

'What's the problem?' said Bragg.

'There are two problems. There's no rock under the city, so they have to use special foundations, and pump continually, to stop tall buildings from sinking. And if the pumps stop because they're underwater, and a hurricane's pushing on the buildings –'

'They could collapse. Fantastic!'

'What's the other problem?' said Siah.

'The flow over the levee is so enormous, I'm afraid it'll cut a channel through it. If that happens we'll have a ten-metre-deep torrent which would wash New Orleans into the Mississippi.'

No one spoke. The disaster would become a catastrophe and there wouldn't be enough body bags in the United States for all the dead.

CHAPTER THIRTY-ONE

'I'll approach from the rear,' said Jack. 'That way, if anyone's watching from the main gatehouse, they won't see us.'

He turned the chopper over the location of the rear gatehouse, fingering the area with a searchlight beam as a search and rescue chopper might have done. Nothing could be seen but roiling water. A long section of razor wire-topped wall slid under. Irith wondered how many of the guards had taken refuge inside the facility buildings.

'What about the missile defence system?' It was Bragg's voice in the headphones.

'We've had a bit of luck there,' said Thornton. 'The first surge raced across into that corner and tore the walls open. Part of the structure has collapsed, including both launchers. I can't see the rest of the bunker lasting more than an hour.'

'That's the only good news we've had in the last week,' said Levi. 'But approach the roof from the other direction, just in case.'

'Might seem less suspicious if I flew directly to the top of Building Three,' said Jack. 'As though I was doing a rescue.'

'I want to land on the roof without anyone knowing,' said Levi. 'We have to assume that there are guards and Security operatives inside. Should they see the chopper land, they'll be on alert. If we have to fight our way in, we won't get in at all.'

'There won't be anyone looking out the windows,' said Jack. 'They'll be in the centre of the buildings, sheltering behind solid walls.'

'The guards will have body armour and visors.'

'They'll keep away from the windows when there's a hurricane on the way,' said Jack. 'How about this? We go high, out of sight, and drop straight down on Building Three. If someone happens to be looking up from the other buildings, and there's a flash of lightning, they may see us, but I doubt it. And if they do, they'll be praying we've come to rescue them.'

'Best we can do,' said Levi. 'Go for it.'

Lights burned here and there in the three towers but the floodlights were out and the surrounding area was eerily dark.

'They've still got emergency power,' said Levi. 'Set down on top of Building Three, Jack, close to that cooling tower. The door's around the other side.'

'Do you want me to wait on the roof?' said Jack.

'Better not, in case guards come up the far stairs. The second roof door is across there. Go up and hang around in the dark, or set down somewhere else, if you can find a safe place. I'll call you.'

'You'll have to be quick. The way Jemma is headed, I could be grounded within the hour.'

'I'm not sure that'll be enough time,' said Levi, shifting in his seat.

'It'll have to be. It's 10.03 now. I'll be down again at 10.50. If you're not back by . . . 11.05, I'll assume you're not coming.'

'If that changes, let me know. When we get onto the roof,' Levi announced, 'don't touch the door. Chances are the alarms aren't functioning, or are going off continuously, but I'll check the set-up first. I may be able to hack it.'

'I thought we were going to blow it,' said Thornton.

'This is the new plan, remember? If we can get in without them knowing, all the better. Thorn, you'll drop the communications tower, as agreed. Try and make it look like it was the wind. Sever the cables, too. The landlines are already out so, with the tower down, they'll be reduced to mobiles. The jammer will take care of them.'

Levi had an all-weather laptop on his lap and was connecting cables as he spoke. He closed the lid. 'I'm ready to go.'

'What about the surveillance cameras on the roof?' said Gretel.

'They look outwards, not towards the roof, and probably have no power. Let's hope so.'

Irith didn't find that particularly comforting and, from her frozen expression, neither did Siah. Irith clasped her shoulder. Siah tried to smile but failed.

The chopper jerked wildly, rose straight up and just as swiftly, dropped sharply. A gust drove it sideways across the roof towards the air-conditioning building and cooling towers. Jack spun it around and set down. Irith expected it to slam into the concrete but it bounced and settled, rocking on its four wheels.

The wind was a shriek but the thunder of water pouring over the levee was louder. The sight, from only a few hundred metres away, was awesome. The water was a deluge to wash the world away. And if the levee broke, a wall of water would tear the facility buildings off their foundations as if they were made of Lego. Irith shuddered and turned away. She couldn't bear to look at it.

'Thanks, Jack!' said Levi.

'Wait for me, Irith,' shouted Bragg. 'You can't go by yourself.'

He slid the door open and jumped out. Thornton passed him one of the boxes. Carrying it on his shoulder, Bragg disappeared into the sideways-driving rain. Thornton went after him, equally burdened.

It took only two minutes to get their gear into the shelter of the wall surrounding the roof door. Irith went down last, hanging onto the steps with a bag over each shoulder and feeling singularly useless.

Bragg appeared out of the darkness and picked her up, bags and all. 'Put me down!' she yelled, but he probably couldn't hear her.

Even with his strength, he made hard work of getting the thirty metres across the roof. A wild blast spun him around and almost tore Irith out of his arms. He went up on his tiptoes, and for an instant she thought they were going to be blown over the side. Then he dropped into a crouch, pulling her down, and the gust passed. Irith was glad he had carried her. And the eye of the hurricane was still a hundred kilometres away.

He set Irith down in the corner and went back with Thornton for the petrol. There were twelve five-gallon plastic jerry cans. They lurched across the concrete, a jerry can in each hand, and stacked them in a sheltered angle of the wall.

Irith looked over her shoulder. The chopper was gone and she hadn't heard it. The roar of the wind was wilder here and the sky was full of flying paper and cardboard. When the hurricane struck it would carry wood, roofing iron, tiles, metal and glass. Anything not securely bolted down would be torn up and hurled across the sky – jagged missiles that would pulverise flesh and bone.

Thornton turned on a couple of flood lanterns, handing one to Siah and the other to Bragg. They held them steady while Levi unpacked his gear, then illuminated the door, which was solid steel set in a steel frame. The rain was like standing under a fire hose.

Crouching in front of the door, Levi opened his laptop. 'Thorn, do your stuff. Gretel, get the jammer in place. Siah, give her a hand then come back here.'

Thornton went off to blow the communications tower. Gretel and Siah lugged a long box along the wall, pulled out an array of aerials and crouched down again. Irith could see them clearly, when the lightning flashed.

Bragg moved closer, sheltering Levi with his body. Levi beckoned to Irith. She crawled along the wall. He shouted something but she couldn't hear a word.

Irith put a hand around her ear. His face was stark in the glare from the floodlamps. He thrust the computer into her hands and moved them into position so he could see the screen. Water trickled onto the keyboard. She hoped it truly was an all-weather machine.

Siah reappeared. Levi inserted his probes into the door. Moving the screen so he could see it better, he wiped his glasses and bent to the door again. Irith settled into a more comfortable position. Water had worked in around her close-fitting hood and was running down her chest and back. The temperature hadn't dropped at all. Her clothes were saturated with sweat and she felt faint.

Crack! Crack! She saw muffled flashes from the direction of the communications tower, itself invisible in the dark, then the roof shook. The tower was down.

Levi inspected the tip of one probe, grimaced, wiped his glasses then pulled out the probe and replaced it with a thinner one. He studied the screen, shaking his head.

Irith checked her watch: 10.14. Eleven minutes had gone by already.

'Might be easier to blow a hole through the wall,' Bragg screamed.

Levi shook his head and continued working the probe. Thornton came back and picked up the spare floodlamp. Irith watched the screen, which she could just see. It lit up. She caught Levi's eye but he gave nothing away. After packing the probe in place with lumps of putty he began typing furiously, hitting the keyboard so hard that she had trouble holding the computer steady. He stopped, tilted it so the water ran off, then resumed.

The others were just shadows in a half-circle around the door, silhouetted by the lightning: the two men in the middle, Thornton taller and broader than Bragg, Siah filling in the gap to the right. Rain streamed off their hoods. The wind grew louder.

Levi moved closer to the screen. Water beaded on his glasses and eyebrows, and dripped from the end of his nose. He didn't bother to wipe it off. He typed three letters, paused, then some numbers and hit the return. Irith held her breath. Could it be this easy?

Evidently not. He dashed the water off his face, hit the return three times in quick succession, and began to type afresh. At the end he cocked his head to one side, as if listening for something. Surely that was just a mannerism? Nothing could be heard above the storm.

Levi adjusted the probe and frowned. Thornton checked his watch, moving uncomfortably. Irith could guess what he was thinking. *Stop buggering about. Let's blow it to the shithouse and get inside before it's too late.* For once, she agreed.

Now Levi was tapping away again. He hit the return, looked up at Irith and smiled. His lips formed the words that she couldn't hear. 'Done it!'

Irith expected the door to come open but of course it didn't. Levi packed up his gear and slid it into his backpack. He twisted the handle and pulled. The door didn't budge.

Levi cursed, gestured at Thornton and jerked his thumb at the lock. Thornton grinned, all teeth like a Cheshire cat in the darkness. Crouching in front of the door, he pushed Irith to one side and began to unpack his gear. He worked quickly, methodically.

Thornton shaped the grey explosive with his fingers and packed it around the lock. Irith couldn't understand why the force would not just blow outwards. Still, he knew what he was doing.

Irith could feel her heart crashing in her chest. The building would have well-trained guards. If the troops from the barracks had also taken refuge inside, they could number in the dozens. Only Gretel, Thornton and Bragg were experienced in that kind of fighting. Irith knew she was barely competent, despite her weeks of training up north. A handful of guards, taking them by surprise, could wipe them out in a few bloody seconds.

She could imagine every detail: the bullets tearing through her flesh, the agony, the slow, desperate dying. Beside her, Siah was frozen in fear. Gretel loomed out of the darkness, seeming pleased with herself.

'Move that gear out of the way,' Thornton roared, waving his hands at them. 'Get to cover.'

They scurried to carry the gear to shelter, then took refuge around the corner. Thornton came after them, the firing mechanism in his hands. In the dark Irith couldn't see what it was.

The explosion was barely audible above the wind and the cascade over the levee. Thornton put his head around the corner, then beckoned. They grabbed their gear. The door wasn't visibly damaged, but it was ajar.

They went inside, leaving the jerry cans where they were. Levi pulled the door shut. The noise outside died to a dull roar. He pressed a probe into a wall socket. 'I don't sense any alarm, but get ready for anything.'

Bragg handed Irith a long plastic cylinder, like a large diameter map tube.

'What's this?' she said.

'Your assault rifle.'

Irith recoiled. 'I'm not doing any more killing.'

Bragg stared at her. 'Then you should have stayed in your room. But since you didn't, take the bloody thing and be prepared to use it.'

Irith drew the weapon from its case. It was of a kind she had never seen before – short and stubby, with seven barrels grouped together and no magazine.

'What the bloody hell is this?' she muttered.

'It's a Metal Storm assault rifle, the fastest in existence. All electronic and jam proof. The bullets are already stacked in the barrels.'

'How does it work?'

'The usual way.' He flicked a little recessed switch forward. 'Forward is single shot. Vertical, burst. Backward is continuous fire – eight thousand rounds per minute. Only use that in a real emergency or you'll be out of ammo in a few seconds.'

Irith couldn't speak. She was too afraid. Too sure how this was going to end – with her as a bloody corpse. *I'll take it*, she thought, *but I'm not going to use it.*

Thornton and Bragg moved to the front, weapons at the ready. Gretel was immediately behind them, then Siah, as pale as paper, with Levi and Irith at the rear.

'What's the plan?' said Gretel to Levi.

'We locate the quarantine floors. Irith identifies the terminator virus labs and looks for evidence to incriminate Lindstrom or the Congress. That's our passport to survival, remember, so we give her as long as possible. Siah stands guard. Gretel, help Irith. You may need to hack into their system. Thorn and Bragg will bring down the incendiaries. Thorn sets them up, we clear out and on the signal he blows the jerry cans, creating a firestorm that will destroy everything on those floors and, almost certainly, the whole building.'

'What if Thornton and Bragg are killed by all their armed guards?' said Irith.

'You'll have to tip the petrol on the floor and rub your little tits together until it ignites,' Gretel snapped. 'Stop making difficulties, you little shit!'

'Thank you, Gretel and Irith!' said Levi. 'We can only do our best, and if we don't succeed, we won't have to worry about anything.'

They crept down the stairs. 'Be alert for booby traps –' began Levi.

'Thanks, *mother*,' said Bragg.

'Which were the virus culturing floors?' whispered Siah to Irith.

'Just floor six, if we can rely on the data. The research floors were three to five.'

'And we're coming down to floor eight?'

'Yes.'

Everything was in darkness. Irith checked her watch. Nineteen minutes down.

'I don't like this,' said Bragg.

'There's a light on across the far side. It's probably an emergency light,' said Levi. He held out a small rectangular motion detector. 'I'm not seeing anything.'

'Is that ultrasonic or infrared?' said Bragg.

'Neither, it's video-based,' said Levi.

'Then how the fuck is it going to work in darkness?'

'It'd work up your backside,' Thornton said, 'and that's the darkest place I can think of.'

'Pipe down!' hissed Levi. 'It'll work, Bragg.'

'Stick it around the door to the eighth floor,' came Thornton's voice. 'I'd hate them to come at us from behind.'

'All right. Stay where you are and keep us covered. Irith and Siah, come with me. Be on the lookout and ready to fire.'

The dark, though intense, was broken by flashes of lightning visible through small high windows. Irith walked beside Levi, trying not to touch the trigger on her assault rifle. It would be too easy to shoot by accident.

'Nothing,' said Levi. 'Hang on. What's that?'

Irith's finger jerked and she almost let off a burst. 'Where?' she hissed.

'Down to our left.'

His lantern carved a solid beam through the air. Something moved down the far end and Irith's heart turned over. She jerked her rifle that way but it was just the rags of a curtain flapping at a broken window, and water cascading down the sill.

'Should've brought an infrared motion detector,' said Levi. 'These video ones give too many false alarms.'

'I had one,' said Siah, 'but it wasn't working properly.'

The beam went out. 'Nothing here. Let's go down.'

Irith's heart was thumping so hard that it was painful. They re-joined the others and crept down the stairs to the seventh level. Light burned in an office on the far side of the floor.

The tension was less this time, although she still felt a profound anxiety, a build-up of tension that was almost sexual. With a thrill of horror she realised that she wanted to use the gun. It would be a release.

Levi was bothered, too. She could tell by the way he walked. He was normally so relaxed, so fluid. Now he moved like an automaton and when he turned his head in her direction, his pupils were the size of marbles.

They crept around the corner. The first lighted office was empty. They moved on to the second. Also empty. The third was across the far side.

'Movement!' Levi hissed, waving his hand behind him. 'There's someone in the office. Don't move. Don't make a sound.'

CHAPTER THIRTY-TWO

'How many people are there?' said Siah with commendable calm, considering that she could barely hold her rifle steady and her teeth were chattering.

'Can't tell,' Levi replied. 'Get ready, Irith.'

They sneaked across the corridor. Before they reached the door Irith heard, over the screeching of the wind, the sound of country and western music. She cast Levi a glance but he wasn't looking her way. She pressed forward, put her rifle around the door and followed it with her head.

A woman sat at a desk halfway across the room, with her back to Irith. She was tapping at a keyboard, every so often looking up to check a small screen in front of her. 'Stand By Your Man' whined out of a golf ball-sized device on the desk. A long extension cord snaked across the floor and under her desk. Emergency power, presumably.

The woman was young and her dark brown hair was bound in a ponytail. She stopped typing, her hands poised above the keyboard. She had seen Irith reflected in her screen.

'Don't touch anything or I'll shoot,' Irith hissed. 'Roll the chair backwards and turn around, and you won't get hurt.'

The woman didn't move. 'Come on!' Irith gestured with the gun.

'I can't move without moving my feet,' she whispered.

'Then move them very gently. Don't try to set off any alarms.'

'What alarms?' The woman pushed the chair backwards and slowly turned around. Her face was so pale that her blue eyes seemed to be lit from behind. She looked exhausted, and absolutely terrified.

The way I must have looked just a few months ago, Irith thought. *Or a few hours ago. Or now, for that matter.*

'What are you doing here?' said Levi.

'I'm Sheryl,' the young woman said in a southern accent. 'I'm a research assistant. I had some work to catch up on.'

'At this time of night?'

'I work two jobs. I'm behind in my work here and there's never enough time to get it done. I came in early this morning ... then the hurricane warning came and I couldn't go home, so I figured I might as well catch up.'

'Come with us, please.' Irith jerked the gun in the direction of the door.

'Who are you?' said Sheryl, her eyes darting from Levi to Irith to Siah.

'Where are the quarantine laboratories?' said Levi. 'For the terminator virus project.'

'What's that?' said Sheryl.

'The project that's going to be tested tomorrow.'

'Oh, that. In Building One. This is Building Three.'

Levi and Irith exchanged glances. If the woman was telling the truth, their intelligence was badly wrong. Had they been fed misleading information? And if they had, what other data might also be unreliable?

'What happens in this building?' said Irith.

'Administration, the library, computer modelling, preparation laboratories,' said Sheryl, her eyes going everywhere.

'You're sure?' said Levi.

'I've been working here for two years,' said Sheryl. 'All the quarantine labs are in Building One.'

'Which floors?'

'Three to six, I think. I've never been over there.'

'What about the culturing laboratory? That'd be a high-security quarantine laboratory.'

'I don't know.'

'How many people are in this building?' said Irith.

Sheryl licked her lips. 'I think I'm the only one, now. When the flood came through, the water was about ten feet high. The basement and the lower floors were flooded.'

'Why did you stay?'

'There's no way out 'til the water goes down. And I'm so far behind in my work I'm afraid of being fired.' She looked as if she was going to cry. 'I've got two kids; if I lose my job –'

'How many people in the other buildings?' said Levi, glancing at his watch.

Irith checked hers: 10.29. This was taking far too much time.

'There were a lot in Building One, because of the ceremony tomorrow. The building was damaged and I think they went across to Building Two. It's the furthest from the levee.'

'What ceremony?'

'A presentation and a special demonstration. I don't know what. It's top-secret.'

'So there are a lot of officials here for the test?'

'Yes. VIPs. Foreigners. They came in early and were trapped here.'

'Where would they be in Building Two?'

Sheryl shrugged. 'Above the second floor, where it's dry.'

'How many people would be in the virus centre in Building One, now?'

'It was evacuated across the aerial bridge. They were afraid it might fall down. It should be empty . . .'

There was a slight hesitation, as if she was not telling all she knew.

'What about the guards from the front and rear gates, and the ones on patrol?' said Irith.

Sheryl stubbornly closed her mouth. Gretel appeared between them. Irith hadn't known she was there.

'Fuck this!' said Gretel, thrusting her multiple barrels against the woman's head. 'Spill it, kiddo, or I'll paint the wall with your brain cells.'

Sheryl made a choking sound in her throat. Siah had gone even paler and looked as if she were about to faint, then began to pant, sucking at the air like an asthmatic. Irith motioned for her to stay back, trying to shelter her as best she could.

'The guards?' Gretel tapped Sheryl's forehead again.

'A lot were drowned when the flood came through.'

'How many?'

'Maybe ten or fifteen.'

'How many guards were there altogether?' said Gretel.

'About thirty, normally . . .' Sheryl trailed off.

'Normally?' said Gretel in a voice as hard as agate.

'They brought in extra ones, two days ago. Another ten, at least.'

'Where are they now?'

'Some were trapped in the front gate guardhouse. Some would be in Building One or Two.'

'How many?'

'I don't know.'

'If an educated guess could save your life,' said Gretel, 'how many would you guess?'

'Fifteen,' whispered Sheryl, her eyes darting this way and that. 'Or twenty.'

'Bind and gag her,' said Levi.

Sheryl opened her mouth to scream but Gretel cracked her over the side of the head. Sheryl clutched at the desk and managed to hold herself upright, but the fight had gone out of her. Gretel bound and gagged her and they took her back to the stairs. Irith's watch read 10.35. Thirty-two minutes gone.

'What took you so long?' Thornton hissed.

'This,' said Levi, indicating Sheryl. 'She said the labs are in Building One. We'll have to check that.' He laid a hand on Gretel's arm. 'Next time,' he said quietly, 'stay at your post. When I need your intervention, I'll call for it.'

They continued down the steps. On the sixth level they discovered what looked like an abandoned barricade, a collection of desks pushed together.

'What the hell is this?' said Bragg.

Gretel ripped off Sheryl's gag. 'Well?'

'They were expecting an attack on the facility,' Sheryl gasped.

'When?'

'Three days ago.'

'When was this abandoned?'

'Just after the levee overtopped.'

'This is bad,' said Levi. 'They expected an attack and spread false information about the facility. They may have withdrawn from here but I'll bet they've got defences in Building One, hurricane or not. What do you know about that, Sheryl?'

'Nothing.'

'Are you sure?'

'I'm just a research assistant. They don't tell us anything.'

'But you come through Security every day,' Levi said mildly. 'What's it like?'

'Tougher than Fort Knox,' said Sheryl. 'You can't get from one building to another, or into the high-security sections, without going through a three-level checkpoint.'

'Three-level security? What, specifically?'

'Iris scanners, face recognition, then a palm print reader. It's foolproof.'

'But it must be off now,' said Levi, 'since there's only emergency power and they've evacuated everyone into Building Two.'

Sheryl shrugged. 'I wouldn't know.'

'What else do you know about Building One?'

'Nothing. I've never been inside.'

'But people must talk.'

'Not here. If you talk, they find out and the next day you're fired. I only know what I've seen with my own eyes, and since nightfall I haven't moved from my desk.'

'The doors into this floor are wide open,' said Levi.

'It's not a high-security floor.'

Levi called everyone into a huddle. 'I don't like this. The hurricane may have changed everything, but I wouldn't want to risk the mission on it. Odds are there are guards on the bridge, or inside Building One. What do we do?'

'First we check this building,' said Thornton. 'In case she's lying and the terminator virus labs *are* here.'

'And we've only got twenty-three minutes to do it,' said Siah, still breathing heavily.

They went through the remaining floors as quickly as they could. The sixth floor consisted solely of administrative offices with workstations. There could have been evidence here but there was no time to search for it.

The fifth floor held laboratories but had only low-level security and it had taken considerable storm damage. A whole row of windows on the eastern side of the building had been smashed by flying debris, and air pressure had blown many of the other windows out. The laboratories looked as though they had been attacked with a giant vacuum cleaner. Some of the benches were swept clean. On others, the equipment had been blown into piles that were now junk. The floor was littered with glass, metal and pieces of ceiling insulation. Water ran out the doors and down the stairs.

'This is just a preparation lab,' said Irith. 'It's not what we're looking for.'

'So she was telling the truth,' Levi said with a glance at Sheryl. 'That's something.'

'So far,' scowled Gretel.

The fourth floor was also a laboratory, and in much the same condition. The third floor, the research library, was a mess. All the windows were broken, the rain was pouring in and there was so much water on the floor it looked as if a flood had washed through. They grouped outside the security doors, around the corner from the aerial bridge. The checkpoint was in ruins, the door hanging from one twisted hinge, although the bridge to Building One was intact.

'Keep back,' said Thornton. 'They could still be watching the bridge.'

'It's 10.50. Fifteen minutes left,' said Bragg. 'If we have to fight our way in, we're not going to do it in time, even if we win. And with fifteen or more guards in there, that's about as likely as me giving birth.'

'We're not going to start a war,' said Levi. 'I'll call Jack. He'll be down by now. We'll break in through the top of Building One.'

'We can forget all the hacking-in bullshit,' said Thornton. 'We slam down onto the roof, blow the top door to the shithouse, hurl in your capsicum mist and blast our way down. Then we drop our jerry cans on each floor, blast them to buggery and piss off.'

'Mr Subtlety,' grinned Bragg.

'This time you get your wish, Thorn,' said Levi. 'A monster explosion. Hope it makes you happy.'

'I'm delirious with joy,' said Thornton.

Levi punched a code into his phone and put it to his ear. He shook it, frowned and punched the code again.

'No answer,' he said.

'What does that mean?' said Bragg, looking unsettled for the first time.

'It means we're fucked,' said Thornton.

'Maybe the wind has brought down a communications tower,' said Levi. 'Maybe something's blocking the signal, or Jack's radio's out.'

'Maybe he's crashed and burned to mutton,' said Gretel.

'Thanks, Gretel,' snapped Levi.

'I don't suppose it could be your jammer?' Irith said tentatively. Everyone else seemed to understand what was going on, while she had no idea.

'Not this frequency,' said Levi. 'Thorn, you're the fittest. Run up to the roof and see what's the matter with Jack's radio.'

They waited. Irith wiped her face. She was sweating like a pig. 'How do people wear armour all day?'

'They don't in this climate,' said Bragg, 'or they'd collapse from heat exhaustion. That may save us.'

'Unless we collapse first.'

Within two minutes Thornton was back. 'Jack's gone! The wind must've been approaching his limit. It's strong enough to blow your balls off up there.'

'Then we've no choice,' said Levi. 'We'll go across the bridge to Building One, fighting our way in if we have to. Let's see if we can see anything.' From his bag he brought out a pair of night-vision goggles, put them on and pressed them to the window.

Despair descended on Irith at the thought of a gun battle. The guards would be well trained. It would be like a slaughterhouse and they were the sheep.

'There's a group of people not far from the other end of the bridge,' said Levi. 'I can't see them clearly.'

'How many?' said Thornton.

'Maybe six, maybe eight.'

'What about elsewhere in the building?' said Bragg.

Levi scanned it from top to bottom. 'Can't see anyone, but unless they're close to the windows I wouldn't pick them up. Night-vision goggles aren't much good in rain this heavy.'

They approached their end of the aerial bridge, keeping under cover. Everything was in darkness. Wind howled through the twisted metal, banging the one remaining door. Lightning flashed, revealing that the metal roof of the walkway had been torn off halfway along. The glass side walls were gone too, and the rain was torrential.

The corner of Building One closest to the bridge had collapsed, although the floors above were intact. Water streamed between the buildings, clotted with floating debris – timber, wall sheeting, boxes and once, Irith was sure, a woman's body. She looked away.

'Prime conditions,' said Bragg. 'I can't wait.'

'Good! You can lead the assault,' said Levi.

CHAPTER THIRTY-THREE

'Before you go,' said Levi, 'I'll just do a sweep for sensors on the bridge.' He did so. 'I've detected a couple but they're not working. Guess they weren't waterproof. Got the capsicum grenades?'

Bragg patted his pocket. 'Yep. Chili con carne tonight.'

'Whoopy-do,' said Thornton.

'How do they work?' said Irith.

'A jalapeno chilli is five thousand Scoville heat units,' said Bragg. 'This stuff is ten million and it penetrates everywhere. You can't see, can't breathe, can't move.'

'How are we going to get across?' Siah said.

'Pray they don't know we're here,' said Bragg. 'If they're waiting for us, we're fucked.'

'Brain fricassee,' said Thornton. 'Have you picked up anything, Levi?'

He was crouched over his computer. 'There's all sorts of stray emissions floating about, but I'd expect that in a building full of scientific equipment, even with the power down. Nothing consistent with surveillance, although that doesn't mean they're not watching. They may just have better equipment than we do.'

'That's comforting,' said Bragg. 'What about radio comms?'

'Thousands of units. It's impossible to sort them all out, but most would be police and emergency services, a long way away.'

'What about ones used by the guards?'

'Can't tell, because of the jammer.'

'That's a pity,' said Bragg. 'We might have located them by their radios.'

'I judged it was better to prevent any message getting out,' said Levi.

'How did you propose to communicate with Jack, then?'

'Using a special frequency that we're not jamming.'

'Maybe that's why you can't contact him now,' Irith muttered.

Bragg said something under his breath. Irith, who was beside him, laid a hand on his. He squeezed it and grinned. She felt surprisingly cheered.

'It may not be as bad as you think,' he said.

'Thanks, Bragg. If we get out of here, I'm going to give you the biggest hug you've ever had.'

'A hug!' He snorted. 'A Panzer division couldn't stop me now.'

'We knew there were guards,' said Thornton, 'so we're no better off. Let's get in and do the business.'

'Signal when you're in place,' said Levi. 'Cover them, Gretel and Siah. Irith, keep watch.'

He handed her his night-vision goggles, Excalibur E8008. Irith hoped they were a good brand.

Bragg and Thornton moved off on their bellies down the walkway. They had practised it at the farm and went surprisingly quickly. Soon they were just dim wriggling shapes in the green field of the goggles, which overexposed to white in every lightning flash.

'It's 11.10,' said Irith to Levi. 'We needed two hours, not one.'

'If the wind drops, Jack'll be back. We've got to make good use of the extra time.'

'Is it likely to drop?'

'You can't tell with hurricanes.'

'What's it doing now?'

'It's ninety kilometres east, still tracking towards the north side of the lake. It's slowed right down.'

'Is that bad?'

'Means high wind for longer – and a lot more rain.'

Thorn and Bragg were halfway along now, at the point where the roof had been torn off. Irith could sense Gretel and Siah beside her though she could not see them.

'They'll be crawling through broken glass,' said Siah, chewing the ends off her fingers.

'How are you feeling?' Irith said in her ear.

'Like the world's biggest coward, just before she runs screaming into the night.'

'Can I go first?'

Siah managed a wintry smile.

Levi held a small piece of equipment in one hand and was turning a dial.

'What's that?' said Irith.

'Something top secret that fell into my hands. It's an infrared ghost generator – sends out dozens of man-shaped infrared ghost images. Very confusing to the enemy, if you use it at the right moment.'

Irith searched the adjacent building, hoping the goggles could pick up something. Beyond the two crawling figures, both doors into Building One had been torn off by the deluge that had almost ripped the walkway from its anchors. Inside all she saw was green shadows, mostly rectangular – building pillars and furniture. 'I can't see any guards, but I'm not always sure what I'm looking at.'

'Night vision takes a lot of familiarisation,' said Levi. 'And it doesn't work well in heavy rain. You might do better with the infrared goggles.' He passed them across, Excalibur IR500. 'If what you're seeing is alive, it should be brighter than the surroundings.'

Irith rubbed her eyes, put the goggles on and something pale and elongated ghosted across her field of view. Someone moving inside Building One.

She lost it but picked up another. This one was much clearer; closer. She could tell it was a man by the shape of the body. There was something in his hands – long and dark and pointing along the walkway.

'They've seen Thorn and Bragg!' Irith grabbed her rifle.

'Where?' cried Siah and Gretel together.

There was no time to tell them, nor to think about her vow. Irith put the weapon to her shoulder, flicked the switch back, sighted on her memory of the second figure and pulled the trigger. The muzzle flash lit up the area as she moved the rifle across and back and across again, firing over Thornton's and Bragg's heads.

A returning flash, and glass shattered at their end of the walkway. Irith kept her finger on the trigger, moving the barrel back and forth until the rifle chattered into silence. She had emptied all seven barrels. Their ends glowed in the darkness, faded and everything went black. She'd lost her night vision.

Gretel pulled Irith down hard beside her. 'There's a time to stand and a time to run and hide,' she said in the sudden silence. Ejecting Irith's spent barrels, she snapped in a fresh set. 'Next time, save some for later.'

Irith stared at the floor. She'd sworn not to shoot and she'd done it again. Had she killed the man? She felt numb.

Clang, clang, clang! An alarm had gone off somewhere in the next building. Irith waited for the returning fire that would tear them to pieces. It didn't come. Then a *crump*! simultaneous with a burst of light well inside the doorway of Building One.

Someone cried out. Levi was counting under his breath. '. . . Seven, eight, nine, ten.' He flicked the ghost generator switch.

Suddenly Bragg and Thornton were on their feet, running along the walkway, their weapons blazing. Irith pulled the goggles over her eyes. The scene swarmed with ghostly images although most were transparent, not particularly confusing. She could easily distinguish Bragg and Thornton. Their muzzle flashes were white. Other figures staggered across the field of view, not firing.

'Come on,' said Levi. 'The capsicum mist has done its work but it doesn't last long. Masks, everyone. And let's just pray they haven't been able to call for help, or there'll be a squadron of Security choppers overhead before you can scratch your backside.'

Irith pulled the mask over her eyes, nose and mouth and followed the others across the walkway. They couldn't run; there was too much debris on the floor.

As they reached the place where the roof had been torn open, a screaming wind threw them against the frame of the side wall, and it was like being punched in the ribs. The rain scythed at them, making it impossible to stand up. They had to go the last twenty metres on hands and knees.

By the time they reached the entrance to Building One, the battle was over. Bragg held a lantern on the scene while Thornton checked the casualties. Four guards were dead, although it wasn't clear whether from Irith's burst of fire or from the subsequent attack. Another three had a variety of ugly wounds. The remaining seven were on the floor, gasping and choking from the capsicum mist. Their faces were scarlet, their eyes weeping and noses running. Some had previous injuries, presumably incurred during the flood. None wore body armour; they hadn't been expecting the attack.

Thornton and Bragg disarmed the guards, rolled them onto their bellies and plasticuffed together everyone who could walk.

'Siah,' yelled Thornton, 'get across and guard the bridge to Building Two. Don't get shot.'

Siah froze, her masked eyes staring. Then, with a jerky movement she edged between the workstations and disappeared. Thornton took up his weapon again.

Irith stepped closer to Levi. 'I don't think she's coping,' she said quietly. 'We should try to shield her.'

'I've been doing all I can,' said Levi.

'We can't afford to nurse her,' said Thornton. 'She's got to tough it out.'

'Nor can we afford to push anyone beyond their strength,' said Bragg. 'As every good leader knows.'

'Now what?' said Bragg.

'We drive these guards across the other bridge to Building Two, then I'll work my magic on it. *Boom!*' said Thornton.

'What if they can't walk?'

'They'll die,' Thornton said loudly.

One of the soldiers was recovering from the capsicum mist. He was short and solid, like a weightlifter. 'What's your name, fellow?' said Bragg.

'Chick,' he said hoarsely. Every mucous membrane in his body was inflamed, his face was scarlet and blistered, his eyes dripped and his nose had a continuous flow.

'Chick?' Bragg sneered. 'What sort of a girlie name is that?'

Chick lashed out with a boot the size of a bucket but could not see well enough to strike. Bragg caught it, threw him on his back and put his own large boot on Chick's throat.

'Doesn't look as though you were expecting us?'

Chick wiped his nose on his sleeve. 'We were, until the hurricane. You were lucky.'

'We made our own luck. Where's your body armour?'

'In the barracks.'

'Not much use there. You pricks are amateurs.'

'If we hadn't lost twenty-one men in the flood we'd have ground you to little pieces.'

'You haven't got the balls for it,' said Thornton. 'How many more of you are there?'

'Find out, asshole!'

'We will. Gretel, get across to the other bridge with Siah, in case his mates are coming across.'

Chick's eyes darted in that direction. 'They'll already be on the way.'

'Then they'll get a nice welcome. Get moving.'

'They'll kill us.'

'So will I,' said Thornton. 'This way you get an extra few minutes of life. Leg it!'

'Where's Sheryl?' said Levi.

'I don't know.' Irith looked around. 'She didn't come across the bridge. Do you want me to go and find her?'

'She'll be safer where she is, and we'll have one thing less to worry about.'

They got the prisoners staggering, under the weight of their injured buddies, across the width of the building to the bridge on the other side. The bridge was intact, although the glass walls were cracked and leaking, and the doors of the security checkpoint were wide open. Siah, crouched in the darkness, swung her rifle at them.

'Easy!' cried Thornton. 'It's us.'

She laid her head against a concrete pillar, the rifle sagging floorwards.

'I didn't say you could take a holiday! '

Siah swung it up towards the bridge, avoiding his eye. The prisoners stopped and Chick turned around.

'Don't see any sign of your buddies, *Chick*,' said Bragg. 'I guess they're in the bathroom, shitting themselves.'

'As soon as you move,' Chick blustered, 'they'll cut you to little pieces and feed you to the alligators.'

Irith shivered. That was one hazard she hadn't thought about. There were thousands of alligators in the Louisiana bayous and hurricanes promised good eating.

'That's why you're going across first.' Bragg grinned.

Chick was sweating. 'They'll shoot.'

'Then you'd better signal them not to,' said Levi.

'How am I supposed to do that?'

Levi folded his arms. 'Your problem, matey.'

Chick nodded. 'I've got a signalling flashlight.'

'Get it, Irith,' said Levi.

She drew a slender grey torch from one of Chick's pouches.

Levi turned it on, then off again. 'Signal, "We're coming across," and nothing more,' he said to Chick.

He nodded. Levi turned the torch on and held it out. Chick signalled furiously. Levi knocked the torch out of his hand. Bragg cracked Chick over the head with his barrel, driving him to his knees.

'On your feet,' snapped Bragg. 'You're going across first.'

They uncuffed him from the others, pushed him out onto the walkway and forced the other soldiers after him, the able-bodied carrying the uncuffed injured.

Irith stood well back, watching through the nightscope on her rifle. Green shadows moved in the distance. 'Bragg, get out of the way!' she screamed.

Bragg threw himself sideways. Someone fired a burst from Building Two; bullets whined off walls and building columns. One of the prisoners dropped the injured man he was carrying and went down, screaming and holding his belly. The other prisoners kept crawling, dragging him by the cuffs. The man who had been dropped kicked feebly.

'They shot one of their own,' said Levi when the firing ceased. 'Because he was in the way.'

'Means they'll do anything to get across,' said Bragg.

'And when they do . . .'

'We'll have to blow the bridge,' said Thornton. 'And it can't be done from here. I'll go out the second-floor window and climb up underneath, while you keep up a covering fire.'

'How the hell are you going to do that, in this weather?' said Bragg.

CHAPTER THIRTY-FOUR

Irith acted as spotter while Bragg, Gretel and Siah fired at any movement and immediately moved to a new position.

Levi looked bleak. 'I hadn't planned on a long gun battle,' he said. 'We'll run out of ammo.'

Irith felt guilty at the way she had wasted hers. She looked at her watch, 11.42. 'Any news from Jack?'

'No.'

The injured man had stopped kicking and lay in a dark puddle. There had been no firing for several minutes. 'What's going on?' she whispered.

'I don't know.'

'Could the enemy be calling for help?'

'I doubt it. The landlines are out, we've brought down the communications tower and the jammer should have lain a cone of white noise over the compound. But they'll have a contingency plan. And they still outnumber us.'

He ducked instinctively as someone fired from Building Two. Bullets chewed pieces out of a desk to Irith's left. Gretel fired back and there was an immediate burst of return fire, followed by a cry from their left.

'Siah?' called Levi. 'Are you all right?'

'Yes,' she said unsteadily. 'Something whacked me on the forehead. Not a bullet, obviously.' She let out an hysterical peal of laughter.

'Put your bloody helmet on.'

Nothing happened for ten minutes. Irith, sure the enemy had some secret and bloody plan to counterattack, sweated.

'Thorn is taking too long,' Levi said to Irith. 'Give me the goggles. Go down and see what the delay is.'

'I'll go,' said Gretel, who was among the tumbled desks to their right.

'I need you here. Get moving, Irith. It's midnight.'

Thornton had gone down the steps to the second floor, planning to climb up underneath the bridge and blow the two concrete beams that supported it. Irith couldn't imagine how he was going to do that in this weather, but he had many talents and no one had trained harder during their three months up north.

She crept down the steps in the dark, not daring to use a torch in case they shot her through the window. If they had night-vision gear they might anyway. Several steps from the bottom, she splashed into water. The lightning was practically continuous now – did that mean the hurricane was almost on them?

To her right was an open window and, because it was on the lee side of the building, the wind wasn't as strong. She splashed across to it and looked out. Something spattered her visor. She wiped it off and it streaked red. Blood. Irith looked up. It was seeping from the side of the walkway, then down the wall to a point where the drips were blown at her.

She prayed that it wasn't Thornton's. She craned her neck, feeling incredibly exposed. The body armour only protected what it covered, and an armour-piercing round would go straight through it.

Irith thought she saw a shadow move underneath the walkway, over the far side. Thornton. A rope streamed out in the wind. He'd tossed a grappling iron over the top, swung himself up and in underneath.

After several attempts, she caught the end of the rope. She was psyching herself up to swing out, afraid the wind would slam her into the wall, when she saw movement up above. Someone had slid out from Building Two onto the intact roof of the walkway. The lightning flash was at just the right angle to carve out his silhouette.

Irith watched his creeping progress. To cling there in the wind he must be using climbing irons or magnets. Had he seen Thornton, or was he intending to attack Levi and the others?

The guard moved to his left and she lost sight of him. She dared not scream a warning to Thornton – if he heard, the attacker would too. Nor did she dare go back for her rifle. By the time she returned, he could have shot Thornton. She had to warn him, and that meant climbing up.

She took off her outer vest, which was too cumbersome to climb in, and tossed it up on the steps, but kept the helmet and visor. Her vision was restricted but at least it kept the rain out of her eyes. She pulled in the length of rope, looped it twice around her waist, tied it and swung out.

The wind slammed her against the wall, taking the skin off her knuckles. She whirled around on the rope and was thumped against the wall again. The helmet took the worst of the impact, fortunately, although her head spun. She lost her grip and fell, but was brought up by the rope around her waist and hurled at the wall again.

This time she broke the impact, though at the expense of her knees. She fended off the wall with her feet and pushed herself in under the bridge. Thornton was a good four metres above her, a tough climb. Despite her training up north, she wasn't strong enough to climb wet rope. She slipped, changed her grip and slipped again. Steadying herself by hanging onto an open window, Irith tried to work out a plan. She was feeling for handholds when the rope was jerked upwards. Before she could tell who had her, Irith was deposited onto a pair of climbing irons hammered into the wall.

An arm like an iron bar went across her chest and Thornton hissed in her ear, 'What the fuck do you think you're doing?'

'There's a guard crawling along the top of the walkway,' she shouted back.

'What, up there?' The wind shrieked and he had to yell it.

She pointed. 'Lost sight of him a couple of minutes ago.'

He cursed under his breath, then crushed her shoulder with one paw. 'Thanks, Irith.'

'What are we going to do?'

'I'm nearly finished. Keep watch.' He gave her his rifle. 'If anyone comes over the side, plug them.'

The wind tried to pull her off her footholds. He put her hand on another iron, at chest height. 'Grip that.'

'How am I supposed to shoot one-handed?' she muttered. She tried to point the rifle but the wind kept pushing it away.

Thornton, who was bare-headed, was working above his head with what looked like a caulking gun, squeezing thick threads of brown gunk into a gap at the base of one of the supporting beams of the bridge. 'C12 extrudible plastic explosive,' he said when she glanced at him. He was using a lot.

There came a burst from upstairs. Thornton pressed in a detonator and swung across to the other beam. Irith waved the gun around uselessly. If the soldier came down the far side, he could shoot Thornton before she saw him. She had to find him first.

She looked back. Thornton was still working in the darkness. Slinging the rifle over her shoulder, she reached for the first handhold, pulled herself up, got her toe in a gap and forced up again. It was much harder than her training; a hundred times harder in the dark, wind and rain.

The beam shuddered and Irith recalled the collapsed pillar on the far side. Was the building being undermined? The water seemed higher now; it was gnashing at the second-floor windows, and a wave passed between the buildings, foaming and crashing. Perhaps more of the perimeter wall had collapsed, like the wall of a dam. Or – the realisation was heart-stopping – the levee might be failing. If it did, none of these buildings would survive.

The wind died long enough for her to pull herself three-quarters of the way to the top. She couldn't go much further. Up there the gale would pluck her off.

She went up another small step. A large gap appeared between the bridge and the recessed wall of the building and she squeezed backwards into it, slowly pushing herself up so she would make no shadow, no silhouette when the lightning flashed.

Irith's eye level rose to the top of the bridge, then slightly above. She raised the weapon to her bruised shoulder and, as the lightning flashed, scanned the bridge. Nothing. Where was the soldier? Was he creeping along one side, or was he underneath?

She waited for the next lightning flash, and when it came the guard was on top of the bridge, just metres from her. He must have been wearing magnetic boots because he was standing upright in the wind. He drew his arm back. A thick, stubby cylinder bulked out his hand; some kind of grenade, she assumed. He was going to hurl it through the broken window, down onto Levi, Siah, Bragg and Gretel.

Then the guard saw her. He tried to stop his throw in mid-swing but was caught off-balance. One foot tore free and he fell to one knee with his mouth open. Irith fired and her bullets carved a jagged line through the roof towards his feet. He threw himself backwards, the wind caught him and he went over the side, hurling the grenade away before he hit the water.

She screamed, 'Thornton, grenade. Hang –'

A waterspout exploded upwards, then the shockwave shook the building so violently that she was sure it would topple. The explosion of water was like a series of hammer blows to her legs and chest. She forced herself back into her cavity, clung on desperately, and prayed.

The world came back to normal. She wiped off her visor, looked down and could not see Thornton. She scrambled down, around the corner and onto the irons, imagining what the others must be thinking upstairs.

'Thornton?'

She heard a strangled gasp, a long way below. The deluge had torn him off his perch and he was swinging wildly on the end of his rope, feebly fending himself off the wall with his feet. There was firing above them, from both ends of the bridge.

She climbed across. 'Are you all right?'

'Terrific! I've knocked half my fucking teeth out.'

'Sorry,' she said, thinking he was blaming her. 'I –'

'Give me a hand.'

'What do you want me to do?'

'Pull on the bloody rope!'

'I'll never lift your weight.'

'I just need a bit of help. I've hurt my wrist.'

She heaved, though it was like trying to lift a refrigerator. He came upright then hauled himself up the rope one-handed. How immensely strong he was. Back on his spikes, he said, 'Thanks. *Again*. Steady me while I check the detonators.'

He poked the nearest one with a finger, swaying on the spikes. Irith clutched his arm, knowing that if he fell she would go too.

'It's all right,' he said, slurring because of his broken mouth. 'I'll check the other one and we'll clear out.'

He edged past, slipped and sprang to the next spike. Irith was sure he was going to fall but the cleated boots held. He inspected his work with a torch not much bigger than his index finger. 'Let's go.'

This was the part Irith had been dreading. 'I can't do it by myself. The wind kept blowing me into the wall.'

'I'm not sure I can get to that window either.' He measured the distance with his eyes, then unfastened her rope and let it go. 'Where's your vest?'

'I left it behind. It was too awkward to climb in.'

'Bloody idiot,' he said, though not angrily. 'I'll try and go in backwards. Come here.' He pulled her to his chest with his injured arm.

'What are you doing?' she yelped.

'I'm going to swing out and crash through that window there. Won't be as easy as it looks in the movies, or as safe, but I think we'll manage. Ready?'

'No,' she said in a small voice.

'Good. Put your arms around me, under my coat, tuck your head in and hang on.'

She did so. He counted *one, two, three* as he judged the gusts of wind, then pushed off. Irith couldn't resist the urge to look up as they swung around on the rope. For an instant she thought the wind was going to drive them into the side of the building but they curved sharply and swung at the window.

Shards came at her face, smashing into the visor of her helmet, then they were through, sliding off the end of the rope to land with a splash in the water. Glass went everywhere, a fragment stabbing through her trousers, and the water closed over her head. She hit the floor, then Thornton was pulling her up and standing her on her feet. The water was up to her breasts; his waist.

She steadied herself against the wall. Thornton swayed.

'Are you all right?' she cried.

'I'll lean on your shoulder for a while. Let's get up the stairs. This isn't a good place to be when the C12 goes off. I used quite a bit of the stuff.'

They staggered up the steps, onto the third floor. Gretel came running out, shrieking, 'Thorn, Thorn!'

There was a burst of gunfire from the other end of the tunnel. Irith heard the thud of bullets hitting Gretel's chest plate; she was lifted off her feet and hurled backwards. Levi, Bragg and Siah fired together. Gretel rolled over, crawled to safety and threw her arms about her brother.

'That was a stupid thing to do,' said Bragg.

She paid him no attention. 'I was sure you were dead, Thorn.'

'It was close enough,' he mumbled. His nose was squashed flat. He felt inside his mouth. 'Only two teeth gone. Feels like a dozen.'

Bragg and Siah gathered around. 'Couldn't you do it?' said Siah.

'I did it, but if it wasn't for Irith we'd all be dead. You OK, Gretel?'

She pulled the Kevlar plate out of the pocket of her vest. It had two gouges in it, roughly over the location of her heart. 'Just very bruised.'

'They're coming!' yelled Levi, firing up the tunnel.

Irith threw herself behind a toppled workstation and unslung Thorn's rifle. The guards were charging, at least a dozen of them, judging by the muzzle flashes.

'Thorn!' roared Bragg over the racket. 'Blow the fucking bridge, for Chrissake!'

Thornton put a hand in his pocket. Nothing happened. The guards were halfway along the bridge.

'What's the matter?' Levi screamed.

If that many guards made it through they would all be slaughtered. Irith fired at one of the leaders and knew she had hit him, but he didn't fall. These ones had their body armour on.

Two explosions, almost simultaneously. Brilliant red flame erupted, the colour of a firework display, but was blocked out by boiling clouds of dust. There was a grinding and tearing noise, rubble hurtled through the air and two holes appeared in the wall, one large, the other small.

As the bridge fell, a soldier was projected through the air at them as if he had been swept with a broom, still shooting. A bullet screamed off the very top of Irith's helmet and it was like being thumped on the head with a mallet.

Siah fired a long burst. The soldier fell on his face a few yards away. No one else came through. When the smoke and dust cleared, the bridge, and the soldiers, were gone, and no one could be seen at the other end.

'Better check the side of the building, in case they're climbing up,' said Levi. He had a mobile to his ear and was tapping the case.

'They all went into the water with the bridge,' Siah whispered. 'Even if they survived that, in body armour and boots they wouldn't have a chance.'

Irith's head throbbed. She took off her helmet. The titanium was dented on the top but the inside was undeformed. She ran a fingertip along the groove.

'They're good value, these titanium helmets,' said Bragg. 'That would have blown your –' He broke off. 'Sorry, Irith. Might be an idea to put on the jacket, don't you think?'

She shook her head, trying to clear it. She felt dazed. 'I've no idea where I left it.'

'It's down on the stairs.' Thornton fetched it and put it on her.

'It's 12.19,' said Levi briskly. 'We're an hour and a quarter overtime and the job's still to be done. Let's get on with it.'

The man on the floor rolled over, coughing blood. It was Chick. Siah's burst had cut through his body armour and the blood underneath him would have filled a saucepan.

'You won't – get away with it,' he gasped, spitting red saliva.

'How so?' Levi said mildly.

'Three people – alive missile bunker. When – chopper comes back – blow it – out of sky.'

'Both launchers are in the water,' said Thornton. 'They won't be firing anything.'

'Got – shoulder-launched – missiles,' said Chick weakly. 'Put one – right up – asshole – from there.'

'Really?' said Thornton. 'What kind?'

Chick set his lips.

'You won't be alive to see it.' Levi bent over Chick, who gave a wrenching spasm and closed his eyes. 'You're dying.'

'Least – I did – my duty.'

'You served a bigger monster than Stalin and Pol Pot,' said Levi.

Chick didn't move again. Siah let out a wailing cry. 'I killed him!'

'What's the matter with her now?' said Thornton.

'She shot him and now he's dead,' said Irith.

'That all?' said Thornton. 'I thought it was something serious.'

They moved into the centre of the third floor, where it was quieter and drier. Levi was checking the weather with his laptop. He turned one of his lanterns on, then dimmed it until the glow illuminated a circle around their faces. 'We've silenced the opposition. The hurricane has wobbled east and the winds have dropped a bit, but they could rise at any time. Let's get the jerry cans and do the job we came for, before it comes back.'

'Might be an idea to call Jack and see where he is,' said Bragg.

'He's on the roof now,' said Levi. 'He came back a few minutes ago.'

'Better warn him about the shoulder-launched missiles,' said Bragg.

Levi stopped. 'Pity we don't have a rocket-propelled grenade. I don't fancy Jack's chances now the three at the missile bunker know we're here.'

'We'll have to take it out,' said Thornton, who was holding his arm out while Gretel bandaged his wrist.

She dropped the bandage roll. 'No! If you go into the water, you'll die.'

CHAPTER THIRTY-FIVE

'I've got an idea,' said Thornton. 'I think it can work.'

'Don't be stupid.' Gretel jerked at his arm. 'You've done enough.'

'We've all done enough, but the job's not done.'

'Why does it always have to be you?'

'I'm the explosives man, and the champion swimmer.'

'What's your plan, Thorn?' said Bragg, his voice barely audible over the roar of the wind.

Thornton led them to the nearest window, pointed across the flooded compound and waited until the next flash of lightning. 'See the corner wall, there, and the missile bunker with the side torn out of it?'

Irith could just make it out with her nightscope, through the rain. Taking the night glasses from around Levi's neck, she focused them. They picked up several brighter blobs, probably people, and a high, curving arc of debris in front and to the left of the bunker.

Thornton took her nightscope. 'There's a shoulder launcher on a stand. Looks like a Mistral fire-and-forget set-up. It uses a two-stage solid propellant rocket motor, and it's good against helicopters out to 4000 metres, using infrared guidance. They're French made. Pretty reliable.'

'How reliable?' said Bragg.

'A kill rate of ninety-two per cent.'

Bragg whistled. 'That's good.'

'Would be less under these conditions – high wind, torrential rain and lightning all around, but we can't risk it. It has to be taken out.'

'Do they have to go outside to fire it?'

'They could fire through the hole in the wall,' said Thornton. 'Wouldn't be very comfortable in there at the moment.'

'More comfortable than in the chopper, if they hit it,' said Bragg.

'See the way the current flows? It swirls around these three buildings, and between them, which is why this one is partly undermined –'

As if to emphasise Thornton's words the building gave a little shudder.

'. . . *partly* undermined.' He grinned, revealing the bloody gap where his two front upper teeth had been. Gretel wailed. He put an arm around her. 'It's all right, sis. A couple of teeth are nothing.'

'The streamline passes where we entered from Building Three,' he continued, 'swirls out then races diagonally across the compound, round by the bunker and out where the southern wall used to be. I'll catch the current across, then paddle to the rubble pile to the left of the bunker.' He pointed. 'The flagpole goes up directly behind it. I'll work along the rubble in the dark and take them by surprise. They won't be expecting any attack that way.'

'Because it can't be done,' said Gretel. 'Thorn, please . . .'

'I think I just saw an alligator!' cried Irith, who had the night glasses.

'Doubt if they'll be feeding in this,' said Thornton. 'Tomorrow's their day.'

'Everyone who's gone into the water today has drowned.'

'The currents will be slower now, and the guards who drowned were wearing body armour, boots and helmets, that must have weighed twenty kilos. I'll just be wearing pants and shirt, and something to give me buoyancy. I was a champion surf swimmer, remember?'

'You're right,' said Levi. 'It has to be done and you're the only one who can do it. Get ready, Thorn. We'll go up to Jack and bring the fuel drums over. Irith, you're a damn fine shot. Stay here and keep watch. If anyone moves in Thorn's direction, shoot them.'

Just like that. In spite of all she had been through, it still shocked her.

'I'll defend him to the best of my ability.' It was a better way of thinking of it.

'See that you do.' Gretel squeezed Irith's shoulder, hard, and it was not the friendly gesture Thorn's had been. She embraced her brother as if she was never going to see him again.

'Good luck,' said Levi. Bragg and Siah echoed him, then they were gone.

'Do you really think you can do it?' said Irith. 'That current looks nasty.'

'Won't know until I try.' His eyes met hers and for the first time they were equals together. It was a strangely warming feeling; their night together in the Minnesota might never have happened. 'Hopefully the current will take me all the way, and I won't have to swim more than a few strokes.'

'You've got a sprained wrist.'

'Most of the power comes from the kick.' He stripped off the ballistic vest but kept on his rubber-soled shoes. 'I'll need some buoyancy.'

They found some plastic water bottles in the canteen kitchen. He emptied them, screwed the caps on tightly and Irith taped them to his chest and back, under his shirt. He checked a long knife strapped to his calf. 'That's everything, except the bomb.'

From a backpack he took another cylinder of C12 and squeezed the contents into a reinforced container. He carefully disconnected an aerial on the outside of the container, took a detonator from a shockproof plastic case, rotated the activator and pushed the detonator into the explosive. Finally he screwed the cap on, sealing it all around.

'All I have to do is connect the aerial and press my firing button,' Thorn said. 'I won't connect the aerial until I'm ready to use it. A stray radio signal on the right frequency could set off the detonator. Bad result!' He grinned his bloodstained grin.

Irith tried to smile but couldn't.

'I'm ready,' he said. 'Let's see what I can find to get me across.'

'I saw a length of plastic pipe down below,' she said. It was a three-inch grey pipe, capped on both ends and a couple of metres long. She passed it up.

'Perfect.' He carried it across to the side of the floor facing Building Three.

The gale blew in through the broken windows, hot, humid and salty. As Irith moved through the piled furniture she caught an occasional stinging whiff of capsicum mist.

Thorn blacked his face with crayon and looked for a way down. 'There!' He pointed through the collapsed section. 'That looks easy enough.'

'Have you got the bomb?'

He patted the little backpack that sat high on his shoulders.

'And the firing mechanism?'

'Better check the seals.' Thornton opened the plastic case and studied its O-ring under the bright lantern light. 'The mechanism is supposed to be waterproof but I prefer to be sure.' He took the firing mechanism out and pressed the test button three times. The LED glowed each time. He packed it away.

'That's it. I'm off,' he said casually, walking towards the collapsed area. He stopped and turned. 'Goodbye, Irith. I don't expect I'll be coming back.'

'But . . .' She looked up at him. 'You said to Gretel . . .'

'What else could I say?'

'About Minnesota ... I'm sorry.' With hindsight, it was such a little thing to make a fuss about.

'I was a bloody fool.'

'I'll never forget it,' she said.

He hugged her to him. 'It's been great knowing you, Irith. Look after Gretel for me.'

'I'll do my best.' Now there was a challenge.

He kissed her forehead with his battered mouth, turned away and did not look back.

The lightning was less frequent now, and with each flash it was harder to pick him out. Finally, she lost sight of him in the rubble. Irith picked up her rifle and trudged across to the other side of the building, where she could see the bunker.

Taking up position on a pile of desks close to a broken window, she got ready. The wind had shifted and it was like being outside in the rain. She put her dented helmet on and pulled up the neck flaps of her vest. Irith sighted through the nightscope at the bunker, adjusted for the range, about 130 metres, and checked again.

A pale shape moved behind the broken bunker wall. She scanned across the water but did not see Thorn. She noted two markers and tried to calculate how quickly a piece of floating debris was carried between them; the current was moving fast, a couple of metres a second. A champion swimmer might hold his position in the water for a minute or two against it, but could not swim any distance upcurrent.

She suppressed the thought that Thorn had drowned already, alone and out of sight. There could be anything in that water – broken timber, wrecked vehicles, tangles of razor wire. Alligators.

He probably had not made his way along the other side of the building and out into the current. Irith moved her scope to the left, focused on the point where he should appear, and waited.

She almost missed him; he was further out than she had expected. The grey tubing did not show, but in the darkness between flashes the nightscope picked up a brighter blob that was his upper body. What was it like out there? Did he feel confident in his great strength, or was Thorn's heart pounding as wildly as hers?

The current carried him towards the corner of the standing wall and the bunker. He was aiming for the steep beach of rubble on the northern, upcurrent side. The tubing bobbed to the surface ahead of him and was carried swiftly away. She caught her breath, gripping her rifle so hard that it hurt. Thorn was swimming at a slight angle to the current, using it to carry him to the rubble.

He got to within a few strokes of it before an eddy whirled him past. Now he had to swim against the current, and he couldn't possibly do it. The water whipped him backwards. Irith felt she could read his heart-bursting strain in the motions of that small green blob in her nightsight.

Thornton made ground; a metre, then two. He went backwards another metre, recovered it, then forward another. He was almost there. Again, he was flung backwards. She cried out. He made a supreme effort and she saw, clearly, his hand touch the rubble. The current tried to tear him away and she could scarcely bear to breathe. She imagined him desperately hanging on with one hand while he tried to kick his way to safety.

Then, suddenly, he was head and shoulders on the rocks. He dragged himself further up, lying flat on the rubble. She fancied she could see his great chest heaving. He had made it. Tears poured down her cheeks. Thorn had done it! An Olympic champion could have done no better.

He did not move. Minutes went by and still he lay motionless on the rubble. Irith began to worry anew. She stood up, trying to see what was the matter, but could extract no more resolution from the nightscope.

Someone moved out from behind the broken bunker wall, pointing a long object. Irith aimed at the figure and was psyching herself up to kill when the nightscope overexposed. A rocket blasted away, a brilliant point of light that was gone in a fraction of a second. By the time she reached the window there was no sign of it. She couldn't shoot at the guard; her night vision was gone.

Had he fired at Jack's chopper? She must assume so, but there was no way of telling if the rocket had hit. She wouldn't hear an explosion beyond the building, nor distinguish its flare from the almost continuous lightning.

They might all be dead but she could not think about that now. She turned back to the bunker but could only see the afterimage of the rocket's flare. Minutes passed before her night vision began to return and then she could not see Thornton at all.

Irith scanned back and forth across the rubble. A man-sized shape darted across a gap, then disappeared. Her finger tightened on the trigger but she dared not shoot. It was probably him.

There was a thump beside her. Irith looked around wildly.

'What's happening?' Gretel said in a cracked voice.

'Thorn got there, but before he could attack the bunker they fired a missile into the sky; lost my night vision. Someone's moving about but I don't dare shoot.'

'Aah!' Gretel cried, peering through her nightscope. 'He's going to die.'

Irith caught a muzzle flash from the far end of the rubble. Thorn didn't have a gun. She sighted but released the trigger. He might have captured a weapon.

Everything was dark at the bunker now. 'They've shot him,' Gretel wailed.

Irith felt like slapping her across the face. She was making things worse.

The bunker erupted in a huge explosion that ruined her night vision for a third time.

'He's done it!' Irith yelled.

Debris rained down on the water. Nothing burned, but for minutes afterwards, the former bunker was a series of ragged white blobs in the nightscope, much hotter than the surroundings. Other blobs and shapes were scattered across the rubble – hot debris from the explosion. Some might have been bodies but there was no way of telling. Nothing moved.

Gretel stood up and now her face was expressionless. 'We'd better go,' she said in a dead voice.

'Where?' said Irith, unable to come to terms with Thorn's death.

Gretel was as mechanical as a robot. 'Levi and Jack have ferried the petrol over in the chopper. Bragg's carrying the jerry cans down now. It's your turn, Irith, and you'd better not fuck up.'

'But ... the missile ...'

'It took out a burning house at West End. Weather isn't ideal for infrared missiles.'

They moved up the stairs, which were littered with glass and rubble. The fourth and fifth floors of Building Two were dimly lit, and there were stark faces at the windows. Perhaps they expected to share the fate of the soldiers on the bridge.

They reached the fourth floor. 'Where are the labs?' There had been none on the third floor. Once again their information had been incorrect.

'How the fuck would I know?' snarled Gretel.

Her weapon was pointed at the roof. Irith could not imagine what she was thinking, or feeling. She was a closed book. But, Irith realised with a shiver, not a person she wanted to have behind her in Gretel's present state.

The entrance to the fourth floor was closed but not locked, and there was no security checkpoint at the entrance, so it was unlikely to house the facilities they were looking for. She stepped inside, her rifle held out, and flicked a switch on the wall. The emergency lights came on. She saw a series of preparation laboratories though none contained the kind of equipment she was looking for.

On the way out, she encountered Levi, Bragg and Siah. Siah looked like a walking corpse, with bloody fingertips and staring eyes.

Irith felt for her. 'Nothing here that needs to be destroyed,' she said.

'Let's go up. The hurricane's drifting our way again. It's 12.54 am. We've got twenty minutes.'

'What happens then?'

'Winds stronger than Jack's flight threshold. He'll have to go, and this time I wouldn't bet on him getting back. Let's get the job done and get out.'

'I can't wait,' said Irith.

CHAPTER THIRTY-SIX

They headed up the stairs. The building shook occasionally from the force of the wind, and the flood tearing at its foundations. How much more could it take?

'Sheryl said everyone had been evacuated to Building Two, didn't she?' asked Levi.

'Yes,' said Irith.

It meant nothing. Any number of people could have come back before Thornton blew the bridge.

The entrance to the fifth floor had an airlock and was a quarantine facility, although it only had low-level security. It was unlikely to be doing the kind of work they were looking for.

'There's a light on at the back of the lab,' said Siah. 'And the airlock door's open.'

Levi slid an arm around the door and pointed the motion detector inside. 'Nothing,' he said after a long interval. 'Let's go in.'

They went through the airlock. The open doors indicated there was nothing hazardous inside, or at least not any longer. 'I really hope 27 August was the right date,' Irith said under her breath.

'I was thinking the same thing,' said Levi beside her. 'Spread out, everyone, in case there are guards in hiding.'

They fanned out between the benches, some of which had recently been cleared of equipment. They saw no one.

'Nothing to worry about here,' said Irith, after walking from one side of the laboratory to the other. 'Let's go up to the sixth.'

The sixth level was locked and had the three-stage security system they had been expecting, although with the main power supply off only the iris scanner was working. Levi hacked in and opened the doors within a minute. Inside, they found an airlock, emergency decontamination showers, and racks of survival suits and breathing apparatus. The laboratory was divided into five sections, each with a variety of equipment, benches and biological safety cabinet rooms.

'It's a Biosafety Level Four laboratory, the highest level of safety for handling infectious disease organisms,' said Irith after inspecting the safety cabinet rooms. Each had double doors separated by decontamination showers. 'The walls, floor and ceiling form a sealed shell. This must be where they did the development work on the virus. We'd better destroy it, to be sure.'

They continued to the seventh level, whose entrance also had a three-stage security system.

'Is this the culturing laboratory?' Levi asked.

'Has to be,' said Bragg. 'Open it up, Levi. I'm itching to burn it and go home.'

'Shouldn't take long.' Levi was connecting probes to his laptop. 'What do you expect inside, Irith?'

'Like the previous floor, only more so. Double airlocks and a negative pressure, stand-alone air-conditioning system with three-stage air filtration. All the virus-handling work will be done in Class Three Biological Safety Cabinets. There should be a variety of equipment including gene and protein sequencers and synthesisers, incubators, freezers, various kinds of microscopes –'

'I get the picture. If we blow the doors, do we risk dispersing the virus from the containment tanks?'

'It'll be kept in lined steel containers,' said Irith, 'and they needn't be that big. Since the virus is so contagious, there's no need to create much of it. Their stock could probably fit in a large thermos flask.'

'Really? I thought there'd be drums of the stuff. I flask could be hidden anywhere.'

'There's a hurricane coming and Thorn is still out there!' snapped Gretel. 'Let's blow the place into orbit and piss off.'

Clearly, she did not believe that Thornton was dead. But he had to be, after that explosion.

'Bragg and Gretel,' said Levi, 'bring down the rest of the jerry cans and the detonators. Don't arm them until I say so, then make sure the airlocks and fire doors are closed. We've got to synchronise this carefully or we'll incinerate ourselves. Siah, stay with me and keep watch.'

'If you're up to it,' sneered Gretel.

Siah closed her eyes in anguish and rocked back and forth.

'Do your job and keep your mouth shut, Gretel!' Levi hissed.

Gretel and Bragg ran up the stairs. Levi attached his probes to the door and had it open within seconds. He sat back. 'It wasn't locked.'

'Maybe the power failure has affected all the security systems,' said Irith.

'The door's got power. Be careful.'

'I killed that poor guard, Levi,' Siah choked. 'I can't – take – any more.'

'You've got to keep going,' said Levi. 'We need you, Siah.'

They went through the airlock. To their left were three fully enclosed emergency showers, a room containing isolation suits with masks and air cylinders, and a bank of autoclaves. Further on were a number of biological safety cabinet rooms. To the right, through an open airlock, were offices with workstations and terminals. In the centre was a meeting room. Through the door, Irith could see chairs, a whiteboard and a long bench running across the room, in front of a raised platform.

'Any idea where the virus would be kept?' said Levi.

Irith was checking the rooms as they passed. 'In one of the safety cabinets.'

She had checked the first two cabinet rooms and was just passing the meeting room door when the motion detector gave a series of rising pings. 'What was that?' cried Levi.

A man rose from behind the long bench. He was tall and lean, almost cadaverous, and his eyes had a manic stare – Per Lindstrom. His clothes were wet, his hair wild, and there was a purple bruise over his right eye. He swayed but steadied himself.

'What took you so long?' he said in a rasping but hypnotic voice.

'Lindstrom!' Levi cried.

'Good to meet you at last, Levi.'

'I wish I could say the same.'

'You should.' Lindstrom swayed again. Was he suffering concussion from the head blow?

'You were expecting us?' said Levi.

He sounded disbelieving and afraid, and that alarmed Irith. Levi's right hand trembled.

'Did you really think you could get away with everything you've done, undetected?'

'I did, as it happens.'

'More fool you.'

Lindstrom reached below the bench and pulled a small, dark-haired woman to her feet. There was a lot of grey in her hair, and lines of exhaustion on her pale, round face.

'Mum!' Irith cried.

Jemma had aged in the past six months. A strip of cloth was bound across her mouth so tightly that it left white marks across her cheeks.

'Jemma!' said Levi.

'Stay where you are,' snapped Lindstrom, raising his left hand so they could see the plasticuff, and the two metres of chain, connecting Jemma to him. His hand shook and, as he struggled to conceal it, his voice slurred a little. Could he be drunk?

'I've got an explosive device strapped to my chest.' He tapped his breastbone. 'One thump and it goes off, and she's dead too.'

'Doesn't sound like you,' said Levi.

'My work is done. I never planned to hang around after it was finished.'

'What do you mean?' cried Irith.

Lindstrom ignored her. He had gained control of his speech but now spoke too loudly, even accounting for the racket outside. 'You're too late, Levi. The virus has been shipped out already. It'll be dispersed across the world within days and there's nothing you can do about it.'

Levi looked as though his innards had been sucked out. Everything they'd done had been for nothing. Yet, beyond hope, Jemma was here. Irith had to be strong now; there had to be a way to save her.

She cast a glance to her left. Siah was hyperventilating again, her mouth opening and closing, her throat working. Her rifle was pointing at the floor. She had been pushed too far and Irith could not rely on her for anything.

'I don't believe you,' said Levi, though his voice was dead. 'If the virus was gone, you wouldn't still be here.'

'I always planned to be here at the end,' said Lindstrom, 'once it was too late to stop the virus. I plan to go out in a spectacular fashion.'

'You're lying,' Levi said unconvincingly.

'You might have beaten me if you'd attacked when you got here,' Lindstrom taunted. 'But you didn't. Were you too afraid?'

'We were waiting for suitable weather,' said Levi.

'The blonde,' Lindstrom indicated Siah, 'looks as though she's having a heart attack. Run while you can!' he sneered, waving the gun at her.

Siah had bitten through her lip and blood was trickling down her chin. She looked around wildly, making a moaning sound in her throat.

'No, Siah!' cried Irith.

'Don't listen to him,' said Levi. 'He's –'

'I told you, Levi,' Siah burst out shrilly. '*I can't do it!*' She stumbled away, then ran.

Irith closed her eyes but when she opened them everything was the same. Lindstrom still there, Jemma still his prisoner, Siah gone. And Levi, who had saved them so many times, helpless to do anything.

Lindstrom began to laugh. 'What a pathetic mob you are! I overestimated you, Levi. August 27 was a dummy date. You should have come three days ago.'

Then Irith saw that her mother's eyebrows were going up and down, as if she were trying to convey a message. Jemma shook her head, twice. Was Lindstrom lying? Irith felt a surge of hope.

'What is your great spectacle?' said Irith. She had to keep him talking, for Jemma had turned slightly away from Lindstrom and was trying to get her free hand, which was bound to her side, up to the gag. Her fingers made signals at Irith. She *was* trying to tell her something.

'Irith Hardey,' Lindstrom said, turning to face her. He swallowed several times, as if trying to clear a blockage, and when he finally spoke the slur was back. 'It's a pleasure to meet you at last – there's more to *you* than I'd thought. The same could have been said about your mother, back in the bad old days. Thank heavens she's seen the light; she's my strongest supporter now.'

Jemma shook her head. She had raised her left hand to her face and was tugging at the gag.

Irith waved her gun in the air as a distraction. 'Then how come you have to bind and gag her?'

Lindstrom put his hand towards the centre of his chest, tapping gently. 'Put down the gun!'

'You're not going to blow yourself up,' she said. 'Not until you've had your triumph.'

'People always underestimate me.' He pulled an automatic out of his pocket and pointed it at Jemma's head. His hand had a slight tremor. 'Drop your weapons, both of you. I'm not alone.'

A man stepped out from behind the wall to their left, dressed in a Congress Security uniform. A bloodstained bandage enveloped his forehead but the gun in his hand was steady and aimed at Irith. A woman appeared to the right. She was also uniformed, but her left arm was in a sling and heavily bandaged. She carried a small handgun.

'You *have* been through the wars,' said Levi, still holding his rifle, although he had lowered the barrel.

'Nature makes fools of us all,' said Lindstrom. 'I bow to her wisdom.'

Irith put her assault rifle on the bench beside her. The woman came forward for Levi's rifle. Irith glanced sideways as he pressed a recessed button on the stock. He was up to something.

The woman took hold of the barrel and received a shock that hurled her backwards against one of the desks, her legs thrashing. He swung the rifle and shot the other guard in the chest.

Lindstrom thrust his gun barrel against Jemma's head. 'I'll shoot,' he roared. 'Drop it.'

Levi dropped the rifle.

'I take no chances,' Lindstrom went on, controlling his voice with an effort. 'I never have. That's why I also have *this*!'

He raised his right hand, revealing a cluster of steel cylinders, each a few centimetres in diameter and about twenty-five centimetres long, bound together with white duct tape.

'It's the rest of the virus. Your mother and I plan to make a demonstration with it, live, over the city.'

'What did we ever do to you?' Irith cried.

'Your mother thwarted me, a long time ago, and because she did, the Earth has suffered cruelly. Had I prevailed, nature would already be repairing the damage of the past. Instead, more is being destroyed every day. She has to pay her debt to the Earth. You all do. That's all there is to it.'

'You're a lunatic out for revenge!' said Irith, aware that it was a stupid thing to say. Lindstrom wasn't mad at all, and she should be making an impassioned plea for humanity's survival, but the words wouldn't come..

'How biblical your thought patterns are,' slurred Lindstrom. 'I don't hate your mother, or you, or anyone. This is retribution, not revenge.' He was calm now, and his words all the more chilling for it. He waved the automatic. 'Give me your mobile, Levi.'

After a brief hesitation, Levi went forward and put it on the table. Lindstrom shoved it in his pocket.

'That's all?' Irith cried. 'That's why you destroyed my life, and Jemma's?'

'I haven't destroyed your lives yet. That's the last act.'

Jemma finally got a finger under the gag and wrenched it down. 'The virus isn't gone,' she croaked. 'He's got it in there. Things went wrong and that's all there is.'

Lindstrom swung around and slammed the bundle of cylinders into the side of her head, though his jerking arm made it into a glancing blow.

Jemma kept yelling as she fell. 'He didn't know you were coming. The hurricane trapped him. I tried to tell you what he's –'

He thumped her with the cylinders and she fell silent. Irith and Levi ran forward but Lindstrom stamped his foot and a transparent safety screen shot up from the floor in front of the bench. Levi was quick to recover his rifle but the bullets bounced off the screen.

Lindstrom heaved Jemma over his shoulder and turned away, the deadly cylinders dangling from his other hand. He now moved with a disjointed, almost dance-like gait. He had to be drunk, surely?

Suddenly Levi's phone crackled into the silence.

'Levi!' said Jack. 'Wind's above the threshold. Got to go *right now*. I'll be back when it drops, whenever that is.' Lindstrom cursed and lurched through the far door. The great lock spun and closed.

'He planned to take the chopper,' said Irith. 'That's why he wanted the phone.'

'Stand back!' yelled Levi. Pointing his Metal Storm rifle at the screen, he set the switch to continuous and pulled the trigger.

The racket was unbelievable. He moved the barrel in a circle, the impacts eroded the glass, then he kicked out the centre of the circle. 'At eight thousand rounds per minute you can chew through almost anything. Assuming you have enough ammo.'

He snapped in a fresh set of barrels and began to climb through, but jerked his hand away from the gouged and shattered rim. 'Shit! That's hot!' He threw his vest over the glass and pushed himself through.

Irith did not follow. There was no point in Lindstrom heading for the roof now. He'd either hide or make a stand, and they could not attack him without risking Jemma's life.

'Irith!' Levi yelled. 'Run down to Bragg and Gretel. Don't let them blow the incendiaries, for God's sake. I'll go after Lindstrom.'

'Be careful,' Irith cried.

'Don't worry.'

Irith turned away, then spun back. 'What did Mum mean by, "I tried to tell you"?'

After a hesitation, he said, 'She was my mole in Lindstrom's office.'

'You risked Mum's life?'

'You pestered me to find out more about the terminator virus. And Jemma was happy to do it. If it hadn't been for her –'

'But I didn't know it was Mum! Why didn't you tell me?' Irith knew she was being irrational but couldn't help it.

'There's no time for this, Irith. Search the computer files and find out what the terminator virus really is. But first, stop Bragg!'

Irith ran for the stairs on the other side of the building. She saw no one on the way up to the roof door, which meant they had to be down on the sixth floor. She crashed down the stairs and raced through the open airlock. Bragg was taping a detonating device to one of the jerry cans. Gretel stood by, finger on her trigger.

'Stop!' Irith screamed.

He stood up, rubbing one knee. He was unnaturally calm. 'What's the matter?'

'Lindstrom's here, hiding somewhere in the building. He's got Mum as a hostage,' she gasped out, 'and the virus too. I've got to get into the computers and find out what it really is. And Jack's had to go – the wind's too strong – so we're stuck here till he can come back.'

Bragg took her hand. 'Slow down. Go through it from the beginning.'

She explained. 'And Lindstrom's got Levi's phone, so he'll know when Jack is coming back, but we won't. I've got to find out about the terminator virus.'

'Pity we blew the bridge,' said Bragg. 'We could have gone over to Building Two and interrogated a few scientists.'

'And Siah's cracked,' Irith said. 'She ran off somewhere.'

'She kept telling us that she wasn't up to it,' said Bragg. 'We should have listened.'

Gretel opened her mouth but Irith rushed out, 'I've got to get into their computer system, *now*.'

'Gretel can do that. I'll go and help Levi.'

'Thanks, Bragg.' He had already turned away. 'Gretel?'

'Thorn's out there somewhere, all alone and injured,' Gretel said icily, 'and you –'

'And he'd want us to finish the job,' Irith roared. 'Just get me into the computer system and you can piss off.'

'How am I supposed to do that with the power off?'

'You're supposed to be the computer genius! There's emergency power to the security system, and there's bound to be a backup system, or batteries, in a place like this. The biological safety cabinets still have power.'

The rifle shook and for a ghastly second Irith thought Gretel was going to shoot her down, then she stalked out. Irith slumped onto a stool. Her head was pounding and the shrieking wind made it worse. She waited, rifle pointed loosely at the door. Where could Siah have gone? She had to help her too, but this was more urgent.

The hurricane was definitely intensifying. Lightning flashed in sheets, the building shook continually and the walls were struck by barrages of flying debris. How much more could it take? She imagined the walls being steadily undermined, the foundations sinking into the saturated ground, then the building slowly toppling into the torrent that foamed all around them. Time was ticking away and every minute she expected to hear a blast that would end Jemma. Though . . . she might not hear it at all.

Now feeling claustrophobic in the steamy room, Irith went across to the nearest window. They were necessarily small on the quarantine floor, triple-glazed and made of toughened glass. Even so, it was a dangerous place to be. At any moment the hurricane could hurl a piece of debris through it.

Something caught her attention, whirling over the lake like a waterspout. It was a waterspout or a tornado, and lightning revealed a large object in it, spinning upwards. It looked like a motor cruiser. She checked her watch as she moved away from the window: 1.30 am.

Then she heard gunfire, somewhere above. She ran to the other side of the building and peered up the stairs. They were empty, but through the window something caught her eye. A taut cable now stretched from the top of Building Two to theirs, and an armoured guard was sliding across it. They had fired a harpoon line into the wall. She ran back for her rifle but, by the time she reached the window again, the guard was gone. No doubt he wasn't alone.

Gretel was back, dragging a yellow power cable. She seemed calmer now. She plugged a power board into a terminal, connected a printer and said, 'Be quick. The emergency generators are underwater and everything's running off the backup batteries, but if the water comes up much further they'll go out as well and they're too heavy to move. I've connected power to the mainframe downstairs. Shouldn't take long to get you in.'

'They're coming across from the other building, on a cable,' said Irith.

'I saw. Keep guard!'

She stood in the doorway, knowing she was no match for trained guards. More firing came from upstairs. 'How's it going, Gretel?'

'Won't be long.'

An anxious ten minutes went by. Bragg hadn't returned, but in a momentary lull in the hurricane there came a burst of gunfire that echoed hollowly, as if in a stairwell.

'Go and see what that is!' said Gretel.

Irith crept to the airlock and put her head around the door, but saw nothing. As she was heading up the stairs, deathly afraid, Gretel called, 'Come back! I'm in.'

The chances were that the gunfire marked her mother's bloody death, or Levi's, Bragg's or Siah's. Irith was desperate to know, but there was a job to do and no one else could do it.

Gretel thrust past her and pounded up the stairs. Irith ran to the computer and tapped through the directories, which were similar to those she had used in her own university. She found the genome engineering directory and went through the list of files, but could find no file name that seemed relevant to the terminator virus.

Nor, though she scanned all the directories she could access, did she see any category that might link the work done here to the Global Congress, or Lindstrom. It was bound to be here somewhere but it would take weeks to scan all the files. At best, she had an hour or two.

Irith glanced over her shoulder. If the guards had prevailed, she might be the only member of the team left alive. And she wouldn't even see them coming.

She went back to the genome engineering directory, plodded through the list of thousands of files and opened the most likely ones. Most were tedious technical descriptions, analysis protocols, standard operating procedures and the like. Then she found a large text file headed 'Terminator Virus'. All it contained was a mass of letters – A, C, G and T. A genetic code. The file date was only two weeks old so it was probably the final version.

It was the strangest genome she had ever seen, and quite unlike the version she'd studied in the cabin in Minnesota, although it did contain a terminator gene sequence. Normally, viruses used for genetic engineering were based on existing viruses with a few genes added or deleted, but this one was unlike anything she'd come across before, or anything she could find in the standard library of sequences. It was as if the virus had been engineered from scratch.

It did what other vector viruses did. It was designed to enter a cell, inject certain genes into the cell's genome, make copies of itself, release them to infect other cells in the human body and to infect other humans, then render the infected cells immune against further infection by the virus. In other words, it was a messenger virus designed to change the human genome. But it was a most sophisticated one – it inserted the terminator virus at precisely the right place in the genome to cause sterilisation.

The power went off, but came back on at once. Irith's heart gave a painful lurch. So much to discover and so little time. And the building had developed a continuous shudder, like a washing machine on the spin cycle. Debris was striking the outside walls all the time now. The hurricane was getting closer. She glanced over her shoulder at the power cable snaking out the door. It was 2.39 am. The power could go off any minute.

This had to be more than just a simple terminator gene, which was neither quick enough nor extreme enough for what she knew of Lindstrom. There had to be more to it.

It took ages to find it and, when she did, she had no idea what it meant, although it had been staring her in the face the whole time. The genome had one tiny section designed to cause part of a particular gene to replicate itself several times. It could even have been an error in the engineering, though Irith didn't think so.

Which gene did the virus affect? It was one on chromosome four, but human chromosome four was one of the largest and contained thousands of genes. Before she could identify the target gene, something struck the outside wall, hard, and a line of windows burst, spraying chips of glass everywhere. The power went off and this time it stayed off.

CHAPTER THIRTY-SEVEN

Irith needed just a few more minutes. She ran down the stairs, following the yellow cable, but on the second floor it ran underwater, and that was that. On the way back she ran into Levi, who was heading through the seventh-floor airlock, carrying a crude assemblage of circuit boards, chips and wires mounted on a piece of plastic. A wire ran to an earphone in his ear.

'What's going on?' she cried. 'Is Jemma –'

'She's alive, as far as I know. Lindstrom had a hiding place and it took a long time to find it. Before we did, he signalled his remaining guards in the other building and they tried to come across on a cable.'

'I saw one of them,' said Irith.

'A few made it before we broke the cable. We stopped them, though in the meantime Lindstrom got out a back way. We haven't found him yet.'

'What if he's called for outside help?'

'He can't. I pressed in a six-digit lock code before I gave him my phone. It won't even let him call 911. Unfortunately ... it does allow Jack to call in.'

'What about Siah?'

'Not a trace of her.'

The earpiece buzzed. Levi adjusted it, frowning as he tried to hear.

'What the hell is that?' said Irith.

'A crude radio. I put it together to try and contact Jack. I'm picking him up but I can't transmit to him.'

'What's he saying?'

'The hurricane turned north-east, toward Biloxi, around two o'clock. He'll be back as soon as the wind lets up.'

'How soon will that be?'

'Another hour or two,' said Levi. 'New Orleans is spared yet again.'

'Where are the others?'

Crash! Another row of windows burst on the far side, spraying glass and water everywhere, and the sudden windblast lifted Irith to her toes. Air pressure popped several windows just outside the airlock. They ducked around a corner towards the restrooms, where there were no windows.

'They're doing guard duty. Come in here, it's the only safe place now.'

They dragged a table into the women's restrooms and huddled under it in a pool of water. Levi kept fiddling with his radio but could not get it to transmit on a frequency that could bypass the jammer. Irith explained what she had discovered.

'So,' said Levi, 'if some small sections of a gene were replicated a few times, what effect would it have?'

'That would depend on the gene and the section that was replicated. In most cases, probably nothing. The human genome is full of replication anyway, and what's called junk DNA.' As Irith spoke, an elusive thought tugged at her, but it was gone before she could uncover it. 'And in a messenger virus that's been so carefully engineered, why this effect at all?'

'Must be close to dawn,' said Levi. 'Keep working on it.'

She looked at her watch: 3.40. 'A good hour and a half yet.'

The earphone crackled again. 'It's Jack!' said Levi. 'He'll be here in ten minutes. Irith, go up the southside stairs and try to signal him. Keep a sharp lookout. Lindstrom will have received the message, and he wants that chopper. I'll round up Bragg and Gretel. They'll probably be on the other side – and Siah if I can find her. We'll do our best to stop him.'

'Be careful. He's got Mum.'

'She means a lot to me, too.'

That was food for thought but there was no time to think about it. Irith ran up the stairs, feeling faint in the heat. Ballistic clothing was not suited to this climate. She tore off her outer vest and dropped it on the landing.

She turned the handle of the roof door but it did not open. She pushed harder. The door moved a fraction, then slammed back – the wind was too strong. Irith put her back to the door, bent her legs and forced with all her strength. What was Lindstrom doing to Jemma? What had he already done in the months he'd held her?

There came a hollow, echoing burst of gunfire, though she could not tell where it had originated. She resisted the urge to run across to the other stairs. If she could gain the roof before Lindstrom did, she might take him by surprise.

She strained until it felt as though her heart was going to burst. Nothing happened – the latch was holding the door. Feeling stupid, she got her hand to the handle, pulled it down and the door came open just far enough for her to squeeze into the gap. The wind caught the door and she thought it was going to slam and cut her in half. She forced with her arms and was through.

As the door banged, the wind thumped her against the concrete wall, cracking her head. She scanned the roof space. The chopper was hovering about ten metres above, although hovering was a poor description of the wild gyrations it was going through. Surely Jack wasn't trying to land in this? Lightning flashed from all directions, striking buildings to the east. The rain was cold now, and she welcomed it.

The wind was stronger than when they had arrived and there was no way she could run across the roof to the chopper. She would have to creep around in the shelter of the wall and crawl downwind.

A lighted rectangle appeared on the far side of the roof. Bragg and the others, or Lindstrom? She made out a very tall shape, clearly Lindstrom by the stalking gait, and a small one beside him. Jemma had recovered enough to walk – or to be dragged. The door slammed.

A lantern flashed upwards at the chopper. Irith hoped that it was the wrong signal and Jack would move away, but the chopper continued to hover. He did not know about Lindstrom.

He dragged Jemma out into the open, keeping low. Irith could see their silhouettes against each flash of lightning. Again the lantern flashed. She'd foolishly left hers on the computer terminal and could not send Jack a warning signal.

The chopper tilted, moving slowly towards the roof. The wind hurled it one way, then another. Surely it wouldn't be able to get down in these conditions? But it kept coming – he was a master and seemed to anticipate every gust.

Where were Levi and the others? Were they dead from that burst of gunfire in the stairwell? It was up to Irith now.

The chopper settled and Lindstrom pushed towards it, dragging Jemma. A gust blew her off her feet but the wrist chain held her. The wind was in Irith's face, pushing her against the wall, and she dared not shoot at Lindstrom. There was no way to reach them. He was going to get away with Jemma – and the virus.

A portable floodlight came on from the leeward side of the air-conditioning cooling towers. He whirled, trying to see who was there. Jemma struggled to break free but he flailed at her with the gun and she fell to her knees.

A woman advanced into the beam of the floodlight, her pale hair glowing in the light. Siah! She was carrying a rifle but it was not aimed at him.

'He's got Mum. Don't shoot!' Irith cried, but she couldn't have been heard.

Crouching low, she scuttled around in the shelter of the perimeter walls until the wind was behind her, then began to waddle across the roof. She had no idea what she was going to do once she got there.

Lightning froze Siah, mouth open like a fairground dummy. She appeared to be shouting at Lindstrom. Lindstrom raised his automatic and fired. Siah's rifle flew through the air and disappeared. She did not go after it; she just stood there in full view.

'Siah!' Irith screamed uselessly. 'Go back!'

Irith tried to target Lindstrom but the wind pushed the clustered barrels all over the place. The risk of hitting Jemma, or the chopper, was too great.

Siah walked forward, leaning into the wind and suddenly Irith understood. Siah was trying to atone for what she had done, but Lindstrom would simply shoot her down.

'Siah, don't!' Irith screeched.

Siah moved steadily towards Lindstrom. They were only twenty metres apart. Then fifteen. Ten.

Lindstrom took careful aim, holding one hand steady with the other, and fired. Siah jerked but kept going. He aimed again but Jemma wrenched the chain and the wind pushed him backwards, tumbling him over her.

Irith dragged herself across the roof. She was almost near enough to shoot when Lindstrom threw his arm around Jemma's neck, aimed at Siah and fired. She fell. He turned away, dragging Jemma towards the chopper, fighting her and the wind all the way.

Irith clawed her way out to Siah. 'Why did you just stand there?' She lifted Siah's head onto her knee. 'Why didn't you shoot?'

In the lightning's glare, Siah smiled weakly. 'I killed a man. I had to face Lindstrom unarmed, to make up for it. Run, you can still stop them.'

Irith glanced across. Lindstrom was dragging Jemma towards the chopper, two steps forward, one back. It might just be possible to take him by surprise.

'I can't leave you.'

'I'll be all right now.'

'That's what Thornton said.'

'Run, or it'll be wasted.'

Irith kissed Siah on the forehead and laid her down in the rain.

When she was only metres from Lindstrom, the far door opened and two figures burst onto the roof. Gretel raised a weapon – Irith saw it clearly in the lightning – but Bragg knocked it down. A lantern blinked on and off, carving beams through the thick air to the chopper. Jack must have got the message, because the engines screamed. The chopper lifted slightly, skating sideways across the roof in the gale. Lindstrom got there first and heaved Jemma in through the open door. A gust almost pulled her out again. As the chopper took off, he threw himself in.

The chopper thumped down and shapes struggled inside. The engines died, roared and died again. Irith struggled to her feet and ran, but the wind caught her, bowled her across the concrete and slammed her into metal. It felt like a fallen flagpole. She pulled herself along it, trying to reach the chopper from the other side. She scuttled underneath and reached the steps.

Lindstrom laughed out loud and, with a mighty yank, heaved her in. Her rifle fell on the concrete. Evidently he had made clear his threat about the explosive, for Jack, who had turned around in his seat, made no effort to attack.

Lindstrom pulled up the steps but left the sliding door open. The automatic was in his other hand, the one still chained to Jemma. He pointed the gun at Jack. Lindstrom's hand shook but he overcame it.

'Take off and head for Uptown. Above the Superdome will do nicely. Don't try anything clever. I'm planning to end it tonight and I'd be happy to take you all with me.'

'Yes, sir!' Jack yelled over the wind. 'Whatever you say, sir.' He saluted and turned to his controls.

The engines screamed and the chopper lifted, lurching wildly through the air. More wildly, in fact, than it had before. Irith reached for the seatbelt.

'Leave it!' rapped Lindstrom, shaking the gun at her. 'You've got work to do.'

There was something strange about his movement, as if he had done it to disguise a tremor that he couldn't control.

Jack's voice came over a speaker. 'I don't like the look of that.' He put the nose of the chopper down and Irith could see out the front. 'The levee's eroding rapidly down there. It's going to fail.'

'Nature reclaims her own,' said Lindstrom, slurring again. 'Keep moving.'

'If it fails, the current will cut straight through the levee,' said Jack.

'The Earth fights back,' said Lindstrom, swinging the automatic to sight on Jack's ear. 'Fly!'

The chopper swung around, lurching and swaying across the sky. Lindstrom swayed too, although that could have been the rough ride. He shrugged off a backpack and passed it to Irith. 'There's a netcasting video camera inside. Get it out. Don't try anything or your mother dies.'

Irith removed the camera from its case.

'Put the strap around your neck,' said Lindstrom. 'I'd hate it to fall out.' She did so.

'Do you know how to use it?'

'Yes,' she said faintly, clutching at a seat as the helicopter shot up vertically. When Lindstrom lost control he spoke, and moved, like an old drunk, but he wasn't drunk at all. Nor did he appear to be affected by drugs. From what she knew of him, he led an ascetic life, shunning all forms of indulgence. So what was his problem, and was there any way she could use it against him?

'It's foolproof, in any case,' he said. 'Automatic everything. All you do is point and pull the trigger.'

'I'd be glad to pull the trigger on you.'

Lindstrom sneered. 'You had your chance earlier.'

'What am I supposed to do with it?'

'Jemma and I are going to empty the virus over the Superdome, and you're going to broadcast it live, *to the world*.'

'You're a maniac!'

He shrugged. 'No doubt history will think so. But as long as I know I've done the right thing, that's all that matters.'

Irith had to keep him talking while she tried to think of a way out.

Jemma caught her eye. 'I'm sorry, Irith.'

'You should have told me what was going on.'

'Yes, I should have. But it was the past and I didn't want to think about it.'

'Shut up,' said Lindstrom.

Jemma swung around. 'Get stuffed! There's nothing more you can do to me and I don't have to take it any longer.'

'There's plenty I can do to your daughter,' he snarled, 'so think very carefully before you open your mouth again.'

CHAPTER THIRTY-EIGHT

'Roll the camera, Irith,' said Lindstrom. 'Your video is going straight to an override netcaster. Everyone who's using the net, anywhere in the world, will see it.' He looked into the camera, jerking from side to side and now unable to control it.

'This is the final President's Page,' he slurred into the mike. 'Brought to you this time not by my regular presenter, Jemma Hardey, but personally. Today we're broadcasting live from a helicopter above the hurricane-ravaged city of New Orleans, USA.'

He signalled with his hands. Irith pointed the camera out the door, panning over the deluge coming across the levee, the flooded streets and bruised skies, while Lindstrom gave a running commentary interspersed with environmental propaganda. He had to shout to be heard.

'It's Armageddon for New Orleans, a forerunner of what is to come for all of us. This disaster is self-inflicted – the result of human interference to a thousand kilometres of the Mississippi. New Orleans has been living on borrowed time for fifty years, and now that time has run out.'

He gestured to Irith to pan back to his face. The focus changed smoothly as the camera passed over the pilot, the controls and settled on Lindstrom again. He spoke clearly now, though the effort showed in the set of his jaw and the rigid tendons of his neck.

'You may be wondering why this is the last President's Page when I've years of my term to run. I'm not a time-serving politician like the ones you're used to. I've done all I came into office to do. Today you'll share the moment with me as I complete my final project, one I've been planning for twenty years.'

He pocketed the gun and raised the cluster of steel cylinders. It looked like a cartoon bundle of dynamite.

'It's called the Terminator Project,' he said to the camera. 'Human overpopulation has wiped out two-thirds of the world's animals and plants, polluted the land, the sea and the air, erased countless ecosystems and brought Earth to the brink of climatic collapse. Overpopulation has ravaged our world, enslaving those animals deemed useful to humanity and exterminating the rest. We've had a global government for twenty years and it's made not a jot of difference.

'A long time ago I determined that there was only one solution, and since I'm a humane man, I aimed for a humane solution.' Lindstrom smiled, though the angled teeth and the curl of his lip gave him the look of a raptor. 'This!' He shook the cylinders in front of the camera. 'A human terminator gene that will ...' he seemed to lose his train of thought '... will, via a contagious but almost undetectable viral infection, render every human male sterile within weeks.

'Twenty years I've had people working on this project. We've had many setbacks but we never faltered, and we overcame them all. We had to; it was the only way to save the world from the worst pathogen of all – humanity!'

He wiped sweat off his brow. His voice was hoarse from shouting. 'Many people have tried to stop us in the past twenty years. None succeeded, although Jemma Hardey came closest.' He pointed with a finger and Irith swung the camera onto her mother's ravaged face.

'That's why I take such pleasure in having her with me at the end, and her daughter, Irith, behind the camera. Jemma will be ... will be the instrument of humanity's destruction, and Irith will record it for an all-too-brief posterity.'

He swallowed, which took a great effort, and continued, loudly and carefully.

'It wasn't easy to craft the virus, but it had to be done. But after it was complete, I had second thoughts. What if someone found a way to repair the damage ...' Again that appearance of confusion. What could the matter be? '... the damage, or make a vaccine to protect those who hid from the epidemic? I would have wiped out the many in favour of a privileged, undeserving few.'

Irith looked over the camera at her mother, whose brow crinkled. Was Jemma trying to tell her something? Be prepared for anything, her mother had taught her, and when an opportunity comes, *seize* it. A chill made its way up Irith's spine. Her heart was racing. She caught Jack's eye. He had turned halfway around in his seat.

'There had to be a better way,' Lindstrom went on, holding the cylinders out. 'A permanent and humane solution ... solution.' He swallowed, struggled then mastered himself. 'I sent my scientists back to the drawing board and just six months ago they found the answer. It took another three months to design the new virus, work out how to reproduce it in the required amount, and how to handle it safely. Then they had the task of culturing sufficient stock, checking it for purity and packaging it. That was all finished just the day before yesterday. It's 27 August in New Orleans. Doomsday.'

So he *had* been lying before. Irith glanced at the clock on the cockpit dashboard: 4.15 am. She caught Jack's eye and dropped one eyelid. He nodded stiffly.

'In these ten slim cylinders,' Lindstrom went on, 'I had prepared enough ...' A very long pause this time, and she could see how much it took to control his illness. '... enough of the virus to do its work on all humanity. The winds fanning out from this hurricane will pass across the United States. All I have to do is empty the cylinders out the door and nature will do the rest.'

'What is the "better way"?' Irith said softly.

'I'm glad you asked that, Irith,' Lindstrom said to the camera. 'This new virus changes the human genome, male or female, in every cell, making it impossible for humans to reproduce. Over a few decades it will terminate humanity.

'Within a day and a half of someone contracting the virus, it will have done its work, though it will remain viable in the environment for years. Many animals will host it, at no harm to themselves – it pleases me that nature will help to bring down its oppressors. And when it's all over, and *Homo sapiens* is gone, the virus will disappear, bringing to an end what biologists call the Sixth Extinction – the one caused by humanity. An appropriate irony, don't you think?'

Irith was sick with horror. Was she already infected? She felt a tightness in her chest, a difficulty in extracting oxygen from the air.

'Camera!' he snapped.

She refocused on his face. 'You're a monster.' She felt faint. She could hardly breathe.

'You believe humans have rights, yet no other creature does.' He spoke to the camera again. 'Not one animal will shed a tear for humanity.

There will just be a great, collective sigh of relief, that the nightmare is finally over.'

'Humanity has done great things,' Irith said, knowing she had to present the case for her own kind. 'Look at all our great works, our art, our culture, our literature and music. Our science. Our civilisation!'

'Humanity *has* built great civilisations, but in doing so it razed the forests, polluted the air and strip-mined the fish in the sea. The very foundations of civilisation are drenched in blood.'

'But there's more to us,' she said desperately. 'We're unique.'

'Every species is unique, by definition,' said Lindstrom.

'We're *more* unique! Other animals just live out their preordained cycle of birth, reproduction and death, as every species before them has for billions of years. We're different, and that's why humanity should be given a chance. We shape and create the world —'

'To the ruin of every plant and every beast.'

'But we do good, too. Humanity has done good and worthwhile things.'

'It doesn't balance the evil and destruction.'

'We can change.'

Lindstrom turned away. 'Of all possible arguments, you've chosen the one my ears are closed to. *People* can change, but the nature of humanity is fixed. Greed and destruction will always prevail, for human lust will always triumph over human altruism. Say no more..'

'Please give me a chance to prove you wrong.'

'You can't, and no one knows it better than I do. I devoted my life, my fortune and my unshakable will to changing humanity for the better, and everything I did failed. Humanity cannot change. It must always increase, and destroy other life to make room, until there's nothing else left. Earth cannot survive it, but Earth *must* survive and there's only one solution: humanity has to make way.'

There was another solution, although it would prove him right. Violence was the only answer she had left, no matter how much she despised people who resorted to it. Lindstrom had to die, and she was the only one with a chance of doing it.

He showed his teeth again. 'I might have listened, had you presented a good enough case for the survival of the human race. I've also sought one. But there is none. Humanity is not worth the price.'

He turned to the camera and now spoke with simple dignity. 'This project has been my life, and now it's time to end it. But I am not a madman. I simply believe that the Earth is worth more than we are. Neither have I done this for myself. In all my years as a member of the Congress, and as President, I took not a penny in salary or perks. I've lived what I preached, as ascetic a life as it is possible to live. I leave no fortune, no possessions, no more than my flesh and bones.

'That's all I have to say.' He turned away and began rifling through his pack.

Irith was still trying to work him out. If he wasn't drunk or affected by drugs, then it had to be some kind of neurological degeneration. But what? There were many conditions that could cause such symptoms.

As she watched him twitch and sway, a possibility occurred to her – one so hideous that the little hairs stood up all the way down her back. And Levi's strip of paper was the key, the message that Jemma had taken such risks to get out of Lindstrom's office: 'IT'S IN THE CAG–'.

And suddenly Irith *knew*. It didn't mean 'cage', or any other word beginning with those letters. CAG was the genetic code to produce glutamine, one of the twenty amino acids that were used to form all the proteins in the body – the basis of life. It was a common code that occurred in hundreds, if not thousands, of places in the human genome, and in some genes it could be repeated many times. And, she realised with mounting horror, it occurred in one particular gene near the end of chromosome four: the Wolf-Hirschhorn gene.

Lack of the gene caused the rare and invariably fatal childhood illness, Wolf-Hirschhorn Syndrome, but that wasn't it. People who had the gene were normal as long as its CAG code was repeated no more than thirty-five times. More repeats invariably caused neurone degeneration that resulted in loss of motor skills, progressive dementia and eventual death.

Huntington's disease.

It could not be prevented, nor could it be cured, and it always ended in madness and death. And the more CAG repeats above thirty-five, the quicker the onset. With fifty CAGs, Huntington's disease would begin by the age of twenty-seven. Worst of all, its victims had many years to suffer the inevitability of going mad.

A terminator gene with a difference.

'You bastard!' she screamed. 'You absolute, utter, lying bastard! The missing word was *repetition*.'

'I've no idea what you're talking about,' said Lindstrom. 'Now —'

'Just days ago we had a secret message from your office.'

'Days ago? From *my* office?' One side of his face froze, then he turned to Jemma, reaching out with a shaking hand. She drew back as far as the chain would allow her.

'How?' he said.

Jemma did not bother to answer.

'The message was, "It's in the CAG repetition",' said Irith, 'but the last word was cut off. That's what the Terminator Project is really about, isn't it? You sick arsehole! You've got Huntington's disease and you're planning to inflict it on the rest of the world, in some kind of twisted revenge for your own misery.'

Lindstrom reeled and suddenly he was twitching involuntarily, the gun shuddering in one claw-like hand.

'It's obvious there's something wrong with you,' said Jemma. 'The aggression, paranoia, hostility and delusions. The twitching and slurring. The weird movements that you try to disguise but can't quite manage. The withdrawal from public life. How long have you known, Lindstrom?'

'A few years,' he slurred, out of control now.

'And since you're condemned to this horrible death,' said Irith, 'you thought you'd do the same for the rest of humanity. So you hid this little sequence in the terminator virus. No one would ever have noticed. After all, all it does is replicate one tiny segment of DNA three times, and what could that matter?

'But it replicates the CAG sequence in the Huntington gene, in every cell in the body. Ten repeats becomes twenty, twenty becomes forty, then forty, eighty. Any more than thirty-five repeats and you're doomed. No one on Earth would be safe, because no one starts with less than six repeats. Six, twelve, twenty-four, forty-eight – doom! The whole of humanity condemned to the most ghastly of lingering deaths. You utter shit!'

'I admit it,' Lindstrom said at last, and that seemed calm him. 'I've had to go through it, but that's not why I did it. This isn't about me, Irith.'

'It can't be stopped,' said Irith, biting off each word as if it were infected, 'or cured, or reversed. The only people unaffected would be those poor kids without the gene, and they're doomed anyway. And if the virus should happen to redouble the CAG sequence in another gene by mistake, that would cause another of the polyglutamine brain diseases, and get them anyway.'

He now looked serene and the twitching had stopped. 'I thought it more humane to keep that to myself.'

'You lying bastard. You wanted no one to know until it was too late to find a solution.'

'Whatever!' he said. 'But I've got the gun, and the bomb strapped to my chest, and there's nothing you can do to stop me.' He turned to Jemma. 'Pick up the cylinders and unscrew the tops, one by one, slowly and carefully. Pilot, keep the chopper as steady as you can.'

'Sir!' said Jack, like a recruit answering a sergeant-major. He looked over his shoulder at Irith and raised one eyebrow.

It gave her heart. He had a reputation, after all. She prayed he lived up to it, for she could not even hint at what *she* hoped to do.

Jemma picked up the bundle of cylinders. She had to use both hands. Taking hold of one of the caps, she twisted but her fingers slipped. She tried again, then looked up at Lindstrom.

'I can't get a grip. My fingers are too sweaty. The caps are on very tightly.'

He cursed under his breath. 'Of course they're on tightly. They're meant to be shipped across the world. Try harder.'

Jemma was making an opportunity for Irith, and she had to take it. Irith flicked her eyes sideways. Jack was watching in his mirror. His knuckles were white on the controls.

'Give it here,' snapped Lindstrom, slipping the automatic into his pocket.

Jemma held out the bundle. As he reached for it, the chopper lurched sharply and Jemma fell against Lindstrom, who knocked her out of the way. She landed hard and it knocked the breath out of her. He stumbled backwards, off balance.

Irith swung the video camera on its strap with all the force she could muster, and he did not see it coming. It smashed into his face and something went crack, his nose or his front teeth.

He fell to his knees, blood pouring from his nose, and the wind blew it all over his face and into his eyes. Jack rose in his seat but a wild gust struck the chopper, spinning it through 360 degrees, and he had his hands full keeping it in the air.

'Get rid of him, Irith,' Jemma choked.

'How?' cried Irith.

'Kick the bastard out the door.'

Jemma was lying on the floor as if she could not get up. 'But you're chained to him.'

'It's the only way. Do it now, before he recovers.'

It *was* the only way, and Irith knew it – Jemma's life for the survival of humanity. She tried to tell herself it was the right, thing to do. Lindstrom was on his knees, gasping and spitting blood. He was a monster and it would be worth anything to be rid of him – almost anything.

Her eyes met Jemma's. 'I've had a good life,' said Jemma. 'I'm ready.'

Irith took a step towards Lindstrom. Jack let out an inarticulate cry; he was standing up in his seat, staring at them, and light glinted on the cross about his neck. She felt sure he was trying to tell her something.

'Irith,' Jemma wailed, pulling herself up. 'Do it now!'

But she could not send Jemma to her death. 'I can't, Mum. Not even to save the world.'

Lindstrom struggled to his feet, wiping the blood off his face. 'You begged me to give humanity another chance, Irith. You said you'd do anything. But when the opportunity came, you didn't have the guts.'

'The price was too high,' Irith whispered.

'You're not half the woman your mother is.' He whirled.

Jemma had recovered and was raising the cylinders to smash them into the back of Lindstrom's head. He clawed the gun out of his pocket. The wrist chain shone in a lightning flash. Jemma stood frozen, her arms above her head. He spat out blood and broken teeth.

'If I go, she goes,' Lindstrom said in a gurgling gasp, pointing the gun at Irith. Red bubbles frothed at his nostrils. 'Move a millimetre and we all go together.'

He tapped his chest. 'Pass me the cylinders, Jemma. Very carefully.'

CHAPTER THIRTY-NINE

Jemma bowed her head, then lowered the cylinders and held them out. Lindstrom stood head and shoulders above her.

As he reached for them with his free hand, Jack cried, 'Now!' and the chopper lurched, throwing Lindstrom towards her.

Jemma slammed the cylinders into his belly, driving the wind out of him. He bent double, then wrested them from her. His other hand, holding the automatic pistol, was shaking violently. He tried to aim at Jemma but the gun was all over the place. She kicked him in the knee then tried to force him out the door. His arm flailed and the gun went off.

Irith was struck in the chest so hard that she was knocked over backwards. It felt as if her breastbone was crushing her heart against her spine. The pain was excruciating and it was a struggle to breathe. Her vision blurred and nausea churned through her belly. She wanted to throw up but it hurt too much.

Jemma and Lindstrom were still struggling, Lindstrom trying to bring the automatic to bear on her. Jemma got one hand free and punched him in the throat. He choked and tried to club her with the gun. She brought her head up under his chin, snapping his head back into the wall. He went down and dropped the gun, which fell out the open door.

Lindstrom landed close to the door on his backside, still clutching the cylinders. He snatched at the rail. Jemma slammed her foot against his shoulder and, as Irith cried, 'Mum, no!' Jemma thrust him out.

The chain pulled her after him. Jemma struck the floor on her knees and slid towards the door, then Lindstrom caught the dangling steps with his left hand and locked his arm through them.

Irith dragged herself forward, against the worst pain she had ever felt, and grasped Jemma's legs. 'Mum, what are you doing?' she croaked.

'I'm solving the problem. Someone's got to.'

'But you'll be killed,' Irith wailed.

'There's no other way. I'm sorry, Irith. Let me go or you'll fall too.'

Jemma took hold of the door rail with both hands and tried to shake Irith off.

Irith tightened her grip. 'If you go, you'll be taking me with you.'

The chopper jerked wildly, the wind flinging Lindstrom one way and then the other. The strain must have been terrible; the edge of the step had chewed through his shirt and was cutting into his arm. He was in great pain, but pain had not stopped him before and nothing would stop him now.

He was trying to unscrew the tops of the cylinders with his free hand but they were covered in blood and rain, and his fingers kept slipping. The chopper was being blown all over the sky. Jack had tilted it to the right, to make it harder for Jemma to be pulled out, but any lurch could tear Lindstrom's arm off the steps and then his weight would drag her over. And Irith too, if she did not let go.

She hooked her left leg through the mounting of the nearest seat and hung on. The camera had wedged under the seat to her left, pointing at the door, and the Record button was still locked down.

Lindstrom banged the tops of the cylinders against the steps, trying to free them. 'Damn you!' he bellowed, gripping one of the cylinder caps and straining so hard that his nose began to bleed again.

Jemma slid down into a crouch and reached behind her for the video camera.

'No,' Irith cried.

She hurled it at Lindstrom's head. It bounced off and fell into the night. The impact left a red mark on his forehead but he was still hanging on, still struggling with the caps. His body might be a shuddering machine but the will that had driven him for the last thirty years was as strong as ever.

Jemma cried out and tried to pull free of Irith. Irith tightened the leg hooked through the seat and held her back.

Boom! Something clanged off the cylinders, tearing them out of Lindstrom's grip. He snatched desperately for them and got a finger in under the tape binding them together. They swung there for a moment but his arm began to twitch violently under the weight and he could not control it. To his agony, the wind snatched the cylinders away.

'They'll smash ... open when they land,' he gasped, as if trying to convince himself. 'They must –'

'No, they won't.' Jack had turned right around in his seat and he was flying the chopper blind. A Colt 45, a long-barrelled antique from the nineteenth century, smoked in his left hand. 'We're east of the Spanish Plaza, hanging over the Mississippi, and they'll go straight to the bottom.'

'There's still a chance,' screamed Lindstrom. Blood was streaked from one side of his face to the other. 'But not for you, Jemma. You're going to die with me.'

The chopper turned away from the river and lifted, and the tall buildings of the city centre spread out below – the World Trade Centre, the casino, the Sheraton New Orleans, no fewer than three Holiday Inns and, ahead, the Louisiana Superdome. Lindstrom clawed his way up the steps, hanging on with both hands. His bloody eyes showed manic determination. The shaking and twitching had stopped and he was eerily controlled. He reached the top and pulled himself up.

'Don't come any closer,' said Jack, pointing the gun at Lindstrom's chest.

'I might have lost,' said Lindstrom to Irith, 'but there'll come a day, very soon, when you'll wish I hadn't.'

She felt a sudden chill. 'What are you talking about?'

'You think you've lived through a disastrous climate change. It's nothing – *absolutely nothing* – compared to what's coming.'

He stood up straight so that his bent head touched the top of the doorway. Then, with a shrill laugh, he threw himself out backwards.

The chain snapped tight, jerking Jemma to the door and Irith across the floor. Jemma clutched at the door rail but Lindstrom's weight was tearing her fingers free, one by one. Irith slid further across the floor. Jemma was going to die and so was she. The weight was too great.

Jemma had only two fingers on the rail when the revolver boomed again. Jack's bullet struck the chain, breaking it, and Lindstrom fell away. Jemma lost her grip and started to topple out. Jack flipped the chopper onto its side and she fell back on top of Irith. Irith threw her arms around her mother and bit down on the pain.

The chopper spun on its axis and its floodlight caught Lindstrom momentarily. He was stabbing furiously at his chest as he fell, but there was no explosion. The mechanism must have been damaged. He vanished into the darkness below them.

Jack brought the chopper level. 'Close the door please, Jemma. Then resume your seats and fasten your seatbelts. We're expecting some turbulence.' He chuckled grimly.

Jemma slammed the door and fell into her seat. Irith remained where she was. Now that the crisis had passed, she lacked the strength to get up. Her chest was a mass of radiating pain. She wondered if the impact had caused a heart attack.

'Irith, what's the matter?' The blood drained from Jemma's face. She threw herself out of her seat to kneel beside her daughter. 'He shot you? Why didn't you say?'

'It's all right,' Irith whispered. 'I'm wearing a vest.'

Jack was standing up at the controls again. 'Get it off,' he snapped. 'The impact can still kill you through a bulletproof vest, and that's a miserable little one, if you don't mind me saying so.'

Jemma tore open Irith's shirt and peeled off the vest. A metal slug clacked on the floor. Irith looked down but couldn't focus. Jemma probed gently. 'The impact was at the top of the breastbone, Jack, a hand span above the heart.'

'Directly over the heart and she'd be dead,' said Jack.

'She's cracked some ribs, and maybe the breastbone as well. You've got a bruise the size of a soup plate, Irith.'

'And I imagine every hospital is full for a hundred miles around,' said Jack.

Jemma helped Irith into her seat and strapped her in. Every movement sent pain stabbing through her chest. She took her mother's hand and they put on their headphones.

'Hurricane Jemma,' said Jack. Another chuckle.

'Thank you, Jack,' said Jemma. 'I won't forget it as long as I live.'

'I won't forget what you did either, ma'am,' he said. 'Nor you, Irith. No one will.'

He turned the chopper around in a series of expanding circles, like a search pattern. The side winds tossed the big machine like a kite but he kept it steady. Lights blinked in a line below them. He went down a little, hovered and aimed the floodlight.

The mast of a broadcasting tower was illuminated atop one of the city buildings, and a man hung in the network of iron. Lindstrom's body was impaled on the metal frame near the top of the tower. Irith's stomach heaved.

'Is he dead?' she whispered.

'If he ain't,' said Jack, 'he won't last long. The hurricane will strip him down him to the bone.'

He flicked off the light and turned away.

'I don't feel so bad now,' said Irith. 'Just very, very sore.' The mission was far from over. What if Levi and Bragg had fired the building and there was no chopper to pick them up?

'With that kind of impact, you can't always tell,' said Jack. 'I'll see if I can find a hospital bed –'

'My friends are down there,' Irith said hoarsely. It hurt to speak. 'We've got to pick them up first.'

'I hadn't forgotten them,' Jack said mildly. 'Well, if you're sure you're okay . . . ?'

'I'm fine,' she lied.

Something wordless passed between Jemma and Jack.

'We'll go back,' said Jack.

'And then?' said Jemma.

'Search and rescue is what I do, ma'am. And body recovery. There'll be plenty of that today and tomorrow, and for a week or two after that.'

He turned toward the Pontchartrain facility. At least, Irith assumed he had. She lacked the energy to keep her eyes open. She slumped in the seat, holding her mother's hand.

They lurched and bumped their way across the sky towards the edge of the lake. The radio crackled. 'Jack? Jack?'

'It's Levi!' said Irith.

'What the heck's he using?' said Jack. 'A crystal set?'

'Something like that,' she murmured.

'Mission accomplished,' said Jack. 'It's all over and we're on our way back.'

'What about Jemma and Irith?' crackled Levi.

'Safe. You ready to be picked up?'

'We'll be on the roof in five minutes.'

'I'll check the levee and be right with you.'

There was no reply. 'Levi!' Irith yelled.

'He's gone,' said Jack. 'Radio's given out, I'd say.'

'You didn't tell him about Lindstrom and the virus.'

'We'll be picking him up shortly.' He whirled off towards the levee.

'But they'll blow the incendiaries. They don't need to, now. They might all be killed.'

'I can't contact him. Come up here next to me, ma'am,' Jack said to Jemma.

'Call me Jemma.'

He held up a pair of night-vision binoculars. 'Be my spotter, Jemma. Check out the roof while I take a look at the levee.'

Jemma slid into the seat beside him and buckled up. Irith began to fret. Thornton was the explosives expert. What if Bragg did something wrong and blew them all up? And brave, terrified Siah was dying on the roof, all alone. Irith had never seen such desperate courage. She began to cry and, once started, she could not stop. She closed her eyes and gave way to it.

'I'm going to fly along the levee for a few miles,' said Jack, oblivious, 'and see how it's holding up. If the armour layer has been eroded, the overflow will cut through the clay core in minutes, and then God help the city, because no man can. We'll go down as far as the causeway, then back past Lakeview and the university to the Lakefront Airport. If there's a break anywhere in that section, it's bad. Outside that, not quite so bad.'

He pointed out the main features as they passed, although the sky was almost as wet as the lake and there was little to see. 'There's the ruins of the Spanish Fort down to your left, on the bayou. Not much to see there. Below us now is the coastguard station. Looks like it's been abandoned. Whoa!' He fought to control the machine in the wild wind.

Irith opened her eyes and saw a trio of tornadoes off to her right, out over the black lake. Lightning flickered all around them.

They cruised west along the levee. Jack pointed down with a stubby finger. 'That used to be Lakeshore Drive. By morning there'll be nothing left of it.' The road that had run parallel with the levee now looked like the base of a waterfall.

The levee turned sharply south for five or six hundred metres, then west again. Outside the corner, huge waves crashed over the breakwater, smashing luxury yachts and powerboats into kindling. 'City Yacht Harbour and Orleans Marina,' said Jack. 'They can't last either.'

The restaurant where Irith and Bragg had eaten lunch only the day before yesterday was gone as if it had never existed. A voice crackled in the headphones. Irith could not make out what was said.

'I'll check it out shortly,' replied Jack. 'That's the Pontchartrain Causeway.' He waved his hand up ahead, but Irith could see nothing through the drenching rain.

She vaguely remembered the causeway from early on the morning they'd arrived in New Orleans. A bridge that seemed to go forever, not far above the water. Everything except this endless night was a blur.

'Looks all right down here,' said Jemma, peering through the binoculars.

Jack looped around a radio tower and headed back, this time on the lake side of the levee. 'The main danger is between West End, where the yacht harbour is, and the Lakefront Airport. I saw some erosion near the airport earlier. Should have checked it out straightaway,' he muttered. 'Don't know where my brains have gone tonight.'

'You've done fine,' murmured Jemma, studying him rather brazenly.

Irith had never seen her mother be so forward and was not sure she approved. She had drifted into a haze of pain when Jemma's cry roused her.

'Down there! Do you see it, Jack?'

'I see it.'

He tilted the chopper on its side. They were opposite the facility and directly below them Irith saw a dip in the cascade streaming over the levee. It had not been there earlier. On the city side the dip formed a distinct U shape and from it a torrent of brown and white water arced for twenty metres through the air, then formed a current racing across what had been the northern wall of the facility.

'This is bad,' said Jack.

He reached forward and flicked switches on the instrument panel. 'Jack Gantry here, flying the Whooping Crane. I'm above the levee at Lakeshore East and this is an emergency! Is that you, Wendy? Get onto the Emergency Operating Centre, the coastguard, Port of New Orleans and the Corps of Engineers. There's a break in the levee opposite the Pontchartrain Viral Research facility. It's thirty feet wide and at least ten deep, and growing fast.'

The radio crackled. Irith couldn't make out the words.

'I'll beam you the video.' He flicked more switches. There was more crackling.

'The people in one of the facility buildings are at risk – a partial collapse already. Can you send a chopper?'

Crackle, crackle.

'Oh!' he said. 'That long? I've fuel for an hour and a half. I'll be around, unless the levee fails completely. If that happens there won't be enough choppers in North America to lift everyone out of the city.'

Jack hovered just south of the levee. 'Would you say the cut is wider, Jemma?'

'Yes, and deeper. Looks like four metres to me.'

'You mean . . . thirteen feet. And it's flaking away on either side. Must be fifty feet wide now.' He muttered to himself. 'The Corps will never stop it, in these conditions.'

'It's going to be a catastrophe,' said Irith. The triumph against Lindstrom seemed like a year ago.

Jack turned around in his seat. 'There's one possibility, so outlandish it's not in the emergency plan. Just something people talk about when they've had far too much to drink.'

'What's that?' said Jemma.

'Sinking a ship across the gap,' said Irith.

He looked over his shoulder, startled, and flashed those white teeth at her. 'Probably wouldn't be effective here. The bottom slopes gently away from the levee and a ship couldn't get close enough. I had in mind plugging the levee by driving a freighter head-on into the break.'

'Wouldn't that collapse it?'

'It could make things worse, if it wasn't done carefully.'

He got on the radio and relayed his idea. There was a long silence then the voice on the other end said, 'Can you get across here?'

'The five minutes are up,' said Irith. 'We've got to pick up Levi and the others.'

'Got a rescue to do first,' Jack said into the mike. 'Fifteen minutes.'

They were racing back to the facility when twin explosions blew out every window in the sixth and seventh floors of Building One. Roiling clouds of flame shot with blackness burst out in every direction, momentarily overcoming the wind, and enveloped the building on either side. Debris crashed into the water. The wind pushed the flames back, they were blown to nothing, then there was just the inferno inside and black smoke belching out of every aperture.

'Oh, shit!' said Jemma.

Irith could only stare at the conflagration and pray.

'I thought they'd overestimated the amount of gasoline,' said Jack, circling the building. His floodlight crisscrossed the roof but they saw no one on it. He made another pass and sagged in his seat. 'There's no one on the roof.' He circled the roof twice more, searching the fumes, then shook his head. 'I'll have to go.' He turned east.

'Where are we going?' said Jemma in a wisp of a voice.

'City of New Orleans Emergency Operating Centre. They're having a meeting about the levee break now. We're going to pick up a few of them; most of their choppers are still grounded. How are you feeling, Irith?'

She could only think about Levi, Bragg and the others, trapped in the burning building. Or dead.

'I'm fine,' she said dully, though she was anything but.

They landed in a car park beside a low, long building. Three people pushed against the wind, climbed in and introduced themselves. The lanky, bristle-headed man was from the US Army Corps of Engineers, the squat jowly woman from the Port of New Orleans, and the short, haggard man in uniform was from the Coastguard.

Jack flew back to the break in the levee, which had grown to five metres deep, though it was no wider.

'That's bad,' said the man from the corps.

'Can it be plugged?' said Jack. 'There are a number of freighters on the lake that might fit the bill.'

'Risky!' said the woman from the Port of New Orleans. 'And we'd need a lot of permissions.'

'Better get them in a hurry,' said Jack. 'If the levee goes there won't be a city left to save.'

There was a flurry of communications, going all the way up to the Governor's Office. A long interval of silence followed. 'He'll probably have to speak to the President,' said Jack. 'He's taken a keen interest in the hurricane. He's the Emergency Coordination Centre in Washington.'

The Executive Order came through. 'Do it!'

'By the time we get a freighter there it could be seventy, eighty, even ninety feet wide,' said Jack.

'What class of freighter do we need to plug that break?' asked the man from the corps.

'Handysize Bulker class,' said the jowly woman. 'They've got a beam between eighty and a hundred feet, draught thirty-two to thirty-eight feet.' She called up a list on her laptop.

Three candidate vessels were nearby: a grain carrier, a bulk fertiliser ship and one carrying petroleum coke. 'They'd all do,' said the man from the Corps.

'And all non-toxic cargoes, in case the ship breaks up.'

'God forbid,' said Jack.

'Apart from their fuel oil, fertiliser would be the worst from an environmental point of view,' said the woman. 'Anyway, the fertiliser carrier doesn't have a master aboard, so it'll have to be one of the others. The grain ship, *Lafcadio Hearn*, is fuelled up; the coke carrier isn't, so we can't use it. Take us there, Jack. And tell them to get the engines going.'

'I imagine they're already going.' Jack headed north, towards the centre of the lake. There were dozens of vessels visible. 'Which one is it?'

The woman from the Port of New Orleans gave him a bearing and Jack turned onto that heading. The freighter was a long way out. They hovered over the tossing *Lafcadio Hearn*. 'She's got a beam of ninety-one feet, draught of thirty-six feet, six inches.'

'Should do nicely,' said the man from the corps, although he sounded worried.

'I'll put you down on the chopper platform,' yelled Jack into the headphones. 'Can't winch you down in this, even if I had a winch hand.'

The man from the Corps gave a muffled squawk as the chopper heeled over and dropped sharply. Irith held her breath. The deck of the ship was going one way and then the other, the chopper bucking wildly in the air. It dropped, hovered, drifted left then right and the wheels touched. The deck heeled sharply and the chopper skidded sideways.

'Make it quick or we'll be over the side!' yelled Jack.

The three officials threw themselves out the door. Jack lifted and hovered above the ship. Nothing happened for some minutes.

'What's taking them so long?' Irith said aloud. Her chest had settled down to a dull ache.

'Seventy million dollars' worth of ship and another thirty million in cargo. If they do it, in an hour it might only be scrap. There's a lot of talking to do. Not to mention the people being asked to put their lives at risk.'

'Can't it be commandeered under emergency powers?' said Jemma.

'It *is* being commandeered, but there's still talking to be done.' A lantern blinked from the freighter. 'Okay,' said Jack, and they began to move off.

He flicked on a floodlight, turned on the video, adjusting it until he had a clear picture, and beamed it to the Emergency Operating Centre as he flew along the levee.

Jemma studied the ship with her binoculars. 'The *Lafcadio Hearn* isn't moving.'

'Takes a while to get a ship going.'

They hovered over the break in the levee. The cut was down eight metres now and eighteen wide, and the torrent pouring through was unimaginable.

Jemma took Jack's arm. He looked across at her and smiled.

Irith scanned the burning building. 'The fire's almost up to the roof.'

'What about the other buildings?' Jack was totally focused on the levee.

'They're not burning ... Oh, I see what you mean. They look all right, structurally. The people inside should be safe for a while.'

'How long will it take the freighter to get here?' Irith asked.

'Another nineteen minutes,' said Jack.

It was 5.35 am and it should have been getting light, but under the black, overcast sky it was as dark as ever.

'Can we take another look at the roof?' said Jemma.

'Sure, though since they weren't there before –'

'They might have been behind a fire door.'

'It'd have to be a strong one to withstand that blast.'

'It's a Class Four quarantine facility,' said Irith. 'It's built strong.'

Jack spun away to the top of Building One. The wind was stronger than it had been lower down, and gustier. He circled the top of the building, probing the roof with his floodlight. It was hard to see. Banners of oily smoke whipped across, steam rose from the roof, and the rain lashed down harder than ever.

'I don't see them,' Jack said.

'How can you be sure?' said Irith. 'Go round again. I can't believe they're not there. They were going to blow the jerry cans from the roof.'

'Maybe the remote failed,' said Jack.

'They wouldn't all have gone back down.'

He went round again, then shook his head. 'Sorry, ma'am. We'd better get back to the levee.'

'One last time,' said Irith. 'Please.'

He circled around again and as he passed the north-eastern corner, the windward one, the smoke cleared momentarily and a light blinked three times.

'*There they are!*' Irith screamed. 'In the corner. Put down, Jack.'

'I saw it, ma'am,' he said calmly. 'Going to have trouble landing in this, though.'

'Do you have to land?' said Jemma.

'Yes, because I don't have an experienced winch operator. And if I did, the wind's too strong to lift anyone with it.'

He dropped towards the corner of the roof. The building was an inferno inside.

'That's one helluva hot fire,' said Jack. 'The whole roof could collapse. I can't land on it.'

'Can you hover above it?'

'Easier said than done in this weather – but I'll try.'

The chopper drifted sideways across the roof. A gust sent it rotating backwards and he had to lift suddenly to avoid the air-conditioning building and the cooling towers.

'Have to go round again,' he said to Jemma. 'One unexpected gust and we're into that lot, and that will be it.'

Again she touched his arm and something wordless passed between them. Jack went around the other way, lifted to go over the wall that surrounded the top of the building and set down with a bone-jarring thump thirty metres from the corner. The whole roof seemed to shudder.

'Oops!' he grinned. 'Didn't mean to do that.'

Irith held her breath. The roof held, for the moment. She reached out to slide the door open. 'Aah!'

'Irith?' Jemma yelled.

'It's okay. Just hurts . . . when I move.'

'Leave it to me.'

A clot of greasy smoke boiled out through the open roof door on the far side. It was hurled at them by the wind, and just as quickly dissipated. The roof shook and shook again. Jack turned on his floodlights. Flames flickered in the doorway. A crack zigzagged from the eastern wall across the concrete towards the cooling towers.

Jemma scrambled from her seat, slid the door open and pushed down the steps.

'Come back!' roared Jack. 'The roof could go at any minute.' The engines roared and the chopper lifted a foot off the concrete.

Jemma turned towards him, her pale face stark in the lights. She was terrified of falling into the flames. 'I'm not leaving without them, Jack,' she mouthed, then, crouching low, ran toward the corner. The smoke obscured her.

Jack cursed and rotated the chopper until it faced the centre of the roof. The concrete had cracked all around the cooling towers. One tower tilted, water poured out onto the roof and steam belched up in thunderheads.

Irith looked around frantically. Why weren't they coming? She unbuckled her belt and lurched towards the door. Every step hurt. Jack cursed, long and fluently, but did not stop her.

She half fell down the steps, landing on the lowest. Pain sheared through her chest. In the direction of the flashing lights she had seen earlier, shadows moved. They must be injured but there was nothing she could do for them. If she went across, someone would have to carry her back.

There came a small explosion from somewhere below and the roof door breathed fire like a flamethrower. Metal screamed, the cooling towers groaned and part of the roof broke away under their weight. There was a momentary diminution of the flames as a hundred thousand litres of water deluged the floor below, then a cloud of superheated steam the colour of boiled soot belched from the hole. It reached out to the chopper to steam them alive.

The wind drove the steam away. Another small section of roof fell. Jack lifted the chopper another trifle, rocking wildly. 'The roof's falling. Get inside, ma'am. I'm going, with you or without you.'

Irith knew she was going to regret it but she wasn't going without her mother or her friends. She slid off the bottom step onto the shuddering concrete.

CHAPTER FORTY

Irith peered through the gushing steam. 'They're coming, Jack,' she yelled. 'I can see them.'

Bragg appeared first, staggering under the weight of a bloody burden recognisable only by her blonde hair: Siah. Behind them lurched Gretel, her shirt bloodstained, then Jemma, supporting Levi. They were all ragged, charred and streaked with soot.

A slab of roof collapsed on the other side of the building. Flames leapt high and fumes stung their eyes and noses. Jack drifted the chopper towards the shambling group. The roof seemed to ripple underfoot. The soles of Irith's boots began to smoke – her feet were burning hot.

'Irith!' screamed Jack. 'It's going!'

She hopped the six steps to Bragg, urging him to the steps. 'Come on!'

He reached the ladder but could not get up onto the lowest step, which was thigh high and jerking back and forth as the chopper was pushed by the wind. Irith tried to help him but he was too heavy.

Gretel pushed past as if Irith wasn't there, put a hand in the middle of Bragg's bloody backside and heaved him up.

'Shit oh fucking shit!' he groaned, almost dropping Siah. He was stuck on the steps without the strength to lift his burden.

Irith hopped up and down, trying to ease her burning feet. On the far side, slabs of roof were peeling away from the supporting beams and plunging into the inferno below.

Gretel climbed over Bragg, took hold of his arm and hauled him and Siah in. Irith helped Jemma drag Levi to the steps. He was practically out on his feet. They pushed him up onto the lowest step. Gretel jerked him inside. Jemma followed. Irith crawled up the steps, last of all. They were hot to the touch.

Crack! Boom! The remainder of the roof collapsed, blasting a mushroom cloud of boiling smoke and flame at them. Bragg hauled Irith in and the chopper shot up, hurled this way and that on an updraught so violent that it was fighting the hurricane for supremacy. The steps were too hot to pull up.

Jack, barely in control, wrestled the machine sideways as the flames roared higher, then they were away. Before they reached the levee, the lower floors of the building began to collapse, one by one, each sending another blast of flame and dirty steam out in all directions. The northern wall fell in. The rest followed and the flames were consumed by the flood.

Jack circled over the foaming levee, taking stock. 'There's a first-aid kit under your seat, Irith.'

She drew it out. Everyone was coated with greasy soot that made the whites of their eyes and their teeth stand out. Levi's clothes were charred rags, his face and hands a mass of blisters, and the halo of hair around his bald head was burnt to a crisp. His legs and feet were also blistered, though not as badly, and he was sagging forward against his harness.

'Explosion broke through the quarantine doors,' Bragg croaked. 'He's lucky to be alive.'

'He doesn't look good,' Jemma said anxiously.

'A bit of concrete fell on his head as we were coming out. '

'Where were you?' said Irith. 'We looked for you just after the explosion.'

'Still down there. The bloody remote wouldn't work so we had to set it off with a grenade. The explosion blew out the airlocks and one of the fire doors, and blocked the stairs. We had to fight our way across the eighth floor to the other stairs. It got a little . . . warm.'

Siah, who was lying on the floor, writhed and coughed blood down her front, which was already saturated. She moaned but didn't open her eyes.

'I thought she was dead!' said Irith.

'Better if she was!' snarled Gretel.

'Shut your mouth, you stupid bitch!' Irith said furiously. 'I've had more than enough of you. We all owe our lives to Siah and you'd better acknowledge it.'

'What the fuck are you talking about?'

'She attacked Lindstrom on the roof, to give me time to get to him. He shot the rifle out of her hand but Siah just walked right up to him, unarmed. It was the bravest thing I've ever seen. He shot her down. If she hadn't done that, I would never have reached the chopper and he would have won. How is she, Bragg?'

'Not good. She took a bullet in the ribs. It went through the edge of her lung and out her back. The second bullet passed through her side, just missing her intestines. She's lost a lot of blood.'

'How did you find her?'

'She'd crawled across to the roof door.'

Siah opened her eyes, looking up at Bragg.

'You bloody fool,' said Bragg, wiping her brow. 'What did you do that for?'

'Had to make up for – evil I'd done – without more – violence.'

'You warned us,' said Bragg, 'and still we pushed you, too far. Any of us might have done the same, in different circumstances.'

'But you didn't.'

'You saved us, and that's what matters. Rest now.'

'Goodbye,' Siah whispered. 'You're the best friends in the world. I –' Her head slumped sideways.

Irith let out a cry of anguish.

'She's still breathing,' said Bragg.

'Is she going to die?'

'She's bleeding internally, but I can't tell how bad. Jack, we need a hospital, fast.'

Jack got on the radio, then said, 'Every emergency room in the state is bursting at the seams. They'll call when they find a place.'

'It'd better be soon,' said Bragg.

'What about you?' said Irith.

'I'm all right,' he said dismissively.

'He's been shot in the arse,' said Gretel. 'That's what you get for going the wrong way, buster.' She almost smiled.

'I was trying to save your bacon! Christ, it hurts.'

'Shot in the arse,' said Irith. It wasn't funny but she laughed anyway.

'It's nothing,' said Bragg, belying his words by shifting onto one cheek and wincing. 'Gretel's the one who needs the attention.'

She had her arms across her chest, partly concealing her own injury. Her shirt was red down the front and she was gritting her teeth.

'Better give me a look,' said Jemma.

'It's . . . not as bad as it looks. Went through my boob, in one side and out the other. If they were a bit smaller . . .'

'First time you wished for that, I'll bet,' snorted Bragg, pleased to turn the attention away from himself.

'If you had to carry them around you wouldn't be so fucking keen on them,' she snarled.

Gretel lifted her shirt. The small entry hole had already sealed over. An exit wound the same size was still bleeding but her whole breast was bruised black and purple. Jemma cleaned the wounds, pressed a stick-on bandage on either side and left it.

'How come you didn't have your vest on?' Irith said quietly.

'How come you took yours off?' Gretel retorted.

'What happened with Lindstrom?' Bragg said quietly.

It reminded Jemma of his chilling final words. What could they mean?

'He's dead. And the cylinders are lying on the bottom of the Mississippi,' said Jemma. 'Unopened. I dare say a determined search could find them.'

'In such a flood they'll likely be washed out to sea,' said Jack, 'and buried under a hundred feet of mud. How are you feeling, Levi?'

'I've had better decades,' he said wryly. 'What have you lot been up to?'

Irith told their story in as few words as she could. Exhaustion had crept up on her and she could barely hold her head up.

'And Lindstrom?' Levi tried to sit up. He looked as if someone had run a blowtorch over him.

Irith related his fate, even more briefly.

'Poetic justice,' said Levi. 'It's over, then.'

'Your work might be over,' said Jack, 'but mine isn't.'

'You can start by going back for Thorn!' Gretel said, with frightening intensity.

They looked at one another. 'I didn't see him after the explosion,' said Irith.

'If he were dead, I'd know it,' Gretel said inexorably. 'He risked his life for us and we owe him.'

'Jack,' said Levi, sounding a little more like his old self, 'could you take a quick turn over the corner of the wall, where the missile defences were?'

Jack tapped the cockpit clock. 'I've got to talk the freighter through the cut in a couple of minutes.'

'If there's a chance he's still alive, we've got to look.'

The chopper swung around, plunging steeply down towards the corner of the wall. As they approached, Jack turned the floodlights on. There was little left of the bunker, apart from the flagpole. Most of the rubble beach Thornton had crawled up was submerged.

'The water level must have risen a couple of metres since he went,' Irith mused. The highest point was only a metre and a half out of the water.

They turned around the flagpole, then again, flying at about ten metres. Irith scanned the rubble. Nothing. Jack went around again. There wasn't a sign of life.

Gretel's face was as white as paper. 'He's not dead.' She looked back as they headed away. 'He's there!' she screamed. 'He's alive. Look!'

Jack spun the chopper around. The massive figure of Thornton was caught in the beam of the floodlights, crouching in a hollow in the rubble. He waved weakly and climbed to his feet.

'Better hurry,' said Bragg. 'The water's rising quickly now.'

Jack went back over Thornton. Bragg slid open the door. The wind shoved the chopper around in a semicircle, the downdraught knocking Thornton to his knees. He looked up, white-faced.

'Thorn!' cried Gretel, screwing up her face as if she could feel his pain.

His right arm hung limply, probably broken, and they were close enough to see the agony on his face. Splotches of blood stained his chest and arm.

'Must have been hurt in the explosion,' said Levi. 'What can we do, Jack?'

'Nothing. There's nowhere to land.'

'I can man the winch,' said Bragg. 'I've done it before.'

'Wind's too strong. Sorry, Gretel. It can't be done.'

'Please try, Jack,' she wept. 'He's all I've got and I can't live without him.'

Jack went round several times, frowning. 'Even if I could hover over him, he can't fix himself into the harness with only one arm. Someone would have to go down, and that's impossible in this wind.'

'I'll go.' Gretel was out of her seat in an instant.

'You're injured,' said Levi. 'You can't –'

'It's my tit, not my hand!' Gretel snapped. She grimaced as she moved. 'Bragg has to man the winch and you puny lot couldn't lift Thorn.'

'Can you?' said Levi evenly.

'He's my brother. I'll pick him up and run with him if I have to.' She flexed her arms and gasped.

Irith could only imagine how painful such a wound must be. Every movement would pull at it.

Gretel strapped into the harness and Bragg began to lower her down. The wind jerked the chopper back and forth. Gretel, on the end of the cable, swung through wild arcs, once right up in front of the chopper. Irith caught her breath. A harder gust might drive her into the blades, and then they would all die.

'It's hopeless,' yelled Jack. 'Pull her up and I'll go round the other side. It may be easier that way.'

Bragg winched Gretel in, screwing up his face at each lurch of the chopper. Blood seeped down the back of his leg.

'Hover next to him,' Gretel yelled over the roar of the motor. 'We'll pull him in.'

'I can't hover that low in this wind,' said Jack. 'We'll either end up in the water or chop him in half.'

'Can you get lower than you were before?'

'Not much. I've got to stay well out of the way of the flagpole.'

They tried again. This time it seemed to work better – Gretel's boots actually touched the rubble, only a dozen metres away from Thornton, before she was dragged out over the water. The chopper dropped suddenly, dunking her, and the current pulled her under. Bragg wound the winch and she came up in a cascade of water.

The flood level was definitely higher; the exposed patch of rubble had shrunk visibly. Gretel swung in an arc on the rope, circling her brother, who had fallen to one knee. Irith could see her frustration. So close, yet she couldn't get to him.

'He doesn't look good,' said Irith.

'Looks like he's got internal injuries,' Levi said quietly.

'Go!' yelled Jack. 'The cut's collapsed again.'

A wall of water rushed towards them, a good metre high. Bragg wound Gretel down. Again the wind swung her away from her brother. The chopper lifted, pulling her straight up about ten metres. They watched the surge rolling towards the rubble as Jack struggled to bring the chopper down again.

Another gust pushed them further away. Thornton stood looking after them, a forlorn figure on a patch of rubble just a few metres long. It shrank to nothing as the wave hit him from behind and knocked him off his feet. When he came up there was only water under him, and the current carried him away.

Even over the roar of the engine, Irith heard Gretel's shriek. She was kicking and struggling in her harness, her hands working at the release.

'Pull her up before she does something stupid!' Jack yelled.

Too late. She freed herself, dropped into the water, bobbed up again and thrashed towards her brother. He tried to swim to her but made little progress. Gretel, with a superhuman effort, closed the gap. She reached out, and he did too. Their hands touched, clasped for a few seconds, then the current tore them apart.

Thornton went under and they lost sight of him. Gretel churned the water to foam, trying to find her brother. She slammed into a submerged obstacle, was pulled under and did not come up.

The chopper followed the streamline of the water but found no trace of her, or Thornton. Finally Jack turned away, shaking his head. Bragg wound up the harness and closed the door.

'I was afraid of that,' Jack said. 'This is the worst part. The ones you lose in spite of everything.' He looked over his shoulder at the silent faces. 'We'd better get going.'

Irith closed her eyes, regretting her earlier outburst. In spite of all their conflicts, the twins had been good to her. They'd saved her life. She wiped away tears but they kept flowing.

Bragg slipped in beside her. 'How's Siah?'

'Still breathing.'

He took her pulse. 'Forty-eight!'

'That's pretty slow.'

'Yes,' said Bragg, 'but she's very fit. Any news on the hospital, Jack?'

'Not yet.'

They approached the levee. The air was full of spray and foam, horizontal rain and flying debris. Dawn was breaking but they could not see the approaching freighter.

'How long before it gets here?' said Irith.

'Two minutes.' Jack turned to get a clearer view of the cut. 'It's going to be touch and go. The cut's eighty-five feet already, maybe ninety. The *Lafcadio Hearn* is only ninety-one. If the cut grows wider than the ship, it could even make it worse.' He called the freighter, and described the shape and dimensions of the cut.

'What happened on the stairs?' Irith said quietly to Levi. 'Why did it take you so long?'

'We should've made sure of Lindstrom's guards. The woman must have been playing dead. She ambushed us in the stairwell. Gretel was a tiger, I've never seen anyone move so fast. She saved our lives.'

'No one would ever question her courage,' said Bragg.

'No one would. I'm very, very sorry,' said Levi.

Irith turned to Bragg. 'So what happened to you?'

'I got shot in the ass. Very undignified.'

'Running away?' she joked, and regretted it instantly.

'If I'd known what this night was going to be like, I'd be in Timbuktu by now.'

'We heard someone moving in the stairwell,' said Levi. 'We couldn't work out if it came from above us or below. Bragg thought it was up the stairs, so we ran that way. The woman from the lab came from below.'

'Sheryl?' said Irith, not thinking straight.

'No, the woman who was with Lindstrom earlier. Bragg threw himself in front of me and took the bullet.'

'Nonsense,' said Bragg. 'I stumbled, is all.'

'I know what I saw,' said Levi. 'We went down in a heap. She would have killed us both, had Gretel not done for her.'

'One minute,' said Jack.

'I can see the ship,' Jemma cried. 'It's lined up perfectly.'

'Well, of course it is,' said Jack mildly. 'It's coming at three knots, which ought to be about right. It should hit the bottom as it approaches the cut. That'll slow it. Hopefully just the right amount.'

Now they could all see the freighter. Since it was coming head-on, it was difficult to judge the speed. Jack drifted the chopper east along the levee, speaking to the captain in a low voice, guiding him in.

The *Lafcadio Hearn* closed rapidly. 'Fifty metres, forty, thirty …' said Bragg.

It slowed with a lurch and lifted half a metre in the water. It slowed more as the bow reached the levee, then lifted again.

'Shit!' cried Bragg. 'It's going too fast. It's going to go right through.'

Irith thought so too. She clutched at his arm. The bow was through now, the width of the vessel meeting the sides of the cut. There came a grating rush and mud squirted vertically all along the sides of the freighter, to be blasted away by the wind.

The freighter slowed rapidly. Nearly a third of it was through the gap. The torrent was cut off. The freighter was barely moving now. With a screech of metal against the gravel of the levee, it came to a stop, the bow slightly up in the air. The gap had been plugged.

Inside the chopper everyone cheered and clapped each other on the back. Despite the pain in her chest, Irith threw her arms around Bragg. He felt like her dearest friend. Tears poured down her cheeks.

'Careful of my butt,' he grunted. 'The bullet's still in there.'

'Well, that's that,' said Jack. 'Let's just hope the plug lasts.'

'Why wouldn't it?' said Irith.

'The waves move the ship a little each time, which will slowly erode the levee from the sides and underneath. Eventually, the plug will fail.'

'How long would that take?' said Levi.

'Depends on the weather,' said Jack.

'The hurricane is moving north-east, away from us,' said Bragg. 'Landfall is expected to be on the state border just west of Gulfport, in about an hour. It's twenty past six now, so that'll be around seven-thirty. The winds are abating and the storm surge should ease fairly quickly.'

'How quickly?' Irith asked.

'Over the next eight to ten hours.'

'That long?' said Irith.

'It's a lot quicker on the coast, but all the water pushed up the lake has to flow back. However, unless Jemma changes direction again, by nightfall the worst will be over.'

'What happens now?' said Irith.

The radio crackled. 'I've got a bed!' said Jack.

'Where?'

'Tulane U Hospital and Clinic.'

'Is that far?' said Bragg. 'Siah's pulse is dropping.'

'A couple of minutes.'

Shortly they landed on the hospital roof, where an emergency team was sheltering inside the doors. They whisked Siah off, leaving everyone staring anxiously after her.

'Let's go,' said Jack. 'The rest of you will have to make do with first aid.'

'Suits me,' said Levi. 'I'd prefer not to draw attention to us. Let's go home, Jack.'

'I'll drop you on the roof of your apartment block,' said Jack, 'then grab a couple of hours' sleep. I can hardly keep my eyes open. Then I'll refuel and get on with what I do best – picking people out of the water.'

By the time they were over the apartment block, the winds had eased to sixty knots. Water continued to flood over the levee and would do so for most of the day, according to the storm-surge predictions. The freighter, worked back and forth by wind and waves, no longer plugged the gap as well as it first had, but the Corps was putting a team in place to deal with that. It was 7 am.

'I'm dog-tired,' said Jack. 'Too tired to be flying.'

'We've got spare rooms, food and good coffee, if the gas is still on,' said Irith.

He landed on the roof, secured the chopper and they went down. 'I never expected to be coming back here,' Irith said as Levi opened the door of the apartment.

'What did you expect?' said Jack.

'Until the hurricane came,' said Levi, 'we couldn't think of any way to get into the facility except by blowing a hole in the levee. That was our original plan. Afterwards, we expected to be running for what remained of our undoubtedly brief lives. We had to lock Irith in her room because she refused to go along with it.'

Jack's bright eyes searched Levi's face and the strangest look crossed his own leathery features. 'You never said that, old friend. You never even *thought* it.'

Jemma took care of Levi's burns and abrasions and Irith attended to Bragg's. It was a quick operation compared to the one she had performed on Gretel in London, but painful for them both, for every movement sent spikes of pain through her chest. The bullet, a slug from a low-calibre automatic, was undeformed and, despite his grimaces and increasingly terse instructions she had it out of his muscled buttock in a few minutes.

They had breakfast at the long table in the conference room. While they ate, Levi filled Jack in on the past few months. The tale was a revelation to Jemma too, although as soon as Jack began to yawn she said, 'Where was that spare bedroom?'

Irith showed him the way. Jemma went, too. 'I'll keep you company, Jack.'

Irith was astounded. Her mother was normally so reserved and slow to trust. She looked in ten minutes later. Jack lay on the bed, fully clothed apart from his shoes, with Jemma curled up beside him. He had his arm around her and they were fast asleep.

CHAPTER FORTY-ONE

'That was quick – Jemma and Jack, I mean,' said Irith as she passed Levi in the hall. His face was covered in burn cream.

For a moment he looked very sad, but it passed. 'She's been waiting a long time.'

'It's wonderful how the expectation of imminent death concentrates the mind.'

'Isn't it?'

They went back to the table. 'We'd better do something about poor Vaiha,' said Irith.

'It's already been done. Jack and I took him up to the chopper, in a body bag, while you were attending to Bragg. Jack'll give him a respectful burial at sea. Poor man. I'll never forget how I let him down.'

'Nor I,' said Irith. 'And you'll make sure he's credited with that factoring algorithm?'

'Of course.'

'What happens now, Levi?'

'It's too early to tell. The Global Congress has taken a battering since your broadcast and can't survive. The sanctions against Britain have been dropped, and an apology offered, but France, Belgium, Germany, Canada, Japan and Korea have already withdrawn, and another dozen countries are planning to, including Australia.'

'I'm surprised America hasn't.'

'It will.'

Irith's chest was throbbing. She carefully laid her head on the table. 'Well, it's over. I wonder what that's going to change?'

'Everything, and nothing. What will you do now?'

'Go home and get on with my life.' But the statement sounded wrong as soon as she said it, like trying to go back to childhood. 'I've no idea, Levi.'

'Nor I. I've been working towards this day for more than twenty years. Now it's over, I feel all washed out.'

'Maybe you just need to vegetate for a while.'

'I don't think I'd know how.'

She sat up. 'I've often wondered who was behind you, and what *they* wanted.'

'I'm sure a lot of people are going to ask the same question.'

'Are you going to answer it?' said Irith.

'Not to your satisfaction. There were fewer of us than you might think, plus we had a number of anonymous supporters who provided money we couldn't raise ourselves. There were never more than a few dozen of us, and half died in the raid on the underground command centre in London.'

'What are you all going to do now?'

'Nothing. We were democrats, Irith. Freedom fighters, to use an unfashionable term. Now that the Global Congress is finished we'll destroy our records, wind everything up and fade away. It's up to the politicians now.'

Was he telling the truth? Could they give everything up that easily? Irith decided that she didn't care. She was going to start living, at last.

Three hours' sleep and Jack was up again. Jemma went with him.

From the roof, Irith watched them fly away. It was 10.45 am. The sun had come out briefly and the levee was an awesome sight. She could see kilometres of it from her window and the lake was spilling over it all the way. The storm surge had fallen dramatically, but it was still a metre and a half over the top and the pounding seas as high again.

The city had been transformed – every street was a canal and the water was getting higher all the time. Once it flowed in, there was no way of getting it out, since all the pumps were underwater.

A number of buildings, large and small, had collapsed, others were tilted and several were smoking ruins. There were boats everywhere, collecting people from balconies, rooftops and windows, taking them to refuges, and sometimes capsizing in the rough conditions. There were bodies in the water, too. One time she saw a raft of them. And coffins from the old raised cemeteries. And alligators.

The rooftops were crowded with people and, now that the winds had abated sufficiently, Irith saw hundreds of choppers, ferrying them to safety. At least, most of them. As she watched, a little Bell Jet Ranger shot up from between two apartment buildings and flew straight into a Sikorsky. The big chopper's blades hacked through the plexiglass bubble of the Jet Ranger, which turned over, leaking bodies, plunged into an apartment wall and burst into flames.

Soon the whole block was burning. People leapt out of the windows and off the roof, into the water. The Sikorsky's pilot tried to save his machine but the blades sheared off and it dropped like a brick into the water, breaking apart on impact and sinking. No one got out.

Irith had to go inside. She lowered herself carefully onto her bed and closed her eyes. Her chest still hurt, although if she breathed shallowly it was bearable. She desperately needed sleep, but her mind kept replaying the endless night, over and over again.

··•●•··

'Get up!' said Bragg.

She woke with a start. 'What's wrong? It's not Mum?'

'She's with Jack. We need to be ready for evacuation.'

'Is there any news on Siah?'

'No.'

As Irith tried to sit up a sickening pain speared through her chest. 'Shit!'

'What's the matter?'

In all the drama after the rescue, Irith had not mentioned her own injury. She unbuttoned her pyjama shirt and pulled it open. The black bruise now covered half her chest.

'Lindstrom's gun went off,' she said, 'and I was in the way.'

'When you buy a bulletproof vest, they don't tell you that being shot is like being hit with a sledgehammer.' He took a closer look. 'So while you were operating on me ... Why didn't you say?'

'You took a bullet,' she said.

'Bloody idiot!' he said, buttoning her up. 'Better put those away or it'll cause me a problem.'

'And we wouldn't want that to happen.'

He lifted her and propped her up with the pillows. Irith felt close to him and wasn't sure how to deal with it. 'How's your arse?'

'It felt better with the bullet in. Did you have to be so rough?'

'I had to get it out quickly.' She managed a small smile.

'Why so?'

'A girl could be overcome by a backside like that.'

'That's a somewhat ambiguous statement.' He frowned, as if bothered about something.

'What's the matter?' said Irith, beginning to worry that there was some bad news she hadn't been told. 'Is Siah . . . ?'

'There's no news. It's the levee.'

Pain prevented her from turning that way. Bragg took her in his arms and, once the throbbing settled down, it felt good. She looked out the window. It was about 5 pm, windy and with a thin cover of ragged cloud. There were helicopters everywhere, thousands of them. A hundred metres east of the plugged levee, another gap had formed, wider than the freighter, and brown water was foaming through it. A third gap, near the university, grew before their eyes.

'The levee is crumbling,' said Bragg. 'It's only an earth wall and it was never designed for this.'

'What's going to happen?'

'The discharge through the gaps is undercutting the base of the levee, as you'd expect, and nothing can be done while water's flowing over the top. Once the earth and clay core is undercut, it collapses and keeps collapsing. If the storm surge doesn't drop quickly there'll be more holes in the levee. And bigger ones.'

'Is it likely to drop?'

'Not quickly enough.'

'Are we in danger here now?'

'Depends on what happens.'

'What do you think is going to happen? You're the engineer.'

He did not answer. Irith followed his gaze. Another gully had formed a few hundred metres west of the facility, and it grew incredibly quickly. In less than a minute it reached the top of the levee. A chunk of bank ten metres wide crumbled and the lake water cascaded through it, forming another waterfall.

'Is there nothing to be done?' said Irith.

'They might tow in a prefabricated barrier, with tugs, to fix a small break, but in these conditions there's not much they can do about a big one. Half a dozen freighters have been commandeered and are being brought up now. See them there?' He pointed. 'But I don't think it's going to make any difference.'

No more levee breaks had formed in the area they could see, though the existing channels were widening all the time. Two freighters had been anchored next to the breaks but it made no difference to the flow, and these breaks were too wide to be plugged by driving a ship into them.

Bragg pulled up a chair for Irith, found her a pair of binoculars and stood beside her. 'Would you like something to eat?'

'I don't think I could keep anything down.'

He went out. Irith focused the binoculars. The gap immediately east of the facility had grown rapidly and now only a small peak of levee, no more than ten metres across, separated it from the break plugged by the freighter, the *Lafcadio Hearn*. What would happen when it went?

Another freighter was standing by preparing to pass a line across to tow the *Lafcadio Hearn* to safety. But what if the peak of the levee collapsed first?

As she had that thought the remnant of levee slumped, then the lake poured through and cut it all away. Thousands of tonnes of compacted earth disappeared in a few seconds and a deluge flooded towards the two remaining towers of the facility, Buildings Two and Three. Building One was just a smoke-stained mound of rubble in between.

A big chopper had landed on top of Building Two, presumably to ferry more trapped employees away. Irith focused the binoculars. She had forgotten all those faces at the windows last night. For them, the nightmare was still going on.

It was Jack's chopper, and as it settled on the roof a crowd of people ran towards it. They seemed to be fighting each other, forcing their way through the chopper door and even hanging onto the wheels.

Irith caught her breath. Bragg appeared beside her with a cup of tea. She took it gratefully.

'I didn't think that peak could last,' he said.

The deluge shook the base of Building Three and Irith saw pieces of masonry fall from the walls. 'If the rest of that levee section collapses, will the flood tear down the buildings?'

'I hope it doesn't go that quickly.'

She looked again. 'Hey! There's Mum!' Irith's chest throbbed and she could barely hold the binoculars up. *Go, Jack*, she prayed. *Go, quickly!*

A fight broke out among the people who could not find a place on the chopper. An armed guard forced them off at gunpoint but they surged forward, knocking him to the ground. A man raised his gun and pointed it at the chopper. People got out. Someone stepped down onto the roof and tried to talk to the rebels. Someone small. Jemma!

Irith turned to Bragg. 'Mum's got out of the chopper. Why would she do that?'

He put his arms around her, careful of her chest. 'She's a clever woman. She knows what she's doing.'

'If she's so bloody smart, why'd she get out?'

Half a dozen people were pushed out of the chopper, which took off. 'Jack's going without her!' she wept.

'It's the right thing to do. He'll be back.'

Another huge slab of levee collapsed, this time on the left side of the *Lafcadio Hearn*. It was no longer jammed against the levee but was now in the middle of a waterfall, held only by the small section of earth under its keel. The *Lafcadio Hearn* swung around, side-on to the gap which was now the length of the ship. The second freighter, which had pulled in close behind in the shelter of the levee, fired a line. The crew at the stern of the *Lafcadio Hearn* caught it and reeled it in, transferring it to a winch to pull in the heavier line, and then the towing cable.

'Shit!' said Bragg.

'What is it?' she whispered, drying her eyes.

'They can't do it in time. The freighter's going to go right through.'

The water was churned to foam behind the *Lafcadio Hearn* as its master gave the engines full astern. It edged backwards, then stopped. It moved a little further into the gap, grounded, then moved forward a few metres more. Minutes seemed to pass like hours.

Irith looked back and forth from the levee to Building Two. There were still a couple of dozen people on top. It would take several trips to ferry them all away and Jack's chopper wasn't in sight. No, here it came. She focused on Jemma, who was standing on the roof with everyone else around her in a semicircle. Irith almost smiled. Jemma had been a teacher and a school principal, and she was very good at organising people without offending egos.

The chopper put down. Ten people walked in a line and climbed in. There was no rush, no panic, no fighting. The chopper took off again.

Fourteen remained, plus Jemma. Two more trips.

The towing cable snapped taut as the second freighter went full ahead. Both ships were stationary now. The *Lafcadio Hearn* could make no way against the current which, falling ten metres in a hundred, was prodigious.

'Can they do it?' Irith said in a wisp of a voice.

'Impossible.' Bragg held her more tightly. 'They haven't thought it through. They should be pulling the stern to the left, alongside the levee. They're trying to pull thirty thousand tonnes up a ramp, and the engines can't do it. Now he's going too hard. It'll pull the stern underwater. Something's got to –'

Water cascaded over the stern of the *Lafcadio Hearn*. 'Shit!' said Bragg. 'Pray that the cable breaks. Pray . . .'

His mind was three or four steps further on than hers. Irith had no idea what was going to happen, except that it looked like a disaster.

The cable didn't break. The *Lafcadio Hearn's* stern lifted sharply and its bow went down, grounding on the bottom. The torrent caught it, pushing it sideways into the gap. It was going to roll. The cable held it upright for a moment. The towing vessel was pulled backwards and then the cable snapped, lashing out like a flail and clearing its stern deck of containers, structures and people in one bloody, scything second.

The *Lafcadio Hearn* rolled through the gap, came up again and was driven bow down onto the point where the northern wall of the facility had once been. The shriek of tearing metal reached them seconds later. Irith counted every one of them.

'Pray it sticks there,' said Bragg.

It did, stern in the air, for the moment.

'The other freighter seems to have stopped,' Irith exclaimed. 'Why would it do that?'

'Perhaps the cable has tangled in the propellers . . .'

Then it was caught by the torrent and hurled stern-first through the gap. It struck the *Lafcadio Hearn* near its stern with another delayed, tearing scream. The *Lafcadio Hearn* came free and was driven sideways towards the tower of Building Three.

'Pray it grounds on something,' said Bragg.

Another huge slab of levee gave way and the torrent rolled the *Lafcadio Hearn* directly at Building Three. The building shuddered but they could not see the point of impact, which was on the western side of the building, away from them.

'It's all right,' said Irith. 'It hasn't done much damage.'

'I'm afraid it has,' said Bragg. 'Buildings aren't designed for side-on impacts. It's going to come down.'

Building Three began to crumble slowly, from the far side. Irith's eyes flicked from it to Building Two. Jack's chopper was just taking off, leaving five people on the roof. Jemma was one of them.

Building Three was struck from the eastern side by the second freighter, which slammed into it stern-first. The building collapsed suddenly, raining huge blocks of masonry everywhere, some as far as Building Two. Waterspouts rose thirty metres into the air.

Building Two shivered and the people on the roof were thrown off their feet.

'It's all right,' said Irith. 'They're safe.'

She spoke too soon. The second freighter was lifted on another immense surge of water. The bow ground around the rubble of buildings Three and One, and speared directly in through the front entrance of Building Two, enlarging it to ten times its previous size. The structure shook violently. A crack ran up the wall, all the way to the roof, and the people there were thrown off their feet again. The crack snaked across the roof as the freighter wedged the building apart, before coming to rest with its bow inside.

The building continued to shudder and quake, and bits fell off, including most of the metre-high roof wall. The crack across the roof continued to widen. Jemma was on one side of it and the other four people on the other.

Bragg enveloped Irith in his arms, so gently that she felt no pain. 'It's going to fall,' he said. 'And Jack is still minutes away.'

Jemma's side of the building began to tilt, widening the gap to a couple of metres. The building moved out about ten degrees then stopped. The gap was three metres wide now.

'Jump!' Irith screamed. 'Jemma, please jump.'

Through the binoculars, Jemma looked as though she was steeling herself up to do that. 'Mum's afraid of heights,' said Irith. There was a terrific pain in her chest, as if a broken bone was sticking into her flesh. She tried to ignore it.

Bragg took her hand. 'She's a strong woman – the bravest I've ever met. Apart from you, of course.'

'Don't be absurd,' she said absently.

Jemma seemed to measure the gap then went back. She ran, but stopped after a few steps. She went back a little further, ran, this time stopping on the very brink.

'Three metres is too far,' Irith said, crushing Bragg's hand.

He winced but didn't withdraw. 'It's not *that* far. A ten-year-old kid could do it.'

'She's over fifty, Bragg, and running uphill. She'll never do it.'

Jemma went back further, but this time just stood there. Her side of the building shuddered and tilted another few degrees. The gap was now four metres and the slope steeper. The jump was impossible.

People on the other side of the gap were calling out to Jemma but she walked to the down side of the building and looked over, as if preparing to jump into the water. The building quivered and puffs of dust spurted up through the gap. A trail of smoke followed. There was an explosion inside, near where the bows of the ship would be. Flames burst out one wall of the building and oily black smoke boiled up.

Jack's chopper appeared. *Hurry, please.* Irith squeezed Bragg's hand harder but it did not help. The chopper hovered above the other side of the building. The sliding door was open and as Jack turned, Irith could see the winch man standing by. *Pick Mum up first.* Realising she was holding her breath, she sucked in air so hard that it hurt.

'He'll try to save the four before the one,' said Bragg.

The chopper dropped towards the flat part of the roof but, when it was still ten metres above, that side of the building collapsed from the bottom up, enveloping the entire structure in smoke and dust. The people disappeared.

'They're dead,' wept Irith. 'All of them. Mum's dead.'

The chopper shot sideways towards the tilted side of the building and someone went down on the cable, drifting into the cloud of dust. The chopper crept along the length of the roof as if trawling for fish, until it reached the other end. Irith's heart was trying to escape through her side. The suspended man emerged from the dust, was winched halfway up, then lowered and the chopper repeated its trawling operation. When it reached the far end, the chopper hovered and he was drawn slowly up again.

Irith let out a great cry and buried her face in Bragg's chest.

He shook her, gently. 'Irith.'

'Leave me alone.'

'Irith, look!'

At the tone of his voice a shiver began in the centre of her scalp and spread outwards. She brushed the tears from her eyes and put them to the binoculars. The suspended man rotated on the cable, holding a small figure against him. There had been no time to put her in the harness, so he had taken Jemma in his arms.

They were drawn up into the chopper. The door slid closed and it sped away to the next crisis point. Irith stood up and, heedless of her throbbing chest, kissed Bragg full on the mouth.

'You're crushing my hand,' he said a moment later, pulling it free and shaking it. 'Not that I mind, you understand.'

'Sorry.' She put her arms around him. 'Thank you, Bragg.'

'I didn't do anything.' He did not pull away, either.

The tilted half of Building Two stood for another ten minutes before collapsing as suddenly as the other side had. A minute later, all that was left above water level was three piles of rubble and the wrecked freighters.

They spent another hour at the window. The levee continued to collapse until the break was more than a kilometre wide and had eroded down to the full depth of the levee. Nothing could be done to plug such a gap. Even after the storm surge went down, the water would keep flowing until the level in the city was the same as the level in the lake. New Orleans, which lay many metres below lake level, was finished.

'Lindstrom was right, in a way,' said Irith. 'Nature is taking its course and nothing can be done to stop it.'

'Not a thing. Let's go up to the roof. We'll get a better view from there.'

He had to carry her, because Irith's chest had become more painful as the day wore on. It took a good while for him to get up the steps. There were dozens of people on the roof, watching and waiting silently. Bragg put Irith down near the edge.

Levi came up beside them, laptop in hand. 'I've just heard from the hospital. Siah's going to pull through.'

'Thank God!' said Bragg. 'The way she looked this morning, I didn't think we'd see her again.'

'It was a close thing,' said Levi.

Irith looked over the edge. The sun was low in the western sky. As it dropped through four fingers of cloud, golden rays streamed across the city, illuminating thousands of little flying sparks, everywhere she looked. They were like jewels in the sky, or iridescent beetles.

'I didn't imagine there could be so many helicopters in all the world,' she said. 'What a beautiful sight.'

'There were nearly ten thousand in the air a few hours ago – the greatest armada since the fall of Dunkirk. And they're still coming.' Bragg wiped away a tear. 'The US President made a personal appeal, and it was answered. Half the choppers in the United States came to the rescue of New Orleans today. We do care about our fellow man, after all.'

'It's incredible,' said Irith, looking down on the flooded city. More buildings had collapsed. 'I would've thought there'd be a hundred thousand dead.'

'The last estimate I heard was nineteen thousand, and that's horrible enough.' He bowed his head for a moment. 'Though when you consider what might have been … As of a few minutes ago, the choppers had taken out one hundred and eighty-five thousand people. Another ninety-two thousand have been evacuated by boat, and there are about a hundred thousand to go, including us. Shall we go down and get ready?'

'Just a little while longer. I never expected to be alive to see today. I want to see the sun go down on New Orleans. I'll never forget this sight as long as I live.'

'No one will, who lived to see it,' said Bragg soberly.

Lindstrom's broken body was found on the rooftop below the communications tower. His flesh had been shredded by the hurricane, although his face was recognisable from the bones. The eyes were gone but the cavernous sockets still glared at the world, their rage unabated.

The cylinders, despite a long search, were never found. Analysis of the chopper's track data revealed that they had fallen into the Mississippi somewhere between the Aquarium of the Americas and the Powder Street Wharf. In the flood, the bundle, or its individual cylinders, would have been washed down the channel into the Gulf of Mexico and deposited at the base of the advancing delta-front.

They would now be covered with as much as thirty metres of mud, and the next flood would bury them deeper. They would never be recovered. The stainless steel might remain in the mud for thousands of years before slowly corroding away.

Seventy-two hours later there were no more people on the evacuation list in the city, although there was plenty to do further inland, and around Gulfport where the hurricane had made landfall. The storm surge had been driven inland more than twenty kilometres, and had flooded wetlands and waterways for many times that distance. Only then was New Orleans able to count the cost.

'It could have been a lot worse,' said Jack, at dinner in their hotel suite in Port Arthur, Texas, the nearest place Levi had been able to find accommodation. 'If the hurricane hadn't turned north we couldn't have done it. If there hadn't been time to get the evacuation plan together ...'

'Most people survived,' said Bragg, 'but few will come back. New Orleans is done for. Even if the United States could afford a trillion dollars to rebuild the city, next year it could happen again.'

'It *will* happen again,' said Siah, who had been carried in only an hour ago. Unable to sit up, she was propped up in bed with pillows. In normal circumstances she would have remained in hospital, but beds were scarce everywhere in the continental United States and those who were recovering had to make way for the needy.

'And again,' said Bragg, 'until the last of the towers have fallen and the Mississippi covers everything in silt. But at least your family is safe.'

'Homeless, but alive,' said Siah. 'I should count my blessings. I killed that soldier and I can't remember anything about it. Do you remember it, Irith?' Siah gave a little shudder.

Irith recalled it all too well. 'Everything is a blur,' she said carefully. It would be a long time before Siah got over her traumas, if she ever did, and it would be the same for herself. 'So much was happening, so quickly.' She changed the subject. 'Does anyone know if Sheryl survived?'

'We picked her up,' said Jemma. 'She wasn't hurt.'

'Well, we did it,' said Levi, raising his glass. 'I never thought we would.'

'Yet you didn't falter for a second,' said Bragg.

'Oh, I faltered many times, especially in the dark days before the hurricane came. I just kept it to myself. How little there is to separate hero from villain,' he mused. 'If the hurricane hadn't come, and we'd gone with –' He broke off at the warning look on Jack's face.

'Let's toast the future, whatever and wherever that may be,' said Irith, who was feeling better. She stood up, slipped, cracked her ribs on the edge of the table, let out a little cry and fell down.

'In your cups again,' said Bragg, chuckling. 'No more wine for you, little Irith.'

She squeezed her eyes shut against the pain shooting through her chest.

'Irith?' He ran around the table to her.

'I think I will go to hospital after all,' she said calmly. 'There seems to be a broken rib sticking into something. Help me up, please, Eustace Power Bragg.' She managed a feeble laugh, then raised her voice. 'E stands for Eustace, everyone.'

'You little cow!' Bragg said grimly. 'You gave your word.'

'That'll teach you to call me 'little Irith'. Lift me up.'

'You're staying right where you are until we get a stretcher. Irith. *Irith?*'

She had fainted.

CHAPTER FORTY-TWO

When Irith came through the arrival gates at Sydney Airport, Jemma stepped out of the crowd and waved. They walked down to the baggage conveyor together and Jemma collected Irith's single bag.

'I can take it,' she said. 'I'm not an invalid.'

'Your pronouncements on that topic don't have a lot of credibility.'

'That was over a month ago. I'm fully recovered.'

'This way,' said Jemma. 'I've bought myself a new car.'

'You've bought a *car*? I've never known you to drive, Mum, except that time we went on holidays up the north coast and it rained every day for two weeks. You always said it was a waste of energy.'

Jemma looked across and smiled. 'I've changed.'

'So I see.'

'This isn't the way home,' said Irith, as they drove out of the airport and turned right towards the coast. Jemma's flat had been in the inner west.

'Along with the compensation package I was offered my flat back, but I'd lived there since you were born and I wanted a complete change.'

'Where are we going?'

'You'll see.' Jemma consulted the navigation screen and set route selection to automatic. It took them north-east.

Irith looked out the window. It was 10 October. The best part of eight months had gone by since Security had taken Jemma from the flat. A lifetime of memories, many of which she didn't want to think about. Gretel and Thornton. Poor, mad Vaiha. . . and all the dead she'd had a hand in.

'After they took you,' she said quietly, 'I vowed that I'd do whatever it took to get you back. And when Janna caught me in the flooded house, I decided that I'd even kill to get free. I did kill, afterwards, but I never knew what it would cost me. I still have nightmares about my dead. Was it worth it?'

'You were defending your life,' said Jemma. 'Or the lives of others. If you can't justify that, nothing on Earth can be justified.'

'What about Lindstrom? He was a monster, yet he really cared. Have we helped to destroy the Earth, by ridding it of him?'

His last words echoed in Irith's mind. *You think you've lived through a disastrous climate change. It's nothing* – absolutely nothing – *compared to what's coming.* And he had been in a position to know. She shivered.

'Bad things may come of good actions, and good from bad,' said Jemma. 'Only hindsight can tell us the answer. And maybe, the way climate is going, it doesn't matter.'

But it did, and Irith had to help. She had to do something to make the future better, not worse.

They wound up a hill and suddenly, over the cliffs, she saw the familiar Pacific Ocean. A tear came to her eye. It was so good to be home. The future was unknown but for the moment she wasn't going to think about that. She had only made one decision in the past month – she wasn't going back to genomics. The science she had once been so captivated by now repelled her.

The car pulled into the driveway of a small apartment block and drove down to the underground car park. Jemma lifted Irith's bag out.

'I'll take that,' said Irith.

'It's not heavy.'

'All I own is a spare pair of knickers and a toothbrush. Makes it easy to start again.'

Jemma's eyes met hers, and she was smiling as if something amused her. They walked up to the ninth floor, the top. Jemma pressed numbers into her phone and pointed it at the door. The lock clicked and she went in, picking up a handful of letters on the way. Irith followed.

The apartment was large and airy, with deep carpets and rich furnishings. The large windows looked up the coast to Sydney Heads, out and down on the Tasman Sea and the Pacific Ocean, and south to the entrance of Botany Bay. A big swell was running and waves thundered against the base of the cliffs. Irith imagined she could hear them through the double glazing.

'So how are you, Irith? Really?' said Jemma.

'My ribs are completely healed.'

'I wasn't talking about your ribs. You suffered more traumas than most people have in a lifetime.'

'I'm all right, Mum.'

'Really?'

'Yes, really. I've had weeks of post-trauma counselling, and that was nearly as bad as . . . all the other. I'm learning to deal with it. What about you?'

'I hardly think about it at all,' Jemma said absently. 'I've got other things on my mind.'

'I'll bet you have. I'm surprised you came back at all.'

'Jack's coming over next week,' said Jemma. 'We're going on holidays for a month, and then I'm going to rethink my life. I'm not going back to teaching.'

Irith considered that and discovered that she was pleased, but sorry too. 'Levi loves you, you know.'

'I've known for a long time,' said Jemma. 'He's a wonderful man and the best friend anyone could have . . .'

'But you don't love him. He seemed to take it well enough,' said Irith.

'He has a philosophical nature. So, tell me about you and Bragg.'

'There is no me and Bragg.'

'Judging by the anxious looks he was giving you on the way to the hospital . . .'

'We're just good friends, and I've got enough to deal with at the moment. There's only one thing I regret.'

'What's that?'

'That I missed the great flypast. When Jack led ten thousand helicopters above the memorial service for all those who died.'

'It was one of the greatest moments of my life,' said Jemma. 'And a powerful opportunity for the President, too. After his personal appeal, and the dramatic rescues, his popularity is at an all-time high. Now the Global Congress is gone, it might be enough to tip the balance against the religious militia and restore democracy in the United States.'

'I hope so,' Irith said absently. She looked out the window again. 'I've always loved the sea,' she went on, feeling rather wistful.

'Really? I didn't know that.'

'Not the coast – the deep sea. I'm fascinated by the oceans – how they work and how they're linked to the changing climate.'

'Maybe you should do your doctorate on that.'

'What doctorate?'

Jemma smiled. 'Why not study what you've always been most interested in? There'll be no trouble getting admittance to a doctoral program in marine or climate science, with your record.'

'What are you talking about? Besides, I'd never afford it and I'm not taking any more money from you.'

'I wasn't offering you any.'

It was a strange thing for her mother to say; downright suspicious. 'What's going on, Mum?'

'*You* can afford it, Irith.'

'I had three thousand dollars and that was confiscated. I don't have a cent to my name.'

Jemma laughed. 'That's been returned, plus modest compensation. Not to mention that your video of the struggle in the helicopter was broadcast worldwide to an audience of over six billion people. The networks are still showing it and, every time they do, you're entitled to a fee.'

'But it wasn't my camera.'

'You filmed it, and as soon as you did, it was *your* creation. You're a well-off woman now.'

'How well-off?' said Irith curiously. They had not been poor when she was growing up, but neither had there been money to spare.

'You can pay for any course you want, at any institute in the world.'

'First I'd have to be admitted and I can't see –'

Jemma had been absently sorting through the letters, and now she picked one out and handed it to Irith. The envelope bore the crest of the University of Sydney.

Irith tore it open. The letter was from the Office of the Registrar.

Dear Irith Hardey

It is with the very greatest pleasure that I am able to inform you that, following reassessment of your honours project, you have been awarded First Class Honours and the University Medal in Bio-engineering. The degree will be conferred at a special ceremony in November this year and I will consult you shortly as to a suitable date.

Yours faithfully

Derick Umpto
Registrar

'Oh!' said Irith. 'Oh!' Tears sprang to her eyes.

'Is something the matter?'

'No,' she said. 'Nothing at all.'

'Something to celebrate. I'll open a nice bottle of red at dinner.'

'Sounds splendid,' said Irith, far away again.

'I'm only sorry that I haven't been able to recover that bound copy of your thesis,' Jemma said. 'It must have been lost in the harbour.'

Irith thought about it and realised that it no longer mattered. *Best place for it*, she thought.

That night, after dinner, they sat in the dark over a bottle of Penfolds Bin 389, watching the moon rise over the ocean. 'It's beautiful,' said Irith.

'And I'm only too pleased I've come to appreciate such things again. I spent too long being brainwashed about the evils of greed and the indulgence of the senses. We all did. We starved ourselves in the name of the planet: physically, mentally and emotionally. Austerity was good; any kind of indulgence bad. Beauty, or pleasure, should never be a shameful thing.'

'No,' said Irith absently.

Jemma went out and returned carrying a small leather case. Inside it was an old and rather battered laptop computer. She lifted it out and handed it to Irith.

'This is for you. I'd kept it all your life. It took quite an effort to get it back.'

'I don't understand.'

'It was your father's and he did most of his modelling on it. He was the first person to forecast the collapse of the West Antarctic ice sheet.'

Irith knew that but she just said, 'Thank you,' and cradled the precious relic on her lap. 'Does it still work?'

'I had it refurbished – largely rebuilt in fact. Though it looks rather daggy and old-fashioned . . .' She trailed off, anxiously.

'I love it,' said Irith. 'I'll think of Dad every time I use it.'

'He'd be so proud of you,' said Jemma. 'He only knew you for a few days but he loved you so. And he'd be pleased that, in a way, you're carrying on his work.'

'I never said I was.'

'The oceans hold the key to the world's climate, and all the research says it's close to a catastrophic tipping point . . .'

It's nothing – absolutely nothing – *compared to what's coming*, Lindstrom had said.

' … but which way will it tip?' Jemma went on. 'And what will the consequences be for the world? We need our best and brightest minds working on that problem.'

'Yes,' Irith said thoughtfully. 'We do.'

Jemma raised her glass. 'Welcome home.'

The Human Rites trilogy concludes in

Book 3: *The Life Lottery*

You can read the first chapter overleaf.

THE LIFE LOTTERY

CHAPTER ONE

The deep-sea submersible *Melvin* had just reached its planned exploration depth – 1,559 metres below the surface of the Tasman Sea and 4.2 metres off the bottom of the eastern flank of the Lord Howe Rise – when the underwater telephone belched. The mother ship was trying to contact them but, like every other bit of technology except that used for spying on people, the phone was decades past its use-by date.

Irith Hardey didn't move from the viewport; if she had, claustrophobia would have overcome her. Besides, she'd been waiting two years for this dive and no intrusion from the dismal world above was going to distract her. Her research was her life, her friend, her lover and comforter.

It could not turn her mind off after she collapsed into bed, though. Nor could it keep the recurring nightmares at bay.

The submersible's floodlights illuminated grey mud between the knobs of tubeworm-encrusted basalt. A white fish swam by, long and thin, like a length of squashed plastic pipe.

'It's for you, Dr Hardey,' said Fred, the pilot.

Irith swore. 'What now? We only left the surface an hour ago.'

Fred passed her the receiver. 'It's Jacques Cuvier.' The expedition leader, on the RV *Thor Heyerdahl*, above.

'It'd better be important!' She took it. 'Irith here.'

Jacques came on the line, his normally mellow voice made adenoidal by the ancient instrument. 'You are to come up, please.'

'Is it an emergency?' Hardly likely, or the surface controller would be talking the pilot through it.

'No. Come up at once.'

Irith's co-observer, Jason Slythe, spun around. 'What's the matter?'

She put her hand over the mouthpiece. 'Surely he can't mean *now*? I've been waiting years for this.' Not to mention writing fifty-three research proposals, and begging and scrounging every cent of the $65,000 per day it cost for the sixty-year-old submersible, all her equipment and the rusting seventy-metre research vessel required to support it.

Jason shrugged.

Jacques said something she didn't catch as the underwater phone gurgled like a toilet flushing. It was always causing trouble; the maintenance budget was totally inadequate. It gave her an idea.

'Hello?' she said loudly. 'Jacques? Jacques?'

'Lost him,' she said, then covered the mouthpiece again. 'Go down to Station One, Fred.'

He adjusted the trim by pumping mercury from the aft tank to the forward one. 'But . . .'

'Jacques hasn't told *you* to come up.'

'No.'

'And it's not an emergency.'

He grinned. Fred was the dependable type, as pilots had to be, but there was enough rebel in him to enjoy someone else breaking the rules.

Irith put the receiver into an empty Milo tin used for storing odds and ends, and taped the lid on over the cord. 'I couldn't make out what he was saying, so we go on with the mission.'

'You're going to be in the shit when we surface,' Jason fretted. He was the worrying type.

'You don't have to worry. You're not in charge.'

The *Melvin* proceeded downslope to 1,642 metres, keeping above the bottom so the wash from the thrusters did not stir up the mud. Irith watched the echo sounder with one eye while using the external video and still cameras with the other. 'We must be nearly on station, Fred.'

'The canyon should come into view any minute. There it is.'

'Ease down into it so I can image the walls.'

The *Melvin* dropped into a gully eroded out of clayey sediment. The lights revealed wavy layering in the walls, dark and light, and occasional lenses of white.

'I knew we'd find it here,' Irith said. 'The hydrate signature was as strong as I've ever seen.'

Further down, the brown sediment was thickly layered with glistening bands of the white material. It looked exactly like ice.

'Follow it down,' she added. 'I want to ground-truth the traces as best we can. Is everything recording?'

'Of course,' Fred said.

The white bands continued to the bottom of the canyon, twenty-seven metres below the sediment surface. The submersible tracked along the bottom for about two hundred metres, then hovered, neutrally buoyant, while Irith tested the water chemistry with her external instruments. She checked that the data was recording, took water samples and sediment cores with the manipulator arms, and stored the sealed containers in the science sample basket outside.

'I'm finished here. Can we track back along the other side?'

Fred was rocking on his seat, gnawing his lower lip.

'Something the matter?' she said.

'The canyon walls don't look very stable, Irith, and the operating regs specify –'

'Of course,' she said. At the bottom of the sea, safety always took precedence. 'Take her up whenever you're ready. I've done everything here I have to do.'

Back at the place where they'd first seen the white material, Fred worked the manipulator arms to break off a chunk of layered sediment and put it in the pressure chamber within the sample basket.

'Enough?'

'Another piece, please,' said Irith. 'Since we've come all this way.'

That proved more difficult than she had anticipated. As soon as Fred closed the grips of the starboard manipulator arm, the white material decomposed in a little explosion of bubbles.

'What about just there?' Irith pointed over Fred's shoulder through his viewport at another icy lens.

He sampled it and worked the remotes to seal the lid of the pressure chamber. It would keep the samples at the same pressure and temperature until they reached the surface.

'Excellent,' Irith said. 'Now, if we can just get a core or two.'

Fred used the sediment corer to extract a two-metre-long horizontal core through the white material, then a vertical core from the top.

'Where to now?' His stare suggested that it was time to obey orders.

Irith heaved a heavy sigh. 'I love it down here. No one has ever dived on the Lord Howe Rise before – it could be a new planet for all we know about it.'

'It'll change if they find a use for that stuff.'

'Methane hydrate,' she said absently. 'Methane gas formed in the sediments over millions of years and frozen into ice crystals. There's billions of tonnes of it here.'

'And it's a greenhouse menace,' said Jason.

'See that?' said Fred. Trails of tiny bubbles were streaming up from the exposed hydrate surfaces. 'It's two degrees outside, yet our lights are making it break down. Let's go.'

'All right.' Irith removed the tape from the Milo lid. 'Hello, Jacques,' she said wearily, as though she'd been calling for hours. '*Melvin* here, come in please.'

'Dr Hardey!' Jacques Cuvier snapped. 'Come up immediately.'

'We're on our way. But why?' The weather had been good when they'd left the surface, and the cyclone season didn't start for months.

'Someone wants to see you urgently.'

'*Me?* Why?'

'The Department hasn't bothered to inform me.'

'Is someone flying out?'

Irith could not imagine why. Thousands of scientists were doing research on climate change and most had more experience than she did.

'They're sending a helicopter to take you back to Sydney, and it'll be here in half an hour. You'd better not keep them waiting.'

'Where am I going?'

'I have no idea, Dr Hardey, but whatever you've done, I'm not happy about it. This mission has been years in the planning, and it's most inconvenient.'

'It's a damn sight more inconvenient for me! It's my research time that's being lost.' She told Fred to ascend to the mother ship.

'What the fuck's going on?' said Jason, as if it were her fault. His precious underwater time was also being wasted. 'This is a real pain, Irith.'

'It certainly wasn't my idea,' she snapped.

At 11 am she wriggled out of the hatch of the *Melvin* and climbed down onto the deck of the *Thor Heyerdahl*. A huge helicopter sat on the pad on the forward deck, its blades spinning. It was an ancient, two-bladed Sikorsky, kept running long past its designed life. There were oil stains down the metal skin, which had been repaired using parts from a machine with a different paint job. It wasn't a comforting sign.

Jacques Cuvier marched across, natty in suit and bow tie. He looked out of place among the casually clothed scientists and technicians.

'Hurry up, Irith,' he fussed. 'The Department's been on the line three times in the last half hour, wanting to know why you're taking so long. They have power over our funding, you know.'

Irith had asked Fred to come up as slowly as possible, making the most of the time she had left. Jacques must have known what she was up to, since the mother ship's sonar logs could locate the *Melvin* to within a few metres, but he merely took her elbow and ushered her towards the helicopter.

'How long will I be away?' she said.

'I don't know. Days, certainly . . .'

'What is it?'

'The helicopter costs $8,000 an hour and it's well overdue for an overhaul. They may not bring you back at all.'

'But my research . . .'

'We've got the plan. It'll get done.'

'It's not the same, Jacques!' she said furiously.

He took two steps backwards. 'I do understand. I've done my best but the Department wouldn't budge. The order comes from higher up.'

'What's that supposed to mean?'

'They wouldn't say.'

'Well, fuck the Department,' Irith muttered. She rarely swore but the situation seemed to require it.

'Pardon?'

'I'll have to pack.'

'There's no time. You'll have to go as you are.'

'What's the hurry?' She looked up at him. Jacques wasn't a tall man but he was a lot taller than her.

He jerked at her arm, uncharacteristically anxious. The Departmental Secretary must have given him a roasting. *Serves him right*, Irith thought, but that was unjust. Jacques was a fussy little man but he knew talent when he saw it and he'd always supported her.

'I've got to go to the toilet,' said Irith.

'Five minutes!' he said hastily.

'Not a second more.'

In her cabin she threw off her overalls and put on the best pants she had here, a pair of jeans that were uncomfortably tight across the backside. *Must get back into exercising*, she thought. Brown boots, a grey blouse and a cotton jacket that made her look like a bushwalker. Irith gave her cropped brown hair a quick brush, which failed to tame it, and her teeth an even quicker going-over, by which time Jacques was rapping on the door.

'Coming!' She threw a spare blouse into her backpack, a couple of changes of underwear, passport and ID cards and, lastly, her battered old laptop. If she wasn't coming back, at least she could get some work done.

In another five minutes Jacques was handing her into the chopper which, she noted, had been fitted with long-range tanks. The *Thor Heyerdahl* was over a thousand kilometres out from Sydney.

'Good luck!' he said as the co-pilot pointed to the rear left seat and slid the door closed.

'Thanks,' she muttered inaudibly.

Three hours later she was in Sydney, but no wiser. A car was waiting at the heliport. A uniformed woman checked Irith's ID with a portable terminal that she took directly from the manufacturer's packaging. In a world dominated by refugee-sponsored terrorism, the security services had the best of everything.

'Would you come this way, please, Dr Hardey?'

'I'd like to know what's going on,' said Irith.

'You'll be briefed on arrival in London.'

'*London!*'

'That's right. Let me take your bag.'

Irith held onto it. 'It's not heavy. What's happening there?'

'I don't know.'

Irith shivered, for it reminded her of her first trip to London, eight years ago, and the subsequent horrors: a blood-drenched hunt through flooded tunnels under the London Docklands, an insurgency school in mosquito-ridden Minnesota, and then the catastrophe in New Orleans –

The faces of dead friends and foes exploded into her mind. Irith took deep breaths and bit down on the memories.

The Life Lottery is available at all online retailers.

ABOUT THE AUTHOR

Ian Irvine, an Australian marine scientist, has also written 32 novels and a book of short stories. Ian is best known for his Three Worlds epic fantasy sequence for older readers, which has been published in many languages and has sold over a million copies.

www.ian-irvine.com

Ian has also written a trilogy of eco-thrillers about catastrophic climate change, Human Rites, and 13 novels for younger readers: the Sorcerer's Tower quartet, the Grim and Grimmer quartet and the Runcible Jones quartet, plus most recently, The Last Christmas.

Contact Ian on Facebook: www.facebook.com/ianirvine.author

OTHER BOOKS BY IAN IRVINE

Epic fantasy novels

THE THREE WORLDS SEQUENCE

THE VIEW FROM THE MIRROR QUARTET
A Shadow on the Glass
The Tower on the Rift
Dark is the Moon
The Way Between the Worlds

THE WELL OF ECHOES QUARTET
Geomancer
Tetrarch
Scrutator
Chimaera

SONG OF THE TEARS TRILOGY
Torments of the Traitor
The Curse on the Chosen
The Destiny of the Dead

THREE WORLDS SHORTER STORIES
A Wizard's War and Other Stories

THE GATES OF GOOD AND EVIL
The Summon Stone
The Fatal Gate

Other Epic Fantasy novels

THE TAINTED REALM TRILOGY
Vengeance
Rebellion
Justice

Thrillers about catastrophic climate change

THE HUMAN RITES TRILOGY
The Last Albatross
Terminator Gene
The Life Lottery

For older children and young adults

THE RUNCIBLE JONES QUARTET
Runcible Jones, The Gate to Nowhere
Runcible Jones and The Buried City
Runcible Jones and the Frozen Compass
Runcible Jones and the Backwards Hourglass

THE GRIM AND GRIMMER QUARTET
The Headless Highwayman
The Grasping Goblin
The Desperate Dwarf
The Calamitous Queen

For lower and middle primary readers

THE SORCERER'S TOWER OMNIBUS
Thorn Castle
Giant's Lair
Black Crypt
Wizardry Crag

The Last Christmas – The North Pole is Melting!

HUMAN RITES TRILOGY, BOOK 1

THE LAST ALBATROSS

WHEN THE ICE MELTS, THE EARTH WILL BURN

IAN IRVINE

Find out what happens next...

HUMAN RITES TRILOGY, BOOK 3

THE LIFE LOTTERY

IN SAVING THE WORLD, WILL THEY DESTROY IT?

IAN IRVINE

ACKNOWLEDGEMENTS

I would like to thank my agent, Selwa Anthony, and Jody Lee, Angelo Loukakis and Julia Stiles for their part in bringing the series to initial publication, and Franscois McHardy, Justine Joffe, Xou Creative and everyone at Simon & Schuster for all their hard work on this new edition.

www.ingramcontent.com/pod-product-compliance
Lightning Source LLC
Chambersburg PA
CBHW032031120726
47901CB00001BA/185